RUBY RED

NIKKI MINTY

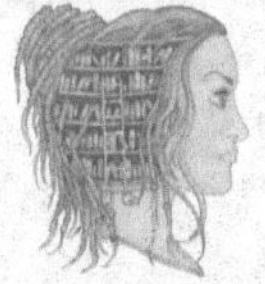

INDICREATES

ACKNOWLEDGEMENTS

I would like to thank my son RJ for helping form the concept for this novel, and my daughter Lyla and brother Trey, for their creative input.

To my partner Kieran, mother Carrie, grandfather Handel and friend Cheryl, thanks for being my loyal beta readers.

Many thanks to Indiana Maria Acosta Hernandez at Indicreates, for creating such glorious, eye catching covers.

And last but certainly not least, I would like to give a big shout out to my editors Amy Cissell and Christopher Barnes at Cissell Ink, for helping to improve, tighten and smooth out the wrinkles in my story. You have been extremely hands-on and helpful throughout the editing process.

To all my other friends and family members who have given me constant encouragement and support during the writing process, I appreciate the love.

Those of you in the reading/writing community who read, enjoyed, and reviewed Pastel Pink, thank you, I'm extremely grateful.

IN LOVING MEMORY OF STEVEN GAVIN

1984 - 2017

AKA Gavo & Stavros

You'll be forever in our hearts

ZADOK'S CAPITALS AND RACES

SUMMER

Extremely hot, barren and two thirds desert. The Royals live in a castle protected by guards, while the rest of the Vallons reside as citizens in the kingdom.

Leader of Summer: *Queen Sjaan*

Race: *Vallon (Power of heat and fire)*

Skin colour: *Black/dark chocolate*

Hair and eye colours: *Red, Orange, and Amber (the colour of the irises continually swirl like molten lava)*

Language: *Similar to German*

Facts: *Vallons are the strongest race and have magical, glowing vertic switz tattoos*

AUTUMN

Very windy, but self-sufficient land. Rukes live by a waterfall.

Leader of Autumn: *Chief Waya*

Race: *Rukes (Power of air and wind)*

Skin colour: *Grey and white (marble effect)*

Hair colour: *Black*

Eye colour: *Blue, Aqua, Teal*

Language: *Similar to Iroquoian*

Fact: *Rukes have wings*

WINTER

Extremely cold, and the only land on Zadok with an ocean. Zeeks live inside the ice caves.

Leader of Winter: *Commander Azazel*

Race: *Zeeks (Power of water and ice)*

Skin colour: *White/white chocolate (with a shimmer that matches the Zeek's hair and eye colour)*

Hair and eye colours: *Purple, Magenta, and Pastel Pink*

Language: *Similar to English*

Facts: *Zeeks are the smallest race on Zadok. Pastel Zeeks are weak with poor eyesight and a short life expectancy*

SPRING

A comfortable climate, mostly forest with a crystal-clear lake near the village. Drakes reside in huts and treehouses in the deep of the forest.

Leader of Spring: *Chief Dakari*

Race: *Drakes (Power of the land)*

Skin colour: *Brown/milk chocolate (with a shimmer that matches the Drake's hair and eye colour)*

Hair and eye colours: *Green, Yellow, and Hazel*

Language: *Similar to Afrikaans*

Fact: *Drakes are the tallest race on Zadok.*

CRUSHED

-HARLOW-

I feel…broken…empty—my throat's constricted. Every intake of breath stabs my lungs. I've been praying Alex will reconsider his decision and return, but it's not looking promising.

He's done with me. I've ruined us. Azazel was right all along; I really am a curse.

I rub my arms, attempting to comfort myself. Little had I known our time together would end so tragically. Last night was a whirlwind of heat and passion. I was on top of the world—and now I'm falling.

A piece of me wishes I could rewind time and take back what I did to Lucas, but I know either way, I would still be mourning. Despite what Alex believes I'm capable of, I couldn't've restrained Lucas. He was too strong.

I'm glad I didn't know that killing Lucas would sever Alex's link to Earth. Had Alex enlightened me beforehand, I might have hesitated and cost Jade her life. Alex means a lot to me, but Jade's family still needs her around. I had to save her, which meant Lucas had to die—and therefore, Alex's ghost had to vanish.

I'm sorry, Alex. The thought of never seeing him again creates a painful lump in my throat. I can't believe it's over between us, and he's left me here, alone and helpless, near the most dangerous part of the forest. He must be terribly enraged if he's willing to let me die. This awful thought rips me apart to my core. So much for being in love with me and doing anything to save me.

He'd said, "Now that I have you, I'll do anything to keep you."

Apparently not. I wonder if he meant any of those nice things he'd said.

The large, imposing trees tower oppressively above me, and I deflate even further. I don't know which direction home is; my internal compass sucks. *How far away are the Zeek safety boundaries from here?*

I'll never make it out before sundown. I'm as good as dead.

With Alex gone, the noises of the forest intensify. Every crackle and snap sends shivers through me.

It's only a matter of time until a predator finds me and rips me to pieces.

I'm no longer afraid to die. A fresh start might be a blessing, but I'm afraid of the pain.

Something crunches towards me and my blood stills. I tense as the encroaching footsteps grow louder—closer. I know it's not Alex; he'd stormed off in the opposite direction. *It's something else.*

A shadow appears above me, and I brace myself for a world of pain. I can't bring myself to turn around and look; I'm too frightened of what I'll see.

I close my eyes and hold my breath, counting down my remaining seconds with every frantic heartbeat. *Please kill me quickly,* I beg. *I can't take anymore torture.*

To my astonishment, a hand gently cups my shoulder. "Harlow?"

My heart jolts and my eyes fling open. *Jax?* I've never heard his voice sound so soft and unsure.

His hand slides from my shoulder down my arm, as he slowly slinks around to face me. "Harlow." Once again, his voice comes out softer than usual. "What are you doing all the way out here? It's dangerous."

My cheeks are hot with tears, and my throat constricts too much to speak.

Jax slides off his bandana, offering it to me to use as a handkerchief. "Are you okay?" His violet eyes stare into mine, filled with worry and compassion. He seems genuinely concerned. Guilt worms its way through me. Again, I've caused him trouble. *I shouldn't have escaped. I've made things worse.*

"I'm sorry," is all I can manage before the tears flow again, and to add to my embarrassment, a humiliating squealy noise leaves my throat.

"It's okay, I'm not upset with you. I've been worried." His eyes examine mine, searching for answers. "Please, tell me what I can do to help."

I'm so choked up; my voice is barely audible. "There's nothing you can do."

His hand strokes my arm, and I quiver. "Come on, let me take you home. It's too dangerous out here."

It's too dangerous at home too, I think.

"Just leave me here," I say with a snuffle. "I'm as good as dead either way. You might as well let the fuegors take me, at least they'll be able to make a meal out of me."

His hand reaches for my cheek, and his thumb gently wipes my tears away. The gesture feels oddly affectionate. It reminds me of Alex. My heart tingles for a moment and then splits painfully down the middle.

"Don't say such things." Jax's gaze is intense. "I'm sorry about the position I've put you in, I truly am, but I promise you I will fix things. Please come back with me. We can fix this together."

I don't know how to fix things; I only know how to break things.

He leans down to scoop me up. I don't argue; I'm too broken to argue. My jumper is screwed up in a bundle next to me. He picks it up and places it on my lap, before rising to his feet.

Goodbye, Alex, I say inside, and then burst into sobs. *I will miss you.*

OUTRAGED

-ALEX AS SLATER-

(Fifteen minutes earlier)

I storm away from Ruby in a fit of rage, punching one of the lower tree branches as I pass by. The rough surface grazes my knuckles, and bark soars through the air like confetti.

Perhaps I shouldn't've called it quits and taken off, but I'm angry. No scratch that; I'm furious. Ruby has completely ruined everything. I've lost my twin brother, my life on Earth… and…well…her.

The most infuriating part about this is, deep down, I know she's right. Lucas had this coming. He killed us both and covered it up, and to my horror, he was about to do the same to her sister and nephew.

He needed to be stopped. She needed to stop him…

But, had he not consumed those five glasses of wine Jade poured for him, he wouldn't've snapped, which means it would never have come to this. He would still be alive.

I shake my head. *You can't pass the blame onto Jade for giving him the wine.* I tell myself. *She wasn't aware of his mental illness. It's not her fault the alcohol turned him violent, nor is it Ruby's fault he's dead. It's his own fault for being such a pathetic weakling and accepting the drinks, and our parents' fault for warping his mind—and if I'm being honest—perhaps it's a little bit my fault too.*

Lucas wasn't born a monster, he was moulded into one after years of constant abuse, and his sinister side only ever surfaced when it was triggered. When he was on his meds and sober, he was okay. He used to mutter to himself and do odd things. He'd rock back and forth, pull strange faces, randomly laugh, talk to his reflection etc.—but he was never menacing or malicious. To me, he was still the scared little boy I grew up with. The one who would hide in our bedroom cupboard to avoid another beating or get me to tell him bedtime stories to muffle out the sound of our parents arguing.

Because Lucas was always a nervous wreck by bedtime, he'd wet his mattress. Our prick of a father would lose his temper and give him a lashing with his belt for being "a worthless little pissant"—his words, not mine. And if Lucas cowered, our old man resorted to threats, telling him, "If you don't clean up your stinkin' mess, you'll be kicked out onto the street like a dog".

Lucas' bed was never cleaned properly, leaving our room constantly reeking of urine—along with old rotting food scraps and black mould. There were cockroaches everywhere. They'd crawled over everything, including us, while we slept. It was disgusting.

Lucas fared far worse than I did. I had a smart mouth and fast legs. I would give our parents a mouthful and then do the runner, not realising Lucas was being punished for my actions.

He never told me how much he'd suffered, or how hard I'd

made things for him until the night he killed me. And since then, I've been burdened by guilt.

It's clear I'm not the only brother who feels guilty. I've received countless apologies over the years. Lucas would rock at the end of his bed and repeat over and over again—*to the point where it got annoying*—"I'm sorry, brother, please forgive me. I didn't mean to kill you; the voices made me do it." I forgive him for killing me, and a small part of me even believes I deserved it. But regardless of his endless apologies, I can never, *WILL NEVER*, forgive him for what he did to Ruby. Bile rises in my throat thinking about it. I'm completely and utterly revolted by the brutal things he did. So much so, I can barely even believe the person who did those heinous things was him. His psychotic behaviour towards Jade, Connor, and Rueben was another shock to my system. It's the third time I've seen him completely lose control.

See. I force myself to see reason. *Ruby did the right thing. He needed to be stopped before he killed someone else. You shouldn't have lashed out and ended things with her. You were wrong.*

By the time Josh and Bianca's parents took Lucas and me in, we were thirteen and had gone through over a dozen foster homes. Some of them weren't much better than the abusive home we'd come from. Mr and Mrs Ralph were the worst of them all, but I made them pay. I threw all of Mrs Ralph's things out onto their front yard and set them alight, and then I took to Mr Ralph's precious Mercedes with a baseball bat. They wanted the authorities to send me to juvie, but after Lucas and I—along with two others— came forward about the ongoing abuse we'd received while living there, they were the ones who found themselves in lock up. *Suckers. I hope they got what was coming to them.* From what I hear, most prisoners don't take too kindly to child abusers.

A lot changed once we hit our mid-teen years, and I probably didn't treat Lucas as well as I should have. I didn't see him as my equal anymore; I saw him as a nuisance. He'd become way too much of a loser-wimp and a liability. I was constantly getting into trouble over him, and I'd always be left having to fight his battles— especially at school. High school was brutal enough, even for the average kids, never mind losers-wimps like him. I wanted to blend in or be popular like Josh. Josh was two years younger than us and the captain of Blaxland High's basketball team. All the other kids loved him.

Lucas didn't care about blending in or being popular, and the older I got, the more I resented him for it. He'd deliberately attract needless attention to himself by wearing black clothes and eyeliner, and listening to dark screamo music by Marilyn Manson and Slipknot.

On the night he killed me, I'd lost my temper with him and finally expressed exactly how I felt. "Why can't you just act normal instead of bringing **needless attention to yourself** all the time?" I'd asked him. "If you wanna look and act like a loser, people are going to treat you like a loser, and I'm not going to keep fighting your battles for you. I'm sick of it. Next time someone goes to beat the shit out of you, I'm going to stand back and let them. Maybe then you'll wake up and start acting normal."

They were harsh words, and I'm not sure if I really meant them, but I was drunk and angry—and I'd had a gutful of putting his problems before my own.

We'd been at a party earlier that night, and a scuffle had broken out between him and two eshay lads. As always, I'd immediately left the popular group I was trying to break into and came rushing to his aid. The fight drew an audience which increased the pressure. I wanted to prove myself by winning, but in the end, I was the one who got knocked down. The lads had knuckle dusters, which gave them an unfair advantage.

As I laid on the ground winded, the lads took off with Lucas' phone and wallet. They'd wounded my pride, and I was humiliated. At that very moment, I hated Lucas. I remember wishing he wasn't my brother.

Someone had called the cops, and as soon as I heard sirens approaching, I scrambled to my feet. Anna, the birthday girl, wanted me to stay to give a statement, but I was over cops and statements. I was over being constantly picked on and questioned about things that were out of my control. Kids from broken backgrounds like ours were always the first to be unjustly targeted.

Before Anna could stop me, I'd snatched up my esky, grabbed Lucas' arm, and hauled him out onto the street.

The party wasn't far from home, and I should've called it a night, but I still had a six-pack of beers left in my esky, and my bruised ego wanted to drown in them. I'd plucked my torch from my pocket and taken a detour through the bush to Elizabeth Lookout, making sure to watch for snakes posing as sticks. I loved the view from the lookout; it was my thinking spot. You could see all the way from Glenbrook to Sydney City.

I wanted Lucas to go straight home. I wasn't in the mood for his company. "Just go home, Lucas," I repeated as we walked. "Leave me alone. I just want to be alone." He hadn't listened, and eventually I gave up on wasting my breath.

He followed me the whole way, his pocket cassette player blaring a very tinny Marilyn Manson.

When we arrived at the lookout, I sat on a step near the edge. Lucas followed.

I'd sighed in defeat and cracked open a bottle for each of us. "Since you've insisted on joining me, you might as well have a drink with me," I'd told him. "And turn that screamo shit off; it's making my ears bleed."

He'd taken the drink, but left the music playing.

Things were amicable at first, but come three drinks later, I saw a different—much darker—side of my brother. Out of nowhere he'd started ranting about how I thought I was better than him, and how it was because of me, he'd been so badly abused by our parents. Between the alcohol and the fact that we were both hurting, things rapidly escalated out of control. We pushed and shoved at one another, both saying shittier things than we should have. Once I'd finished giving him a piece of my mind, he'd lunged at me full force with the deliberate intent of knocking me off my feet. Before I knew it, I'd flipped straight over the safety rail at the cliff's edge. I remember falling to the blaring sound of The Beautiful People, and thinking, *there's no such thing.*

However, my opinion changed when I returned in spirit four years later, to discover Ruby, the beautiful, vibrant angel I couldn't save.

Like I'd told Ruby yesterday, Josh would often come out to Lucas' caravan of an evening to talk about her, and the more I heard about her, the more I wished we'd had the chance to meet before he killed us. Josh carried on about how beautiful, funny, and kind she was, and how foolish he was for taking her for granted. He'd say he hadn't deserved her—that he'd treated her poorly, and she could have done much better than him. Lucas would agree with Josh when he referred to Ruby as kind. He'd say Ruby was the only girl who treated him like he mattered—like he wasn't invisible. He wouldn't say much more than this, but I could see the cogs turning in his head.

After Josh left of a night, Lucas would pop on Ruby's Red Hot Chili Peppers CD he'd stolen and sit at the end of his bed, knees up, rocking back and forth, and apologising profusely.

I've never told Ruby about his apologies. I'm certain she wouldn't be interested. Until yesterday's disastrous love spiel, I've tried to avoid the topic of Lucas as much as possible. I hadn't wanted to ruin my chances with her. I was completely head over heels for her.

It depresses me to think I'd finally won her over, only to lose her again in the blink of an eye. Lucas is dead, which means I can't go back.

I've lost her forever.

You've lost human Ruby forever, I correct. This thought replays in my head twice over, and I feel like kicking myself for being so rash and stupid. Human Ruby might be lost to me forever, but it doesn't mean Zeek Ruby has to be. If I really do love her, it shouldn't matter if she's a human or Zeek, the only thing that should matter is I still have her in my life. Zeek Ruby might not have the face of the girl I fell in love with, but she still has a pretty face, and what happened between us last night was incredible. Seriously, the chemistry between us was beyond anything I've experienced.

I dated a Vallon girl named Raven for a year before Ruby came back into my life, and even during our honeymoon period, our connection was never *anything* like the connection Ruby and I shared last night. Then again, I'm fairly sure it was because of my lifelong infatuation with Ruby, that we could never find a true spark.

Due to inter-relationships on Zadok being punishable by death, I'd assured myself that my secret meet-up with Zeek Ruby was a one-off—and never for one second had I imagined things would lead to where they did. For us to be together in our Zeek and Vallon forms was an amazing experience, but it was also extremely risky and dangerous.

The only time you'll find a Zeek and Vallon together on Zadok is in Summer, under criminal circumstances, when the guards take advantage of some of the prettier slaves. *Sickos!* I've been told they find the look of the Pastels enchanting. They like the way they shimmer. The Queen has no love for the Pastels and turns a blind eye to these heinous crimes. Her only concern is the hazardous potential of half breeds, therefore any slave who falls pregnant by a guard is destroyed.

Pushing these disgusting thoughts aside, I divert my focus back to Ruby. *Is there a chance we could make things work between us here?* For us to have a true relationship on Zadok would be nearly—but not completely—impossible.

If she means that much to you, you will do whatever it takes to make it work, says the voice inside my head. *You were very cruel to her just now, and she didn't deserve it. You need to go back and apologise. You need to find a way to keep her in your life.*

I'm a complete and utter idiot. I love Ruby no matter what. *So what if she's a Zeek? And so what if she killed Lucas?* She says she didn't mean to kill him, and even if she did, it's not like he didn't deserve it. More to the point, she'd been adamant she didn't realise that by killing him, she would lose me on Earth. I should never have stormed off. I should have talked things out with her. She's probably as upset as I am.

Now that I'm thinking straight, an alarming thought springs to mind. *Shit! I've left her alone outside of the Zeek safety boundaries.* It's too dangerous for her to be left alone. She might not be able to find her way back, and she's certainly not strong enough to fight off any of the predators in these parts.

You idiot, I scold. *She could be killed. How incredibly selfish you are!*

I swallow my pride and sprint back—hoping to God she hasn't already taken off into one of the more shaded parts of the danger zone.

When I draw close to the area where we'd camped together, I sense another presence lurking nearby and slip behind a tree. It's the hunter in me. I close my eyes and breathe in deeply through my nostrils, trying to control my heavy breathing.

The reckless, impatient side of me wants to rush in and pounce, but the sensible side of me remains cautious. If there is a predator prowling around, it hasn't gotten to her yet. She's not screaming.

I think one of the Vallon guards have found her.

This thought scares me just as much, if not more. She has a pretty face, so chances are they'll take her as a slave and use her for more than just regular chores. This idea sickens me to my core. If this is the case I'll kill whoever I have to kill to set her free. I won't let any of them lay a hand on her.

With steady breath and light feet, I creep closer. I doubt it's her own kind who've found her; she's too far outside of the Zeek safety boundaries. I know this, because she told me. She'd even gone as far as to show me on her map.

Eventually, I'm close enough to make out the rumble of a guy's voice. After shifting a few steps nearer, I catch sight of long, purplish-black dreadlocks hanging down the back of a warrior's leather vest. The hair colour is instantly recognisable. It's Jax, Azazel's son. The Commander's son. *Son of a bitch!*

He is crouched down in front of her, with his back to me, and I squirm as his hand rubs tenderly against her arm.

I feel an urge to do something about it, *but what?* If I were to lay a hand on the Commander's son, it would cause an outright war.

"Please, tell me what I can do to help?" he asks.

I wish she would tell him, "You could help by leaving."

It's a petty thought considering I'm the selfish jerk who'd left her out here alone and vulnerable.

He's the one who's found her. He'll rescue her. He'll become her new hero now.

Okay, inner voice, enough with all the taunts!

I shift further along, trying to catch a glimpse of Ruby's face to see how she's responding to Jax's touch. I need to know if my jealousy is warranted. When she'd spoken about Jax her eyes lit up, and her voice held a sense of awe.

According to our conversation yesterday, they've been spending a lot of time together. She says she has a lot of respect for him and admires what he's trying to achieve. This bothers me, and I had made sure to let her know it.

I'm suspicious of Jax's intentions. No Purple—especially the son of a Commander—would put their life on the line for a Pastel for selfless reasons. Purples don't care about Pastels. They're throwaways to them. His own mother Azazel had over a hundred of them sent to us as a peace offering. *How am I supposed to believe he is so different? That he wants to help the poor Pastels? I can't.*

Jax isn't the noble Zeek he's leading Ruby to believe he is. A quick look into any—and all—of the history books ever printed about the Commanding family tells me he's up to something underhanded. They're sneaky snakes, and I hate snakes. I'm certain he's after Ruby for more than her help. He has to be. He wouldn't be out here searching for her otherwise.

What I'm uncertain of, though, is if she can see he's interested and is choosing to deny it, or if she's totally oblivious.

Her face finally comes into view, and it's hard to gauge whether or not she's happy to see him. Her lips are held in a tight line, and her eyes are red and puffy from crying.

Because of you, my inner voice says. *You hurt her, just like your brother hurt her. You're no better than Lucas.*

Shut up!

Guilt courses through me. I should be the one crouched down consoling her, *not him.*

I wonder what she's told him about how she got here, or why she's crying. Oddly enough, the truth would be less believable than a lie.

"Just leave me here," she says. "I'm as good as dead either way.

You might as well let the fuegors take me; at least they'll be able to make a meal out of me."

His hand reaches for her cheek and I have to fight the urge to leap out from the trees. "Don't say such things," he tells her. "I'm sorry about the position I've put you in, I truly am, but I promise you I will fix things. Please come back with me. We can fix this together."

His use of the word "together" claws at me.

I rock on the balls of my feet. It's taking all the willpower I can muster not to leap out and pounce on him.

Eventually Jax stands and bends down to scoop her up.

Shit! I need to talk to her, *but how?* I need to tell her I'm sorry, that I still really love her. I know the risks, but I want to make us work. *I can't lose her.*

If she leaves with him now, I'll have no way of contacting her. Things really will be over between us. *This is my only chance.*

You're too late, says my forever-taunting inner voice. *You missed your chance and blew things with her. Now you have to let her go before you start a war between your races.*

3

HOME SWEET HOME

-HARLOW-

Jax's biceps are bunched like hard pieces of steel beneath me, as he carries me all the way to the edge of the forest. He's covered a fair distance, yet he's barely even broken a sweat. He might not be as big and solid as Alex—or any Vallon—but he's still extremely strong.

Sitting in the snow at the edge of the Winter border is a Zeek warrior sled. And seated up front, with his legs resting on the front rolled edge, is Oscar. When he spots us coming, he jumps to his feet. His tired, bored expression changing to one of delight. This surprises me.

"You found her," he says with relief. "And she's alive."

An instant chill claws at my bare arm as we cross over the border. It's not an unbearable sensation like it would be for my human body, but it's uncomfortable. An icy breeze sends snowflakes drifting through the sky, and a small one lands on my hot, tear-stained cheek, melting instantly.

"Where was she?" Oscar asks. "Kieran and I checked every square inch of the forest yesterday, according to our containment maps. We didn't see her anywhere."

"She wasn't inside the safety boundaries."

"What?"

Jax gestures with his head to a folded fluffy blanket in the back of the sled, and Oscar is quick to shake it out and lay it down across the back seat.

"How on Zadok is she still alive?"

Brushing off Oscar's question, Jax places me down on the back seat, leaving his lower arm under my neck as support. He nods to my lap. "Can you please put her jumper down as a pillow?"

Oscar snatches the jumper from my lap and shakes it out to fold neatly. To my bewilderment, something dark falls to the sled floor. Seeming unconcerned, Oscar pops my jumper under my head as a pillow, before leaning down to pick up what's dropped.

"Here." He throws a small leather pouch back into my lap. "This fell out of your jumper."

My pulse quickens. This isn't my pouch, it's Alex's. It's the pouch containing the vertic switz jar and needle. *I wonder how it got tangled up in my jumper?* It's lucky the jar didn't smash and drain red fluorescent ink all over the sled floor or I'd have a hard time explaining myself.

Jax grabs another smaller blanket from the front floor and drapes it over me. "Try to stay covered." It's the first and only thing he's said to me since scooping me up in the forest.

I nod my thanks to both of them and then close my eyes before any more tears leak out and embarrass me. I feel tired, broken, and depressed, and I could easily drift off, but as the sled pulls forward, Oscar whispers something and my ears prick.

"What was she doing all the way out in the danger zone?"

"I don't know; I haven't asked her." There's a deep rumble to Jax's whisper. "Either she got lost, or she was looking for a way to..." He doesn't finish.

A blast of snow-laced air hits my face and swirls my uncovered dreadlocks. I hitch the blanket up to cover my hair but keep my ear exposed so I can continue to eavesdrop.

"She must have been scared. Even I get nervous out there. Some of the creatures we've come across when doing our extreme danger training have mouths bigger than Zannah's head."

Despite how depressed I feel, I can't help but to smile at his little dig.

"You're lucky Zannah's not around to hear you say that," Jax warns. "Or she'd take to you with her blade."

Oscar's laugh is tinged with bitterness. "Yeah, I bet she would." He pauses a moment before jumping back to his original point. "But seriously, how did Harlow survive the night alone? Not even you could survive a night alone in the danger zone. We'd need a whole team camping out there to have a chance at surviving."

The sled hits a few big bumps, and I'm thrown about on the seat. I don't mind so much this time around, especially with all of these soft, fluffy blankets curled around me. Compared to my very long and painful trip out to the forest, this feels as if I'm travelling first class.

"Like I said, I haven't spoken to her," Jax answers. "She was a mess when I found her. After everything that's happened with Electra and then Rae, I think she's scared and confused." He lets out a long breath before adding, "I think she feels worthless."

"Well, what do you plan on doing with her when we get back? Nothing's changed since she left; she's still in danger. You both are. I've overheard whispers in the passageways. Everyone is talking about what happened on the boat. No one can believe you stepped in to save her. They're saying you should've let Rae throw her overboard. They say she's been nothing but a nuisance since the day she was born." Jax must have given him a sidewards glare or something, because he's quick to backpedal. "Don't get me wrong, I get why you're doing all of this, and I'm here to back you one hundred percent, but I'm afraid your tactics might need some tweaking. If you're killed, the rest of us are doomed. Your mother and Electra will turn the caves into a bloodbath for all the Pastels—and 'Pastel lovers' as they like to call us."

"Don't worry, I'm already on it," Jax assures him. "I have a new plan. But let's discuss the matter later, shall we? My first priority is to get Harlow back into the caves unnoticed, and then after she's had a decent night's sleep, I have a few ideas I'd like to put forward to you both."

I must have fallen asleep after this, because all I'm left with are snippets of nightmares. I see Lucas' face, his eyes wild with rage. He disappears and then I see Alex, his expression wounded. His face morphs into Electra's face, and along pops Ogre and Rae. The three of them taunt me and laugh hysterically before knocking me down with their fists. "You're dead!" they shout in unison. "You're dead!"

Their images eventually fade away, and Jax appears. Blood drips from his mouth, and there's a blade handle sticking out from his chest.

I wake up to screams, my screams.

"Harlow…shhh…shhh." Strong hands take hold of my arms, stopping them from whipping the air around me. They push them down at my sides, holding them tight. Startled by my own outburst, my eyes flit open to find Jax's face hovering just above mine, and for a second, I forget to breathe. "You're okay," he says, his breath warm on my face. "We're back in the caves now; I'll keep you safe."

Cheeks flushed, my eyes evade his. "I'm sorry. I didn't mean to…"

"I know." His strong, warm hands release me, and he draws back.

"Why don't I carry her back to her family cavern?" Oscar suggests. "You can't be seen with her, especially like this. As I said, Zeeks like to talk."

The image of the blade's handle sticking out from Jax's chest replays in my head.

"Oscar's right," I say, levering myself up. "You shouldn't be seen with me." My eyes flick between them. "Neither of you should. I'm small, you can hide me in one of your camping packs."

Jax looks hesitant. "Are you sure you're willing to do that? It'll be tight."

"I think it's a good idea," Oscar cuts in before I can answer. "I'll take her back in one of the packs, and you head to the training grounds before anyone gets suspicious of your whereabouts."

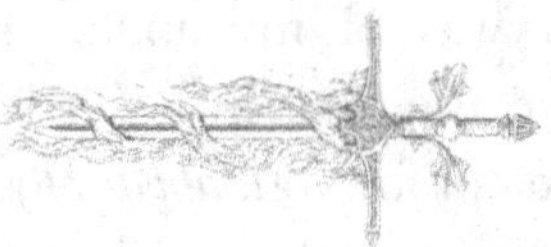

The ride back to my family cavern is extremely squishy, but being squashed in a pack beats the alternative. Jax needs to stop helping me. It's become a one-way street. There's nothing I can do to help him. I'm only a hinderance to him, and I don't need another death on my conscious, especially his. Alex and Zavier might think he's using me for selfish reasons, but I'd like to believe his intensions are honourable. That he really does care about us Pastels.

"What do you have in there?" Floss asks. "An army's worth of supplies?"

I feel the pack being placed down gently. "No, I have your sister."

"What!"

She sounds shocked, although I can't tell if she's glad shocked or upset shocked, and maybe it's for the best. At least this way I can pretend to myself she cares.

Oscar unzips the pack, and I pop my head out to discover I'm on my bed inside my nook. I tumble the rest of the way out with absolutely no grace at all.

"Thanks Oscar," I say with burning cheeks. "Can you please tell Jax I'm sorry if I caused him any trouble?"

His brows shoot up, and he crosses his arms. "*If* you caused him any trouble?" His words are mocking, not unkind.

"*That* I've caused him trouble," I return sheepishly.

His expression relaxes to a lazy smile. "I wouldn't worry too much about it." His arms drop back to his sides. "I think he holds himself partly responsible for you taking off."

This makes me feel worse. "He should have just left me out there," I blurt. "There's nothing I can do to help his cause. I'm more of a nuisance than anything else."

"I don't think Jax sees it that way."

"What Oscar is trying to say is," Floss intrudes, sticking her head through the entryway of my nook, "Jax was never going to leave you out there, because he is in love with you, and everyone in our colony knows it, except for you, *apparently*."

Oscar presses his lips together and says nothing, but I am *so* infuriated by her stupid-little-comment, I pick up my pillow and peg it at her face. "Butt out, Floss! This has nothing to do with you."

She deflects the pillow with her hands. "It has everything to do with me, I'm your sister."

"Since when?" I'm shaking with pent-up emotions. "You've never been a true sister to me. You're only trying to humiliate me in front of Oscar."

Oscar's hands fly up in submission. "You know what, you two go for it. I'm out of here."

"Don't worry, I'm done." Floss turns on her heels. "It's nice to have you back, sis," she mutters as she leaves.

The prickle of tears stings the corners of my eyes. *No, no, no, no. I can't cry again, not now, not in front of Oscar. I have to keep my composure.*

It's not only Floss' comments that I'm upset about, it's everything. My life has become a complete and utter mess, and I have absolutely no one I can talk to about any of it. Not even Alex. *Especially not Alex.* I've lost Alex, and I've become a danger to Jax. The idea of confiding in Zavier flitters through my mind, but I'm quick to reject it. I can't do it to him, he has enough of his own problems to worry about.

Oscar's eyes trace my trembling body with knitted brows. "You should try and catch up on some more sleep before tomorrow. You seem a little edgy." His tone is concerned, not nasty. "Jax and I will be back early in the morning to discuss a few things."

"I thought it was too dangerous for Jax to be near me?"

"It is. But he says he has a new plan to run by us. We'll have to wait and see what he's come up with."

After exiting my nook, I hear him tell Floss to be mindful of whom she shares her opinions with before leaving our cavern.

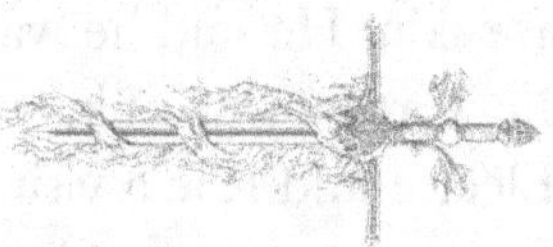

After a night spent sobbing into my pillow, I wake up the next morning with sore puffy eyes and a major case of depression. *Not a good look.*

I give my face a few cool splashes of water, trying my best to avoid my sorry reflection. Alex's comments about Jax poke at my glum, sleep-deprived mind, making me re-question Jax's motives, along with my faith in him. When Jax had come to see me the night before last, he'd seemed different somehow—warmer. The visit had felt more intimate than usual. I shake away the memory, afraid of the feelings it stirs inside me. I don't see how someone as important as Jax could possibly be interested in someone as insignificant as me, especially when he's got an entire colony of beautiful Purples like Zannah to choose from. I dare another glance at the mirror. Even with my delicate bone structure, all I see reflecting back at me is the washed-out face of a pitiful Pastel. Annoyed, I spray a handful of water across my reflection, distorting it. Jax isn't showing me attention because he's in love with me, he's doing it because he pities me. He feels guilty for putting me in the line of fire.

Alex says Jax is either into me or using me as his pawn, so I guess this leaves me as his pawn.

I don't want to believe this, but I don't know what to believe anymore. Both possibilities seem wrong.

I'm covered in dirt, and my hair is decorated with twigs and leaves. I'd love to ignore the way I look and curl up in bed, but Jax and Oscar will arrive soon, and I need a proper wash before they get here. After stripping down, I examine my figure. Bruises of all shapes, sizes, and colours mark at least thirty percent of my body. Between the fuegor, Electra, Ogre, Rae, and my lovely little sled ride out to the forest, I look like a living breathing—not so pretty—work of art.

Alex had been absolutely appalled when he'd seen the ugly bruises marking my bare skin. He said he was glad I'd taken him up on his offer to use the vertic switz ink, and when I was strong enough, I should pay Electra and Rae a visit. *Oh, Alex.* I still have no idea how sincere his feelings were towards me, but I long for him, regardless.

I rotate from side to side. As far as I can tell, nothing at all has changed since I used the ink. I'm still short and scrawny. *I wonder how long it will take for the tattoo to show any effects. More importantly, I wonder if I'll live long enough to see it.*

"Hurry up," Floss grumbles, giving the wooden door to our washroom a loud thump. "There are others here who need to use the washroom too, you know."

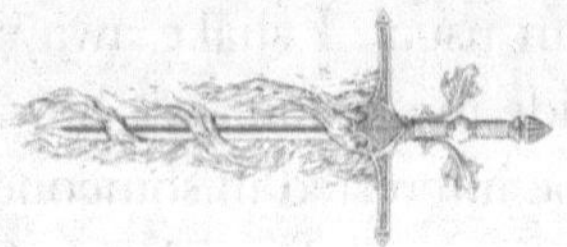

At six A.M., Jax and Oscar arrive at our family cavern, and as usual, they receive an exuberant, over-the-top greeting from my father. He hasn't spoken to me once this morning—and for the first time *ever*—I couldn't give a damn. I've finally decided I don't need his approval, because he hasn't got my respect. I pity him with his petty wants and needs. He's never going to be satisfied with what he's got; he's always going to crave more.

"Look at that idiot, would you?" Floss spits under her breath. She steps up beside me. "How humiliating."

I sigh. "Yep, he's at it again."

"I don't even think Jax likes him." She sniggers. "Look at the way his jaw is set. He looks like he wants to clobber him."

We share a secret look in agreement, and together we grin. It's kind of nice to connect. Perhaps she is interested in being more of a sister to me after all. It would be amazing to finally have her as a friend. I'm not going to pin my hopes on it though. I know better than to trust her mercurial personality.

Jax has brought Sphinx along, and next to Oscar stands a husken I've never met before. It's slightly smaller than Sphinx with more white bleeding through its purple coat.

Oscar's husken steps over to my father and gives his leg a curious sniff. He glares down at it in disgust, and I can tell he wants to kick it away, but he doesn't. He wouldn't want the warriors to see his nasty side in action. "What's happening with Rae?" he asks. "When is she coming back? We are handling our three-Zeek hunting team fine, for now, but it's easier and more efficient when there's four of us."

My mother gapes—appalled by his question. "You want Rae back?"

"Actually… I have a few things I need to discuss with you all, regarding this matter." Jax's voice is firm, bordering on hostile. "Where's Fau?"

As if on cue, Fau enters our family cavern. "I'm here," he says, leaving his two heterochromia huskens, Lollie and Gypsy, by the entryway.

I've never seen so many lion-sized huskens together in one small space. My father must be on the verge of a coronary.

"I'm here to inform you that Rae will not be returning to your hunting team. I have reassigned her to another team for the best interest of everyone."

"But she's a strong and valued team member," my father argues.

Jax's expression hardens. "She also tried to throw both of your daughters off the boat at Elgar's funeral—which would have killed them. I believe keeping Rae on your team would be a conflict of interest."

My mother's eyes meet my fathers, a mix of anger and resentment emitting from them. "I agree with Jax. Our daughters' safety comes first."

I haven't had much to do with my parents since their disagreement during our "family dinner". They'd put up a good front for the sake of onlookers at Ogre's funeral, but the tension between them at the moment is rife with hostility.

"Due to the inconvenience of this sudden change, I'm assigning Floss to be your new team member," Jax continues.

"What?" my father and Floss say in unison, however, I'm pretty sure they are expressing different kinds of "what's".

Jax turns his attention to Floss. "I know you were interested in becoming a hunter before you were assigned as a fruit picker. Do you still feel the same way?"

Her eyes flick to mine before answering. "Yes. I want to be a hunter."

"Good." He glances back at Saul, who doesn't look at all happy about this new arrangement. "I'd like you to take Floss out hunting today. Her training can start immediately on the job. You are the best hunter we've got, so I'm sure taking on a new recruit won't be an issue."

He's stroking his ego. *Smart.*

Jax gazes across the room. "Is everyone on board and satisfied with this new arrangement?"

Nods and "yesses" fill the cavern, my father's too, only his doesn't sound sincere.

"Well in that case, you lot can all get going, while I speak to Harlow about her new arrangements."

Floss is excited and quick to move, but no one else is. They are all curious about my new work placement, and quite frankly, so am I. *Please don't let it be another purple job.*

Jax stands fixed, lips sealed, watching, waiting for them to leave. He's obviously not willing to discuss my new work placement in front of them. *I'm grateful.*

It doesn't take long for my mother and Fau to take the hint and head out, but my father lingers.

"Are you sure this is the right decision?" he asks. "Floss isn't the kind of Zeek I would choose to put on my team."

Jax sticks to his guns. "I'm sure. It makes the most sense. She's your daughter, which means you can also give her some added training at home. It will only be a matter of time until she's as good as Rae."

"What's the story with *her* then?" My father points without looking at me. "Are you going to fill us in on her position too?"

"Yes," Jax's jaw ticks, but he keeps his expression neutral. "I will fill you and Krista in on all the details when you get back from hunting this afternoon. However, this is a matter I would prefer to discuss with Harlow alone first, if I may."

Saul gives a reluctant nod, his face reddening with irritation. "Very well then."

When my father finally leaves, Jax gets me to take a seat on the lounge, and I prepare myself for the worst. You always get someone to sit before serving them with bad news; it's common knowledge.

"So…" he starts, and for the first time *ever* he appears nervous. "I have some good news, and some not so good news."

"Okay?" I swallow hard, fidgeting with the sleeve of my jumper. "Let's start with the bad news."

"To keep you safe and out of the spotlight until things cool down, I think it might be best if I send you down to live and work on the lower level with the rest of the Pastels. This won't be permanent." He rushes out the last sentence. "I just need a few more months to build a bigger army of sympathisers to stand alongside me on this." He kneels down in front of me, and takes hold of my hands, sending my heart into an unnatural rhythm. "I'm so sorry." Regret fills his deep voice. "I feel like I've let you down badly. I hadn't realised things would come to this. I hadn't predicted Electra would retaliate the way she did. She's more involved with Nix's gang of radicals than I'd realised."

His violet eyes search my face, creased with concern at the corners. "You're not saying anything."

"I'm not worried about being sent down to live with the Pastels," I say, and I mean it. My father's prejudiced opinions no longer have pull over me. I'd rather be sent down to live and work with the Pastels than sent up to live and work with the Purples. Perhaps after a while they might start treating me as if I'm one of them. I might finally belong somewhere. "You can leave me down there forever if it will make your life easier. It's not like I belong up here. There's nothing I will miss."

"I told you she would take it well," Oscar pipes in from behind us.

Acting as if he's been busted doing something wrong, Jax releases my hands.

"My father was a good man," he tells me. "His mission was to make life more pleasant and equal for all Pastels, but he died before he could succeed. I was hoping I could continue on with his legacy, but by the time I was old enough to take any action and be heard, Nix had already brainwashed and persuaded a large percentage of our colony that Pastel lives were worthless, and a drain on our society."

Count your mother in too, I think, but don't say. *I wonder if he knows it was his mother who had his father killed. Or how she'd sent over a hundred Pastels to Summer—as a peace offering—to be used as slaves.* I don't want to be the one to inform him. *How do you tell someone their mother is pure evil without upsetting them?*

"I want Electra to think I'm abandoning my beliefs and she's won this battle, even though she hasn't won the war. It's the only way she's going to leave you alone."

"I'm not afraid to die," I say, and it's mostly true now that I've hurt and lost Alex. A new beginning with no memory of my Human or Zeek life might be just what I need. "Don't bow down to Electra if it's only to save me. If you want to put up a fight and bring about change for future Pastels, then I'm happy for you to continue using me as your pawn."

"My pawn?" He eyes me with shock. "Who said that you were my pawn? Was it Zannah?"

Oscar takes a step forward, his face contorted. "Of course it was Zannah, who else would be spiteful enough to say something so ridiculous?"

"No." I shake my head. "It isn't something Zannah said." *It's something Alex said.* "It's coming from me."

The look of hurt flashes across Jax's eyes. "Do you really think this is what I've been doing this whole time? Using you as my pawn?"

I glance down at my hands, annoyed at myself for letting Alex's comment make me question Jax's integrity. "No, I guess not; and it doesn't really matter what I think. You need to do what's right for you, not me."

"I want to do what's right for both of us—and the colony. I will fix this, I promise you, but I need a more time."

His intense gaze locks on mine, and an awkward silence lingers a moment before Oscar says, "Why don't you give her the good news."

"Right." Jax rises to his feet. "Three things," he says. "First of all, I've spoken to your friend Minty and her parents, and they've agreed you can move in with them."

What? I think I preferred the bad news, and I'm afraid it shows.

Jax cocks his head in question. "She's your friend, right?"

"Right." I don't have the heart to tell him the truth.

"Secondly," he continues, "I've got you working in the Bean-Brew Cavern. Zavier will be out of action for another six weeks or so, and with Minty's arm fixed in a cast, I figure she's going to need all the help she can get."

I force a smile, attempting to look pleased.

"Lastly," he adds, and then turns his attention to Oscar's husken. "Lucy," he beckons. "Come here, girl." The husken scurries over.

"You will be responsible for Lucy."

"What? Me?" This time I don't need to fake a smile. My whole face lights up with excitement. "Seriously?" This really *is* good news. "But she's a warrior husken, and I'm not a warrior."

"The Bean-Brew Cavern will be re-opening again tomorrow, and the warriors and I have decided two of our huskens should be sent down as guard dogs to help avoid any further incidents from occurring. Lucy will stay with you and Minty, and Bell will be sent to live with Finn—the other head chef. This way they can work the same rotating rosters as you lot do, four days on and four days off. As a working dog, all of her food will be provided for her. All you have to do is care for her and take her with you wherever you go."

I feel like springing out of the lounge and throwing my arms around him.

"Lucy," I call, and she comes straight over. My eyes dart to Jax's. "Can I pat her?"

A semi-smile plays on his lips. "Why are you asking me? She's your husken."

I reach out and bury my fingers in the thick fur around her neckline. During one of our walks home, I'd told Jax that I was disappointed my father hadn't taken one of the heterochromia huskens, and how I'd always wished I'd been able to grow up with one.

I wonder if he remembers, and if that's why he's arranged this?

"Thank you," I say.

"There's no need to thank me. Just promise me you'll be careful, and if any problems arise, you'll reach out instead of running away again."

I nod. "Okay."

"We won't be seeing as much of each other for a while, but if things get out of hand, or you do really need me, let Oscar, Kieran, or Zannah know, and I'll come right away."

"I don't know that I would trust Zannah," Oscar mutters under his breath in the background.

My heart deflates. I don't really know what Jax and I are to each other. I doubt if I could even call us friends. All I know is I've grown to care about him a lot, and I will miss him. Sphinx too.

"Oscar has left an empty pack by the entry for you to pop all your belongings into before you go. You should be safe walking to Minty's with Lucy by your side. She'll protect you. It's what she's been trained to do." He gives me one last apologetic look and then turns his gaze to Oscar. "We'd better go. It's nearly six-thirty."

Lucy's ears prick and something occurs to me. "Hold on, do Minty's parents know I'm bringing a husken with me?"

"Yes, I've told them about Lucy," Jax assures me. "And they are glad to have the extra security around of a night, especially after what Elgar did to Minty."

Relief floods me. "Okay, perfect."

The ghost of a smile stretches along his lips. "Goodbye Harlow." *Ouch.* Alex's final words had been the same, only he'd called me Ruby, not Harlow. Two devastating goodbyes in less than two days. *I'm going backwards fast.*

Putting on a brave face, I wave goodbye to the three of them as they leave. My hand rests on Lucy's back. Despite everything, I am glad to have my long-awaited companion. At least one of my dreams has come true. "It looks like it's you and me, girl."

My room doesn't have much in it, only my threadbare clothes and my carving of Lollie from Fau. I might have to get another carving done of Lucy to match, and I know just the guy who would be capable of doing such a thing. Come to think of it, *I wonder what's happened to RJ? I hope he's safe.* I should have asked Jax about him. I should've asked about Zavier and Trey too.

The sack of clothes Jax acquired for me sits in a pile at the side of my bed. With a disappointed sigh, I scoop everything up and dump it on Floss' bed. She'll be excited to find these precious items when she gets back from hunting. I'd like to keep the black jacket with snowflakes and matching boots. I feel an odd attachment to them because Jax recommended I wear them. "I think it will look good on you," he'd said.

I push the memory aside. It would be selfish to keep them for sentimental reasons. I have no use for them anymore. I can't wear them on the lower level; all they will do is ostracise me further.

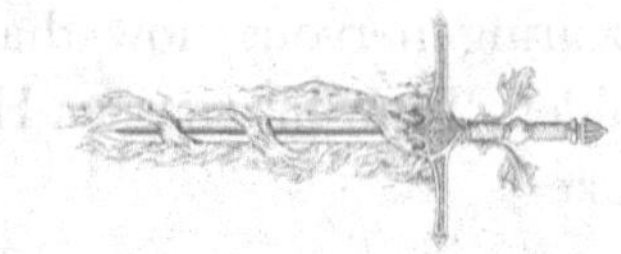

Before heading down to Minty's, I swing by the medical chamber to see Zavier. I miss the way things used to be between us before everything turned to chaos. Now it feels like there's a wedge between us. Soon there might even be a Floss wedge to split us apart even further. I still can't believe she likes him. Sure, he's cute and fun to be around, but it seems out of character for her to go for someone below her status. She's always been so mean to Zavier, calling him a bottom feeder.

As I get to the medical chamber entry, I tell Lucy to "sit". She does, and something inside me tingles. I hadn't expected her to be this obedient for a mere Pastel. "Wait here and don't let anyone pinch my pack, okay," I add, dumping it beside her.

I have Alex's leather pouch tucked away in my pocket. I couldn't risk leaving it in my pack. I still have no idea where I'm going to hide it, especially now that I'm moving in with Minty.

When I get to the front desk, an unexpected face greets me. "RJ? What are you doing working here?" I smile, relieved to see him.

"Jax got me a job in here," he leans in closer and whispers. "He says it will be much safer. There are a few other Pastel sympathisers on staff. He also said he's going to have me trained to become a medic. He believes I've got the brains for it."

"For certain," I agree.

The same doe-eyed Purple I'd witnessed flirting with Jax a couple of weeks back makes her way over to the desk. Going by her tag, her name is Harper.

She slides smoothly into the seat next to RJ. "How's it going over here?" she asks, voice chipper. "Were you able to help this young lady?"

RJ looks up at the labelled floor chart in front of him, all the while tapping his pencil on the desk repeatedly. "Zavier is in bed fifteen," he says, appearing nervous now that he's got someone watching over his shoulder. "I saw him earlier. He looks much better. Hopefully he's still awake."

"Thank you, RJ."

4

GET ME OUT OF HERE!

-ZAVIER-

"*H*ey, you."

My eyes peel partially open to find Harlow standing above my bed. She's gazing down at me with a warm, affectionate smile. My heart melts. It's been awhile since she's smiled at me this way. I've missed it.

She looks different. She's had her hair knotted into dreadlocks. It suits her, but I don't like that it reminds me of Jax.

"What are you still doing in bed, you lazy bludger? I'm amazed they've managed to keep you here now that you're awake. I thought you'd be up and crawling to the exit on all fours." She pulls a chair up close and sits. "I know how much you detest this place."

A chuckle escapes my throat before I can stop it, and my whole chest feels as though it's about to burst wide open. "I'm only sticking around for the free food," I croak.

"Is that so?" A playful smile curls her lips. "I'm not surprised, I've heard the food they serve here is way better than the sludge they serve up in the Bean-Brew Cavern—*just saying*."

I cast her a mock-annoyed glance. "Ha, ha, ha, when did you get so funny?"

She folds her arms on top of the bed rail, then leans forward to rest her chin on them. "You're the only one who finds me funny."

"Talking about sneaking out, I heard you took off to the forest. Why? What happened?"

"I've been feeling a little bit cooped up lately, I needed a breather, is all." she says, playing it down. "But I'm back now, and I'm glad to see you're awake and in good spirits. I've been worried about you."

I attempt to shuffle up the bed, but a sharp pain rips through my side, stopping me in an instant. I groan. "I've been worried about you too," I say. "Jax said he found you out in the danger zone. What the frost were you doing all the way out there?"

As expected, Harlow blows off my question with one of her own. "Does this mean you and Jax are on speaking terms now? *Funny*, I didn't think you liked the guy."

"I don't," I retort. "But, when it comes to matters concerning you, I have to talk to him. You hang out with him more than me these days."

Guilt flashes across her face. "Yeah, I know. I'm sorry we haven't gotten to hang out as much lately, but that's all about to change."

"What do you mean?"

"I mean, I'm coming down to live on the lower level, with you and all the other Pastels."

"Really?"

She nods. "Really."

You'd think I would be happy about this, but I'm not, and I

doubt she could be happy about it either. I don't want her to come down to the lower level and live in a tiny little hovel like the rest of us Pastels. She's part Magenta. She has the right to stay where she is. Magenta caverns aren't huge, but they are certainly spacious compared to Pastel caverns.

I wonder where this new arrangement has come from? A theory comes to mind, and I try to push it away, but I my brain continues to run with it.

Jax and Harlow have been dating and some Purples have cottoned-on. This is why she's been roughed up lately, and why Jax has been uncharacteristically concerned about her wellbeing. Due to the Commander's death policy regarding inter-relationships, Jax had chosen to break things off with her, and she'd been so devastated by his decision, she'd taken off to the danger zone.

Now that he's found her and brought her back to safety—to clear his own conscience, I bet—he's sent her down to live with the rest of us Pastels, hoping no one else will suspect there'd ever been anything between them.

The image of Jax dumping the sack of her clothes by our cavern entryway snaps to mind, and the answer is clear. I feel like an idiot. *They really have been involved in a secret affair all along. Silly girl.* I don't know whether to feel mad or sorry for her.

"Where are you going to live?" I ask, because irrespective of what she's done, and how bitter I feel about it, I still really care about her. "Do you need a place to stay? You can have my bed if you want, I can stay on the couch."

"It's okay, Jax arranged for me to stay with Minty."

"Minty?" I jerk up and an excruciating pain shoots through my side. "What? Why? Is he trying to punish you or something?" I'm only half joking about the last part, but nevertheless, I find his choice of residence a little odd. Minty is an absolute bitch to Harlow. Plus, Minty knows too much. This is going to be problematic. I don't think Harlow should stay there.

Harlow fiddles with the bracelet I made for her. "Jax is under the impression Minty and I are friends."

"How? You two don't even speak unless you *absolutely have to*."

"Well, we did *absolutely have to* after Ogre nearly killed you. Believe it or not, Minty was the one who convinced Jax he should let me into the kitchen to see you after the incident. She told him you would've wanted me there." Harlow's eyes touch my face, and she winces at the sight of it. I can only imagine how terrible it looks. The intense pressure of fluid built up around my cheeks feels tight and painful. "I know you're not fond of Jax," she continues. "But if it wasn't for him, you'd be dead. He saved your life. He patched you up and then carried you here from the Bean-Brew Cavern."

I groan in frustration. "Don't tell me that."

I didn't know this. Nobody told me. All Jax had said was, "Elgar did a serious number on you, you're lucky to still be alive." He never mentioned he was the one who saved me. *Cocky bastard.* He must've assumed I already knew and was trying to show off.

"It's true," Harlow insists, which only irks me further.

I brush off the comment. I don't want the added pressure of owing Jax anything. Especially now, when I've finally figured out what's been going on between them. I'm completely disgusted with the guy. He used Harlow, and now he's tossing her aside like she's nothing.

"You don't have to stay with Minty, you know," I say, steering away from the subject of Jax. "You can come and stay with Lexan and me. I'm sure Lexan would be more than happy to take you in."

"I don't think I'll fit. I've got a husken now. Her name's Lucy. Jax gave her to me this morning. He says she's to be one of the guard dogs at the Bean-Brew Cavern."

Even after everything she's been through these past couple of weeks, she still seems to think the sun shines out of Jax's arse.

"How delightful," I say, sarcasm dripping from my voice. "There's nothing like a bit of mutt hair mixed in with the chicklet omelettes."

She gives me a slight nudge, which hurts. "Oh, come on Zavier, lighten up. If it makes you feel any better, I'm going to be working at the Bean-Brew Cavern too."

"You are?"

"Yeah. Who would've thought, huh? We'll be able to hang out all the time once you get better." Her hand slips over mine and she gives it a light squeeze. "I've really missed you, you know?"

"I know. I've missed you too."

A comfortable silence lingers between us, before I say, "I can't wait to get out of here. You were right before. If I could move well enough to crawl my way out of the exit, I would. Between us both getting hurt, I feel like I've been living here, and I honestly can't stand the place. There's always something beeping, or some self-important Magenta whinging, and those Purple medics think they can keep telling me what to do."

Harlow gazes over at Medic Sylvie, who stands a few beds down from mine, discussing—with a young Magenta patient—which activities he should avoid doing for the next few weeks. Sylvie sees Harlow looking and gives a slight nod.

"Things have been rough lately, that's for sure," Harlow says, returning her attention to me. "And this place does suck, but you should really listen to the medics. Most of them are nice, and as crazy as it sounds, they are looking out for your best interest. It's their job."

Sylvie finishes up with the Magenta guy and comes wandering over to us.

"What have you done?" I groan. "Why'd you have to lure her over here? Good friend you are. I've been trying to associate with these Purples as little as possible."

Harlow tenses, appearing as distressed as I feel. "I didn't mean to lure her over here," she says, biting a nail. "I was only looking to see which medic was on out of curiosity."

I wonder if the reason she's distressed has anything to do with her breakup with Jax? He'd made her feel like she belonged with the Purples at one stage of the game, and now he's sent her to live with us lower-class citizens. She's probably ashamed. It's understandable. He's made a mockery of her.

"Hello, Harlow," Sylvie says as she nears. Her lips twitch at the corners, like she wants to share a smile but can't bring herself to do so. "How's your leg?"

Harlow shifts uncomfortably where she sits. "It's feeling much better now, thank you."

"Just remember, you still have internal stitches, and we don't want them ruptured, so don't go doing anything too strenuous."

Harlow nods. "Got it, thanks."

Sylvie steps up to the head of my bed. "And how are you feeling today?"

"I feel amazing." My voice is mocking. "You should really write up the paperwork to send me home."

Ignoring me, her eyes drift back to Harlow's. "He's charming, this one, isn't he?"

Harlow nods in agreement but says nothing.

Noticing Harlow's unease, Sylvie says, "Okay. Well, being as I'm not needed here, I'll leave you two to get back to—whatever it was—you were talking about before I rudely interrupted. Take care, Harlow."

"Well, that was nice and awkward," I blurt, before Sylvie's even made it out of earshot. "Are you ever going to let me in on the truth about what happened to your leg? Or are you just going to keep getting all weird about it whenever someone mentions the topic near me?"

A jumble of expressions flash across her face, and I can't tell if she wants to laugh, cry, or punch me. "We both have things we haven't shared with each other lately," she says, and I flinch, not sure exactly what secret she is referring to, "but let's save the story swapping for when you get out of here. You should concentrate on resting at the moment. You need to heal if you want to get out of here." She gives my hand one last squeeze and then stands. "I should probably go. My husken is waiting at the entry for me."

Her playfulness from earlier is gone, and I feel responsible. I haven't been all that nice to her since she's been here. I've been picking at her, but I can't help it. I'm disappointed, bitter, and hurting all over.

"Harlow wait," I call, as she turns to walk away. I can't let her leave like this. I'd prefer us to part on a positive note. "I forgot to mention I like your new hair-do. It suits you."

"Thanks." Her cheeks flush. "Floss did it for me."

"Sorry, I think my hearing must have glitched for a second. Did you just say Floss did it for you?"

"Yeah, she's been a little bit nicer to me lately."

Talk about a major turnaround. *Exactly how long was I passed out for?*

5

FRENEMIES

-HARLOW AND HARLOW AS RUBY-

I arrive at Minty's to discover she's the only one home, and to top it off, her greeting is even more wretched than I'd expected. "Oh, look," she says bitterly. "It's Precious and her furry friend Invader, finally coming to join us lower-level subordinates. How devastating this must be for you."

My insides sour, but instead of biting, I keep my face neutral and ask, "Where do we sleep?"

She points to an opening off the main living-kitchen-dining area and my mood plummets further. It's a small dual nook, separated down the middle by a short nib wall. I'm used to having an open nook, all nooks are doorless, but I'm not used to having an adjoined open nook. The sight of my new living space leaves me feeling exposed. *There's no privacy.* I sneak a quick glance at Minty's side. It's spotless, with minimal personal items. Going by what Zavier's told me, Minty is fanatical when it comes to cleanliness.

I haven't been to Minty's since Zavier came to stay for six weeks after his parents died, and that was forever ago. This cavern is bigger than the one he lives in now, but not by much. The living-kitchen-dining room is two metres longer, and there's the adjoined sleeping nook. It's bigger because Minty's grandmother used to live with them in the beginning, but sadly she passed away after Minty turned seven.

"I don't believe Invader will fit in there with you," Minty says, pointing out the obvious. "You'll need to make her up a bed in the living room." She steps over to the lounge and hands me a bunch of blankets with her good arm. "My parents said you can use these scruffy ones for the husken. They are too tattered to use on our beds."

"Her name is Lucy," I say. "Not Invader."

"Good to know." Her tone is deadpan. "I'd like the area between our nooks to remain clean and tidy, and make sure to keep Invader's nose out of my stuff. That goes for you too. We might have a friend in common, but this doesn't make us friends."

A depression sweeps over me. I thought I could handle this new arrangement, and I thought I could handle Minty, but being in her company feels even worse than I remembered. She makes Floss seem friendly by comparison.

I lay the blankets out for Lucy and then pop my pack into my new, sad little nook.

Lucy follows me inside, taking up the whole floor space. I hope she knows how to reverse, because it's the only way she's getting out of here again. I unzip my pack and take out the carving of Lollie.

"This is Lollie," I whisper, and Lucy pants in reply. I place the carving on my nightstand, hoping it will make me feel a little more at home. "As soon I earn some tradable goods, I'll see if I can get a carving done of you too."

Lucy stays for a scratch behind the ears and then backs out in a slow and awkward fashion. At a lost for what to do, I follow.

I pause by the shared entryway when I see Minty standing inside her nook. Her glasses are off and she's swinging them around by a single arm, seeming to contemplate something. Hopefully, it's not how best to get rid of me. Her face looks younger without her specs on. Sweeter. *It's deceptive.*

"What time will Herman and Ollie be home from work?"

Her swinging glasses come to a sudden stop, and she glances up at me. "About five-thirty, give or take."

I wither internally. Five-thirty seems like forever away, especially when I'm stuck here alone with Minty. I've never known the ice caves to feel this icy.

Minty stares at me a moment, eyes scrutinising, and then flops onto her bed, appearing as deflated as I feel.

"For your information, I didn't ask to be sent here." I rest my back against the wall. "Jax thought we were friends."

"It is what it is." Minty sighs. "I shouldn't be here for much longer, anyway. Tatum and I are saving up to get a place of our own."

There's a chance I won't be here for much longer either, I think. *Especially if Rae and Electra are still out for my blood.* Jax seems certain once they learn I've finally been put where I belong, things will blow over and they'll leave me alone. *I'm not convinced.* He didn't see the way Electra's face turned to stone when she gave me the agonising brain freeze, or how Rae's eyes turned killer wild as she tried hurling me over the rail of the boat.

I have Lucy for protection now, which is reassuring, *but will she really protect a Pastel over a Purple if Electra comes to finish me off herself?* Lucy is a warrior husken. You'd imagine she would be trained to protect Purples above all other Zeeks. I won't know the answer to this until it happens—if it happens. *Hopefully, it won't.*

By five-thirty Herman and Ollie arrive home, and I smile with relief as they greet me with a much warmer welcome. They even seem pleased to meet Lucy.

"Wow, she's much bigger than I thought she'd be." Ollie says, giving Lucy an affectionate pat behind the ears. "And her fur feels much coarser than it looks." She glances up at me, her faded pink eyes tired and sunken. For someone who is only in her late thirties, she looks much older. She has heavily indented crow's feet stretching halfway down her cheeks. *It sucks to be Pastel. We age much faster than our years.* "I've never seen a husken up close before," she admits. "They're rarely brought down to the lower level."

"That, and Mum never leaves this cavern unless she absolutely has to," Minty chimes in, sounding snarky. "She doesn't believe in living life to its fullest; or doing what makes you happy."

"I don't believe in overdoing yourself," Ollie corrects. "And you, Little Lady, have been overdoing yourself lately."

Minty scowls at her comment. "I might be 'little' in stature, but at least I'm not 'small minded' like some."

"Minty," Herman cuts in, pointing a bony finger at her. "Be nice to your mother."

"Okay, Old Man, I'll play nice," Minty shoots back, her tone sickly sweet and mocking. "But can you please ask Mum why she is willing to take in Harlow and her large, furry friend but still won't even allow Tatum to come over for dinner?"

"Can we not have this discussion right now?" Ollie says, casting her a prickled glance. "We have a guest."

"She's not a guest, she's a boarder. We're stuck with her indefinitely."

I sit on the dining room chair bowing my head—pretending to be invisible. I don't want to be pulled into this conversation. Things are already uncomfortable enough as it is. Clearly, I've stepped into something that's been brewing long before I got here.

"Just say it," Minty insists. "You can't accept who I am."

Ollie's voice tightens. "I said not now, Minty."

"Not now—or ever, *right?*" Minty retorts. "You're such a…"

"Minty," Herman warns once more. "Take a breather."

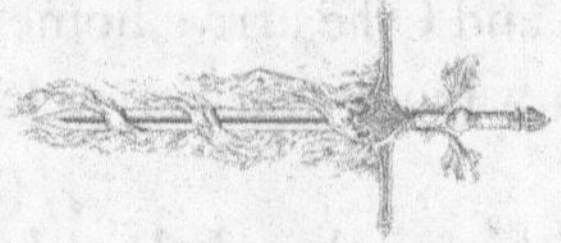

My first dinner with Minty's family is almost as pleasant as the family dinner I'd experienced the night before Ogre's funeral. There's no pushing or shoving, but Minty and Ollie are at each other's throats the entire time, their tongues flicking at one another with sharp, hurtful remarks. Herman tries to defuse the situation multiple times, but eventually Minty angrily excuses herself, and takes off to her nook.

Ollie apologises about Minty's attitude, but I think she's as much to blame for the tension. I hadn't known she was struggling with Minty being gay, *but how could I?* Minty never speaks to me, unless it's to say something snide and horrible.

As much as I feel sorry for Minty—knowing her mother doesn't accept her for who she is—it feels reassuring to know I'm not the only Zeek in our colony who is a disappointment to her parents.

Some bowls and sacks of food were delivered for Lucy earlier this evening, so after helping Ollie to clean up, I give Lucy her dinner, take her to the toilet, and then hop into bed.

"Minty, are you awake?" I whisper. If it wasn't for the thin nib wall, our beds would be joined.

"No," she answers with a growl.

I bite my lip, wondering why I'm even trying. "I went to see Zavier today," I continue, regardless of her negative attitude towards me. "He was awake."

She doesn't answer for a long time, and I imagine she's going to ignore me, but finally she asks, "How was he?"

"He still looks terrible, but he's as spirited as ever." I smile to myself. "He can't wait to get out of there. He's already mapping out escape plans."

"I think it's going to be awhile before that happens. Tatum said he can't even sit up."

My visit to Zavier hadn't gone completely as I'd hoped. He

wasn't horrible to me, but he also wasn't his usual friendly self. He'd seemed bitter towards me, which—if I'm being honest with myself—is fair. Zavier was there for me unconditionally when I was down and out, yet I haven't been there for him.

"Minty… What exactly happened to Zavier?"

She lets out another groan. "It's late, Harlow. I'm tired."

I glance at my watch. The lighting in my nook is dim, but I can faintly make out the small black hands on its face. It's only ten to eight. "It's not that late."

"If you are so interested, then why didn't you ask him?"

Feeling slightly chilly, I pull my blanket up over me. "I didn't know if he'd want to talk about it. I didn't want to embarrass him."

"He got into a fight with Elgar, protecting your sister," she says matter-of-factly.

I'd like to be given more info, but she doesn't elaborate, and I don't want to push my luck by pestering her. I'm actually surprised she answered me at all.

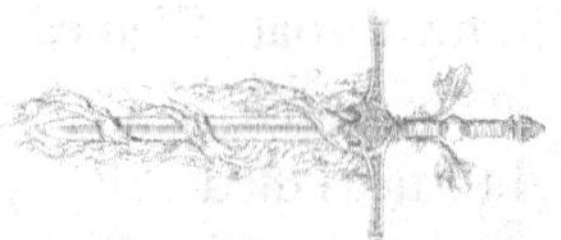

The sound of cups clinking and chattering voices stirs me awake, and I can smell the sweetness of cakes mixed with the strong aroma of coffee. *Yes, please.* What I wouldn't give for a caramel expresso and a big slice of orange cake. My mouth waters at the thought.

I blink several times over to discover I'm standing in the middle of a crowded café. Two small kids charge through my lower half unknowingly, racing each other towards the play park.

"Here's one latte and one cappuccino." I turn to see a young freckly nosed waitress setting down two steaming hot mugs in front of a pair of blondes. I glance between the two, registering Jade's face.

"Thank you," they say in unison, and the waitress moves on, juggling her tray of beverages through the mass of noisy patrons.

I focus my attention back on my sister, wishing I could join her in the literal sense. What I wouldn't give to have her love and support right now.

She slowly sips at her latte, brows dipped while her friend gossips about someone by the name of Lou, and her messy divorce with Reggie.

Desperate to feel a part of something, even if it's only one sided, I step closer. However, to my shock and bewilderment, Jade appears to notice me. She gasps wide-eyed, spraying an entire mouthful of coffee all over her friend.

"Jade!" Her friend jumps up from her chair, gaping in disbelief. "What in the world...? I only just bought this cardigan. It's a Chanel."

"I'll get you a tea-towel," a nearby waitress says and scurries off.

Disregarding her friend, Jade's eyes lock on mine, wide and semi-crazed. "Ruby? Is it really you?"

My breath catches in my throat. "You can see me?"

She stares as she rises from her seat. "Yes, I can see you. I saw you before too. The night Lucas died... But you left. I thought I was going crazy."

I remember her head whipping around to face me, and her crying out my name, but I was too preoccupied with what was going on with Alex to take in the significance. She can see me. *My sister can actually see me.* This changes everything. *I have my rock back.*

"Jade?" Her friend's brows pucker. "What's going on? Who are you talking to?"

"Carrie, it's Ruby," Jade says, and there's a delirious note to her voice. "She's here, I told you she rescued me the other night, and she's here again.... Right now."

The waitress comes dashing back with a tea-towel and hands it to Carrie. "Here you go, Miss."

It suddenly occurs to me we have an audience. I gaze across the tables to find all eyes on Jade. *Oh dear, this isn't good!* While I am thrilled Jade can finally see, nobody else can, and at the moment she looks bat-shit crazy.

"Jade, wait. Stop," I say, and her eyes flick back to mine, still semi-crazed. "Nobody else here can see me, only you. You need to stop speaking to me and politely excuse yourself."

"But—"

"Shhh." I raise my finger to my lips. "I want to talk, I really do, but now is not the time. Look around. You're causing a scene and scaring your friend."

Whispers have replaced the clinking and chatter.

"But you will stay with me?" Jade asks, voice wobbling. "You won't leave."

"No, I won't leave, now please stop speaking to me in front of everyone."

"Sorry," Carrie says to the table next to them. "I think my friend may have had one too many coffees this afternoon." She tucks her chair in, throws a fifty-dollar note on the table, and then takes Jade by the arm. "Come on, let's go."

Carrie drags Jade out the front, and I'm relieved, because Jade didn't appear to be moving of her own accord. I've never seen my sister act this out of control before; it seems completely out of character. The Jade I grew up with was always calm and collected.

"For heaven's sake, Jade, what was that?" Carrie asks under her breath. She pulls Jade to the side of the pavement, making room for pedestrians to pass. "I know you're having a difficult time processing the truth about Lucas and the tragic circumstances surrounding your sister's death. But that there was—"

"I'm telling you, it's Ruby, she's here. I can see her." Jade points in my direction. "She's standing with us now."

"Maybe stop telling her," I say. "I don't think she's ready to hear it."

Carrie's eyes flash to where I'm standing, and I can tell by her focus she's looking straight through me. She wraps an arm around my sister, her frustrated expression softening to one of concern. "I shouldn't have invited you out today. It was too soon. I was hoping it would be a distraction, but I can see now, it was too much." She doesn't believe I'm here; I can tell. She thinks Jade is losing it. "Come on, I should really drive you home. I don't think you are in the right state of mind to drive yourself."

Jade nods agreeably and then spins to me. "You'll come with us, won't you?" A young couple passing by, stop to give Jade a questioning look.

"Sorry, she doesn't mean you two," Carrie tells them, which only confuses them further. They glance about, frowning, and then continue along the path, whispering between themselves.

"Yes," I say. "I'll come with you. Now let's hurry and get to the car before you cause mass hysteria in the street."

When we get to the car, Jade tries to open the back-passenger door for me, but I assure her it's unnecessary.

"Please," I say, praying this time I'll get through to her. "Just act as if I'm not here until Carrie drops you off at home, and we're alone."

Thankfully, Jade's place is only a ten-minute car ride from the café, and the fresh air blowing in from the open car windows seems to snap her back to reality.

As Carrie walks Jade to the front door, Jade acknowledges her crazed actions from earlier. "I'm sorry about spraying coffee all over your new cardigan. I haven't slept much since Lucas..." She doesn't finish. "I must have been hallucinating. I'll pay for the dry-cleaning or buy you a new one."

That was a good move, Jade, I think. *And it sounds credible.*

"I'm more worried about you than the cardigan," Carrie says with a shiver. "Are you going to be okay?"

Jade nods a little too eagerly to appear convincing. "I'm okay."

"Don't be mad," Carrie says, "but I've messaged Byron. He's on his way home."

"Oh... Right... Thanks."

"I'll stay with you until he arrives. We can talk."

Jade straightens, nearly dropping her phone. "No, it's fine, you don't need to stay."

"I want to," she insists.

"Honestly, I appreciate your concern, but I'd rather be alone right now. I need some time to myself to collect my thoughts."

Carrie looks hesitant but gives in. "Okay, but I want you to call me if you start hallucinating again, promise? Remember, I'm always here if you need to talk."

While Jade promises and gives Carrie a hug goodbye, I wander over to the living room to find Fat Cat curled up in a ball on one of the lounge arms. He looks peaceful, much different to the hissing arch of spikes he'd always been whenever Alex was around. My heart gives a painful twist, and my eyes sting with tears. *Alex. I can't believe I'm never going to see him again, that he's lost to me forever.* If only I could rewind time. Now that I know it's possible, I would jump into Jade's body earlier. I would try to knock Lucas out without killing him. I would…

Stop! I force my thoughts away from Alex before they become too agonising to bear. *He's gone and there's nothing I can do to bring him back.*

I refuse to spend my precious time with Jade blubbering like a baby. I'd like her to believe I've moved on to a better place, and I am happy. It's what's best for her. She needs to find peace.

After shutting the front door, Jade comes bounding over. "Rubes," she says, diving in for a hug. I try warning her I'm permeable, but she doesn't listen, and stumbles straight through me, tripping on the coffee table which sits directly behind me. I reach to catch her, and for a split second I make contact, but my fingers lose traction, and she crashes to the floor with a painful thud.

"Far out, Jade, are you okay?"

"Owww." She puts her hands to her heel. It's the same heel she'd cut open during her struggle with Lucas. There is a large plaster covering it, which now appears to be filling with blood. "That hurt," she says with a wince. "I think I might have popped a stitch."

"Geez, Sis, what are you doing?" I say. "You need to be careful and start listening to me. This isn't like you. You were always the cautious and in control twin. I'm the wild reckless one, remember?"

Or at least, I used to be.

She gazes up at me, her forehead crinkled. "How come I went straight through you, yet when I fell, I felt you fleetingly touch me?"

"I can't always make contact; sometimes it works, and sometimes it doesn't."

"Why?"

I shrug. "I wish I knew. It would make things much easier if I could control it."

"I can't believe you're really here. This is completely insane." She shakes her head, looking as if she's still struggling to process everything. "I thought I could feel your presence for ages before I saw you, but I was worried it was all in my head. I wasn't sure if it was possible, or if spirits were even a real thing." Her words all roll together. "How are you here? And how is it I can suddenly see you now?"

I take a seat on the lounge, nearest to where she remains on floor after her fall. "I don't really know the answers," I say. "But I can only assume it's because you let Lucas back into your life. Perhaps I was brought back to help protect you?"

"You did protect me. You saved me." Her eyes glisten with built up tears. "Without you, I would've been the one who went flying out the window. You shoved me out of the way before Lucas could get to me."

"I would have done something much sooner if I could have, but like I said, I can't always make contact. I had no idea I could jump into your body like I did. It took a lot of failed attempts before I was actually able to do something helpful." My insides knot at the memories of my and Alex's heads colliding, and I feel like bursting into tears.

Keep it together. I can't bring myself to tell Jade what my action cost me. I don't want her to think I regret saving her, because I don't. I just wish I didn't have to lose Alex as a result.

An important thought suddenly occurs to me. Only Alex, Jade, and I know it was me who killed Lucas. Everyone would automatically assume Jade killed Lucas.

"What's being said by the authorities regarding Lucas' death?" I ask. "Are you in any trouble over what happened?"

"No, they've classified my actions as self-defence."

Relief fills me. "They were my actions, not yours," I remind her. "Remember this, okay. I killed Lucas. This is on me. I don't want his death weighing down your conscience."

She grits her teeth forcefully before saying, "Don't worry. If I could have killed him myself, I would have."

I let out a deep, pained sigh. I wish she'd never moved back here. She should've stayed in Coffs where she was safe. The darkness and hatred I see in her expression doesn't seem healthy, and I don't want it to end up consuming her.

"How's Connor?"

"He's a little shaken, and he has a few bruises, but he's doing pretty well considering the circumstances."

"And what about Rueben?"

"He's taking it hard. Connor says he was close to Lucas. He'd never seen him lose control like that before. It was a shock to all of us. None of us knew he was a schizophrenic. Josh only told me after the incident." Her eyes study mine. "Did you know?"

"Not when I was alive," I say.

"I'm so sorry I'd never suspected Lucas was your killer. I thought he was our friend."

"You couldn't have known. He covered his tracks well." I consider telling her that Lucas killed his own twin brother too, but decide against it. I don't know if Alex would want this information to be common knowledge, and at the end of the day, it isn't my secret to tell. "Don't worry," I say. "I thought he was our friend too."

"Are you stuck here? Is your spirit unable to move on?"

"No, I've moved on. I just come back now and then to check in." It's a partial truth.

"Where do you go when you aren't here?"

I don't know what—or how much—I should say. *Are there rules on what I'm allowed to disclose? I have no idea.* And anyway, I don't know if I want to tell her the whole truth. With me already gone, chances are she won't remember this life once she passes on, so why set her up for disappointment by telling her that the next life sucks.

"Somewhere pretty and far away," I answer. The caves are pretty, so it's another partial truth.

"Have you seen Nan and Pop Hughes?"

Enough with all the hard questions, I think. "No, not yet, but it's a big place. I'm sure I will eventually."

Okay, next topic. "What about you?" I ask, "I want to hear more about you. Like how did you meet Byron, and what's it like being a mum?"

Jade tells me she met Byron at a party during her Uni days. They got to talking and hit it off right away. "I was so completely awe-struck that I would turn into a klutz around him," she admits with rosy cheeks.

She shares the details of their first date, and how she'd embarrassed herself by knocking a glass of red wine all over his new outfit.

"If it's not coffee, it's wine," I tease. "Remind me not to sit opposite to you when eating out."

Now that she's recovered from her fall, Jade pulls herself up onto the lounge beside me, and after settling in comfortably, she fills me in on all of things I've missed these past eighteen years. She even gives me a bit of info about Josh's new partner Sarah, telling me she is part Maori and works as a vet nurse.

"Actually, I can show you a picture of them." She pulls out her phone, clicks on an app she calls Facebook, and types in Josh's name. When she's done, she swivels the screen towards me, revealing a picture of the pair standing together by the Sydney Opera House. A strange feeling sweeps over me as I stare at the photo. Josh looks completely different. He has a crewcut and a beard. *Weird.* My focus moves to Sarah next. She's friendly faced with dark skin and a stocky build.

"I can see where Rueben gets his looks from," I say.

After catching me up on a few of our other old friends on Facebook, Jade apologises for keeping me a secret from her family for so long.

"When you died, it was like a big piece of me died too," she admits. "I couldn't handle it. I spent every afternoon of the following year searching every square inch of the bushland behind our house, hoping to uncover a piece of evidence the police missed. I was obsessed with being the one to shed some light on your killer's identity. I wanted to find out who they were and make them pay. But after coming up empty-handed for twelve months straight, I fell into a spiral of depression. At one stage I even contemplated suicide." She lowers her eyes like she's ashamed. "I knew I had to snap out of it before I did something stupid. I didn't want our parents to be devastated any further. They were already completely distraught over losing you, and if they lost me too, I was sure it would be the end of them. I took the coward's approach, because it was the only way I could cope. I moved away and completely shut you out of my thoughts."

"You're not a coward, and I don't blame you for shutting me out." I put my hand over hers, wishing I knew how to make contact on command. "I don't know what I would've done if our roles had been reversed. I've struggled being away from you. You're my rock."

"You're my rock too."

Jade reverts to the topic of my new whereabouts—or "afterlife" as she quaintly puts it—bombarding me with question after question. I try my best to stay evasive, but thankfully, or maybe not so thankfully, a couple of loud barks begin drawing me back to Zadok.

"What's happening to you?" Jade asks. "You're flickering."

"I'm sorry, but I've got to go."

"Will you come back?"

I don't get a chance to reply.

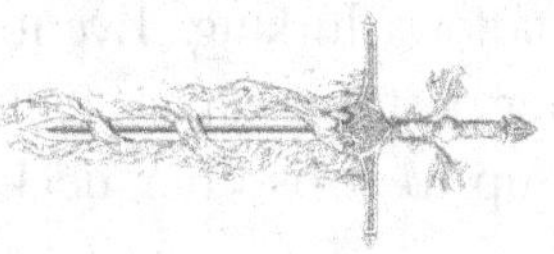

I spring out of bed to find Minty already up and scoping the area outside our adjoined nooks.

"What's going on?" I whisper.

She brushes me off with her hand and tells me to shoosh.

Lucy stands at the cavern entry, her tail raised straight and ears pointed forward. I go to walk over to her, but Minty grabs me by the shoulder and reefs me backwards.

"I think someone's out there," she whispers.

Herman stumbles out of his nook with only pants on, and I'm shocked to see how scrawny he truly is. He has the most prominent pigeon chest I've ever seen. "What's going on out here? What's the husken barking at?"

Minty snorts. "Go back to bed, Old Man, before you hurt yourself. We've got this covered."

"Do you?" He shoots her an irritated glance. "I don't know much about huskens, but going by Lucy's stance, I'd say she's still quite distressed about something, wouldn't you?" He walks over to Lucy—who's crouched in a ready to attack mode, and Minty and I follow close on his heels. "Did either of you see anything?"

"I thought I saw someone run out of the cavern." Minty says, "But I can't be sure if it was real, or if my eyes were playing tricks on me."

Herman goes to step past Lucy, but Minty grabs his arm and pulls him back with a jerk. "What do you think you're going to do, Lightweight? If there really is someone out there, you'd best go run and hide."

"Do you always have to be so condescending?"

"You look like a bag of bones," Minty mutters. "Do us all a favour and put a shirt on. My stomach's growling just looking at you."

I gaze around the cavern opening, unable to detect any movement or suspicious shadows lurking. Eventually Lucy's ears lower back to normal, and her posture relaxes, telling us the threat is gone.

"Hey girl." I step up to stroke her neck. "Who was out there? Who'd you see?"

"Whoever it was, I think they're gone," Herman says.

Minty crosses her arms over her chest. "Yeah, for now maybe."

6

DAMN YOU, ALEX

-HARLOW-

As the days pass and I'm introduced to my new job, Minty seems to grow more impatient with me.

She snatches the spatula out of my hand. "You're flipping the fluffy cakes too soon and making a mess of them. You need to wait for them to be completely bubbled first."

"I'm sorry, I didn't realise."

"And what about the gravy? Have you forgotten about it?" She fixes me with an irritated glance. "Go and give it a stir."

"Okay, okay."

I walk over to the bubbling pot of gravy and give the wooden

53

spoon a whirl. It's only my fourth day here, and I already hate it. There's a ridiculous amount to do in such little time. Minty is on my back constantly. Everything I do is too slow or wrong. My incompetency is partially her fault, though. She's not exactly the best trainer, she just expects me to already know everything.

I glance at my watch. It's quarter to six, which means it's only forty-five minutes until pack-up time, *thank goodness.* I can't wait to have four days off.

"Have you checked on the order for table five? It should be done by now."

I nod. "Yes, it's done."

"And what about table nine?"

I pick up the ladle, scoop out some gravy, and splash it over the plate of roasted deetra and vegetables. "Yes, Minty, I'm on it."

The new Pastel waitress who'd started the same day as I did opens the kitchen door and sticks her head in. She is short like Minty, only younger and friendlier. "Harlow, there's someone here to see you. She wants to know if she can come in and speak to you for a second."

I frown, stunned. "Who is it?"

The waitress gives an embarrassed shrug and glances behind her. "I don't know. She didn't give me her name, but she looks exactly like you only Magenta."

Floss is here to see me? I wonder what she wants?

"We don't have time for social calls," Minty shouts from behind me. "There are still too many orders to be done."

"Bring her through," I say, overriding Minty.

I head back to the bench to find Minty glaring at me. "What's your problem?" I ask. "I am fully capable of working and talking at the same time. And it's not like it's a friend who's dropped in for a social call. It's only my sister."

"Rude…" Floss says, as the wooden door swings shut behind her. "And here I was, thinking we were buddy-buddies."

We are barely sisters half the time, I think.

"What's up?" I crack an egg to fry. "I'm sorry, but I've got to keep working or someone is going to get upset." I shoot Minty a pointed look when I say this. She glares in retaliation but doesn't bite.

Floss' eyes do a sweep of the kitchen, and going by her creased brows, I sense disapproval. "You know Rae's out there, right?"

I tense at the mention of Rae's name. "No, I didn't."

"It's a shame she got here before I did." Floss raises a mischievous eyebrow. "Otherwise, I could have let you know what table she was sitting at, and you could've spat in her food."

"Floss." I screw my nose up. "Is this really what you came in to tell me?"

I wait for Minty to snap, and tell her to get out, but surprisingly she ignores Floss' comment.

"No, I came to say thank you for the clothes."

"Oh…" I hadn't expected a thank you from her, but I appreciate it. "You're welcome."

"I know you helped to get me the hunting job too," Floss adds. "Only our family knew I wanted to become a hunter. You must have told Jax."

She's right, I had.

"Is it living up to your expectations?"

"Honestly…" She lets out a long breath. "No, not really. I don't like watching the animals being killed."

A dark laugh escapes me. "What *exactly* did you think being a hunter was all about?"

"I hadn't really thought about what the job would entail; I was more worried about the glory. I wanted to be well-respected like Saul. I wanted him to be proud of me." She scowls. "But now I don't care so much."

"Yeah, well that makes two of us."

"Don't forget the chicklet wrap for table nine," Minty orders. "It needs to be done pronto."

Doing as I'm told, I go over to the cooler and pluck out a wrap and salad.

Floss follows, kicking aside a dropped og peel I haven't got around to sweeping up yet. "You know, Saul might not have reacted when we were told you'd been sent down here, but mum was quite upset. As crazy as it sounds, she's actually been much nicer lately. She's outside waiting if you want to see her?"

"No." I shake my head. "I don't want to see her."

I'm glad our mother is being much nicer to Floss—she needs her love and support right now—but I can't forgive her for all the years she's bowed down to our father and put him first. She should've fought for us from the very beginning. We are her daughters, and she saw how poorly he treated us. She's weak and selfish. I resent her even more than I resent him.

"Fair enough. She was pretty sure you wouldn't want to see her." Floss' voice drops to a whisper. "I don't think she and Saul will last much longer. They don't even sleep in the same nook anymore. Mum has been sleeping in your nook."

"Why do you keep calling him Saul?"

"Because, as far as I'm concerned, he's not my father."

Minty lets out a loud choking noise. "Okay, that's it, catch up time is over." She raises a pointed finger to the wooden door. "Floss, out!"

"Stand down Minty, I'm not going to *spill* anything." She casts an amused look in Minty's direction. "Anyway, I was about to leave of my own accord. I wouldn't want to stay in this cramped little kitchen any longer. I'm feeling claustrophobic." She gives a mock gasp and tugs at her collar, before gazing back at me. "Don't forget Rae is out there," she reminds me, and I'm amazed to hear a hint of concern in her voice. "She's been giving me the stink-eye, so I'd tread carefully if I were you."

"I will."

"By the way, I saw your new warrior husken on patrol out the front, she's a beauty. Make sure to keep her by your side when you leave."

As soon as Floss exits, Minty bites. "Since when are you two so chummy?"

"I still wouldn't call us chummy," I argue. "But things are certainly much more amicable between us these days."

Minty's brows narrow, and I imagine she is thinking of another snide comment to spit at me, but instead she asks, "Are you going straight home after your shift?"

What's it to her?

"Nooo…" I answer, slowly and cautiously. "I'm going to visit Zavier."

"In that case, we'll close up together, and Tatum and I will come with you."

I cock my head in confusion. "What? Why?"

"Floss is right; you should be careful around Rae. I'm pretty sure she's the Zeek I saw dashing out of our cavern the other night."

I scratch my head. "I'm surprised you care. I didn't think you liked me."

"I don't, but Zavier does, and he will be dirty with me if I don't look out for you. Now, hurry up and sort out table two's desserts."

After cleaning up the kitchen, I take my hairnet off and toss it into the bin. Minty gapes and gives Tatum an obvious nudge.

"Seriously?" I throw my hands up in exasperation. "What've I done wrong now? Is there a certain way I'm supposed to bin a hairnet?"

Ignoring my question, she leans into Tatum and asks, "Is it just me, or has Precious' hair darkened a shade since yesterday?"

Tatum carefully examines my dreads. "You're right," she says. "Her hair does look a little darker." Her gaze drops from my dreads to my eyes. "How long has it been since you washed it?"

I shrug uncomfortably. "I don't know, a couple of days maybe."

"Didn't you wash it this morning?"

"I have dreadlocks Minty. I don't need to wash them every time I have a wash."

It's a lie, I did wash them this morning, and I had noticed they looked a little darker. I'd also noticed my figure looked fuller too—

but not by much. Thankfully, they'd never be able to pick it in these baggy rags I'm wearing.

I hope my hair doesn't get too much darker or it will start attracting attention. Alex never mentioned that my pigments would change. He'd only said my physique would. If I'd known, I might have reconsidered.

"Did you put something in your dreads to make them look darker?" Minty eyes me curiously behind her glasses. "Are you trying to make yourself look more like a Magenta in a ploy to worm your way back up to the middle ranks?"

I usually take what Minty says with a grain of salt, but these particular comments hit home. I'm sick of everyone believing I'm chasing after more than I deserve. I am not my father. "Oh, come on, Minty, stop being such a bitch and give me some bloody credit. I'm not as precious and pathetic as you seem to believe."

Minty jerks back wide-eyed, but instead of looking offended, she almost looks impressed. "Wow Precious, you're turning out to be a bit of a surprise package."

Tatum's eyes haven't left mine. She's staring, analysing me like I'm a puzzle. *I don't like it.* "What's your problem?" I say to her.

"Your irises look darker too."

Oh God no, not my eyes too. Damn it, Alex! What have you done to me?

"It's because I'm overtired," I bark in defence. "So, can we quit this pick on Harlow session and make tracks already? The sooner I see Zavier, the sooner I can go home to bed."

Tatum apologises, insisting she hadn't meant to upset me.

Minty rolls her eyes in a carefree manner. "Alright, you lot wait out the front while I lock up."

I call Lucy over, and she follows obediently as Tatum and I exit the cavern. Once we're outside, she stands vigilantly by our sides like the fierce guard-dog she's trained to be.

"She's really something, isn't she?" Tatum leans in to give Lucy a pat, but before her hand reaches Lucy's fur, the husken hunkers and growls. Tatum quickly snatches her hand back, her brows shooting up in alarm.

"Lucy!" At first, I'm completely shocked, but I soon come to realise it's not Tatum she's growling at.

"I see he has you well protected." Rae steps out from the shadows, and Tatum and I stiffen. Her presence sends a prickling sensation down my spine. "But there's going to come a time where he has to decide what's more important, his Chief Warrior position, or you."

"I don't know what you're talking about," I say through gritted teeth.

"At least he's grown enough sense to finally put you where you belong."

Lucy crouches down further, baring her sharp teeth. I would love to see her put them to good use, but I hold back on any attack commands. Lucy's here as my shield, not my weapon.

Minty steps outside to find this nasty scene unfolding, and to her credit, she doesn't hesitate to jump straight on the attack. "The Bean-Brew Cavern is closed, Rae," she says firmly. "I think you'd best be moving along before our guard-hound rips you to shreds."

"I think it would be best, if you minded your own business, Shorty," Rae hits back. "Or you'll end up finding yourself in the line of fire."

"My fellow employees are my business, and as far as I can see, you're the one in danger of being mauled here. I suggest you do as I've said and move along before things turn ugly."

Rae's eyes meet mine, slitted and vicious. "Until next time," she says, and then strides off.

JACKARSE

-ZAVIER-

"How are you feeling today?" Jax's booming voice asks, and I groan. "Are you able to sit up yet?"

It hurts like crazy, but I grit my teeth and force myself into an upright position. "What do you care?"

"I care about all the medics, and apparently, you've been making life difficult for them. They want you healed and out of here as soon as possible."

This is music to my ears. "When are they planning on releasing me? Tonight?"

"No, not tonight, but we're aiming for the end of the week.

You'll still have to be on bed rest for the next four weeks, but I don't see why you can't rest at home. Now turn around, I need to check your side."

I don't want him touching me, even if it is for my own good. "There's no need for a check over, I'm fine."

"Why do you always have to be so difficult? I'm here to help get you out of here. It's what you want, is it not?"

I hate that he's the best chance I've got at getting out of this dreadful place. I can't stand him. I resent him with a passion for what he's done to Harlow.

Grudgingly, I bite my tongue and force myself to do as he says.

His fingers prod at my wounded side, and I fight the urge to yelp. "I think you're secretly enjoying this," I mutter.

Ignoring my comment, he says, "The outer wound is healing nicely."

"Save me the details, just jot down whatever's needed on my paperwork to help get me out of here."

When he finishes with his inspection, he lingers, watching with an irresolute expression while I struggle to right myself. I'd assumed he was debating whether or not to help me, but then he asks, "How is Harlow doing?"

Predictable. He's not only here to check on me, he wants info on Harlow. *Frost sake, I hate this guy.*

"If you care so much, why don't you go and ask her yourself?"

"It's not safe for us to be seen together."

"Yeah, and who's fault is that? You should've known where this was going to end up before you even started something. You're so selfish."

His brows shoot up in disbelief. "*I'm* selfish?"

I don't appreciate his mirrored implication. Everything I've done has been to protect Harlow.

"Minty told me Harlow has cried herself to sleep every night since the day she got there. What do you think about that? Do you feel good about yourself?"

His jaw ticks. "I don't understand. She said she wasn't upset about being sent to the lower level."

He's kidding himself, surely. For someone who's usually so switched on, he's acting incredibly thick. *Acting* being the operative word. I don't care if he's the Commander's son, or that he saved my life, he's getting a piece of my mind. Nobody hurts Harlow and gets away with it.

"Wake up and take some responsibility for your actions. She's not upset because you sent her to the lower level, she's upset because you used her up and spat her out." Feeling riled up, I shuffle further up the bed. "And to make matters worse, you sent her to live with Minty."

"What do you mean? I thought she and Minty were friends?" Jax continues playing Mr Innocent and Confused, but I can see right through it.

"Well, it just goes to show how much you really know about her, doesn't it? She and Minty absolutely hate each other."

"Why didn't she…" He pauses as three pastel figures enter the medical cavern and then says, in almost a whisper, "That's her now."

"Oh great." Sarcasm oozes from my voice. "Now you can stop pestering me and go ask her yourself. Although I'm sure she won't tell you the truth. She wouldn't want to upset Mr Sunshine."

Jax's only reply is an irritated grunt before he strides over to meet the three blurry figures.

8

BIG MOUTH!
-HARLOW-

As we step through the medical cavern entry, I'm pleasantly surprised to spot Jax standing beside Zavier's bed. *Wow*, he's even better looking than I remember. The vertic switz ink has done wonders for my eyesight; everything is sharper and crisper, including him.

When he sees us coming, he leaves Zavier's bedside to walk over to us. At first, I'm pleased about having this small window of opportunity to speak to him. It's only been four days since I saw him last, but it feels like forever. However, when he draws closer, I notice his movements are stiff. There's an air of tension radiating off him.

"Good evening," he says politely, addressing all three of us, and then his rigid gaze settles on me. "Harlow, may I have a quick word with you?"

I gulp. This doesn't sound good. "Sure." I glance across at Minty and Tatum. "You guys go ahead. I'll meet you over there."

Tatum simply nods, while Minty's gaze flicks between us, her eyes narrowed in judgment. Eventually she humpfs and gives a disapproving scowl before leaving.

Wonderful. Any progress I'd made with her in the last half-hour is dead and buried. She must assume there's something going on between Jax and me, the same as everybody else does. Little does everyone know, I've stooped much lower. I'm not the Purple-chasing gold digger they all believe me to be, I'm a traitor. I've spent a night with our enemy. The memory of being with Alex makes my heart fall like a stone into my stomach. A piece of me still longs for him and wants him back, but there's also a piece of me which feels angry and ashamed.

"I thought it was too dangerous for you to be seen with me?" My voice comes out choked, uneven.

Jax blows off my question with one of his own. "Zavier is right then, I see. You and Minty aren't friends?"

Zavier, you big mouth!

I give an awkward shrug. "No… Not exactly."

"Why didn't you tell me? I thought I was doing the right thing by putting you with your friend."

"It's fine, really. I don't hate Minty as much as she hates me."

"Don't lie to me, Harlow." Jax's stern tone makes my neck shrink into my shoulders. "Zavier says you've been crying yourself to sleep every night."

I scoff. "What would Zavier know? I've barely seen him."

"He said Minty told him."

Well, nice of her to console me, I think bitterly.

"I'm not upset about where I live or where I work." I reassure him. "I'm just going through something personal right now, that's all." It's a sorry excuse, and I know it, but I don't know what else to tell him. I can't exactly say, *I was falling for a human spirit named Alex who also happens to be Vallon, but I killed his human brother Lucas, which broke his connection to Earth, and this made him SO mad that the Vallon version of him left me in the forest to die… Totally believable, and totally not incriminating!*

Jax's glittering violet eyes regard mine, searching for answers. "It's because of me, isn't it?" He looks upset with himself.

No. He hasn't done anything wrong, I'm the one who's done something wrong. I doubt he'd even be able to look at me if he knew the truth.

"You were never my pawn; I promise. And I'm sorry if I made you feel chewed up and spat out." He bristles. "Like I've told you before, I never knew it was going to come to this. I had no idea I was putting your life in such danger. I was merely trying to bring about change. I thought together we could make a difference."

My spine straightens. I may have been the one to mention the pawn thing, but I never said anything about him chewing me up and spitting me out.

"Where is this coming from?" I ask, and then it clicks. I shoot a dirty look in Zavier's direction—not that he can see it. *Who does he think he is, meddling in my business?*

"I don't know exactly what Zavier has said to you, but I've barely seen him lately, so none of this has come from me. I haven't told him anything about your plans to break down the colour system, or where I was supposed to fit in those plans. He knows nothing."

"It doesn't appear that way."

"I swear to you, Jax, I haven't said anything to him or Minty. The only thing I told Zavier was you saved his life." My blood simmers. "You'd think he would be a little more grateful, the stupid chump!" My outburst seems to catch Jax off guard, and he suppresses a smile. "Please don't take anything Zavier said personally," I insist. "He doesn't like Purples in general. He thinks you're all evil and plotting against us."

"Your friend doesn't have to like me or show me any gratitude. I just don't want there to be any issues between us. If there's a problem, I'd like you to tell me. I don't know how many times I have to say this. I don't understand why you continually avoid sharing important things with me. I want you to trust me."

"I do trust you. And there are no issues between us." My heart pounds at the expression "us". "Everything is fine. Honestly, Jax. I appreciate everything you've done for me, and I have a lot of respect for you."

When I glance up to meet his gaze, an unexpected fluttery feeling fills my belly. However, this intensifies to a churning feeling when I detect him appraising me with a newfound curiosity.

"You look different somehow?" he says, and it's like reality slapping me across the face, telling me to wake up to myself.

Oh no, not you too. I don't want to have to lie to you. I've got enough problems to deal with on the lower level.

"It's been a long day, and I'm tired," I say a little more abruptly than I'd planned. "I'm glad we've had a chance to talk and sort everything out, but I think from here on in you need to stay away from me." I really should tell Jax about Rae sneaking around Minty's family cavern and making threats outside work, but I don't want to want him worrying about me. He thinks he's put me somewhere safe. "Have a good look around," I say instead, keeping it general. "All eyes are on us. If Zeeks keep spotting us together, it'll only be a matter of time before one of us is killed."

"Harlow wait…"

"I'm sorry, I can't," I say, feeling a stab of hurt and guilt. "You need to stop worrying about me and start worrying about yourself. Besides, I have a best friend I need to strangle."

I leave Jax and storm over to Zavier's bedside.

"What the hell, Zavier? How dare you say those things to Jax? You have no right to tell him—whatever it is—you think that I'm feeling."

"Well, someone had to do it, and I knew you were never going to. He needs to be put in his place. What he did to you was wrong."

"I don't understand what it is you think he did? All he's done is try to help me. If it wasn't for him, I would be dead."

"Nice one," Minty mutters under her breath, "Let's thank the guy who got you into this mess, not the one who keeps picking you up off the floor."

"Don't start Minty, because I'm pissed at you too."

"Oh…really, Precious? And what exactly have I done besides help to keep you safe?"

"You made a point of mentioning to Zavier that I've been crying into my pillow every night, and yet, *never once*, did you ask me if I was okay. You just let me cry without consoling me. How heartless are you?"

Minty launches up from her seat with flared nostrils. "Listen here, Precious, we all know what you've been crying about these past few days, and some of us don't want to hear about it. I'm not about to be dragged down and killed because you've made a bunch of bad choices." Her eyes glare into mine. "You've made your own bed, don't expect others to lie in it with you."

"Okay, Minty, tone it down a notch," Zavier cuts in.

"I may have made some bad choices lately," I admit. "But I can guarantee you that none of those choices involve Jax." I can feel the burn of tears coming on, but I refuse to let them spill. "You guys enjoy your catch-up. I'll be waiting out the front with Lucy."

Jax watches as I storm away from Zavier's bed, but he doesn't follow me out, and although this hurts—*a lot*—I'm glad he's finally listening to me. I hadn't wanted to brush him off, *not at all*, but it's for the best. He needs to stop worrying about me. I'm not worth his job or his life.

I hate what people are saying about us, especially when it's not even true. *Okay, so I'm attracted to him, but what girl in our colony isn't?* I know I'm not worthy of him, and I've never made any passes at him. I don't want to be that kind of Pastel.

I plonk myself next to Lucy and finally allow my built-up tears to spill down my cheeks. I can't believe Zavier embarrassed me by saying those things to Jax. I thought we were friends, best friends. I thought we were supposed to support one another, not throw each other under the bus.

He obviously believes what everyone else believes. *Oh well.* Minty can be his best friend now. I've got Lucy. At least she won't go around blindly spilling my business to everyone.

I wish I could go home and curl up in bed, but I don't want to leave Minty and Tatum to walk home without a guard-hound, especially after Minty just gave Rae a mouthful. As much as I'm angry with her, I don't wish her dead.

After a few minutes of sobbing into Lucy's fur, Tatum exits and plonks next to me. "Are you okay?"

"No, not really," I say. "I only have one friend, and we're fighting."

"Zavier did the wrong thing, and I told him so." She gives me a gentle nudge. "But he didn't say those things to Jax to hurt you. He said those things believing he was standing up for you. He's honestly distressed about upsetting you. He loves you."

"He's got it all wrong." I say with a sniffle. "You've all got it wrong."

"Well, maybe it's about time you open up to him. He's just about run himself into the ground trying to save you lately. I think he deserves some sort of explanation about what's going on, don't you?"

"I've already told him we can swap stories when he gets out."

"According to him, Jax is planning on having him out by the end of the week."

"Really? So soon? I thought he was supposed to be here for another four or five weeks."

"Apparently he's making life difficult for the medics. He won't let anyone work on him, and he refuses to do what he's told."

A weak chuckle escapes me. "That sounds about right."

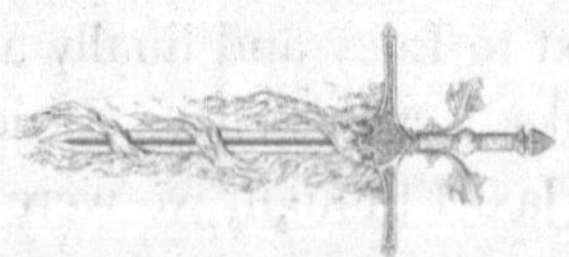

I spend my next four days off hiding out, curled up next to Lucy with a book I'd borrowed from Ollie. It's not my usual kind of book, but it's interesting enough to keep my mind occupied. Needless to say, every time I put it down, even for a second, all of my problems come rushing back to haunt me.

Minty and I are swimming in mega-hostile territory, to the point where she glowers at the mere sight of me, yet for some reason she still insists on coming along every time I take Lucy out for a walk. She claims she's looking out for me due to a promise she made to Zavier. But given my last encounter with Zavier, I don't know how good of friends we are anymore. She may be protecting me in vain.

Like me, she's barely left her family cavern, not even to visit Tatum. *I wonder if she is angry with Tatum for siding with me. I hope not.* While I appreciated Tatum's kindness, the last thing I want is to cause problems between them. I think Tatum is good for Minty; she's the rose to her thorn.

Before my blowout with Zavier, I had planned on visiting him every day over my four days off. I wanted to finish reading him the book he'd started reading to me when I was in a coma. But not only am I still incredibly mad at him, my dreadlocks and irises have darkened another few shades. I know for sure he'd notice the change and ask questions. Minty gives me curious looks and mutters snarky comments under her breath while we take Lucy on her walks, but thankfully she doesn't care enough to ask questions.

I've been using Jax's bandana—which he'd given me to use as a hanky—to cover my hair, and I've been giving as minimal eye contact as possible when speaking to Minty's parents. It's working for now, but it'll only be a matter of time before they, too, notice my darkening pigments.

The bandana smells of Jax and makes me miss him. I hadn't realised how much he'd come to mean to me until I pushed him away. I'm not interested in him in a romantic sense, I'm quick to tell myself, although there's a small piece of me that wonders if this is true. *It has to be true. I could never… Would never…*

I still don't really know how to classify what our relationship was to each other, but he's an upstanding Zeek, and I have way too much respect for him to tarnish him in such a way. Besides, a commanding Purple like Jax deserves better than a lowly Pastel like me. I'm not worth the death sentence.

Thinking of Jax draws Alex to my thoughts, along with a painful stabbing sensation in my chest. He'd calmly laughed off the ramifications we'd be forced to face if we were caught together, saying that the incredible moment we'd shared was well worth the punishment. I'd swooned over this comment, feeling as if I was special. Little did I know the next morning he'd be leaving me for dead.

The more I dwell on what happened between us, the ickier and more ashamed I feel. What Alex and I had shared was nothing more than some risky fairy-tale. I'd acted on the emotions of my heart instead of thinking with my head, and I've come to realise what a huge regrettable mistake it was. Here, he's a Vallon, my enemy. I should never have trusted him. I should have stuck to my initial instincts and pushed him away.

My feelings towards him have taken a complete turnaround. I've gone from feeling hurt, heartbroken, and wanting him back to super angry and resentful. I wish I'd never met up with him. He'd said Jax "was only telling me what I wanted to hear". *Funny.* I wish I'd known he was speaking about himself.

I'd believed he loved me, that he cared, but he couldn't have felt any of these powerful emotions, because he'd left me to die. I hadn't meant to hurt him; I was only trying to help my sister, but he sure as hell meant to hurt me.

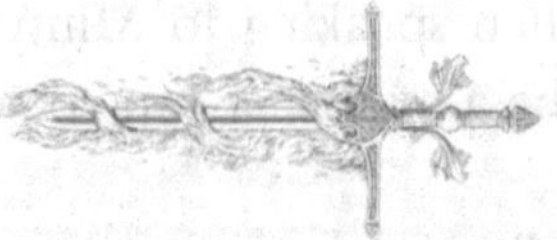

I wake up early for work the next morning to find my deadlocks and irises are somewhere between hot pink and crimson—*not* a natural Zeek colour. I stare at my reflection in gaping horror. My dreads and irises aren't turning Magenta like I'd first assumed, they're turning red. *Far out! How am I going to hide this?* Not just today, but every day. It's going to be impossible.

My eyes trace over my body. It has changed a lot too. It looks much fuller and muscular. I'm delighted with these changes, although I've gotten a little thicker around the waistline than I'd hoped.

After taking a moment to settle myself, I get dressed and pop on Jax's bandana, wishing there was an easy inconspicuous way to cover my eyes. Minty is waiting at the washroom door when I open it, and I try my best to quickly slip past her before she notices anything different. *Not a chance.* It seems my near-red irises have become way too obvious to by-pass.

Her arm snatches mine, tugging me to face her. "Harlow, your eyes," she says, staring into them with alarm. "The colour—"

"I know. What should I do? How can I cover them?"

"Show me your hair."

"No." I snatch my arm back with ease. This catches Minty off guard. My strength has improved two-fold.

Her brow crinkles, and her expression is somewhere between cautious and curious. "What's happening to you?"

"I don't know. I must be sick. Maybe I should stay home today."

My heart thrums in my ears. There's no way I'm going to be able to leave this cavern without attracting attention. My pigments are completely off. Even my shimmer is off. To think, I was sent down to the lower level to blend in, and now my pigments are darker than my Magenta twin sister's. I'd laugh about it if I wasn't so darn upset. Alex hasn't helped save me, he's screwed me—both literally and figuratively. I can't believe I trusted him.

"This hurts to say." Minty looks like she's swallowed an insect. "But I need you. I can't run the kitchen by myself, especially with only one working arm." She heads towards her nook, motioning for me to follow. "Come with me. I think I've got an old set of glasses lying around somewhere. We'll see what we can do to cover your eyes."

"That's it?" I say. "You're just going to help me and not hand me over?"

"Who *exactly* would I hand you over to? Jax?" A mix of frustration and accusation drip from her voice. "And just to clarify, I'm only helping you, so that you can help me. Now hurry, before my parents see you and have a heart attack."

Between the two of us, we turn her old set of glasses into something similar to human sunglasses. Everyone will think I'm crazy wearing shaded glasses inside the caves, but it beats the alternative.

Just before we enter the Bean-Brew Cavern, Minty jerks me back to say, "Head straight to the kitchen and leave the communicating up to me. You look like a complete weirdo dressed this way, and we don't want anyone questioning your poor fashion choices or pulling your accessories off. If they see what's hidden beneath, we're in trouble."

"Don't worry. I'm not planning on speaking to anyone."

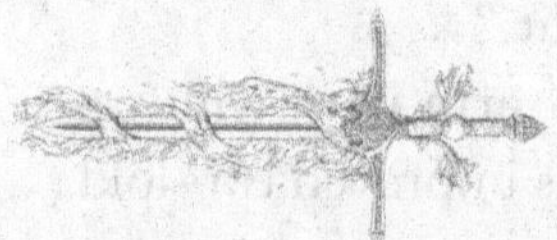

As the next few days pass by, Minty continues to cover for me, not only at work but at home with her probing parents. She's certainly a hard Zeek to read. If she wasn't so intent on being snarky to me all the time, I'd actually call her a decent friend.

"Zavier is getting out today," she mentions, while carefully chopping up an og to juice. "We should stop in and see him on our way home from work. Tatum says he misses you, and I refuse to let you ignore him forever. It'll break his heart." This is the first non-work-related thing Minty's said to me all day.

"Okay," I agree, although a part of me feels like resisting. I'm not entirely ready for all of his questions, especially regarding my darkening pigments.

"Are you going to tell him the truth about what's wrong with you?" She scans me from head to toe, and I detect a curious thought forming behind her scrutinising gaze. "You're not like…pregnant with Jax's child or something, are you?"

"Leave me alone, Minty," I retort, but as soon as the words leave my mouth, I gasp. *How long has it been since my friends last came to visit?* I count back the weeks since my last period and gulp. *Oh God! Maybe I am pregnant? But not to Jax—to Alex. A Vallon.* The thought fills me with instant dread. I buckle over, feeling nauseous and lightheaded. I think I'm going to puke. *No, no, no, no. This can't be happening. I can't be pregnant to a Vallon.*

Having to hide red dreads and irises is one thing, but hiding a bulging belly will be absolutely impossible, and God knows how big this baby will be. It'll probably be bigger than my body can cater for.

"Precious? Are you okay? You don't look so good."

I can't answer. I dash to the bin and hurl.

"*No,*" Minty gasps. "I'm right, aren't I?" Noticing me struggling, she steps over and hands me a paper towel. "I knew it. That's why you've put on so much weight and your pigments are all off. You're pregnant to a Purple."

So much weight. Ouch.

"Minty please," I say. "Don't go jumping to conclusions."

"The signs are all there, Precious. You can't keep fighting this forever."

The more I consider her assumption as a fact, the more my body trembles. *What if the baby comes out looking like a Vallon? We'll both be killed. No!* I feel sick. Really, really sick. Being executed for my mistakes is one thing, but for them to kill an innocent child—my child…

I have no idea what I am going to do. I'm in trouble. BIG TROUBLE. If I'm truly pregnant, it's not only my life that I have to worry about anymore. I will be responsible for someone else's too. *I'm such an idiot. I should never have slept with Alex. Stupid, stupid, stupid!*

I must be a sorry sight, because Minty does something completely out of character. She gives me a few light taps on my back. "There, there," she says, although her words lack genuine compassion. "Let's get through the rest of our shift, and then Tatum and I will take you to Zavier's. You can talk to him about what's going on."

"I don't know if I can talk to him about it," I admit.

"I think you should. Despite everything, he still really loves you, and I know he would do anything to help you. It's how he is."

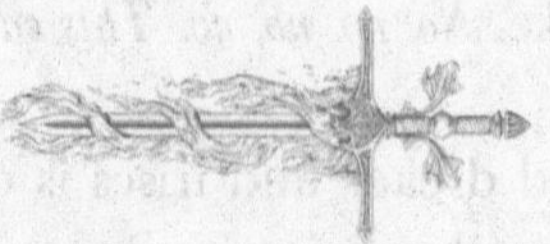

Tatum enters the kitchen right before closing time and Minty greets her with a kiss. I'm glad to see they're on good terms again. Their standoff had been bothering me.

When Tatum catches sight of me, she gawks. Minty gives her a look which says, "don't ask".

I take care of a few last-minute jobs while Minty grabs her pack and shovels a bunch of fresh food inside.

I eye her curiously—although she'd never be able to tell with these dark glasses I'm wearing. "What are you doing?"

"While you and Zavier talk, Tatum and I are going to make dinner for everyone."

I throw the last of the scraps in the bin and give the bench a wipe over. "Aren't you sick of cooking? We've just finished work?"

"We still have to eat, don't we?"

Tatum smiles enthusiastically. "I think it will be fun. Who knows, I might even learn a thing or two. My mum's a terrible cook."

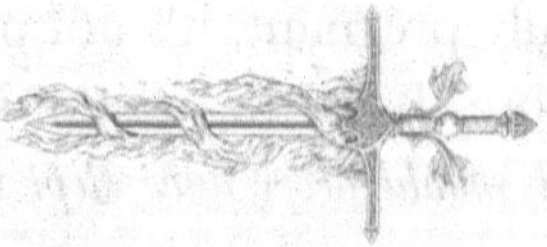

Lexan is sitting on the lounge peeling a deg when we arrive. However, as soon as he notices us, he immediately pops it down and stands to greet us. "The welcome home party has arrived." His voice is warm and cheerful. "It's good to see you girls." He glances between us, stopping at me to do a double take. "Harlow? Is that you under there? What are you wearing?"

Minty jumps in before I can answer. "She's trying out a new look. What do you think? Is it going to catch on?"

"Well, ah… I don't know." He scratches his head. "It's certainly different."

"Different?" A light-hearted scoff leaves Minty's lips. "What would you know, Old Timer?" She gives him a friendly shove. "Come on you. You're going to help Tatum and me cook dinner while Harlow and Zavier catch up."

9

IT'S TIME FOR A HEART-TO-HEART

-ZAVIER-

*H*arlow is here. *Yes.* I've been desperately hoping she would come to see me today, but after the way she'd blown up at me the last time we saw each other, followed by over a week of the silent treatment, I wasn't confident she would. I hadn't meant to upset her, but I was ropable about Jax hurting her, and I couldn't help but lash out. He shouldn't be allowed to use her, only to toss her aside when things get tricky. It's not fair. I hate that he can do it and get away with it, just because he's the Commander's son.

Even though I'd given him a mouthful the last time I'd seen

him, Jax had still shown up to release me today, as he said he would. Although, I imagine it was more for the medics' benefit than my own. Neither of us said a word to each other the entire time he was there. I had a few other issues I would've liked to have brought up, but I bit my tongue for the sake of my and Harlow's friendship. I knew if I kept pushing the matter, I'd only push her further away, and that's the complete opposite of what I want.

Jax had brought Sylvie with him to do my final checks. When they all came back okay, he asked her to do the discharge paperwork, and make sure she sent me home with a couple of nauclea latifolia roots for pain relief.

Harlow ducks her head around the corner of my nook, and I can see now what all the fuss was about. *What is she wearing?* Or maybe the question I should be asking is, *what is she trying to cover up?* I bet someone has hurt her again. She's probably got two black eyes hidden under those glasses, courtesy of her failed relationship with Jax.

"Can I come in?" Her voice catches.

"Of course." I prop my pillow up and shuffle back into a sitting position. Harlow sees me struggling and offers to help, but I wave her off, telling her I'm fine. *What's a little white lie between friends?*

Her mouth is pulled in a tight line. She appears as nervous about this visit as I feel. She said we'd swap secrets once I was out of the medical chamber. I already know what she's going to tell me, and I've prepared myself for it. Although, I know it's going to hurt all-the-more, hearing the admission coming from her own lips.

"I'm really sorry I upset you," I say, trying to break the ice. "Tatum was right, I should have minded my business and kept my mouth shut."

She sits lightly at the end of my bed. "Yes, you should have. Especially because you've got it all wrong. You are blaming Jax for things that aren't his fault."

Here she goes again, sticking up for Mr Sunshine. I feel my anger flare again, and I snap, "Whose fault would you say it is then? Yours?"

I'm way out of line, and I wait for her to snap back at me and take off, but strangely, she doesn't.

"Oh, God." She leans her back against the cave wall and lets out a long breath. "I don't know if I can do this. I…I don't even know where to start."

"You could start by removing the bandana and glasses. Why are you wearing them, anyway? You look ridiculous." It's my second snappy comment in the matter of minutes. You'd swear I was deliberately trying to push her away. *I need to tape my mouth shut.*

"I'm wearing them because I have to." She avoids looking my way. "Zavier, I'm pretty sure I'm in a lot trouble, and I have no idea how I'm going to get through this, even if I can."

As much as it hurts to move, I lean forward to grab her hand. I need to push aside my bitterness and start being nice to her, or I'll lose her. "Harlow, it's okay. If someone's hurt you, tell me. You don't need to cover yourself up."

"It's not bruises I'm covering; it's something else. But I can hardly bring myself to tell you what I've done. I'm too ashamed." A dark, humourless laugh escapes her. "Yet, if I can't tell you, I can't tell anyone. There's nobody else I can trust with my secret."

"Not even Jax?"

"Especially not Jax."

The familiar sound of Minty shooting off orders in the background has me feeling relieved that I've still got a few more weeks of bed rest left before I go back to work. I've never known someone so small to be so bossy.

I shuffle to the side. "Come up here," I say, making room for Harlow. "Minty's too noisy."

She hesitates, taking a second to think about it, before crawling up next to me. "You may not want me this close once you hear what I've got to say."

"Try me," I say.

"I think I'm pregnant."

My body jolts painfully. It's worse than I thought. I swallow hard before responding. "Does Jax know?"

"It's not Jax's. There's nothing going on between Jax and me. I keep trying to tell you all, but none of you will listen."

I don't believe her. "Well, if it's not Jax's, then whose is it?"

"It's Alex's."

"Alex's?" The name rings a bell. It's the name she'd called out to me, when I'd first brought her out of the coma. When I'd asked her who Alex was, she'd told me he was Lucas' brother, and that he'd died before she ever had the chance to meet him. *That was obviously a big fat lie.*

"I know it must sound crazy." Her words all roll into one. "And the rest of what I'm about to tell you is going to sound even more insane."

"Hold up a second…" I say, feeling lost. "I don't know who Alex is. When I asked you who he was, you said he was Lucas' dead brother."

"Yes, that's right, he's Lucas' brother."

"What?" I frown in confusion. "That doesn't make any sense."

"Like I said, I know it sounds crazy—"

"It sounds as if you're confusing fact with fiction."

"It's the truth," she says adamantly. "I wanted to confide in you earlier, but I was afraid you wouldn't believe me, and by the looks of it, I was right."

I rub hard at the base of my skull. "Well, you must admit, it does sound rather unbelievable. I mean, I don't understand how what you're saying could work?" Seeing her disappointed expression, I bite off the rest of what I was going to say and try to go with a more supportive approach. "Look, I'm not saying I don't believe you. I need you to give me more information. Help me understand. Why don't you start at the beginning?"

She nestles closer, her voice lowering. "You know those dreams I used to have as a kid—about my past life and Lucas?"

I nod.

"They've started up again recently."

"Yeah, I figured," I say. She'd called out Lucas' name a couple of times while she was in the medical chamber. She'd even called it out in front of Jax.

"Only they're different now." She fiddles nervously with the sleeve of her jumper. "I've literally been waking up on Earth."

A wave of doubt hits me. This definitely isn't what I was expecting her to say.

When she'd spoken to me about the dreams as young kids, I'd told her I believed her. And to a certain extent, it had been true. I'd believed she really did dream about a past life she'd had, and I'd believed she honestly considered those dreams to be real. What I've never decided, though, was if I completely bought into the idea, or if I just believed she was having super vivid dreams, which felt as if they were real.

"You don't believe me, do you?"

It sounds way too far-fetched to be true, but I'm not about to say so. She needs me right now, and I want to try my best to stay open minded. "You're going to have to fill me in with a lot more details before asking me to make my mind up."

Harlow nods thoughtfully. "I suppose that's fair."

She clears her throat and jumps into a spiel about going to sleep one night and waking up on Earth to see her sister Jade—who is now in her mid-thirties and married with a child named Connor. She says Jade had only just moved back to their hometown of Blaxland, and Jade's son, Connor, had become friends with Rueben, Josh's son, who is also Lucas' nephew.

"Lucas looked after Rueben while Josh and his new partner worked," she says, and then expresses how much this worried her, because it meant Jade and Lucas were seeing a lot of each other.

Eventually Alex is brought up, and she stiffens uncomfortably beside me as she fills me in on the details of how they first met. She says she didn't know if she could trust him at first, but the more time she spent with him, the more she grew to like him, and eventually she ended up falling for him, blah, blah, blah... *Spew*. She throws in way more intimate details than I'd like to hear.

"Okay, so you fell for Alex, and clearly you must have slept with him," I spit. "But I don't understand how you can sleep with him as a human, ghost, or whatever, and then wind up pregnant as a Zeek?"

"This is where it starts to get complicated," she says.

Oh, right, now it gets complicated. Because everything up until this point has been completely straightforward.

"Go on then, spill."

"Alex is dead, just like the Ruby side of me is dead, but his spirit has moved on, just like the Harlow side of me has moved on."

"Are you're saying Alex lives here—on Zadok?" I motion between us. "With us?"

"Yes."

"Who is he then? Is he a Purple? Is this why you've been spending all of your time with Jax?"

"Actually, no." She bites her lip. "Jax is a different story entirely. This is worse than that."

I bolt upright, which hurts. "Worse?"

"Alex is a Vallon." She pulls off her bandana and glasses, and I just about jump out of my skin.

"Frost!" Her dreads and irises are completely red.

"He's a Red," she says.

This definitely wasn't the twist I was expecting—AT ALL. *Damn straight this is complicated!* I'd been sceptical as her story was unwinding, but now—looking at her—I don't know what to think. While I stare goggle-eyed in disbelief, a few dots start connecting. Saul was knocked around by a Vallon who'd wanted him to use a set of voltz on Harlow. Saul had also said the Vallon knew Harlow was in a coma. *Far out...* At the time I thought he was lying, but with this new info coming to light, I'm reconsidering.

"Does Minty know?" I doubt she'd be able to hide it from her. Their open nooks are only separated by a nib wall.

"She knows what I look like, and she's worked out I'm pregnant. The only problem is she thinks the baby belongs to Jax."

Strangely enough, even though I hate Jax, I almost wish it was the case. Her being pregnant to Jax would be less dangerous than her being pregnant to a Vallon. At least if it was Jax's baby, Harlow wouldn't be turning into a Red. I've heard of slight pigment changes in pregnant Zeek women, but this is completely off-the-charts drastic!

"Does Alex know?"

She lowers her head, and her cheeks turn rouge. "No."

"Well, are you going to tell him?"

"No. We're not on good terms anymore." She hesitates a moment. "I killed his brother to save my sister and nephew. It was either kill him or lose them, and I couldn't let it be them."

I blink in astonishment. "You killed Lucas… Your killer." I try to puzzle the pieces together. "How? I thought you were a ghost on Earth?"

"I used my sister's body to push him out a window."

Information overload. This is all way too much to process in one sitting. I don't understand how she could even fall for Alex, knowing he was her killer's brother. It seems like a poor choice on her part. But then again, she went for that Josh guy who sounded like a complete and utter jerk. Maybe bad guys are her type.

After another moment of processing, I ask, "How does Jax fit into all of this? Why have you been spending so much time with him?"

They may not be sleeping together, like I'd first assumed, but there's clearly something secret going on between them.

"Do you remember the day when you found me wounded by the water pool?"

"You mean the day after you cut your leg by falling out of the tree?" I say cynically.

"Okay, so you're right, I didn't fall out of a tree. A fuegor attacked me on my way home from fruit picking."

"What?" This story of hers keeps getting bigger and bigger. "A fuegor? How did you get away?"

She says a Drake woman saved her, and when she got to the caves Jax was waiting for her and helped her to get the medical attention she needed.

She also mentions it was Saul's idea to tell everyone she'd fallen out of a tree, because he didn't want her losing her job. Apparently Jax and Medic Sylvie had been told the truth, but they went along with the cover story.

"But you lost your job anyway," I point out. "And isn't it more heroic to have escaped a fuegor rather than to have fallen out of a tree? I don't understand the cover story."

She considers this a moment and then says, "Fair point. I'm not sure why Saul wanted me to say that. I didn't question it. I just did as he asked."

"Fine, I get that you were doing what you were told, but why didn't you at least tell *me* the truth?" I ask. "I'm supposed to be your best friend, yet you tell Jax the truth and not me. I thought we were closer than that."

"I heard Jax telling you the fabricated story while I was out of it, and when I came to, I figured I'd leave it as is. On reflection, I wish I had told you the truth. I'm really sorry."

Her excuse isn't really good enough. I'd asked her what had happened to her when I'd first found her at the water pool, and she'd said, "It's nothing, I'm fine". I want to point this out too, but I figure it's pointless. What's done is done and we can't turn back time. Plus, I don't want her to think I'm attacking her. I still have more questions I want answered. *I'll let it slide for now.*

"What was with Jax getting you a job at the library?" I ask curiously. "I understand you needed to rest your wounded leg, but there are plenty of other jobs he could have offered you, and he would have known it would cause a stir with the Purples."

When Electra had smugly admitted Harlow had been hurt filling the bookshelves, Jax had snapped at her, saying, "She's supposed to be here on light duties. You know this!" But the library isn't the only place Harlow could've gone if he wanted her on light duties. There are a number of Pastel factory jobs she could have been sent to, and it wouldn't have attracted as much attention. By him granting her the Purple job, it made it look like he was giving her special treatment, and a piece of me still thinks he was. Whether she knows it or not, I think he is keen on her. He's too involved in all of her movements for me to believe otherwise. A Commander's son shouldn't be so worried about one little Pastel.

I suppose if he has taken a fancy to her, I can't really blame him. Even with red hair and eyes, she is still the prettiest Zeek in our colony as far as I am concerned.

"There are a few reasons. Firstly, you're right, I needed a job where I could rest my leg; secondly, he knew my father would have been disappointed in me if I was sent down to work with the rest of the Pastels; and thirdly, he's trying to break down the colour system."

She dives into a bit of backstory concerning the Commanding family, telling me how Arlo had been a Pastel sympathiser, and he was the one who helped to save her life as a baby and let her parents keep her.

"That's why he was killed," she says. "Azazel was the one who gave the order. She saw me as an abomination and thought I would bring about conflict to our colony." The corners of her eyes glisten with tears. "She wasn't wrong."

"Don't you dare go there," I warn. "You're not an abomination."

"Jax said he was hoping he could continue on with his father's legacy." She's fidgeting with her sleeve again. "But it's been much harder than he'd imagined building an army of sympathisers, especially after all the damage Nix caused to our colony before he died." She gazes up, biting her lip, considering something. "You were right about Nix," she admits. "He was the one in charge of blowing up the sewing factory caverns. It wasn't an accident. I'm sorry."

My blood turns to fire. *I knew it.* Nix was born evil, just like his mother.

"I told you, didn't I?"

"You did," she agrees. "Nix was a monster, there's no denying it, but don't go putting Jax in Nix's category. He is nothing like his brother. He's a good Zeek. Like I've said, he has been trying to help us all."

I hate how quick she is to jump in and defend Jax when I haven't even said anything. I bet she thought the same thing about Alex and Lucas—and look how that turned out. She's too trusting.

"Yeah, we'll see."

She elbows me and I wince. "Oh, come on Zavier, you were wrong about him, admit it."

"I still don't like him."

I can tell she's unhappy with my response, but she doesn't push the matter. I don't understand how she can keep insisting Jax has been helping her, because from where I'm sitting, all I can see is how her life has deteriorated since he's been in it. He is still the reason Electra and Rae want her dead, and he's also the reason she's been sent down here to rot like the rest of us.

It takes another half-an-hour for dinner to be ready, and during this time I run some more questions by her to fill in the gaps.

"Are you two all good now, or what?" Minty steps into my nook carrying two fully loaded dinner plates on her good arm. "Because if not, I find food always helps."

Harlow leans over me to help take the plates from her. "Wow, Minty, you've gone all out. This looks delicious."

"You'll have to thank Tatum, she's the one who helped to prepare most of it."

"Yes, we heard. She was under strict orders." I stir.

Minty raises her brows and grins smugly. "What can I say? I run a tight kitchen. You of all Zeeks should know this."

I meet her smug gaze with a knowing one. "This, I do."

"Good, now eat up. I need you back in shape ASAP. Harlow doesn't know how to flip a deg cake or crack an egg without making a huge mess."

As Minty exits, Harlow sighs. "Anyone would think I was training to be a warrior."

Besides the sound of Harlow chewing on her dinner, things fall silent between us, which gives me time to sort through my thoughts. Now that the initial shock has worn off, I'm feeling worried. If Harlow has Zeeks like Rae keeping tabs on her, it's only going to be a matter of time before her secret gets discovered. I don't want her to be killed. I love her, and I never want to lose her.

"Why don't you move in here with Lexan and me?" I suggest. "I don't know what we can do about your hair and eyes, but we can at least pretend that the baby is mine."

"No, I can't do that to you." She shakes her head. "You have enough of your own problems to worry about."

"Well, what's your plan? What other choices do you have?"

She shrugs, not allowing her eyes to meet mine. "I think I need to leave the caves again."

"And go where?" My question comes out harsher than I'd anticipated, but I can't help it. I'm worried about her. She's not thinking straight.

"I don't know."

"You'll die out there," I say bluntly, and I mean it. *She can't leave.*

"It's only a matter of time before I die in here," she retorts. "Rae is waiting to pounce, and if she doesn't get me, my dreads and irises will. I'm sure to slip up at some stage, and if someone notices my pigments have turned red, they'll inform the Commander. She won't hesitate to have my head sliced clean off my shoulders. Plus, if I stay with you, and you lie for me, I will be putting your life in danger too."

"I understand there are no good options," I say. "But at least if you stay here, there are a few of us who will stick our necks out to protect you. Whereas, if you sneak out to the forest without Alex there as your safeguard, you won't make it past the first night."

"What happens if I pretend the baby is yours, and it comes out with dark skin like a Vallon?"

The thought terrifies me, but for Harlow's sake I don't let my feelings show. "We'll cross that bridge when we get to it."

"It would be selfish of me to take you up on your offer."

As much as it hurts, I put my arm around her and pull her in close. "It would be more selfish of you not to. It's not just about you anymore. If you sentence yourself to death, you're sentencing the baby to death too. You need to at least give it a fighting chance."

She gazes at me with anxious eyes. "Minty won't like this."

"Don't worry about Minty," I say. "I'll talk to her."

"Did I hear my name?" Minty steps into my nook and Tatum follows.

"Oh my," Tatum gasps. Her eyes narrow in on Harlow with alarm. "Minty told me your pigments had darkened further, but I wasn't expecting you to look red. Why are you red?"

"I'm pregnant."

Tatum's eyes widen. "To whom?"

Minty crosses her arms over her chest. "This ought to be good."

"What do you think?" Harlow gives me a questioning look. "Should I tell them?"

Before I can answer, Minty instantly takes offence and jumps to conclusions. "We're not thick, so don't either of you *dare* try to feed us with some pathetic story you've concocted. I know you, Zavier." Her angry eyes rest on mine. "And I know where you've been, not to mention the fact that you have always said you would never have kids because you think it's selfish and unfair of Pastels to breed."

"It's not Zavier's, and that's not what I was going to say." Harlow lets out an exasperated sigh. "But it's not Jax's either."

Minty glances between us sceptically, with indented brows. "Whose is it then?"

"I'm pregnant to a Vallon."

Tatum looks as if she's about to faint and plops down at the end of my bed. Minty, on the other hand, looks like she wants to grab Harlow and shake the sludge out of her. "What do you mean you're pregnant to Vallon? Was it consensual? Tell me it wasn't."

"Easy, Minty," I warn. "Don't fly off the handle before you know all the facts."

Minty's eyes spark with anger. "I thought I was taking a big enough risk looking out for her when I believed the baby was Jax's, and now I'm finding out she's pregnant to our enemy. How can you sit there acting like this is not a big deal, Zavier? Vallons are danger-ous. They steal and kill Pastels like us. This is not okay!"

Lexan pokes his head in to see what the fuss is about, and when he catches sight of Harlow he gapes, wide-eyed. "What happened?"

"Oh, it's nothing serious," Minty says sarcastically. "Harlow's just wound up pregnant to a Vallon. No biggie."

"She's what!" A mixture of emotions flash across his face. "How's this even possible?"

Minty's gaze cuts straight to Harlow's. "That's what I'd like to know."

"It's a long story," Harlow says, voice meek. I can sense by her heavy breathing she feels nervous about confiding in Minty, but if she's going to stay in the caves, she has no choice. We are going to need Minty and Tatum's help to keep her secret under wraps.

Minty folds her arms, face tight. "It looks like we'd ought to get comfortable then."

Tatum pats to the spot on the bed next to her, gesturing for Lexan to sit.

While Harlow reluctantly retells her story, Minty lets out a lot of disbelieving huffs and grunts. She also asks harsh questions and makes a lot of snide comments. Unlike me, she isn't afraid to tell Harlow that "going for your killer's twin brother is idiotic".

"Not that I know if I really believe any of this," she'd added tactlessly.

Tatum is curious and asks a few questions, but she delivers them in a much kinder tone. Sometimes I wonder how she and Minty are even a couple. They are polar opposites.

Lexan sits there tight-lipped, and I'm curious to know if he holds himself partly responsible for what a horrible mess Harlow's life has become. I notice his shimmer fade a little as she speaks about the Commander wanting her to be destroyed as a baby. Most of her Zeek problems—up until she slept with Alex—have stemmed from her Pastel colouring. His Pastel colouring. She was born a Pastel to a Magenta because of him. You'd imagine it would weigh on him. And the worse thing is, she still doesn't know he *is* her father. I've never told her, thinking I was protecting her, and now she's gone and done something far worse. At least he'd stuck to the same race. My nose crinkles. I can't believe she went there with a Vallon. All the choices she's made here and on Earth have been totally reckless. I never pinned her as the irresponsible type; I thought she was far more level-headed than that.

When Harlow finishes her story, I tell them about the offer I've made. Lexan agrees with the offer and says she should take me up on it, but Minty looks irritated.

"Everyone out," she blasts. "I need to have a conversation with my friend." Harlow hops up, and Minty is quick to add, "You'd better put your disguise on before you leave. We don't want any passers-by seeing you."

As soon as everyone leaves, Minty plops down next to me and sighs. "Is this really a risk you're willing to take? That girl is a walking death-trap."

"I have to. I can't let her leave the caves. She won't last a night."

"You're taking a lot of risks for this family, and I want you to really consider whether it's all worth it, because you, my friend," she pokes me, "will be the one who ends up getting hurt." She inhales deeply, and her expression grows pained. "What I'm about to say is going to hurt, but it needs to be said. While Harlow may love you as a friend, chances are she will never see you as anything more. What you are asking her to do is play pretend. She's going to use you as her fall guy. So please, if you're asking her to do this under the secret hope that you'll eventually end up together, don't do it, because she will ruin you."

It hurts to think Minty's right, but it doesn't change my decision. Irrespective of how Harlow feels about me, I still really love her and would never forgive myself if I let her leave. I'd rather die with her than send her out to die by herself. "I know the risks, and I know how she feels, but I've made my decision and I'm sticking to it."

"I still don't know if I buy into everything she's told us," Minty says. "But there's obviously some truth in it, because her body is changing, and she's clearly turning red."

"So, what's your stance?" I ask. "Are you willing to keep covering for her?"

She stares ahead, the crease in her brows deepening. "You're asking a lot of me."

"I know, and if you and Tatum want to walk away from this, leave Harlow here, and pretend like tonight's disclosure was just a dream, I completely understand."

"It would be the smartest thing for us to do." She gives me a resigned look. "But you're like a brother to me, and you've always had my back. If you're in, we're all in."

WHO'S THE DADDY?

-HARLOW-

It's been four painfully intense weeks since Minty figured out I was pregnant, and my belly is growing by the day. Minty took my confession about Alex as badly as I thought she would, and she's said a lot of hurtful things. I don't think she one hundred percent believes the whole human-ghost aspect of my story. But, despite her ongoing snippy comments, she's still been insistent on covering for me and keeping me protected, so I can't complain. In truth, I'm grateful to her. She's taking an enormous risk by looking out for me.

After she and Zavier spoke, she came out and told me I was to remain living with her for the next four weeks—until Zavier was fully healed—and then if I still wanted to take Zavier up on his offer and move in and play happy parents, she wouldn't stand in my way.

Besides telling me I should take Zavier up on his offer, Lexan hadn't said much. He'd merely stared at me to the point where it became uncomfortable. I'd considered breaking his stares by asking him if there was something going on between him and my mother, but I wasn't sure if I really wanted to know. Besides, I wasn't exactly in the position to be pointing fingers.

I've only been back to their cavern twice since. Minty had suggested I stay away as much as possible over the four weeks. She said Zavier needed space to think long and hard about the gravity of what he was offering. I'd agreed, knowing she was right. I know deep down I don't deserve his kind offer, and I feel guilty about considering it, but it's the safest choice I have if I want to stay in the caves.

It's a day shy of six weeks since I'd met Alex in the forest, yet it feels like a lifetime ago. It's also been over five weeks since I'd seen Jax at the medical chamber. Oscar has popped into the Bean-Brew Cavern twice to see how I'm holding up, and both times I've successfully ducked him. Jax must have sent him down to check on me. Minty was quick to cover for me, saying I was happy and fitting right in. *I wish.*

I try hard not to think about Alex or Jax. The Ruby part of me is still broken because of Alex, and the Harlow part of me desires things she should be ashamed of.

My round tummy is starting to show through my clothes. I won't be able to keep my secret under wraps for much longer. Zeek pregnancies are shorter than human pregnancies; they only last four months, hence we get big fast.

Minty steps into my nook and catches me rubbing my tummy. "Have you come to a decision? Are you going to take Zavier up on his offer?" Her questions hold a hint of accusation.

I don't meet her gaze; I'm too ashamed. "I think so."

"I know the four weeks are up, but you might as well continue staying here for the next couple of nights being as we are working together," she suggests. "I'll help you take all of your stuff to Zavier's during our four days off.

I eye my lonely pack sitting on the floor in my nook and laugh inside. I don't think moving one pack is going to be all that difficult, but I do think it makes sense to stay for the extra two nights.

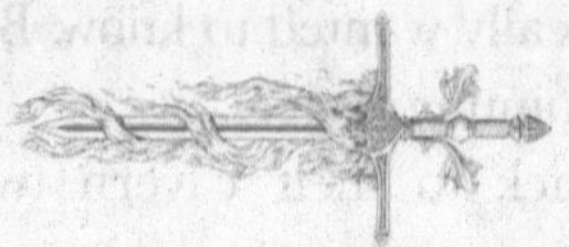

Work is super busy, but I don't mind now that I'm getting the hang of things; it makes the day go faster. The effects of the tattoo have kicked in full force. All my aches and pains are gone and I no longer feel constantly exhausted. I'm as strong as an ox, and my senses are sharp. The only problem is I've grown a foot, which is awesome, but extremely noticeable. Especially when I'm standing alongside Minty.

My small vertic switz snowflake tattoo is the one secret I've kept sacred, and I'd like to keep it that way for now.

"You know, you don't have to go live with Zavier. You and Lucy can stay with us." Minty's comment comes out of the blue and takes me by surprise. "My parents know something's up, but they'd never come forward. They're wimps. My mum prefers to stick her head in the sand. It's what she does best."

"Thanks, that's kind of you, but I'm sure you'll be happy to have your own space back again." I finish chopping the carrot-like vegetable into small dollars and scrape them into the pot. "Our nooks are pretty open. They don't hide much."

"You do realise that Zavier will be taking a huge risk by pretending to be the baby's dad." She glances at my swollen tummy in disapproval. Unfortunately, the apron I'm wearing does more to accentuate the bump than hide it.

"If you think it would be better for me to decline his offer and leave the caves, just say the word and I'll do it. I know he deserves better, but I don't know what else to do besides leave altogether. I've really screwed up."

Minty flips a perfectly circular fluffy cake. "If I tell you to leave, I will be sentencing you and the baby to death, and I can't have that weighing on my conscience." She says this lightly, like she's joking around, but we both know her words carry serious weight. "And anyway, who will I have to pick on once you're gone?"

"I'm sure you could find some other poor Zeek to loathe."

She places the pan back down on the stovetop and gives me a pitying look. "I don't loathe you. I just hate the way you continually lead Zavier on and use him to your advantage. You allow him to think he's got a shot with you, when we all know he doesn't."

I find her comment extremely offensive. I have never led Zavier on. It's not like that between us. We're close, and we love each other, but we're not in love with each other. He's like family to me. *Can't a girl and guy be friends these days without everyone jumping to conclusions?* "Zavier and I are just friends, best friends, and that's all we've ever been."

"Wake up, Precious, it's blatantly obvious. Zavier is in love with you. He's always been in love with you."

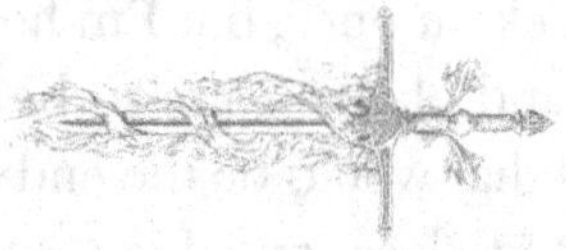

After locking up, Minty and I hear sniggers. Lucy snarls and I glance over my shoulder to find Rae and three other Magentas lurking close by, all eyes on me. There's a beefy male and an extremely tall female, both of whom appear to be in their late thirties like Rae, but the other Magenta with the shoulder-length dreads only appears a year or two older than I am. I don't know him, but I must have seen him around, because his face is familiar.

My chest tightens. Rae's brought her new hunting team with her this time.

They all look rough and ready, the same as she does. *The perfect fit, it seems.*

Rae wanders across, and the other Magentas follow, prompting Lucy to hunker and growl.

"This isn't good," Minty says under her breath. "Don't let any of them snatch your disguise."

It's been weeks since we'd last seen Rae, and I'd hoped she'd given up on settling the score with me for something I didn't do. *Apparently not.*

"Well, well, what do we have here?" Her eyes trace over me from head to toe. "Do I detect a bump under that jumper of yours? My little friend here," she motions to Mr Dreadlocks, "said you looked to be going through some physical changes these past couple of weeks, so I thought I'd come by and check you out myself."

Lucy's growl intensifies, and her lips curl up, baring her teeth.

Oh no, this is bad.

"Walk away, Rae," is all Minty says, and for the first time ever, Minty looks nervous.

If a fight breaks out, we'd have a decent shot at winning. My strength would have surpassed Rae's by now, and Lucy could probably take down two Zeeks at once, but I'm hoping it doesn't come to that. If my bandana and glasses were to be knocked out of place, they'd see the red, and that would be the end of me.

Rae steps a little too close, and Lucy snaps at her in warning. She stops abruptly but doesn't retreat. "Easy, Vicious, I'm not here to fight. I'm just here to look." Her eyes flick curiously between my glasses and bandana. "What are you hiding under there? Your shimmer appears to have darkened a few shades, but it was bound to happen. I wonder how Azazel will feel to discover she's expecting a grandchild?"

"You've got it wrong," I tell her.

She sniggers. "Not even all the huskens in Zadok will be able to save you now. You've made this too easy." She spins to face her gang, her expression cunning. "Come on crew, we have an urgent report for our Commander."

We stay put as they retreat, and it's only once they are fully out of sight that Lucy relaxes.

"What are you going to do?" Minty asks.

"What can I do? It doesn't matter what path I take; they all lead to the same destination. Death." My heart twists painfully knowing it's not only I who will die if I'm killed; it will be the baby too.

"I never thought I'd say this, but do you think we should speak to Jax? Believe it, or not, I don't actually want you to die."

"I can't. It would look even more suspicious if I were to reach out to him now, and I don't want him getting hurt." My voice hitches. "This applies to you too. If you'd prefer me not to come back to your family cavern tonight, I understand. I don't want to drag you down with me."

"If you won't speak to Jax, I think the next best thing to do is to act as if nothing has changed. Rae is known for trash-talking and using scare tactics. Hopefully, she's just trying to call your bluff."

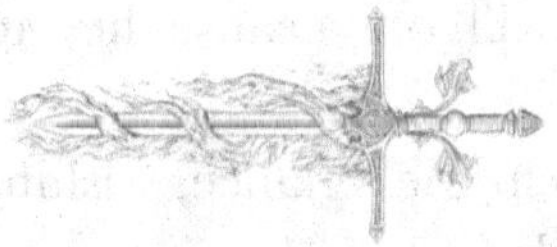

I wake up the next morning feeling even more wrecked than before I went to bed. I didn't get much sleep, and by the looks of the bags under Minty's eyes, neither did she. I'd stared at the creviced ceiling, paranoid I was going to be dragged off in the middle of the night and killed, via the order of our Commander.

Not wanting the vertic switz ink to be found in Minty's house, I'd slit a small hole in the lining of my pack and stitched the leather pouch inside.

Minty steps into my nook as I finish tying my boots. "Are you worried about today?"

I rub my swollen belly, praying to whoever is out there listening *to keep my baby safe.* "I worry about every day."

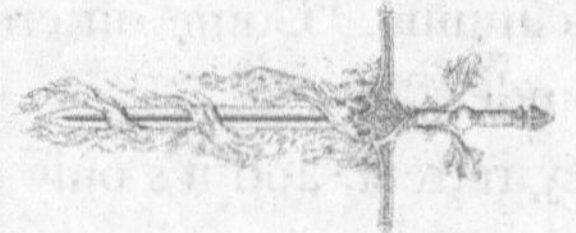

We get through the day unscathed until five-thirty, when Floss flies through the wooden door unannounced.

Her eyes dart straight to my protruding tummy, and she gapes. "It's true! You really are pregnant with Jax's child? How stupid can you get? I warned you about this, but you lied to me and said there was nothing going on between you."

I walk over to her and discover we finally match in height. "I wasn't lying. The baby isn't Jax's."

"I don't believe you." She frowns. "And what are you wearing? Covering your face won't hide your big belly, you know."

"The baby isn't Jax's, I swear. Our relationship was never like that."

"Well, whose is it then?"

I don't know what to say. I can't tell her the truth, and to tell her the baby is Zavier's will only cause her to become more upset with me.

I give Minty a "help me" glance, wishing she would kick Floss out of the kitchen and save me having to answer. "I can't tell you, not right now. Not like this."

"Why not?"

"We should talk about this once I've finished my shift." *AKA, I need some alone time with Minty to discuss the matter before giving you an answer.* "I only have half an hour left. If you wait for me, we'll make you dinner on the house."

Her expression grows wild. "It's Zavier's, isn't it?"

I open my mouth to say something, but no words come out. I'm surprised she would even guess Zavier, given how much my body and shimmer have changed. If I were pregnant to him, there's no way I would've changed this much. She mustn't be thinking straight.

"That's why he and Lexan had acted so weird when I asked

them how you were yesterday." Her eyes bore into mine with hatred, and she gives me a hefty shove. "You bitch! I hate you."

MISTAKEN IDENTITY

-ALEX AS SLATER-

It's been over a month and a half since I watched Jax pick Ruby up and carry her out of the forest—knowing full well it was all my fault.

I've tried to convince myself it's for the best. We could never make it work; it would be too dangerous. But the more time passes, the more I'm struggling to believe this. *I need her in my life.*

When I'd gotten back to the castle, Raven was in my chamber waiting for me in a clingy little pink dress. She said she'd been worried out of her mind, because my older brother Kenneth had told her that I hadn't returned from hunting. *Snitch.*

I'd assured her I was fine and asked her to leave—I wasn't in the mood for company—but she'd refused, telling me she missed me and wanted me back. She'd said she was upset with the way we'd ended things and thought we owed it to ourselves to give our relationship a second chance. She was up in my face, begging, flirting, touching—making me feel wanted.

For selfish reasons, I let her stay. I was absolutely devastated about losing Ruby and was jealous seeing her with Jax. He'd been so close and affectionate towards her, and she hadn't pulled away.

I'd reasoned with myself, it would be better for me to try and make it work with someone I could actually be with, rather than long for someone who was out of my reach. Ruby was gone, and I'd never be able to contact her again. *What was the point of holding on when all it would do is cause me pain?*

My rekindled relationship with Raven lasted a whole week before she left, telling me she felt as if she was dating a beautiful, empty shell. We'd slept together the once, but never again. My heart wasn't in it. I'd wanted to forget about Ruby and try to make things work with Raven, I honestly did, but I couldn't. Ruby was all I could think about. She was all I cared about.

Both Kenneth and my mother were frustrated with me for letting Raven go without a fight for the second time. My mother had said Raven was "one of a kind", and I would live to regret my decision. I think she was the one regretting it, *not me*. Raven is the most eligible candidate there is after Jacinta, Kenneth's partner. She comes from a rich and powerful bloodline worthy of a prince. Our colour system is as rigid as the Zeeks' when it comes to linking, especially with the Reds.

Raven is gorgeous, and she does have a fun side—I'll give her that—but she isn't Ruby.

"Your brother's linking ceremony is in a few days. Might I suggest you work things out with Raven once and for all. I'd like you to bring her as your partner," my mother says in our language, which is similar to German. She may have used the word "suggest", but we both know it's more than a mere suggestion. It's a command. "I don't know why you can't be more like

Kenneth and settle down with a worthy woman who will enrich our bloodline."

"Stop meddling," I tell her. "I'm not in the mood."

I leave my chamber in the north solar and head out to the passageway, trying to hurry, because I'm running late—*again*. The castle walls are made of large sandstone blocks and extend up to a high arched cathedral ceiling, heavily decorated with carvings. Torches line the passageways, and the flickering flames cast eerie, dancing shadows on the walls.

I exit across the castle draw bridge and head to the stables. Kenneth has already hooked the horsens to the cart and is ready to go.

"Nice of you to finally join me," he grizzles. "It's the fourth time this week I've had to pick up your slack. What's got into you lately? You haven't been your usual self. Our mother is starting to worry. She thinks you're trying to make a mockery of her."

"She's already got one golden boy she can control." I toss our weapons, some ropes, and sacks into the cart. "She doesn't need two. And I'm not the heir, you are, so what does it matter what I say or do?"

"You're still a prince," he says pointedly. "And that title alone comes with certain responsibilities."

"Right." I cast him an irritated glance. I hate it when he parrots our mother. "Lucky me, to have been born so blessed."

Our trip into Spring seems longer than usual, or maybe it's Kenneth's company that has me feeling this way. If I hear one more thing about Raven or what our mother wishes I would do or be, I'm going to pick Kenneth up by the throat and hurl him off the cart.

Besides our similar height and build, Kenneth and I are very different to look at. My features are refined like our mother's; I have high angular cheekbones, a decent nose, and a defined chin. Kenneth's looks more like our late father—he has flat cheekbones, a broad nose, and a rather large chin. *Poor ugly bastard.* Sweat drips from his face as he speaks, and I can feel it dripping from mine too. Summer has a scorching climate, averaging 38-49°C temperatures year-round. This is why Zeeks don't fare well here. That, and their bodies are thrown into an entirely different sleeping pattern. When it's daytime in Winter and Spring, it's night in Autumn and Summer and vice versa. Hence, why we hunt at night.

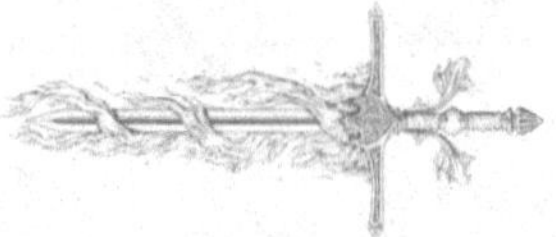

It's been another fruitful night of hunting, and the cart is full to the brim before dawn. Vallons are keen sighted. We're able to see every movement, even on the darkest nights when the moon is hidden. Hunting at night isn't a problem for us; it's an advantage. Most of the bigger, meatier animals are nocturnal, and nine times out of ten, we can take them down before they even know what's hit them.

After tying down the last of the carcasses, Kenneth is ready to head back.

"I'm going to stay out here for a bit," I tell him. I want to explore. "If you unload all the carcasses today, I'll unload tomorrow."

"What are you really trying to achieve out here?" His large, glowing irises turn slitted. "If the Drakes find you using their land in the daylight, you know it'll cause problems between our races."

"I'm not staying out here to cause trouble, I'm staying to keep my sanity. I need a break from you, our mother, and everybody else in our kingdom. Your linking ceremony has everyone going bonkers."

"I'm not covering for you again." He tugs off his black hunting shirt, revealing his glowing vertic switz.

A cynical laugh escapes me. "You didn't cover for me the first time. You went and told Raven."

"Raven was looking for you, and I figured if she kept looking and couldn't find you, she'd alert our mother. I did you a favour."

"Admit it, you were trying to set us up again."

"Please." He hops onto the front bench of the cart and cues the horsens to start moving. "I wouldn't be so cruel. She deserves much better."

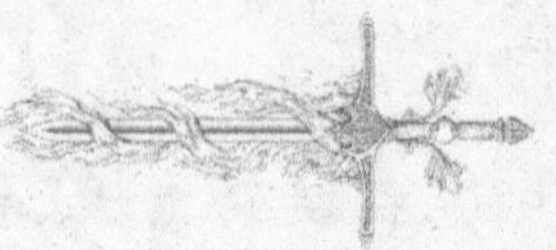

As the first light of dawn breaks through the trees, I make my way over to the Winter border. I want to catch Saul and his hunting team on their way out and have him deliver a message to Ruby for me. I've been considering the idea for weeks, but I've been holding off, hoping that my feelings for Ruby would fade. They haven't, and even though I know it's dangerous, I have to reach out. I want her to know I didn't completely desert her, that I came back.

It takes a while before I spot two separate hunting sleds heading towards the forest. I immediately recognise Saul's because of the set of deetra antlers decorating the sides. Ruby had said he was an egotistical bastard, and it shows. She also said he was well-respected for being a brute. Little does she know he'd turned to jelly when I threatened his life.

As the sled gets closer to the forest edge, I catch sight of everyone inside, and my heart comes to a standstill. Ruby is with him. I hadn't expected this. *What a relief.* I can speak to her directly instead of going through Saul. *It's less messy this way.*

She's certainly changed a lot over the past month. Her fuller face and muscular arms are something I'd been expecting, but her hair has darkened a lot more than I thought it would. She almost looks Magenta. I imagine this would have sparked a few questions among the Zeeks in her colony. *I wonder what she told them.*

I follow them through the forest for quite some time before the sled comes to a halt a few metres away from a small flock of woollies.

Woollies are a good find. Their meat tastes good, and you can use their wool for bedding, clothing, insulation, and floor rugs. This makes them valuable when it comes to trading.

Saul and the other male head to one side of the flock while Ruby and—I'm guessing it's her mother, going by their similar looks —head around to the other side. I follow closely, trying my best to stay light-footed. *Think,* I urge. I need to find a discreet way to separate them. As they get closer to the flock, Ruby's mother gestures for Ruby to stay where she is while she continues on a little further, presumably so they can come at the flock from all angles.

This is too easy. I can't believe it. I don't have to come up with anything. Had I known it would be this simple to see Ruby, I would have done this weeks ago.

"Pssst, Ruby. Rubes," I whisper. She glances about in wide-eyed confusion. Her eyes are magenta too. *Weird.* This hadn't happened to any of the other Pastels who were injected. Their pigments never darkened; they'd merely given off a slight peach tone. It was only faint though, nothing highly noticeable like this. *I wonder if it's because they were injected with the amber vertic switz ink, not red?* "Ruby, over here." I'm positioned behind a tree, but I stick my head out slightly so she can see me. "It's me, Alex."

Her eyes finally catch sight of mine, and she lets out an ear-piercing scream. *What the hell?* I dive out, grab her, and quickly duck behind another tree, pinning her between me and the trunk. She goes to let out another scream, but I stop her with my hand. "What are you doing?" I whisper in frustration. "Are you trying to cause a scene?"

"Floss! Floss, are you okay?" her mother shouts, and I freeze in alarm, realising my mistake.

This isn't Ruby, it's her sister. *Fuck!*

Ruby told me she had a sister named Floss, and that they weren't close. She'd said Floss was born a Magenta, the same as their parents. What she'd failed to clarify though, is they must have been born on the same day, because besides their physiques and colouring, their facial features are identical. *She's a twin.* I let out a frustrated sigh. And here I was thinking it was all so easy.

"Floss," her mother calls again, this time in a hushed tone.

Her body struggles beneath mine.

"Stop," I warn. "I'm going to release my hand for a second, and if you want to remain alive, you are going to tell your mother that you are okay. Got it?"

Her eyes glisten as she nods against my hand.

"Good." I let my hand drop, and she does as I've said, adding, without being prompted, she'd just tripped over a tree root.

"Be more careful," her mother warns, her tone still hushed. "We don't want the flock running off."

Floss' eyes look into mine, and she cringes away. "What do you want from me?"

"I want you to give Ruby a message for me."

Again, she tries wresting herself out of my grip. "I don't know anyone named Ruby."

She's much feistier than her sister.

"Harlow. I need you to give Harlow a message for me."

"Harlow?" Her eyes widen. "My sister?"

"Yes. I need you to tell her I came back, but saw Jax had found her, so I stayed hidden. I also want you to let her know I love her, and I want to make it work, so if she feels the same way, she should sneak out to the forest again tomorrow morning. I'll be waiting for her. Can you do this for me?"

"Why? What does th... Oh..." Her fight instantly subsides as something seems to register inside her. "Oh my, it's yours, isn't it? That makes much more sense."

I frown. "What's mine?"

"The baby."

"Baby?" I feel like she's zapped the wind out of my lungs. "What baby?"

"Harlow's pregnant. Surprise!"

Too stunned to hand out any threats like don't tell anyone bar Harlow you saw me here, I release Floss and step back, almost stumbling over my own feet. *She's pregnant. Ruby is pregnant.*

I expect Floss to take off right away, but she doesn't. Instead, she moves towards me. "Could it be yours?" she asks curiously, and I have to admit, I admire her bravery. "I'd rather it be yours than his."

I frown. "Who else's could it be?"

"Never mind. Going by the changes in her, I'm pretty sure it has to be yours." Floss looks irritated. "That sneaky little bitch. What is it about her, *huh?* What makes her so God damn special?"

Not entirely sure what she's trying to get at, I ignore the questions, and take a few seconds to gather my thoughts. *This can't wait. Screw sending a message. I need to see Ruby now.*

For me to barge into the caves on my own would be a death wish, but if I had a hostage to bargain with and use as my shield, I might make it past Jax's warriors.

My eyes flick to Floss'. "I need your help to get into the caves."

"How?" she asks, taking a cautious step back. "What could I possibly do?"

"I need you to be my hostage."

HARLOW IS MOVING IN TODAY

-ZAVIER-

I smile like an idiot while re-making my bed with clean sheets. I'm over the moon because Harlow is moving in today. As far as I was concerned, she was welcome to move in right away, but Minty had other ideas. She'd insisted we should wait until I was off bedrest and feeling stronger.

I knew I was already pushing the boundaries with Minty by asking her to jump on board with our cover story and keep Harlow's secret. So, to stay on her good side, I gave in and agreed to her argument. It made sense. I was weak and needed time to heal, but I also felt like I needed Harlow. I want our closeness back.

Since that evening, I've seen even less of Harlow than usual, which again, was one of Minty's ideas.

Lexan is at work today. It might be the start of the girls' four days off, but it's only mid-week for everybody else around here. Jax had Medic Sylvie come by yesterday to clear me to go back to work. I'm still in a bit of pain, but I'm mostly okay. I'm fairly certain I'll end up like Lexan, sore and arthritic for the rest of my life due to all of my injuries.

Surprisingly, Floss has come to visit me quite a few times since I've been on home rest. She still has the personality of a yo-yo, but she's much easier to get along with than she used to be. She's been helpful and has even said some warm, uplifting things to me—which is weird given how much she seemed to detest me only a matter of months ago. *Who would have guessed that getting my arse kicked by Ogre would have been the key to winning her friendship?*

As I pick up the last of my clothes off the floor and dump them into my wicker wash basket, I hear footsteps entering the cavern. I walk out with a smile, expecting to see Harlow, but my smile falls flat when I see Jax and his mutt standing inside the entryway.

"What do you want?" I ask with irritation.

He doesn't look like his usual self. His eyes are circled with dark rings, as if he hasn't slept a wink in days, and his jawline is shaded with stubble.

"There are a lot of dangerous rumours going around about Harlow and me."

I tap my fingers against my thigh in agitation. "Yes, I know. I've heard the rumours."

He casts a curious glance in my direction. "Is this why you've been so hostile towards me?" he asks. "Why you accused me of using her up and spitting her out? Were you under the impression there was something going on between us?"

"I'm hostile towards you because I don't like you," I say bluntly. "I don't like or trust Purples. My parents were killed by Purples."

"I'm sorry about what happened to your family." His voice is sincere. "It was tragic. But you can't hold me responsible because of my colouring, especially when I'm the one who saved your life."

I roll my eyes. *Show off.* "Yeah, rub it in."

His brows pucker, and he exhales with a huff, shaking his head in disbelief. "I don't know why I even bother trying to talk to you."

"I wish you wouldn't."

Despite his comment, he continues, "The main reason I've come, is because I'm worried about Harlow. I'd pay her a visit personally if I could, but I'm afraid if I'm seen trying to contact her it will only make matters worse." His mutt comes over to sniff me, and I smack it away. "Just to be clear, the rumours about Harlow being pregnant with my child aren't true. Rae is trying to cause problems. She wants Harlow killed. I thought if I sent Harlow down here as a temporary solution, Electra and Rae would eventually lose interest and leave her alone. It turns out I'm wrong once again."

"Harlow is pregnant," I say, catching him off guard. "But don't worry, the baby is mine. You can let everyone know to back off and leave her alone." He recoils like I've just delivered a hefty punch to his guts. "She's moving in today, actually. She and Minty should be here any minute."

His eyes, now filled with hurt, flash with a thousand questions, but all he says is, "My apologies, I wasn't aware. Congratulations to you both." He clicks his fingers, and Sphinx rushes to his side. "Come on, boy. It's time to go."

13

HOSTAGE SITUATION
-ALEX AS SLATER-

Floss doesn't need to be convinced or threatened to help me, she tags along willingly. It's strange—she doesn't know anything about me, yet she's less afraid of me than Ruby was in the beginning, and Ruby already had the assurance of knowing my human side. If anything, Floss seems excited about being a part of my plan. *Maybe she's a thrill seeker or something—who knows?* She's definitely a lot more audacious than her sister.

The frost-filled air of Winter feels crisper than I remember, and my teeth chatter within minutes of crossing the border. I'm glad I've left my hunting clothes on because they cling tightly to my skin like thermals. I don't know how Zeeks live here. It's bloody freezing.

Floss asks a lot of questions, and I dodge them as best as I can without pissing her off. I need to keep her on my side.

She notices my answers are clipped, and says, "You're not much of a talker, are you?" But it doesn't stop her from continuing to poke and pry.

Going by her bitter string of comments about Harlow—as she calls her—I'm guessing there's a bit of rivalry between the sisters. Ruby had given me the same impression. She wasn't too complimentary about Floss either. She'd said, and I quote, "Floss can be a bit of bitch sometimes."

Eventually the caves come into sight, and I make out five warriors on guard.

"I need to pick you up," I say.

Floss wordlessly raises her arms, allowing me to lift her by her waist. I'm not about to let her know this—in case she gets the wrong impression—but I'm secretly glad to have her warm body pressed up next to mine. While I'm not a fan of Summer's putrid sweaty heat, the frigid air of Winter is biting. My joints are near seizing, and my skin stings.

"As soon as we're spotted, I'm going to put my blade to your throat," I inform her calmly. "Don't worry, I'm not going to kill you, but I need the warriors to believe I have every intention of doing so."

"I'm not worried," she says, and it sounds as if she means it. "If you'd wanted to kill me, I would be dead already."

"How can you be so confident?"

She shrugs against me. "It's not a matter of confidence, it's a matter of care-factor. If you don't kill me, Rae eventually will. She's been eyeing me for weeks. And anyway, no one will care if I die. I don't have men lining up after me like my sister does."

Her comment makes me bristle. I don't know whether she's trying to make me feel sorry for her or get a rise out of me.

Not taking the bait, I simply respond with, "I've heard about Rae. She sounds dangerous."

We get within a hundred metres from the cave entrance before we're spotted, and within seconds, a handful of warriors descend on us with their weapons raised. "Stop!" one of them yells. "Stop where you are, before we put a shard through you."

I thrust the edge of the blade firmly against Floss' neck, making sure not to let it bite into the skin. "If anything or anyone touches me, I will slice her throat." Floss lets out a whimper, and I don't know whether I've actually hurt her, or if she's merely playing her part.

A warrior with cornrows takes a small step closer. "What do you want?"

"I want to speak to Jax. Bring him out." When he doesn't react right away, I yell, "NOW! Before I slice this pretty girl's head clean off her shoulders."

Cornrows nods to one of the other warriors who has a man bun. "Kieran, I'll handle this. You get Jax." His gaze floats between the other three. "The rest of you stay put, but don't attack unless I give the word."

It takes a good fifteen minutes of hard, intense stares before Kieran re-emerges with Jax and his husken.

Jax stalks straight over to where I stand, wearing his stoic warrior mask. His husken treads a step closer, baring its teeth.

"Slater." Jax's voice is cold. "To what do I owe the pleasure of this visit?"

"I'm here to make a trade. Floss for Harlow."

He tries hard to keep an impassive front, but his eyes spark with a hint of curious unease. "What do you want with Harlow?"

"I'm not here to hurt Harlow, I'm just here to retrieve her. We have unfinished business."

His eyes flick to Floss momentarily and then back to me. "What kind of unfinished business are you talking about?"

"The more questions you ask, the closer I get to slitting Floss' throat, so act fast. Your time is ticking."

Floss lets out another whimper. "Jax, please, help me," she begs. *She's good.*

He keeps his composure, and with a firm, steady voice, he says,

"It's okay, Floss, I'm not going to let him hurt you. However…" His eyes glare into mine. "I'm sure we can come to an understanding that doesn't involve me handing over Harlow. What's your price?"

"My demands are clear and non-negotiable. Retrieve Harlow for me, and nobody will get hurt."

"There has to be a price," he urges. "What could you possibly want with her?"

I press my blade firm to Floss' skin. "Tick tock, Jax. I'm not leaving here without Harlow."

His expression betrays him by darkening in defeat. He could order his men to kill me, and they would easily succeed. I'm outnumbered. But he won't let that happen for the same reasons I didn't attack him that day in the forest. We are both too important. We are the sons of opposing Leaders. If either of us were killed, it would start another war, and neither of us wants this.

"Wait here and don't let him move," Jax commands his warriors. "I'll be back with Harlow."

14

THE VALLON IS OUT OF THE BAG

-HARLOW-

I've just finished setting my pack down in Zavier's nook when I hear fast-paced footsteps entering the cavern.

"Where's Harlow?" Jax's voice booms, and I can tell by his harsh tone he's certainly not happy about something.

"What are—" Zavier starts, and Jax cuts him off with a snap.

"I don't have time for your nonsense, Zavier. Tell me where she is."

"She's..." Minty begins.

I step out from Zavier's nook. "I'm here."

Jax takes one look at me and his shimmer vanishes. My stomach twists into knots.

"What's going on? What's happened to you?" His eyes do a double-take at the bandana that was once his.

I know I need to answer. He's the Commander's son, I should obey his orders, but my throat closes up. Jax is too smart to believe this baby is Zavier's, and I'm too afraid to tell him the truth. Not only because of the ramifications, but because I'm terrified of facing his disappointment. I don't want him to hate me or cast me out. I have so much respect for him and I feel… My heart thuds hard and painfully inside my chest. *You shouldn't feel anything for him other than respect,* I warn.

When I fail to answer, he stalks over, takes me by the arm, and drags me back into Zavier's nook.

"Hey!" Zavier yells, but Minty is quick to tell him to shut up and stay out of it.

Now alone, Jax's hands grip both of my shoulders, pulling me around to face him. He leans towards me, and he is so close I can feel his heavy, angry breaths beating down on my face.

"What business do you have with Slater?" His question comes out as a sharp, rumbling whisper.

Stunned, my thumping heart stops dead. Something shrivels inside me. Jax knows the truth, or at least part of it. *I wonder how he found out?* I know for certain none of the Zeeks I've confided in would squeal on me. Besides, I never gave Alex's Vallon name. I've only referred to him as Alex.

"It's a long story." My voice wobbles. "And you probably won't believe it."

His violet eyes blaze in frustration. "Well, I don't have time for long stories, because he's here right now, asking for you."

I jolt. "He's here?" A plague of emotions stirs inside me, making me feel sick to my core. I'd spent so many nights crying into my pillow, hoping against all odds Alex would regret his decision and come back for me, but he hadn't. And now that I've finally pushed past the hurt and heartache, he's here. *Why now?*

An expression I don't like comes over Jax's face. "Yes, and he has your sister hostage. He said if I don't hand you over, he'll kill her."

"He won't kill her," I say with certainty, yet as soon as I've said it, I find myself second guessing it. "Well at least, I'm pretty sure he won't. Where is he? I'll talk to him. I should be able to sort this out." *I hope.*

Without a word, Jax's hand goes straight for my glasses. I try to stop him, but I'm too slow. He snatches the shades away from my face. His eyes enlarge, and a disbelieving huff escapes him. He reaches for the bandana next. I don't bother trying to stop him this time around; there's no point.

"Frost," he says under his breath, and it's the first time I've ever heard him curse.

He snatches up one of my dreadlocks and twists it around in his fingers, his brows creased as he stares incredulously. After several agonising moments, he lets the dreadlock drop, and his eyes fall back on mine.

"I guess I've got my answer." There is no warmth in his words, only hurt. "It's obvious why he's here."

A lump rises in my throat. The pain in his voice is excruciating. "Jax, I'm sorry." A tear escapes. "I'm so very sorry."

He hands me back the bandana and glasses. "Put these back on," he says, his indifferent warrior mask slipping back in place. "You can explain yourself later. We have to save your sister."

Jax exits the nook while I reassemble my disguise. "I'm leaving for the cave entry now," I hear him tell Minty and Zavier. "And I'd like you to walk Harlow to me as soon as you can. I can't risk taking her with me. It will attract too much attention." Zavier goes to say something, but Jax speaks straight over him. "I would also appreciate it if you'd help keep the Vallon situation under wraps from the rest of the colony for now. I don't want this getting back to my mother."

When I come out, I fill Minty and Zavier in on what's happening. Zavier isn't happy about going along with this. He's worried about what will happen to me, but Minty and I convince him it's the safest choice now that the Vallon is out of the bag, *so to speak.*

"And besides," I say adamantly, "I have to save Floss."

When we get to the mouth of the cave, I'm glad to see it's empty of all Zeeks, bar Jax. He stands straight and stony-faced as he waits for us, looking every bit the fierce warrior he is.

"Thank you," he says to Zavier and Minty as we near, and then he raises a palm to Lucy. "Lucy, stay," he tells her. "I need you to protect these two."

"Come here, Lucy," Minty calls, taking Jax's cue. "Come stand with me."

"If we're not back in half an hour, it means there's trouble. And if this is the case, I need you to seek help, but until then, I want you to act as if it's any other day. Got it?"

Zavier's face is scrunched, and he doesn't answer, but Minty nods and repeats, "Got it."

Jax's hard gaze settles on me last of all. "We need to go." He scoops me up and stalks to the exit. "I'd like to get this settled before anyone else catches on to what's happening."

As soon as we get a few metres out, I'm able to see Alex holding Floss, along with the five remaining warriors who have him surrounded. I only recognise three of the warriors, Oscar, Zannah, and Kieran. I've never met the other two.

My heart thumps. It's been over a month and a half since Alex left me in the forest to die. I don't know how or why he has Floss, but she's obviously told him I'm alive, otherwise he wouldn't be here asking for me. *I wonder if he's here because he feels sorry about leaving me, or if he's here to finish me off.* I thought I knew who he was, but now I'm not so sure. A sickening thought enters my mind. *What if he's asked for me to be brought out here, so he can kill Floss in front of me? A sister for a brother, an eye for an eye.*

Please don't let this be the case. Floss might be a bitch, but I do love her. Any remaining confidence I felt earlier completely crumbles. I don't know if I'll be able to sort this out.

"Why him?" Jax finally asks, as he trudges toward them. "Why the Queen's son?"

"What do you mean?" But before he gets the chance to respond, his question registers with a wallop. "Alex is the Queen's son?"

"Who's Alex?"

"I mean Slater," I correct.

"Are you telling me you honestly didn't know?"

"No, I didn't know. I've only ever met him once. It was during the night I'd spent in the forest." It's not a lie, it's just not the whole truth. I have only met Slater once. "He never mentioned he was the Queen's son."

It seems obvious now that it's been pointed out. I don't know how I didn't pick up on this earlier. When Alex first told me he was a Vallon, we'd got into a bit of a heated discussion regarding our warring races, and he was completely up on all the politics.

"Oscar has been hounding me for weeks to find out how you survived the night alone in the danger zone. Now I can let him know you weren't alone." A bitter tone rings out as Jax says this.

I feel terrible. "Jax, I'm sorry."

"I'm sorry too, because you've left me with no choice. To keep the peace and save your sister, I have to hand you over." There's a long brittle pause before he goes on to say, "When RJ told me that together we'd help bring change to our colony, I believed him, and when he said there would be special children born, I'd imagined those children would be ours. I thought if I could breakdown the colour system, you and I could… We could…" he shakes his head. "I was wrong. I've been wrong about everything."

I'm rendered speechless. *Is this Jax's way of admitting he has feelings for me?* I don't understand why he's waited until now to say something.

His semi-admission is agonising to hear, especially when there's a secret part of me that wishes this baby was his too. I haven't wanted to admit it, even to myself, but I like him in a way that's more than platonic, I like him in a way that makes my insides flutter.

A few Zeeks had said Jax was interested in me, but I hadn't believed them. I honestly thought he was only being kind in the beginning because he needed me, and then afterwards because he felt guilty for putting my life in danger. I couldn't see how he would want someone like me when he's got beautiful Zeeks like Zannah to choose from. I would tarnish him. *I am nothing but a worthless, pitiful Past...* Before I can finish thinking it, I realise with a jolt this is no longer the case. I might still be worthless and pitiful, but I'm not a Pastel, I'm a Red. A Red Zeek. Well, if nothing else, I've become a one of a kind. This could be what RJ meant by, "You are special. I've seen it. You will bring about change." I don't want to be seen as special for sleeping with the enemy. I believed I was going to do something good for the colony, that I was going to make a positive difference. I'd pictured myself as the hero in this scenario, not the villain.

At a loss of what to say without making things worse, I let out another lame, "I'm sorry, Jax."

As we get closer, Alex looks me over with concern. "What's wrong with her?" he asks. "Why do you have her all covered up?"

"Those reasons should be obvious to you." There's a dangerous edge to Jax's tone.

I've never heard him sound this threatening. My breath catches in my throat. "Harlow belongs in the caves, as does Floss. Name your price, and I'll see to it you are paid."

The two warriors I'm unfamiliar with are standing on either side of Alex, and as Jax makes this comment, they exchange glances, a silent message passing between them.

"Quit trying to negotiate with me. I'm here for Harlow and Harlow only. Now put her down, let her come to me, and I will release Floss," Alex's harsh voice cuts through the air like a knife.

"We'll put the girls down together," Jax challenges, "and we'll swap them simultaneously."

Alex shakes his head, his eyes fierce. "I don't trust you, and I'm outnumbered. I'm keeping Floss as leverage until I get Harlow."

Jax's grip on me tightens. "That's not going to work for me."

"Make it work," Alex snaps, and it sends chills down my spine. His aggressive tone sounds absolutely terrifying, especially laced with the harshness of his German-like accent. "The sooner you give me Harlow, the sooner I'm out of your hair for good."

"It's okay," I tell Jax. "Let me go. I'll make sure Floss is handed over."

Ignoring me, Jax casts Alex a warning glance. "I don't care if you are the Queen's son, if you hurt either girl, you'll receive a shard to your chest. Do I make myself clear?"

"Crystal."

Jax reluctantly puts me down and allows me to cross the two metres which separates them.

As soon as I'm within arms-reach, Alex releases Floss and shoves her forward, before quickly taking hold of me. My heart pounds erratically as I look back at Jax. I wish I'd known how he felt before I'd gone and made such a mess of things.

Alex holds me close to his chest as he backs away slowly, and I can tell he's worried because his heart is beating almost as fast as mine. I'm not as good of a shield to use as Floss. My life isn't as valuable, especially now. I'll be seen as a traitor.

Alex only makes it a few steps back before I hear the whistle of an arrow-shaped shard zooming towards us. I see it coming before it hits. It's been aimed at my chest by the bulky woman warrior. Fear sparks inside me. Alex sees it too, and moves just in time for it to miss my heart and smash through the meaty section below my collarbone.

"No!" Jax shouts.

A sharp, icy pain rips through my entire shoulder as the shard pierces one side and bursts out the other. The intense burning sensation is phenomenal. An ear-piercing scream escapes me, clawing at my ears.

More whistles sound, and I see another set of shards zooming through the air. One shard is heading our way, but the other is headed towards the bulky woman warrior. I gape in disbelief at the sight of Zannah's risen arm. It's shimmering bright purple with the use of winter magic. The shot at the warrior had been fired by Zannah's hand. I can't believe it; she's siding with us over her fellow warriors. *A traitor and the Zeeks' greatest enemy.*

The bulky warrior-woman's eyes widen, and she falls.

Too stunned to move of my own accord, Alex shoves me aside before the second shard hits. I stumble, semi-dazed. I feel like I'm in a dream. The second shard completely misses me, but nicks Alex's side as it passes. He groans through gritted teeth but doesn't scream.

The other unknown warrior, a guy with a short, stubby ponytail, sends a shard blasting towards Zannah's chest in retaliation. Furthering my state of shock, Alex quickly blasts the shard into water with a ball of fire, saving Zannah as she'd saved us. Oscar and Jax both send shards flying at ponytail guy, taking him down with a heavy thud.

"Harlow!" Jax leaves Floss with Oscar and comes racing over, but Alex jumps in front of him.

"Stay back!"

"Not a chance," Jax roars. "She's hurt." He pushes past Alex without any fear of retaliation.

15

THE AFTERMATH

-HARLOW-

Stars dance across my vision, and I sway woozily. "Jax?" Even after all the disgraceful things he's learnt about me, he still rushes to help me. *Why?*

He sees me swaying and picks up the pace, managing to catch me in his arms. "Easy," he says, gently placing me down on the snow-covered ground. "I've got you."

Once I'm lying flat, he tears at the neckline of my jumper.

Alex instantly takes offence. He steps over and angles his blade to Jax's throat. "Don't even think about it."

"She's losing a lot of blood. I need to see precisely where she's been hit."

"Move aside. I know where to take her to get help."

"Where do you plan on taking her, to Summer?" Jax roars. "She'll die before you get her there."

Kieran sneaks up on Alex and sticks his blade to Alex's throat. "I'd put the blade down and walk away if I were you."

Alex grudgingly retracts his blade, and Kieran steps back, keeping his blade up in warning.

Jax rips my jumper wide open, and when he sees my wound, he curses for the second time in one day. "We need to get her back inside."

"Like hell you do. Your own warriors tried to kill her. She's safer with me." Alex drops to his knees by my side. "Ruby," he says. "Rubes, I want you to come with me. Tell Jax you want to come with me."

"Alex, I—"

Jax cuts me off to drive across his point. "You're not listening." His tone is hostile. "If she doesn't get help soon, she and the babies will die. Is this what you want?"

"Babies?" Alex says. The confusion and shock in his features mirrors my own.

What does Jax mean by babies? Am I having twins? RJ must have told him. Nice of him to tell me.

"You need to go," Jax warns. "Get out of here before my mother sees you and you start an outright war."

Alex shakes his head. "I'm not leaving her."

"You left me before," I croak, and they both glance my way. "You left me to die."

"No, I didn't leave you," Alex says, tenderly touching my cheek. "I swear, I came back to apologise, but he was with you." He nods towards Jax, shooting him an accusing look. "I'm sorry for the way I acted. I was upset with you for killing my brother—and for taking away the Alex part of me, but I do understand you did what you had to do in order to save your sister."

Jax looks down at me in shock-horror. "You killed Kenneth?"

"No," I say, which only confuses him. "I killed Lucas."

"I don't want to lose you." Alex takes my hand in his, and I find myself wishing he would stop touching me like this in front of Jax. "I can't lose you in both lives."

A month and a half ago, I would have given anything to hear Alex say these words, but now they leave me feeling numb.

"Look, I have no idea what's going on here, or why you two are calling each other different names," Jax says in exasperation. "But I need you to let me take her inside now, or I promise you, you will lose her in both lives—whatever that means."

"Alex, please go," I say with gritted teeth. "You need to leave. Now! Before anyone else sees you."

His face twists with hurt. "And what? Leave you here so that you can curl up in bed with him?" A dark gleam takes over Alex's molten eyes as he redirects his focus to Jax. "Don't think I haven't figured out what you're up to," he says. "I know you're after her, but get this, she's mine. You need to back off."

"Alex, stop," I say, lifting my head. It hurts. "She's mine" has a very possessive ring to it and makes me feel more like an object than the girl of his affections.

"You need to go. If you care about me at all, you will leave. I need help. I want these babies to survive."

"I hate to break up this lovers' quarrel," Zannah cuts in, "but we've got bigger problems to deal with and a mega story to concoct, so if we could get all non-warriors out of here A.S.A.P., that would be fantastic."

Alex squeezes my hand, kisses me lightly on the lips, and then stands. "I'll be back for her in a fortnight. You touch her in that time, and you're dead."

"She needs more than a fortnight to heal," Jax argues. "Give her four weeks from today, and I promise you I will bring her to you myself. We'll meet inside the Spring border at dawn. Near the dual fallen trunks. I'm sure you know where they are."

I watch as Alex considers this, his features twisted with angst. "Fine." He gives in. "I'll give her four weeks, but you'd better come, or I'll make you sorry."

Zannah steps forward, her chest puffed. "If he says he'll bring her, he'll bring her. And I'll be coming with him. Now go."

Alex leaves and Jax calls Floss over. "I need you to take Harlow to the medical chamber for me. Tansy should be on the front desk today. Tell her to get Sylvie. We can trust Sylvie. Don't talk to anyone else, got it?"

"Do I really have to carry her all the way there by myself?"

Leave it to Floss to make saving my life sound like so much trouble.

"Minty, Zavier, and Lucy are just inside the cave entry." Jax lifts me up carefully and places me in Floss' arms. "They should be able to help you. Make sure to remind them not to talk to anybody, either."

"Well, somebody's put on a bit of weight," Floss scorns, and I feel a sharp pain shoot through my shoulder as she tries to reposition me. "I think I might need a new set of arms after this."

Feeling embarrassed, I tell her to shut up. Most Magentas are like Purples, exceptionally strong. I've seen Floss pick up logs double her size and toss them out of the way. She's only looking to humiliate me.

"Be careful with her." Jax helps to readjust me in her arms. "Now go, quickly."

It's an excruciating trip back. It feels as though Floss is bouncing me around on purpose.

"How is it you get three men fighting over you, you selfish bitch, and yet I can't get anyone better than Elgar? We look the same—*basically*—only I'm supposed to be superior. I don't understand how this works. What makes you so God damn special?" Her arms tighten, and I groan.

"Floss, be careful, please. You're hurting me."

"Oh, be quiet," she snaps. "You're lucky I'm even carrying you."

As soon as Floss steps through the cave entry, Zavier, Minty, and Lucy come bounding over.

"What's happened?" Zavier asks, and I want to answer, but I feel like I'm on the verge of passing out.

"She's been hurt," Floss answers. "Jax needs us to keep quiet and get her to the medical chamber with as minimal fuss as possible. I'll fill you in on the details once we get her there safely."

"I'll help you carry her," Zavier offers, but Minty pushes him out of the way. "You're still recovering. I'll help carry her."

"What about your arm?"

"I've still got one good one."

The pain I feel as they manoeuvre me across their arms is so agonising, I slip out of consciousness.

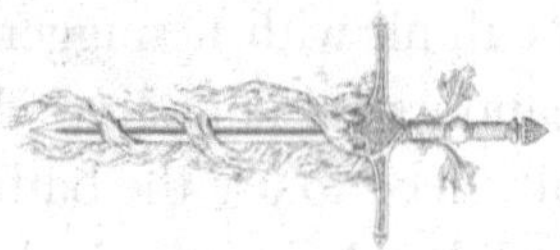

My eyes flutter open to see Jade sitting back in a very posh yet comfortable looking black recliner.

"How many weeks would you say it's been since you last saw her?"

In front of Jade sits a man in his early fifties with short brown hair and glasses. Dr Anthony Murray, according to the metallic plaque on his desk, and below his name in smaller block letters it reads, Psychiatrist. He wears an expensive blue suit with a green shirt and a red-striped tie. Not a good look. Surely, he must be colour blind.

Jade instantly spots me, and her whole face lights up. I can tell she wants to leap out of the chair and come racing over to me, but she holds back. *Good.* I don't want Dr Murray writing her off as insane.

"Jade," Dr Murray says, trying to regain her attention. "Can you see her now?"

I don't know for certain, but I suspect he is talking about me.

"No," Jade replies, but even as she says it, she's still looking right at me.

"What seems to have caught your attention then?" he asks. "You were relaxed a moment ago, and now you seem anxious. Has something upset you?"

"Stop looking at me," I tell her. "Act casual."

"I'm sorry." Jade stands. "But I really, really need to go to the toilet."

"Are you sure it's not nerves?" Dr Murray's tone irks me. He's speaking to my sister the same way a kindergarten teacher would speak to their students. "You've only been in here for five minutes. This is a safe space, Jade; you don't have to be afraid. Remember, anything you tell me is confidential."

Give me a break, I think with a snigger. These therapists and their patronising demeanours are enough to drive people crazier.

"I'm fine, I just really need to use the bathroom."

"Okay, well when you head out into the hall, it's the second door to your left. You should find it easily. There's a sign on the door that says toilet."

"Wow, he must really think you are thick," I tease, and Jade chuckles.

This prompts Dr Murray to jot something down on his little notepad. *Oops.* I probably should've kept my mouth shut.

As soon as we're out the door, Jade starts speaking to me, and I have to remind her that we are still in a psychiatrist's clinic, and there are staff and patients within earshot.

"Let's get out of here," she says. "It's getting late, and the last thing I want to do is waste my time talking to Dr Murray when you're here. It's only my third visit, but I think I'm done. He's not helping me. All he does is talk in circles the whole time. He thinks I'm crazy."

"I agree, you don't need him, but please, stop speaking until we get to the car, otherwise everyone else in this clinic will think you're crazy too."

It's dark outside and raining heavily.

"I don't know why Byron had to go and book the latest appointment available," Jade grumbles. "I'd rather be home, snuggled in my pyjamas, watching Netflix."

Jade's black BMW is parked under a streetlight nearby, and we race over to it to save her from getting too drenched.

"I think Byron wants to leave me," she says, once we're both inside the car. "He's been less affectionate and sending me off to late appointments. He doesn't seem to want me around."

"I've seen the way Byron looks at you," I say. "He's not going anywhere. Trust me, he's smitten. He's obviously worried about you. *Are* you okay?"

"Sort of. I don't know. I've been feeling a little mixed up since moving back here. Everywhere I look holds memories of us growing up." A tear trickles down her cheek. "I miss you and the close relationship we had. You were my other half, my better half, and I'm struggling to continue on without you."

Hearing this makes me feel guilty. "Stay strong," I say. "I'm here with you now and I'll love you forever."

"It's Lucas' funeral tomorrow." Her voice cracks on his name. "I'm not going, even though Byron and Josh both suggested I should. They believe it will give me closure, but I disagree. I know Lucas had a mental illness, but I can't forgive him for separating us at such a young age. I hate him."

I cast her a sympathetic glance. "I'm sorry I used your body to push Lucas out of the window. I'm sure it must be difficult to have everyone you know believe you killed him."

"I'm not upset about what people think. Lucas deserved to die for what he did to you. I'm just upset I didn't figure it out earlier. I can't believe I let him back into my life. Things might have ended very differently if you hadn't shown up. He could have killed Connor!"

I want to wrap my hand around hers and console her, but I can't. "Don't you dare blame yourself for anything. You did nothing wrong. Sometimes people aren't who we think they are," I say, feeling my throat close. The words hit close to home. "You have to try and let go of all this negativity clouding you. Life is too short to be wallowing in regret. You have a gorgeous son and a husband who adores you. I want you to live your life to its fullest and be happy. Please, if you won't do it for yourself, do it for me."

16

WE SERIOUSLY CAN'T GET AWAY
FROM THIS PLACE

-ZAVIER-

We don't have far to go. The medical chamber is on the same level as the cave opening, but this doesn't stop my pulse from thrumming in my ears. Harlow's torn jumper is covered in blood, so in an attempt to conceal the evidence from curious onlookers, I take off my jacket and drape it across her top section. We don't pass many Zeeks along the way, only one Purple and two Magentas. All three stare as we pass them, but thankfully nothing is said.

Inside the medical chamber, we find Tansy running the front

desk, and alongside her sits that unique-looking RJ fellow with his short purple spikes.

"We are here to see Medic Sylvie," Floss informs them with a puff. "It's an emergency."

Tansy instantly leaps from her seat. "I'll get her."

RJ taps his pencil in some sort of nervous, automatic reflex. "She'll be okay," he says without looking up. "She and the babies will be okay."

Babies?

A minute later Medic Sylvie comes rushing over and asks, "What's happened?"

I wish I knew. My heart is running on overdrive. I told Harlow not to go out there. I told her it was dangerous. *She should have listened to me.*

Floss gives Sylvie a sharp look and silently mouths for her to shush. Sylvie takes the hint and gets us to follow her to one of the beds in the back.

As soon as Floss puts Harlow down, Sylvie pulls aside my jacket and winces when she sees all the blood. "This doesn't look good." Next, she peels open Harlow's jumper, and Minty and I both gasp when we see the severity of her wound.

"Frost!" I curse.

She goes to remove Harlow's glasses also, but Minty is quick to stop her.

"You might not want to get rid of her shades or the bandana," she warns with a toothy grimace. "Otherwise, you'll end up giving everyone in here one heck of a fright."

"How much darker are her pigments?" Floss asks, now curious. "Do we look the same?"

"I think she might have surpassed you by a few shades," Minty says, playing it coy.

Sylvie lightly pokes around the wound, her brows knitted. "I need information. What exactly happened to her?"

"Jax said we can trust you, right?" Floss checks before giving anything away.

Sylvie nods. "Yes, you can trust me."

"She was speared by a shard from one of the warriors."

"A warrior did this?" Sylvie's eyes bulge, making her look as shocked as I feel.

I can't believe this. Those Purple pricks! I'd assumed it was the Vallon who'd hurt her.

"Which one was it?" I ask in anger. Not that I'm in a position to do anything about it.

"How should I know?" Floss retorts. "They're not my friends. You'll have to ask Miss Man-magnet when she wakes up. She's the only one who has been privileged enough to be introduced to Jax's inner warrior circle."

"A whole lot of good it did her," Minty remarks.

"I'm going to have to rush her into surgery." Sylvie says, unlocking the brakes on the bed's wheels. "Can one of you go and get RJ for me? He's not trained as yet, but he's trustworthy, and I'm going to need help. Desperate times call for desperate measures."

"Hold on a minute," Minty places her hand on the bed rail. "Just in case you didn't see the bump," she says, pointing it out, "she's pregnant."

"I'll take that into consideration. Thanks for letting me know."

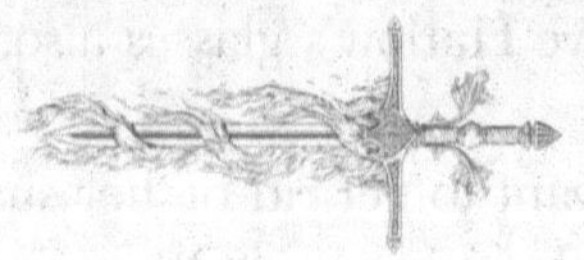

Minutes feel like hours when you're made to wait helplessly while the Zeek you love battles on in surgery.

Floss manages to fill us in on all the details regarding what happened outside, and I have to say, I'm shocked to hear some of Jax's warriors stood up for Harlow and a Vallon over two of their own members. Floss is confused as to why Harlow and Slater were calling each other alias names, and she says Jax was confused too, but because Minty and I know the backstory, it makes perfect sense to us—not that we share this information with her.

Towards the end of her recap, Floss looks green-eyed. "I can't believe Harlow has two super-hot sons of leaders fighting over her. It's not fair. Where's my special someone?"

"I wouldn't exactly call either of them special," I say bitterly. "Harlow deserves better than either of them."

She scoffs, shoots me a resentful look, and then stalks away, kicking a metal trolley as she passes it.

I gaze at Minty in confusion. "What the frost is her problem?"

"Isn't it obvious? You've caught the attention of the wrong sister."

I laugh off her comment, not believing it. "Yeah, right."

I hadn't known Slater or Alex—or whoever I'm supposed to call him—was the Queen's son. Harlow failed to mention that part when she'd told me her story. According to Floss, he'll be back to retrieve Harlow in four weeks. I bite my thumb nail until it bleeds. I don't imagine the Vallon Queen is going to be very happy about having a Zeek for a daughter-in-law. From what I hear, she is crueller and more vicious than our Commander.

Plus, Harlow is sure to fall to pieces when she sees the Zeek slaves working around the castle. I know if I was brought to Summer, I wouldn't be able to bite my tongue and accept their fate. I'd make it my mission to help them all escape.

After a while of sulking by herself, Floss returns to the seat next to me, and without being prompted, she lets all of her problems spill. "I thought being a hunter is what I wanted, but it's not. I hate my job, I hate Saul, I hate that I have no friends, I hate being in permanent lockdown, and I hate being a Magenta!"

"You think you've got it tough," I say. "Try being a Pastel. It sucks to be the laughingstock of your colony. Plus, most of us won't even make it to sixty. Look at Lexan, he is only thirty-nine and his body is already breaking down. Heck, my body is already breaking down, and I'm just shy of eighteen. My everything hurts."

"At least you have friends. There's no point in living longer if you're lonely and miserable. Life is boring when you have no one to share things with."

"If you're that eager to make friends, then why don't you try and be nicer to your sister. She's been desperate to win your love and acceptance for years."

Floss' eyes turn wild with resentment. "Everything always has to come back to Harlow with you, doesn't it? Harlow, Harlow, Harlow. And for your information, I have been nicer to her lately. But it's hard to fully like someone who you are completely and utterly jealous of."

I find it strange to hear that Floss is jealous of Harlow. You'd think it would be the other way around. I know our first teacher did a lot of damage by telling Saul, "Harlow's academic level far surpasses Floss'", but from age six onwards, Harlow has been ridiculed for *pretty much* everything she's said and done. Pastels hated her because they saw her as privileged, Magentas hated her because she was living amongst them, and now all the Purples hate her because of Jax and his inability to hide his feelings towards her.

A warrior with a man bun enters the medical cavern and comes straight over to us. He'd be around the six-foot mark, but because of his man bun, he looks as tall as Jax.

"Where's Harlow?" he asks, his voice a low whisper. "Is she going to be okay?"

Floss straightens where she sits, her expression irritable. "We don't know. She's still in surgery."

"What about you?" His expression is earnest—no mockery. "Are you okay?"

Her whole face instantly lights up. "Yeah, I'm okay. A little shaken, but I'll live."

I realise now—with mild guilt—I hadn't thought to ask her how she was. I'd been too worried about Harlow to consider checking on her. To be taken hostage by a Vallon, especially a Red, would be very traumatic. She'd probably spent that whole time believing he was going to kill her.

"Jax says not to go home until he has spoken with you. Go back to Zavier's after you leave here, and he'll drop by to see you as soon as he's dealt with the crisis outside."

"Your name is Kieran, isn't it?" Floss asks, and he answers "yes" with a nod. "Okay, Kieran," she says with a full-faced grin. "I can do that."

"You should probably go straight to Zavier's too," Kieran suggests to Minty, and I watch Floss deflate a little. "Just to be sure."

Minty glances up at him to answer. "No problem."

After Kieran leaves, I give Floss a nudge and say, "I thought you didn't know any of the warriors' names, *huh*."

"I don't." She bobbles her head with attitude. "I learned Kieran's name by default."

"Fair enough." I pause a moment before deciding to add, "By the way, I'm sorry I never asked you if you were okay. That was pretty mean of me."

"That's okay, I'm used to being treated as invisible when Harlow is around."

Half an hour later, Sylvie comes out to inform us Harlow is okay, and we're able to come into the restricted area to see her.

Harlow is mostly out of it, but her shimmer is back and strong.

"Are the babies okay?" I ask and Sylvie nods, assuring me they are perfectly fine. "So, there really are two of them?"

Again, she nods. "Am I allowed to ask who the father is? I'm guessing he's not a Pastel." Floss, Minty, and I glance between each other in silent question. Finally, Floss must consider Sylvie trustworthy enough to share the big secret with, because she answers, "The father's a Vallon."

Sylvie gasps as though she's been winded. "Well, this explains the colour of her hair and irises."

"What do you mean?" Floss jerks upright. "Give me a look." She lifts Harlow's bandana slightly and peeks beneath it. "It's red." She spins back to face me, her eyes wide like dinner plates. "Harlow's a Red!"

"Keep it down," Minty and I say in unison.

"You two sly jerks already knew the truth about the Vallon before today. You didn't need me to tell you anything." Her whole face twists in anger and hurt. "And nice of my sister to let me in on her big secret."

"She was going to tell you last night, remember?" Minty reminds her. "But you never stuck around. You jumped to conclusions and stormed off."

"But that's only after I asked. She wasn't offering the information."

"Now isn't the time for this," I say, stepping over to Harlow's bedside and taking hold of her hand. "You and Harlow can talk this out later, when she gets better."

"Screw you, Zavier," Floss sprays bitterly, and then she takes off.

Minty rolls her eyes. "I'll go after her."

I don't spend long with Harlow. Sylvie says it's important she gets a proper rest, not only for her own good, but for the babies.

Keeping it brief, I tell Harlow I love her and I'm sorry she was hurt. "I will be back to see you again first thing in the morning, okay." I softly brush my lips against her cheek.

Before leaving, I step to the side and gesture Sylvie over. "I'm afraid of leaving. Is she going to be safe here? If anyone else sees her hair and irises—"

"Don't worry, I'm on until late, and I won't leave her side," Sylvie assures me. "I'll have to speak to Jax about what happens once my shift ends. No doubt, he will be in to see her as soon as he's free. I know she means a lot to him."

I bristle at her comment, but I know she's right. I'm sure Jax will try his best to keep her protected during the night. I just hope his best is good enough. Going by his track record thus far, I'm not feeling overly confident.

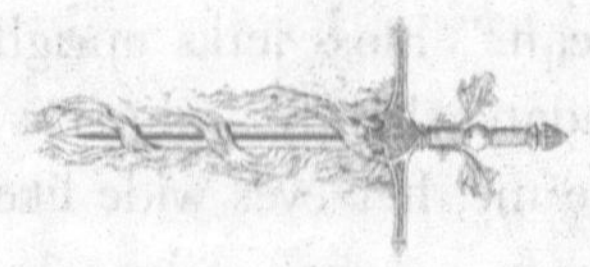

A drop of drool lands on my arm and I grizzle, *gross*. "Minty, can you please get this thing away from me? If it's not panting in my face, it's drooling on my arm."

"Lucy, come here," she calls while giving me a foul look. "I don't know what your problem is. Lucy is beautiful."

"Funny, I seem to remember you telling me you nicknamed her Invader to start with."

"Yeah, well, she's grown on me." She gives Lucy an affectionate scratch behind the ears. "Haven't you, Lucy?"

Floss sits on the lounge, fiddling with the button of her jacket, her expression sombre. She's not speaking to me *apparently*, "because I'm not worth wasting her time on", or at least that's what she told Minty. It's no wonder she doesn't have any friends; she's too hard to get along with. Her behaviour is completely unpredictable. I swear she's neurotic.

To be fair—aside from today—she has been much nicer lately, and at times, I've almost found myself enjoying her company. But the problem is, I never know which Floss I'm going to get minute by minute. She can be super sweet when all is good and well, but as soon as things don't go her way, she instantly morphs into a psycho.

Minty makes the three of us chicklet wraps for afternoon tea. My tummy rumbles as I watch. It's been a long day and none of us have had any lunch. When she's done, she hands me Floss' wrap as well as my own. "Go and give it to her," she whispers. "At least pretend to care."

"What do you mean? I do care, but I think she's being overdramatic. And anyway, this is rich coming from you. Since when do you care? It's Floss."

"I overheard what she said to you earlier today, and oddly enough, I kind of feel sorry for her. I think she craves love and friendship, but she doesn't know how to go about it."

"Fine." I give in. "I'll take it over to her." I stroll over to where Floss sits and hand her the plate with the wrap. "Minty made this for you."

She takes the plate and mutters a "thanks" without looking up.

I sigh heavily and plonk on the lounge next to her. "I'm sorry I didn't tell you about Harlow's secret, but it wasn't my secret to tell."

She stares straight ahead, expression sulky. "It's not only Harlow's secret I'm upset about."

"Well, what else are you upset about?"

"It doesn't matter." Her words come out thick. "It's not like I can do anything about it, anyway."

Jax and Sphinx come strolling in, and for the first time *ever* I'm happy to see them. Firstly, I don't have to finish this awkward conversation with Floss, and secondly, I'm desperate to know what's happening with Harlow.

I set down my plate and leap up from the lounge. "Hey, Jax," I say, and he pauses, momentarily stunned by my pleasant greeting. "Did you see Harlow?"

"Yes, I saw her." He eyes me cautiously. "But I couldn't stay long. She's okay."

Sphinx pitter-patters over to eye off my wrap. I've only had two bites of it, and I'm not about to give it up. "Don't even think about it," I warn, which prompts Jax to call him back.

"Did you and Sylvie manage to sort out who's looking after Harlow tonight?" I'd offer to stay and watch over her myself, but I'm fully aware I'd be of no use to her. I'm no match for a Purple. I'm barely a match for someone as broken down as Lexan. A Purple would only have to flick me, and I'd fall over. My pride shatters. It's no wonder Harlow isn't interested in me. *Why would she pick a weakling like me when she has two staunch sons of leaders chasing after her?* If Jax is double my body mass, I can only imagine how big Alex would be. Vallons are supposed to be huge.

"Yes, I've spoken to Zannah. She's going to keep an eye on her."

"Who's Zannah?"

"One of my warriors,"

"Is that a safe choice?" I shoot him an inquiring glance. "Two of your warriors tried to kill Harlow."

"Zannah took out the warrior who tried to kill Harlow—*without hesitation*. I think it's safe to say I trust her."

If this is true, then I'm satisfied with this arrangement. "Okay, good."

Jax takes a moment to question Floss, and I watch as she laps up the attention. She says Slater mistook her for Harlow—and he was calling her Ruby, which she'd found confusing. *It's a shame he didn't take her to Summer instead.* I immediately tsk myself. It's a despicable thought, and I don't really mean it. Floss can be a nightmare, but there's still something I like about her—just not at the moment.

After filling Jax in on the details surrounding her terrifying experience, they move on to the topic of her parents and what should be said to them. Jax thinks it's best if they come up with a plausible cover story, but Floss—being Floss—says, "I don't need to give them a good cover story, I'll just tell them I walked off the job, I'm over it, anyway. I hate working with Saul. I never want to go back."

Jax's face flushes in annoyance. "I had to pull a lot of strings to get you that hunting position. There are Magentas who've been waiting for years for a hunting role to come up, and I fast-tracked you to the top of the list. Harlow told me you wanted to be a hunter like your parents. She said it had been your dream job since you were kids."

"Yeah, well that's before I knew…"

Fortunately, she cuts herself short, because I'm afraid I know what she was going to say. That's before she knew Saul wasn't her father.

During the few days Floss stayed here, she admitted there'd been a time when she was hell bent on trying to impress Saul. She said she was so desperate for his approval, she'd gone to extreme and dangerous lengths to get it. However, when she came to the realisation Saul wasn't her father—that a Pastel was, and her mother had never told her the truth—something broke inside her, and she'd turned to using Ogre's chemical concoctions.

"I'm not going out hunting anymore," she says with defiance. "I'm traumatised. And I'm not going home tonight either, I'm staying here."

I glance up in shock.

The muscles in Jax's jaw tick, but he keeps his composure as he speaks. "You can have tomorrow off, and I'll see what I can do about swapping your job, but I don't think it's wise for you to stay here. You won't be protected, and it will draw attention."

"I've stayed here for a few nights before, and no one knew any different. Besides, if you think my parents are going to be my big almighty protectors, think again. They don't care. Especially Saul. My mother should walk out and leave the monster, but she won't, she's too weak to take the final plunge. The hostility between the pair is toxic and doesn't make for a healthy environment for me to live in."

"What about your Magenta friends?" Jax asks. "Why don't you arrange to spend the night with one of them?"

"Newsflash, I don't have any friends."

Jax doesn't seem at all surprised by this revelation. "I don't agree with your decision, but I'm not going to stop you from staying here if it's what you really want. Just know you're not protected here. I won't be able to send any warriors down to this level without questions being asked. If anything terrible happens to you during the night, you'll only have yourself to blame."

"Lucy's a trained warrior husken. She can stay and protect me."

"No, she's not staying." His voice is firm, verging on harsh. "Minty will be taking the husken home with her when she leaves. From what I've overheard, she's found herself on Rae's radar too. She'll need Lucy's protection."

Floss smacks her hands on her hips and gives a bratty pout. "Are you saying Minty's life is more important than mine?"

Jax's composure starts to crumble, and the severity in his tone is enough to make Floss back up a step. "I'm saying that Lucy was assigned as a guard-hound at the Bean-Brew Cavern. Minty is one of two head chefs, and Lucy is to reside at her family cavern, just as Bella is residing at Finn's family cavern. Minty is not the one trying to make things difficult here, *you are*."

"Why don't I stay the night too?" Minty offers, trying to defuse the building tension. "Zavier and I have had plenty of sleepovers over the years; my parents will be fine with it. They don't need Lucy. They aren't on anybody's radar."

He frowns, appearing frustrated. "Where will you all sleep? This cavern is tiny."

"And who's fault is that?" I mutter.

"I was born into this colour system," Jax retaliates, each word spilling out like a curse. "I didn't create it. And as soon as I have more Purples on my side, I will have it abolished."

"I'm sure you will," I say cynically.

Jax steps up in my face and for a split second it looks as if he wants to punch me. His usual tolerant nature has disintegrated, revealing something much darker.

"Jax, ignore Zavier," Minty says, snapping him back into control again. "You look tired, we're all tired. It's been a stressful day. I'll stay here with these two tonight, and tomorrow we'll come up with a better arrangement."

His tensed muscles uncoil, and he takes a step back. "Very well." He calls Sphinx over and leaves without any further argument.

As soon as Jax is gone, Minty gives me a mouthful, telling me I need to show more respect. During their brief time living together, Harlow has somehow managed to convince Minty that Jax is this divine Purple who is going to save all of us lower class from squalor. I brush off Minty's lecture, and she exits the cavern, saying she needs to go and let her parents know she's staying the night here.

She tugs Floss by the wrist, dragging her along with her. "Staying here was your idea, so you are going to help carry over some spare blankets."

I watch them disappear and settle back on the lounge with my wrap, grateful for the peace.

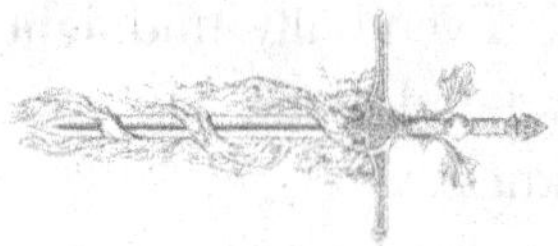

When Lexan gets back from work, we let him in on the day's chaotic events, and I make him promise on my life he won't spill a word to Krista. He gives Floss a fatherly hug and tells her he's glad she's safe before joining me on the lounge for a chat.

We are both concerned about what'll happen to Harlow come four weeks' time when Jax delivers her to the Vallon.

"She won't survive in Summer," he says, telling me what I already know. "Surely Jax can put a stop to this."

"How?"

He glances at me with dead hope in his eyes. Neither of us has an answer that doesn't end in bloodshed.

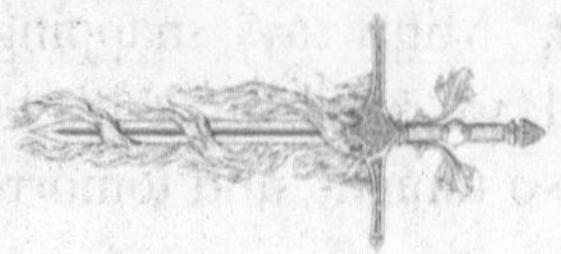

Come bedtime, Minty takes the lounge, which is her size exactly, while Floss sleeps on a pile of folded blankets on the floor. I hadn't felt comfortable about this arrangement, and neither had Lexan. We'd both offered her our beds, but she refused to take them, telling us we needed them more than she did.

"You're still healing," she'd told me. "And you're too arthritic," she'd said to Lexan. "You both need the soft mattresses."

After arguing the matter for a good twenty minutes, I'd given up on trying to be nice. Truth is, my body feels broken, and I'd much prefer the bed than the floor.

I lie awake studying the crevices of my nook. I'm too worried about Harlow and her future to sleep. It kills me to know what's happening to her is completely out of my control. I feel so helpless. Frustration gets the better of me, and I toss and turn for several hours, unable to relax. Eventually midnight passes, and my mind tires of concocting dead-end plans. My eyes and limbs grow heavy, and I succumb to blackness.

I wake up to the unexpected sight of magenta hair in my face.

"Floss!" My arm is draped across her, and I pull it back with a start. "What are you doing in my bed?"

I'm not at all comfortable with this. She shouldn't be in here. I must've been *that* exhausted from all the tossing and turning earlier in the evening, I hadn't heard or felt her crawl in with me sometime during the night.

She grumbles at being woken. "The floor was harder than I thought it would be, and I could hear strange noises filtering in from the passage outside. I was worried someone was out there."

"Well, why didn't you jump on the lounge with Minty?"

She rolls over to face me, wrapping her muscular leg over my waist. "I didn't want to excite Minty; she might have started groping me."

"Just because Minty is gay, doesn't mean she doesn't have standards," I say, in retaliation to Floss' comment.

She cracks an eye open, her tone still sleepy. "Ouch. That hurts." Her eye closes again.

"What are you doing?" I say, "Don't go back to sleep. You can't be in here. If we are caught in the same bed—"

This time both of her eyes spring open. "If we are caught in the same bed…what? Everyone else seems to be having inter-colour relationships, even our own Commander's son is interested in someone out of his colour rank. And it's not like you can say this will put us in danger. We're already in danger because of everybody else's actions."

"Maybe so, but we aren't in a relationship, so you shouldn't be in here."

"But we could be." There's a sense of yearning in her eyes as she says this. It makes me squirm uncomfortably. "We kissed once, remember?"

"You kissed me."

Her eyes narrow. "Whatever. You liked it. I'm the closest thing you're ever going to get to my sister."

"You're right, I liked it," I say, blowing off her jab. "Just about as much as I liked your pickup line, what was it again?" I cup my chin in mock thought. "Oh, that's right, 'If my mother can slum it with Lexan, then I don't see why I can't slum it with you'."

She grimaces. "I didn't mean to say those things. I was high and upset."

"I don't care. Get out of my bed."

"If you're so terribly uncomfortable about having a girl in your bed, then *you* get out. I'm tired, and I want to go back to sleep." She peels her leg off my waist and flips back over, putting her back to me.

There's no way I'm staying in here with her. She's a brat who's looking for trouble. "You're infuriating," I mutter into her ear, while climbing over her to get out.

She ignores me.

I grab a clean shirt and a pair of pants and then throw them on before heading out to the living-kitchen-dining area.

Minty is awake and sitting on the edge of the lounge, twiddling her thumbs. "When I said you should at least pretend you care, this didn't mean, you should invite her into your bed. Don't we have enough problems to deal with as it is?"

"Floss wasn't invited," I mutter in irritation. "I'm going to check on Harlow. You can stay here and deal with her. I need a break."

17

TWINS

-HARLOW-

(Three hours earlier)

It must be early when Jax comes in to see me. He gently whispers my name, and I find it hard to rouse. Partly because I'm drugged up, and partly because I'm too scared to open my eyes and look into his. I'm afraid they'll reveal the disgust and disappointment he feels towards me, now that he's had time to process the true nature of my disgraceful actions. Not to mention, two of his warriors were killed because of the regrettable choices I've made. I've messed up bad.

I wish—now more than ever—I'd never met up with Alex in the forest, and I REALLY, REALLY regret sleeping with him. The Ruby part of me yearned for Alex so badly, I failed to separate our two existences. We are not the same people here. We are not even people—he is a Vallon and I am a Zeek. We're supposed to be enemies, not lovers. IT WAS A TERRIBLE MISTAKE.

Alex might have apologised for leaving me, and he swears he came straight back, but I'm still not sure if I can forgive him. I know I hurt him when I killed Lucas, but he absolutely shattered my heart. I wonder what he wants from me. He can't possibly say he's come back for me because he loves me, because if he really did love me, he wouldn't have waited so long to come back. His kiss still tingles on my lips, and I wish I could wipe the feeling away.

The strangest thing about all of this is how guilty I feel towards Jax. I almost feel like I cheated on him, even though we've never actually been a thing. The feelings were there, I can admit that now, but they were hidden—because they were forbidden—and despite what everyone was saying, I honestly thought it was all one sided.

The idea of Jax meaning more to me than someone I look up to and respect had seemed completely out of reach. Whenever I even dared to entertain the idea, these recurring thoughts would play in my head—*he is a Purple and the Commander's son. He is above you. He is too good for you. You will tarnish him.*

Unable to face him just yet, I keep my eyes closed and pretend to be completely out of it.

"She's been out the whole time I've been here." I recognise the voice as Zannah's. I hadn't realised she was in here with me. I still can't believe she sided with me and killed one of her fellow warriors to save me. I feel appreciative yet somewhat uncomfortable about it. *She's made her opinion of me clear. She not a fan, so why save me?* I would have presumed she'd be happy to be rid of me.

"What are you doing here at this hour? You should be resting. You have a training session to run in a few hours, and you look like death."

I feel Jax's presence move away from my bedside. "I couldn't sleep," he says, and I hear a creaking sound, like he's taking a seat. "It's been a crazy few days, and I've been too worried about Harlow to relax."

"You should start worrying more about yourself," Zannah says with a forceful edge, "or you're going to end up burning out." She waits a beat and then adds, "What's your next move now, anyway? You know you can't keep her hidden in here for the next four weeks, it's too risky."

"I know." There's a long silent stretch broken only by the beeps of machines around us before Jax adds, "Thank you very much for what you did yesterday. I'm grateful to you. I know it must have been a tough call for you to make."

"Stace did the wrong thing. She shouldn't have taken the shot without an order, and I know how much Harlow means to you. I don't understand why you're so infatuated with her, but it's clear you are."

Jax clears his throat. "She was supposed to be killed as a child, but my father saved her, did you know that?" I don't hear Zannah's answer before he continues. "He risked his own life to save hers, and he'd been adamant that she was to be raised on level two by her Magenta parents. I was only four at the time, but we were close, and he'd let me in on everything that was going on. He'd said he saw something special in her worth saving. I remember when I first saw her, I could see it too." He pauses for a breath. "I know it might seem irrational, and I don't fully understand it myself, but I feel deeply connected to her somehow, like she's the missing piece I need to feel complete."

To hear Jax pour his heart out like this is a rare experience and causes a flurry of emotions to burst inside my chest. I want to reach out to him and beg for his forgiveness. I feel absolutely wretched.

"The only problem is you're not the only one who seems to have a connection with her," Zannah points out, and I wince at the directness of her comment.

"Yes, I know," his voice is clipped. "And the worst thing is..." He doesn't finish, and I wish I could read his mind to see what the rest of the sentence looked like. "Anyway, it doesn't matter. I have to deliver her to Slater in four weeks, whether I like it or not."

"What's with the names they were calling each other?" Zannah asks. "Do you have any idea what any of that was about?"

"No, not really, but they said something about her killing his brother Lucas, and I've heard her mention Lucas' name before. She cried it out several times in her sleep back when she was in here because of her leg. She'd seemed distressed when she was saying it, like she was having a nightmare about him."

"Does this mean she was with Slater, even as far back as then?"

"She said she'd only met Slater the once, the night she'd spent out in the forest, and I believe her, but I get the feeling Ruby and Alex have history." He pauses. "I spoke to RJ earlier. He says Harlow remembers snippets of her past life as Ruby, so I can only assume Alex is an old connection from Earth. I don't fully understand how they've re-connected here on Zadok, though, but I intend on asking her for the details when she wakes up."

I'm surprised Jax is accepting of the idea of us having lived as humans in the past. I wouldn't've expected him to be a believer. He is truly the opposite of his mother.

I actually wasn't with Alex as far back as then, but I can't exactly sit up and say this without admitting I've been eavesdropping.

"Well, she's sleeping now, which is exactly what you should be doing," Zannah says, and I find myself wondering what her beliefs are. She doesn't say either way. "You need to go home and have a couple of hours rest before training. You're no good to any of us like this."

"You're probably right." I hear the chair creak as he leaves it. "Make sure you get someone to fetch me if anything changes."

"I will. Now go."

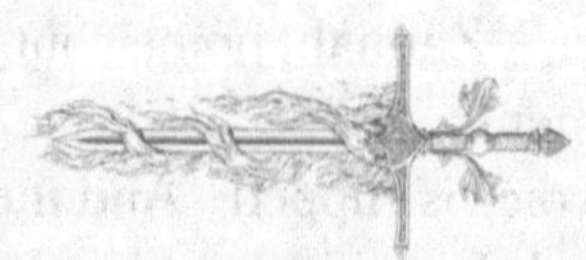

I wake up a few hours later to find Zavier by my bedside.

"Oh hey, you're finally awake?" He leans forward and gives me a smile, a real smile. Despite all the trouble I've caused, he's still genuinely happy to see me. "We seriously can't keep away from this place lately, can we?"

"Tell me about it." I sigh. "Have you been here long?"

"An hour, maybe? Not too long. And being here is better than being at home at the moment. Your sister is driving me crazy."

"What do you mean? Has Floss been staying at your place again?" I go to prop myself up a little, but it hurts my shoulder. I slump down.

He nods and gives me a full recap of Floss' bratty behaviour towards Jax yesterday. Apparently, she'd hard-headedly refused to return to her hunting job and had insisted on staying at Lexan and Zavier's for the night in spite of Jax advising otherwise.

"I woke up to her in my bed this morning," he says, and then pauses nervously as if he's waiting for a negative reaction. When I don't say anything, he continues. "She snuck in during the night when I was sleeping. She said the floor was harder than she'd thought. Lexan and I had tried offering her our beds last night," he makes sure to add, "but she'd refused to take them. If she persists on staying again tonight, I will be insisting on taking the floor. Either that, or I'll ask Minty if we can bring across the spare mattress from her place."

"I'm pretty sure Floss likes you," I say. It feels a little odd admitting this out aloud. "She was jealous when she thought I was pregnant to you."

"Yeah, well, the feeling isn't mutual."

Dropping the topic of Floss, he slips his hand into his pocket and pulls out our magic rock.

"Oh good, you found it." I smile.

"I wasn't aware I had it until the day I was discharged," he admits. "Sylvie handed it to me when she signed me out, telling me she'd found it in the bedside drawer." He returns my smile. "Now it's my turn to hand it back to you, not that it appears to be working at all. *But hey*, it's tradition."

I open my hand, and he recites the words, "It's magic, it will keep you safe."

He pulls up a chair after this and stays for another hour. We chat like old times—the same as we used to before our lives turned upside down. It feels good to finally slide back into our old friendship. Jade might be my rock on Earth, but Zavier is my rock on Zadok.

"I'm really going to miss you when you leave the caves," he admits towards the end of our conversation. "I wish you didn't have to go with the Vallon."

Me too, I think silently.

Zavier must read the thought in my eyes. "If you don't want to go with him, you should stand your ground and let him know that you want to stay. He doesn't own you."

"I could, but I won't last long here. Not with my red hair and irises. It'll only be a matter of time before I'm discovered by our Commander. Besides, I can't put that kind of pressure on Jax. He's under enough stress as it is."

Zavier's expression is a wild mix of hurt, fear, resentment, and disappointment. "I'm afraid you won't fare well in Summer either. I've heard horrific stories about what they do to Pastels."

"Don't worry," I assure him, hiding my anxiety behind a plastic smile. "Things will be okay. Let's just enjoy the time we still have."

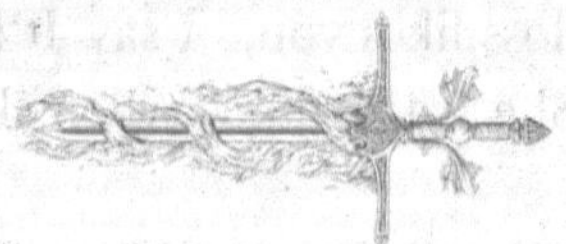

I fall back into an exhausted sleep after Zavier leaves, only to wake up to another visitor a couple of hours later.

"Hello, Harlow, how are you feeling?" says a semi-robotic voice, and I don't have to look to see who it is.

"Hey, RJ."

He steps over to my bedside. "I'm on my lunch break, so I

thought I'd come in to see you. I assisted Sylvie with the surgery on your shoulder, which makes you my first ever patient." He appears pleased with himself. "When I first started working here, Jax let Sylvie know I'm trustworthy."

"Well, I'm glad you're here actually, because I have a bone to pick with you." My tone is playful, but I am actually slightly annoyed with him.

"Oh?" His eyes dart nervously. "What did I do? Have I done something wrong?"

"You told me I was special, that you've seen it, and I would help to bring about change." I cock my head and shoot him a look that says, "You lied". "And then when I asked you how, you said you didn't want to tell me because you didn't want to jinx anything, but guess what, now I've gone and stuffed it all up. You didn't have to tell me everything, I wouldn't have expected that, but you could have at least steered me in the right direction."

He glances at me with a puzzled expression. "But you *are* still going in the right direction."

"How? I'm pregnant to a Vallon, I've got a hole in my shoulder, I've hurt Jax, and just about everyone wants me dead. How the hell can this be the right direction?" My sentence comes out a little more accusatory than I'd planned, and he flinches.

"I didn't want to say too much, because it would've ended up doing more harm than good. Even now, if I say too much about what's coming next, it will send you off course and change everything."

"You say this," I press, "but you were happy to tell Jax about the twins. You even led him to believe these babies would be his."

"I never…never, ever, implied the babies would be his. I told him you would have a set of twins who were very special, and you would help him to break down the colour system. That's it."

"Then why would he just assume they were going to be his?"

"Um, well…" He scratches his head, appearing uncomfortable about what he's about to say. "Some of the receptionists and medics that work here have suggested you mean a lot more to Jax than you should. Maybe he secretly wanted them to be his?" He gives an uneasy shrug. "I don't really know though.; I'm not very good at reading the emotions of others. I generally tend to get things ballsed up and wind up offending Zeeks. I'm more of a facts and figures kind of guy."

I can't imagine Jax jumping to conclusions, especially when it's something as big as this, but if RJ really didn't lead him to believe the twins were his, then I don't know what else to think.

"Actually, being as we are on the topic of your twins, I do have something I feel I should tell you, but you're not going to like it." He clears his throat. "I can leave it for another day if you would prefer? So long as you are aware, though, you will find this out eventually, and I feel it will be much easier for you to hear this information from me, than from…" he hesitates and then just says, "him."

"Okay?" My insides bunch. "I'm listening."

"As you're already aware, being twins comes with a very special bond, but what you may not know is, you as a twin will share a connection with all twins and multiples. It'll never be to the same magnitude as your own personal twin, but the connection of all twins and multiples is always magically there. Twins are drawn to other twins, and that's why you'll find that a couple who has given birth to a set of twins will usually have another close family member who will give birth to a set of twins. Sometimes, even the child who is a twin will have twins, or it will skip a generation and the grandchild of a twin will have twins."

I have no idea where he is going with this, but I continue to nod and listen.

"Scientists of the human world would often say it came down to genetics, and they weren't entirely wrong, but what they failed to realise was these particular genetics were formed because these people had had a connection to a twin in a previous life. A twin from a previous life will often become a twin in the next life, or give birth to twins in the next life. For those who were previously a twin —or multiple of some sort—in the last life, but didn't get the chance to be a twin or a multiple in their new life will often seek a relationship with a twin or multiple or be drawn to a family who has twins or multiples in it, because they feel that invisible pull." He finally takes a breath from his ongoing rambling. "Do you understand what I'm saying?"

"Yeah…kind of. I get the drift."

"You in particular, have a strong pull which draws twins to you, and this is because you've managed to be an identical twin twice running now. Oddly enough, in saying this, the twins you are now carrying weren't only drawn to you because of your strong pull, they were also drawn to you because of the pull of those close to you with a twin connection."

"RJ, my brain hurts. Please just get to the point."

"I do have some good news as well as the bad, well sort of, it depends really. I'm not sure how you'll take it."

"RJ, the point."

"I'll start with the bad new first. It's better to give the…" he sees the frustrated look on my face and snaps straight to it. "The boy you are carrying inside is Lucas, Alex's twin."

My blood instantly runs cold, and my next breath freezes in my lungs, leaving me unable to speak. *NO! No way.*

Of all the messed-up things that have happened to me so far—*in both lives*—this devastating revelation surpasses the lot. I feel ill, violently ill.

"Pass me that bin," I say, pointing at it. As soon as RJ places it in front of me, I lean forward and vomit. The jerky movements of my body heaving causes stabbing pains in my shoulder. It hurts, but not nearly as much as my heart hurts. *How will I possibly be able to love my son knowing he was Lucas?* If this is my punishment for killing him, then it is far more sick and twisted than the crime itself. *Screw you fate, I hate you. I HATE YOU!*

Tears stream down my face. What a horrible tragic mess. For someone who is supposedly "special" I have left a trail of death and destruction, and now I'm bringing someone evil back to life.

"I'm sorry," RJ says. "But I thought you'd prefer to hear it from me now than from Slater—or Alex, whatever you wish to call him—once the baby is born."

"How would Alex even know it's him?"

"He will feel it. He has managed to stay connected with his twin brother all throughout this life, so the bond they share is strong enough for him to recognise his spirit. This being said, Lucas won't remember his past life, because Alex died first, which means he doesn't have a twin attachment on Earth to spark any memories or draw him back to his old life. Lucas will feel the close bond to Slater as his father, but he will never know Slater used to be his twin brother Alex unless he's told."

This is too much. I don't know if I can handle this. *Maybe I shouldn't be having these babies.*

How is it RJ is too afraid to tell me about my future, and yet he isn't afraid to tell me something as gut-wrenching as this? I almost feel like shutting down.

"Let me tell you the next part. Hopefully, it will make you feel better," he says, and I don't imagine there is anything he could possibly say that would make me feel better. "The other baby you're carrying was a girl named Lyla, and by coincidence, she happens to be the former twin sister of Levi, who you now know as Jax."

"What?" This I didn't expect. My mind feels like it's about to explode.

"Jax will instantly feel a connection to your baby girl and want to protect her. He and Lyla were fraternal twins, not identical, which means he didn't get to keep the Earth connection to her, so unless you actually tell him she was once his twin sister, he will just think of her as your child whom he loves and cherishes as his own."

"What does this mean? If you say Jax is going to love and protect her like his own, does this mean I will be staying in the caves? That I won't be going with Alex?"

"It means no matter where you end up, whether it be here, there, or somewhere else entirely, Lyla belongs with Jax. He will keep her the safest."

My brain is going around in circles. I don't know what to think, or what to say.

"I'm sorry I can't tell you more than this," RJ says, not looking at me. "Are you angry with me?"

"No RJ, I'm not angry with you. I'm just very confused right now."

"Oh, would you like me to re-explain it all then?"

"No, definitely not." I let out a hollow laugh. "It's not the information I'm confused about. It's my feelings."

JAX WANTS ANSWERS

-HARLOW-

$\mathcal{S}$ylvie is taking my vitals when Jax walks in at six, which means there's no way I can get out of facing him this time. My insides flutter when I see him. His presence has me feeling more nervous than ever, especially now that I know how he used to feel about me. I wish I'd known the truth about his feelings before I went and ruined everything. He wasn't like Alex; he wasn't obvious about his interest, or at least I couldn't see it—not like everybody else could. I really thought he was only helping me because he wanted my help in return. He couldn't possibly be interested in me the same way anymore, not now, after everything I've done. Chances are he resents me. I know I would if our situations were reversed.

Sylvie says, "hi" and gives him my vital readings, which are all within normal range. "She and the babies are doing well," she reports.

"And what about her shoulder?" Jax asks. "Is it healing well?"

He could easily take a look for himself, but he obviously doesn't want to.

"Strangely, it's improving much faster than I'd expected," Sylvie answers. "But maybe it's because she's got the vertic switz…" She stops short when she notices Jax's questioning frown. "Actually, I'm glad you are here," she changes the subject. "There are a few patients in the main chamber, whom I'd like to take a look at. If you wouldn't mind, I might duck out there for a bit and make myself useful. You can call me when you're leaving, and I'll come straight back."

I know she is leaving to give us some privacy, but I want to tell her, "No, please don't go". I don't want to be left alone with Jax. I'm afraid of facing his condemnation.

When Sylvie leaves, Jax pulls up a chair and sits close to my bedside. "How does your shoulder feel?"

"It's a bit sore, but it's okay."

Unlike Zavier, he doesn't look happy to see me; he is wearing his indifferent warrior mask. He's acting concerned without being too friendly—like he's just another medic checking up on me. This adds more butterflies to my already fluttering tummy. I don't know what he is thinking, which means I don't know what to feel or how to act around him.

I have no idea where to start, so I lead with an apology. "I'm sorry two of your warriors were killed because of me."

"They brought it on themselves. Stace and Haydn acted of their own accord instead of listening to my commands." His reply is all business, no warmth.

I want to ask him what cover story they came up with to explain their deaths, but it's not appropriate, nor is it any of my business. A brittle silence lingers between us, and I wish someone would enter, if only to break the excruciating tension.

"Who is Lucas?" he finally asks. "And why were you calling Slater Alex?"

He's not about to waste time beating around the bush with small talk. He wants answers, and he wants them now.

Damn, I'm so not ready for this.

"This is going to be hard for you to believe, but I remember my life before this one, my human life. I was a girl named Ruby, and on the night of my eighteenth birthday, Lucas killed me."

He arches a curious brow, but aside from this, he remains unperturbed. "Go on."

I start from the beginning, telling him how it all started out with the dreams. Unlike Minty and Zavier, he doesn't constantly interrupt or ask a bunch of questions, he just listens, his face an expressionless mask. It makes me uncomfortable. I rush out the sentences and trip on my words.

When I get to the part about meeting Alex in the forest, Jax stiffens, which is the only insight he gives me to how he really feels. I tell him about the vertic switz tattoo because I feel I must if I want him to believe I hadn't only met Alex in the forest for… *Well*… I blush at the memory of our bodies entwined.

Jax knows what comes next, and I don't really want to say it, so I wash over the details and get to the part where we fell asleep, and I killed Lucas.

"Because I killed Lucas, Alex lost his connection to Earth, and I think he was as upset with me about that, as he was about losing his twin brother," I say, cringing at the awful memory of that morning. "We had a big fight about it when we woke up, and he took off in haste. He thought I'd killed Lucas on purpose as revenge, but I honestly only did it to save my sister and nephew."

Even after I finish speaking, Jax still doesn't say anything. He stares ahead with a faraway look on his face.

"You don't believe me, do you?"

This question seems to draw him back, and his gaze snaps to my wrist. "Can I see it?"

I'm aware he's avoided answering my question, but I refrain from re-asking and hold out my wrist. He slips the bracelet off and stares at the snowflake. *I wonder if he'll notice the J and what he'll think if he does?* I didn't mention the letter when telling him my story, and I'm curious to know if he is switched on enough to realise it was for Jade, or if he'll presume I got it to represent him.

He doesn't say either way, he just stares at it for a while longer and then slides my bracelet back on again.

"I do believe you," he finally replies. "I don't know how I feel about any of it, but I do believe you."

I wish he would say more, even if it's only to tell me how stupid I am. I find his silence and masked expression to be absolutely excruciating.

"I made a terrible mistake," I say. "I know I keep saying it, but I really am truly sorry."

He looks at me with hooded eyes. "Get some sleep. There is somewhere I need to take you this weekend, so these next two days of rest will be vital."

"Where are we going?" I ask anxiously.

"You'll see."

19

I MISS BEING ALEX WHEN I FALL SLEEP

-ALEX AS SLATER-

In the very corner of my full-length mirror, I see Raven staring at my reflection in delighted approval. "Perfect," she says, tossing her long red hair over her shoulder in an attempt to look sexy. "Those colours look great on you."

Admittedly, she actually does look sexy tonight in her fitted red and orange dress, with her thick, wavy hair cascading down her back. But when it comes to listening to what my heart wants, it only calls for Ruby.

Raven is here purely because my mother has forced the issue. She didn't want me showing up dateless for my brother's linking ceremony. She also had this red and orange suit made *especially* to match Raven's dress. It feels a little tight and restricting around the collar, although I wouldn't be at all surprised if she had it made this way on purpose to spite me. I don't want to go to the ceremony, and she knows it, but it's expected of me. I'm not entirely sure what type of punishment she would inflict on me if I skipped it. However, I'm smart enough to know it's not worth the risk of finding out.

All hell broke loose when I'd returned to Summer after my failed attempt to retrieve Ruby from Winter. Kenneth the snitch had purposely given me up, informing our mother that this was the third time in a matter of months I'd disobeyed the rules of the Drakes. The Drakes are aware of our rivalry with the Zeeks, and since Dakari came into power just shy of a decade ago, he has made it very clear he disapproves of the abuse and slavery of the Pastels that goes on here in Summer.

We Vallons know that if our opposing races were to break out into another battle, the Drakes wouldn't hesitate to side with the Zeeks. Not only do they appear to have allied with them in recent years, but the exchange they have in place with the Zeeks is of more value to them than the exchange they have with us. They prefer the constant buckets of seafood over the small bags of minerals.

This all being said, the Drakes are a mostly peaceful race who prefer to avoid conflict if possible, and it's because of this they have a firm set of rules in place when it comes to Vallons hunting and fruit picking on their land. Royals and the Queen's guards are the only Vallons eligible to delve deep into Spring's forest, and we are only allowed to enter between the hours of six P.M. until six A.M. when the forest is free of Zeeks. Our fruit and veggie pickers are permitted to work within the first two metres of the Spring border, but this is heavily regulated. There's always a Queen's guard sent out to monitor them, and anyone who's spotted venturing in any further than those two metres is to be severely punished—by order of the Queen.

If any Vallons were to be found roaming on Drake land during the daylight hours, it could cause an uproar, and Dakari could easily retract his current arrangement with us.

Being as I didn't get back to Summer until nine P.M., my mother was in a panicked rage, and to teach me a lesson for not sticking to the rules she'd sent a legion of her guards to hide at the edge of border and lie in wait for me.

As soon as I crossed into Summer, the guards immediately pounced on me from all angles, catching me by surprise. They even managed to land a few solid punches on me before I recovered my senses and retaliated full force. I managed to get a few good punches in and knocked two of the guards out cold, but given there were a dozen of them and only one of me, they soon knocked me down to the ground. They chained my hands and gave me a few solid kicks while I was down before bringing me to my mother's chambers.

"Why do you always insist on breaking all the rules?" my mother had asked, her tone low and malevolent. "All the young Vallons in our kingdom look up to you. You need to start setting a better example for them, or there will be consequences."

She'd noticed the dried blood on my hunting shirt and asked what'd happened. She knew the wound wasn't inflicted by her guards because the blood was stale and brown. I'd given a smartarse answer and was instantly met with an uppercut to the ribs from one of her guards.

"You are my son and the Prince of Summer," my mother said, cutting to the chase of the lecture, "and your actions reflect heavily on me."

"I may be your son, but I'm no longer a child. Whether you like it or not, I'm an adult, and my choices are my own to make."

She'd shot daggers at me. "The choices you've been making are reckless and affect our entire race. I only need one son to continue my reign. Don't force me to remove you from the equation."

Threats, she's always a tyrant with her threats.

I miss being spirit Alex when I fall sleep; I miss the informality and the freedom. As Slater, I might live in a majestic castle with lots of expensive possessions, but I feel like a prisoner. Being a prince comes with certain expectations and rules, and I am sick of having to abide by them, especially when most of the time I completely disagree with all that is expected of me.

I might not have parents who are abusive junkies this lifetime around, but I still have a mother who is ruthless and rules with an iron fist. Whenever she barks an order, Kenneth obeys without question, and so do all of her guards, but I've never been afraid to challenge her with my opposing opinion.

Even before I knew that Ruby was a Pastel Zeek, I've always had an issue with the Pastels being kept as slaves, and just like Dakari—the Drake chief—I've made my opinions well known. I've seen what some of the animals of my race do to them, and I find it absolutely sickening.

When my mother ordered the ink trials to be done on the weaker Pastels, I hadn't opposed, which had baffled her, but I figured they were dying anyway, and I was curious as to what would happen to them. I thought if the ink made them stronger, they'd be able to stand up for themselves, and it turns out I was right—but it backfired.

One of the injected Pastels who'd been abused by one of my mother's guards took revenge. She and another injected Pastel lured Ash into one of the lower chambers and killed him with his own blade. My mother was absolutely outraged when she found out; and ordered that all the injected Pastels be destroyed immediately. Little did she know, I'd caught the tail end of the incident. I'd heard a few pained cries as I was walking past one of the lower chambers and went flying in to find out what was going on. To my disbelief, I found two Pastel women standing over a fallen guard. His body convulsed as he attempted to curse at them, but his words gurgled incomprehensively as he choked on his own blood. The prettier of the two Pastels was still holding onto the handle of his blade, which she must have plunged into his stomach repeatedly, given the sheer amount of blood all over him and the floor.

"Hurry up and die, you rapist creep," she'd said, thrusting the blade in further.

When she heard my footsteps encroaching, she'd panicked, yanked the blade back out, and spun it towards me. The guard wasn't dead yet, but he was almost there, coughing and spluttering. He would be dead soon enough.

She'd yelled at her friend to hurry up and climb out the window, while she came charging at me with the blade, swinging it wildly with very little control. I easily ducked her attempted blows and snatched the blade from her fingers, tossing it to the other side of the room.

"The piece of shit got what he deserved," I said, and then I turned and left the chamber to give them a chance to escape.

I'd been slightly worried that another Vallon might have seen me exiting the chamber, and I'd end up being accused of the murder, but luckily for me, Ash was a bragger. He'd boasted to one of the other guards, saying he was off to meet one of the tasty little Pastel slaves.

I hadn't believed the rest of the Pastels should be punished for the crime of two women, and I'd fought my mother on her decision to execute them all—but my opinion had no pull. Kenneth and the guards showed no qualms or hesitation and killed them all without question.

Here in my chamber, Raven leaves the edge of my four-poster canopy bed where she's been sitting to step up behind me and brush a loose thread from my shirt.

"Don't," I say, and jerk away. There's a look of hurt in her eyes, and I feel terrible. I don't want to keep hurting her, but I need her to know where we stand. I wish I could feel for her the way she feels about me; it would make life a lot easier. "I'm sorry, but I don't want to confuse things. You are only here with me because my mother insisted I escort you to Kenneth and Jacinta's ceremony, and not because I want to reconcile."

My thoughts snap to Ruby. *I wonder how she is. I hope she and the babies are okay.* I still can't believe she is pregnant with twins, *our twins.* I wish I'd found out sooner. I would have gone straight back for her instead of trying to forget about her and move on.

I'd felt like an arsehole leaving her there wounded, but I knew in my heart Jax was right. I couldn't have gotten her to help fast enough. Leaving her there was the only option to ensure her survival.

I'd considered heading back to the Winter border again the next morning—to find Floss and ask her if Ruby was okay. As much as Ruby had painted Floss out to be a bit of a bitch, I personally found her to be a good sport.

The only thing that'd stopped me was my mother and her guards' watchful eyes. As it is, I'm already dreading the great lengths I will need to go to in a few weeks, not only to sneak out of this hellhole, but to sneak Ruby back in. It's going to take a lot of planning if I want to succeed.

You must resist going to the Winter border until the four weeks are up, my inner voice warns. *It's not worth the risk of getting caught.* Besides, as much as I hate to admit it, I do actually have faith that Jax will take good care of her. He's in love with her, it's blatantly obvious. If Ruby can't tell, then her low pastel vision must be worse than I'd thought. Jax had let his stoic mask slip when he handed her over to me, and in that moment, I'd managed to witness the raw hurt in his eyes. I just hope he's able to keep his hands off her for the next four weeks. I don't want to lose her to him.

"It's time to go," Raven tells me, her voice bitter. "Queen Sjaan told me to make sure you get to the ceremony on time. She doesn't trust you to do the right thing without my guidance."

"Well, you see, that's the dilemma. What she thinks is the right thing to do, and what I think is the right thing to do, tend to contradict."

20

WOW, THAT'S A HUGE STATEMENT

-HARLOW-

’ve spent the last two days Jax-free. Sylvie has stayed with me during the days, and Zannah has stayed with me during the nights. I'd thanked Zannah for doing what she did to save me, and her clipped reply had been, "I didn't do it for you, I did it for Jax". She reminds me of Minty. They are both tough bitches, and not all that pleasant to be around, but they are fiercely loyal to those they care about. We hadn't conversed much, but she'd at least had the decency to tell me Jax hadn't come in to see me because he was busy making all the arrangements for Stace and Haydn's joint funeral, and that he wouldn't be coming the following day to see me, because he'd be spending the day out on the boat for the afterlife ceremony. I was aware he probably could've ducked in to see me for a quick visit if he'd really wanted to, but clearly, he hadn't. I don't blame him. If I were in his place, I wouldn't want to speak to me either.

Zavier, Minty, and Floss had come to visit me both days, and Tatum joined them on the second of those two days. Zavier and Floss had bickered a lot, and Minty needed to step in several times as their referee.

"See what my life has become?" Minty said to me in frustration. "Living with these two is like living with two squabbling five-year-olds."

Apparently, Floss had insisted on staying a few more nights, telling them she was still traumatised and needed time away from our parents to clear her head. She'd said Saul was too uncompassionate and seeing him would only upset her further. I could agree with her reasoning, our father's a pig, but I didn't believe he was the only reason she'd pushed to stay.

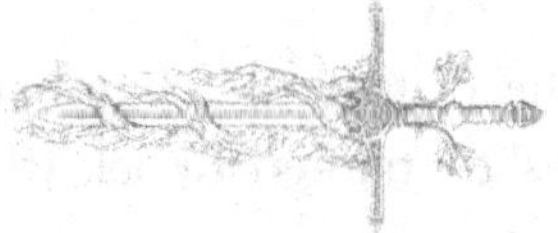

"Harlow," Jax's rumbling whisper wakes me from my sleep. "I'm sorry to wake you, but we need to leave early."

The last time I'd seen Jax, he'd told me he was taking me somewhere this weekend—although he never specified where this "somewhere" is.

He hands me a set of female warrior clothes with a hooded jacket. "You need to put these on. This way if someone sees us walking together, they'll assume you are one of my warriors."

"If she fits in my pants with that swollen stomach of hers, I'm going to kill myself." *Great, these are Zannah's clothes,* I realise.

"Zannah." Jax's voice is firm with warning. "Please don't." His eyes flash to mine, but only for a mere second. "I'll wait outside while you get changed."

Zannah stays put in a seat not far from my bed and watches as I struggle to get dressed one armed. After my third attempt at trying to get her shirt over my head, she lets out a frustrated sigh and comes over to help me. "I can't believe he's even got you borrowing my clothes now." She gives me an examining look-over. "Your body sure has changed a lot, hasn't it?" She doesn't wait for a reply. "A few months ago, my clothes would have swum on you."

We slide on her pants together, and to her delight, she can only manage to do up the bottom two buttons, leaving the top four undone.

"Well look at that," she says, face smug, "We might need to improvise." She folds the waistline twice over. "This should help to keep them up, although I'm sure if they do happen to fall down, Jax won't mind."

Ignoring her comment, I pull the hoodie of the jacket up over my bandana, and together we step out to the open chamber to meet Jax.

"Alright, let's go," he says.

When we get to the exit of the chamber, he calls Sphinx over, along with another husken named Rebel, who is smaller and much darker.

I glance at my watch while we walk; it's a quarter to five. We really are leaving early.

Zannah and Jax chat about the funeral, while I stay quiet and keep my head down. Zannah has a lot of questions regarding the warriors who'd attended and asks if anything incriminating was said by any of the former members of Nix's old gang. Jax says he'd over-heard a few underhanded things being tossed around between Roc, Austin, and Feeney, and he suspects Electra had a lot to do with Stace and Haydn taking those shots, but he doesn't get into any of the details, and I can only assume it's because I'm around.

When we get to the warrior cavern, Zannah says "bye" to Jax and leaves. It looks like it's only Jax and I going out. My nerves light up. I hadn't realised this. I'd assumed she was coming with us.

While Jax hooks up the huskens, I manage to pull myself up into the sled, one armed. Once he's done, he slides onto the seat next to me and calls, "Mush."

The huskens head towards a large, wooden portcullis which has been built into the limestone ceiling. He pulls a lever, and the portcullis draws up, allowing us to enter an open passageway which leads to the outside world.

An icy wind bites at my exposed skin as the sled leaves the passageway, but there's no fresh snow falling at present. The sky is clear, giving us full visibility of the colourful winter lights above. A trio of pinks, purples, and greens swirl through the atmosphere and reflect magnificently off the shiny front roll of the sled.

I slide off my glasses and take a better look. "It's beautiful," I say, more to myself. Eventually my neck gets cold and stiff, forcing me to lower my gaze. The sky might be bright overhead, but here on ground level, it's dark. I'm still able to make out my surroundings though, which is a pleasant surprise. These crimson irises are far more useful than my old pastel ones.

Within the next twenty minutes, the sun begins to peak above the horizon, and I beam internally at yet another beautiful sight. I've never watched a sunrise in Winter. The closest I've got to seeing any kind of sunrise here on Zadok was during the early hours of my overnight stay in Spring, but it hadn't been nearly as breathtaking as this. The pretty pink and orange sun rays were partially blocked-out by the tall trees of the forest.

"For what it's worth," Jax says, finally breaking the awkward silence between us. "I think Alex was completely out of line. You did the right thing by killing Lucas."

I glance over at him, a rush of disbelief and relief filling me. After the silent treatment he'd given me these past couple of days, I hadn't expected him to bring up my story, never mind side with me.

"The major difference between Alex and me," he continues, "is that if I saw my brother do those things to you, you wouldn't have had to kill him, because I'd kill him myself."

Wow. My jaw drops to my lap. That's a huge statement to make and goes to show just how foolish I was to have ever started something with Alex. The way Alex had always been so quick to defend Lucas had irked me right from the start. *How had I allowed myself to fall for him?*

Eventually, we enter the Spring forest and travel silently for several kilometres before pulling into a space between two ultra-large protruding roots. The trunk of the tree is enormous, both in length and width, and the bark is all different shades of brown, some almost pinkish. I gaze up in wonder. It's by far one of the tallest trees I have ever seen.

Jax slides his bulky jacket off and throws it in the back of the sled. "We'll need to walk from here," he says, and then hops out of the sled to unhook the huskens.

I nod and go to hop out too, but it's more of a struggle than I'd imagined. Pulling myself into the sled one-armed had been easy enough, but to get back out requires much more balance. Jax notices me struggling, and within an instant, he stops what he's doing and hurries over to help me. As his strong arms wrap around my waist, a warm sensation flows through me, threatening to set me on fire. The more I've thought about him lately, the more I've come to realise *just* how much he really does mean to me. Sadly though, it's too late. I'll never be able to be with him now. *I've ruined everything.*

He places me down gently, and his hands seem to linger slightly longer than they should—*not that I'm complaining.*

"I'm sorry, that was thoughtless of me, I should have helped you out before seeing to the huskens."

Thoughtless would be the last word I would use to describe him. He is the most thoughtful Zeek I know.

"You're too kind to me," I say, my cheeks burning. "I don't deserve all the help you've given me."

"You deserve more than you give yourself credit for," he says, but his eyes don't meet mine, and I wonder if he really means it, or if he is only saying this to make me feel better because he pities me. "Here, let me help you take your jacket off before you overheat. You should leave it and the bandana in the sled. You won't be needing them."

He gently helps to slide the puffy jacket off my bad shoulder, throws it in the sled on top of his, and then goes back to unhooking the huskens.

As soon as they are free, the huskens take off excitedly—like they know where they're going—and I rush over to Jax and follow as they lead the way. The deeper we get into this section of the forest, the darker and denser it becomes, and soon I'm able to catch glimpses of luminescent creatures. Some have beautiful wings and flutter above us through the trees, while others are reptilian like and scurry across the ground, hiding behind tree roots. Seeing them reminds me of some of the places Alex took me to, only these creatures don't seem nearly as vicious.

"We're outside the containment lines, aren't we?" I ask. "We're in the danger zone."

"Yes and no. There's no true danger on this side, not like where I found you." His tone holds slight accusation. "We're at the edge of the Drake village."

A nervous excitement surges inside me. "Are you taking me to the Drake village?"

"You'll see."

After trekking another kilometre, the Drake village comes into view. On the ground level directly in front of us beyond a tall wooden spiked fence, I see dozens of stilted, thatched huts sticking up several metres from the forest floor. Above them, up in the trees, are hundreds of wooden tree houses, linked together by wooden plank suspension bridges—lit up with natural golden fairy lights.

"Wow," I say. "This place looks like a fairy tale."

Jax gives the faintest hint of a smile. "The village is as tranquil and peaceful as the race who lives here."

As we draw closer, our presence soon becomes known, and two *extremely* tall yellow Drake men come strolling over with their canines to greet us. Their canines are not as big or furry as our huskens. They look similar to greyhounds, slim and muscular, with slick, shiny coats and amber eyes. One of them is black, and the other one is grey.

The Drake men smile at Jax, and the taller one says, "Hallo, my vriend," which sounds similar enough to the Zeek language that I can understand. Neither of them say anything to me; they both merely eye me with suspicion.

"Ek is hier om Dakari ten sien," Jax says in return, and I have no idea what any of those words mean.

The three converse for a while, and in the end, both Drakes glance in my direction, their expressions laced with cautious curiosity. I wish I knew what's been said. I still have no idea why Jax has even brought me here. We'd spoken very little during the trip, although he did mention that he'd managed to get Trey released from the cell on self-defence—which I was very grateful to hear. Other than that, though, things still feel very strained between us.

"Hy is op hierdie manier, volg ons," the taller of the two Drakes says and gives a motioning signal for us to follow.

I gaze about curiously as he leads us through the village. There are plenty of Drakes out and about, simply going about their business. However, as soon as they catch sight of me, they stop what they are doing and gaze over curiously. Despite their different coloured shimmers and irises, they all appear to be very similar in shape and size. They're extremely tall, thin and wiry, with hair shaved close to their skulls and decorative stretched earlobes. The clothing they wear is minimal, just like the woman who'd saved me from the fuegor, but they seem to be fond of jewellery, and their necklines are fully covered with handmade necklaces.

We're taken to a very large hut and are given a signal to wait at the bottom. The one Drake enters, while the other stays and watches over us, and then after a few minutes, we are called to come up.

"What about the huskens?" I ask.

"They'll be fine," Jax assures me. "They've been here many times and know to behave and wait for us."

The inner woven walls of the hut look pretty, and the floor space is decorated with colourful hand-knotted rugs and cushions. A Drake man with a large colourful headdress sits on a cushion covered wooden seat towards the far wall, and beside him is a Drake woman with far more jewellery than any of the other women outside. His eyes and shimmer are a lime-green, yet her shimmer and eyes are lemon yellow. They look important, and I wonder if the man is Dakari the Drake Chief.

"Hoe kan ek jou vriend help?" the important man asks Jax, and I come to the conclusion he's said something along the lines of "how can I help?"

He and Jax converse for a moment before the Drake turns his attention to me.

"What is your name?" he asks, using the Zeek language; however, his accent is so strong, I struggle to understand him.

"My name is Harlow."

"I've heard about you, Harlow." He blatantly looks me up and down. "You're not what I'd expected."

I don't know what to say to this. I don't know what he's been told, or by whom. Quite frankly, I'm surprised he's heard of me at all.

"We've never had a Vallon in our village before," he says. "Vallons are not easily trusted."

"With all due respect, I might be a Red these days, but I'm not a Vallon. I'm a Zeek, and I don't believe all Zeeks are easily trusted either."

He seems to find this funny and laughs. Jax, on the other hand, stiffens.

He looks to my tummy. "You might not be a Vallon, but you are carrying a set of Vallon twins, which means I do indeed have Vallons in my village."

I contemplate pointing out that the babies might both be Zeeks—not Vallons, but I'd really rather not indulge the topic. If anything, I'd prefer to steer away from it.

There is amusement in his voice as he continues to speak. "I'd never thought I would see the day where a Vallon and Zeek—two such warring enemies—would unite of their own accord. This will most certainly go down as a very distinct moment in history."

I don't like where this conversation has gone. I don't want to talk about how I've wound up pregnant to a Vallon, especially in front of Jax. We've already been through the details of this, and it was torturous enough the first time. Jax's jaw is tight, and his stance is rigid. He doesn't want to be speaking about this any more than I do.

Why are we here? I want to ask.

"What do you make of my offer?" Jax asks.

"It's a generous offer, and I accept the terms, but if Harlow turns out to be untrustworthy, the deal will be terminated, and she will be banished from our village for good."

"That sounds fair," Jax replies. "Now is there any chance that I may take her to see the others?"

"Sonja," the man calls, and a tall green Drake woman comes out from behind a curtained wall. On seeing her face, I do a double take, registering the familiar features. "Escort them to the hut of misfits," he says, and chuckles with a rumble that comes straight from the belly.

Sonja takes one look at me, and her eyes grow wide. "Bleek Een?"

I nod.

Like the man, she blatantly looks me up and down. "You're not so bleek anymore."

21

THE THIRD DEGREE

-HARLOW-

We exit one big hut only to be led to an even bigger one. A young Hazel calls Sonja over to him metres before we get there, and she leaves us to make the rest of the way on our own. Rebel looks very excited about where she's going and shoots off ahead, letting off two loud barks. Someone must recognise the sound of these barks and the door flies open to reveal… Stavros, the notorious warrior who killed Nix. I jolt at the sight of him. I hadn't expected this. I'd guessed he was still alive, Jax had hinted as much, but I never imagined he would be living amongst the Drakes.

He jumps down to meet the husken on the ground, and the two of them wrestle for a few moments before he leaps to his feet and comes rushing over to greet Jax with a friendly hug.

"Hey, Brother, I've been wondering when I might see you next." His eyes assess me with curiosity as he pulls back. "What do we have here?" he asks. "You've sure changed."

He knows who I am? It seems everyone knows who I am, and yet I've spent my whole life believing I was invisible. *A pitiful Pastel.*

Stavros has changed a little too. There are no snowflakes shaved onto the sides of his skull—which makes sense—and he's grown a beard. He still looks good though, even in his new relaxed attire. A woman exits the hut opening after him, and I'm even more shocked to see her than I was to see him. My jaw drops. She's a Ruke, a real live Ruke. I've never seen a Ruke before, but I've always wanted to. I've always been fascinated by the idea of having wings.

"Acacia, come down," Stavros calls. "There's someone I'd like you to meet."

Acacia's wings flap softly as she jumps down, lightly fanning the air around us. Goosebumps prickle my arms. *Wow, so cool.*

She looks to be a few years older than Stavros and Jax. At a guess, I would say she's twenty-six, and gosh, she's beautiful. Really, really, beautiful, with high cheekbones and almond-shaped eyes.

Like most Rukes she has long, thick, shiny black hair and skin that looks like white and grey veined marble. Acacia's skin is different from the pictures I've seen in textbooks, it has a slight purple sparkle to it. She also has purple eyes, which I find odd. I thought Ruke's eyes were only supposed to be aqua, teal, or blue.

Acacia's wings fold down as she makes her way over to us, and when she gets to where we stand, Stavros wraps his arms around her affectionately. "Acacia, this is Harlow," he says. "Jax's lifelong-love." *Oh God!* "Tell me?" he asks, gesturing to my swollen tummy, and I cringe internally. "When did this happen?" His gaze falls on Jax, who looks like he wants to curl into a ball and die.

"The twins aren't mine," he says flatly.

Now it's Stavros' turn to look embarrassed. "Oh, I just assumed… I mean, well you're both here…and she's pregnant." His gaze floats between my hair and irises. "And she doesn't look like she's pregnant to a Pastel."

"She's not." Jax tries to keep his voice deadpan, but I can hear the veiled hurt. "She's pregnant to a Vallon."

Shock waves pass over their faces.

Okay, well, this got awkward fast. I bet Jax wishes he'd never brought me here.

"I guess that makes more sense," Stavros finally says. "Pink and purple don't make red."

I take another look at Acacia's eyes and understanding fills me. She is either having—or has had—a child to Stavros.

"Well, regardless of who the twins' father is, it's lovely to meet you, Harlow," Acacia says with a tonal accent. "Say, why don't you come inside and meet Atohi. It will give the guys a chance to catch up on things."

"Sure," I say, glad of an escape.

Inside the hut, she takes me to a cot where a small baby lies sleeping. "We chose to name him Atohi, which in my language means woods. We thought it was fitting, given he was born here."

His hair and skin are the same as hers, but I can't see his eyes or back. "Did he get the purple eyes and wings?" I ask.

"He got the wings, but his irises are more of a bluish-purple, somewhere between my old and new colour. He is the first baby of his kind."

"He's beautiful," I say.

My eyes keep drifting to Acacia's wings. I can't help it. I'm fascinated by them.

Noticing my intense interest, she semi-opens the wing closest to me. "You can touch it if you want."

"Really?" I ask excitedly, and then I blush, embarrassed about how childish I must sound.

"All of the Drakes were fascinated by them when I first arrived here."

I run my hand over her wing. The feathers feel soft and silky. "May I ask how you came to live in Spring? Or is it private?"

From what I've been told, Rukes never usually leave their land.

They don't need to. Their land is the most self-sufficient of all the lands. Their main village is also much further away from the rest of the main capitals, so it would take more than a couple days' travel to get to any of us. The capitals of Summer, Winter, and Spring are all fairly close to one another, situated on the northern end of Zadok's globe in their quadrants. The only thing Autumn doesn't have is an ocean, but it has large rivers which connect to our ocean. The beginning of the ocean starts in Winter and takes up the majority of the southern part of our land.

"When I was around your age, I found myself in an awful situation back in Autumn, so my older brother Wohali helped me to escape. We hadn't known the extreme dangers of travelling through the Spring forest during the evenings, and due to our ignorance, we were attacked by a fuegor." She swallows. "Wohali died saving me."

"I'm sorry," I say, and she politely waves it off.

"The next morning, I was found by a Drake who carried me back to the village. My wing was broken during the struggle with the fuegor, but Roz, the Drake medicine woman, helped to mend it. I was very lucky. I've managed to get my full range back with no permanent damage. I'm still able to fly—not that I often do."

I'd like to hear more about her backstory, but sadly she doesn't continue, so I look at Atohi and say, "Well, it looks like everything has worked out for you here."

"What's your story then?" she asks. Her tone is calm and friendly, almost soothing.

"A regrettable one. I thought I knew who Alex was, but it turns out I was wrong, and now I'm stuck in a bad position I can't escape. My kind wants me dead, and Alex is returning to retrieve me in three and a half weeks to take me back to Summer with him—or at least I believe that's where he will be taking me. He didn't really say."

Her eyes widen with sympathy. "Summer is a dangerous place for a Zeek. A couple of the other Zeeks you'll meet here escaped from Summer a couple of years back. They say it's an awful place. They say, many of the paler Pastels died of heat exhaustion— among other things." Her last three words come out as a whisper.

"I'm worried about the babies," I admit.

"And I bet Jax is worried about you."

"Just so you know," I say, feeling the need to explain myself. "I never knew Jax was interested in me until recently. He never said anything, and even if he had, we could never have truly dated. He is a Purple and the Commander's son, and—until recently—I was only a Pastel. We were from different ranks. I would have tarnished him."

She lets out a light, sorrowful laugh. "I believe Jax was hoping to break down the colour system before letting his feelings be known to you. If you were to start a relationship, he wanted it to be true, honest, and open—not hidden. It's a shame he wasn't able to succeed."

We hear the guys enter and make our way back out of the nursery to greet them.

"What do you think?" Stavros asks. "He's a star, isn't he?"

"He's gorgeous." I gush. "You are both very lucky."

Stavros and Acacia take us for a walk through the large hut and introduce me to some of the others who live there.

First, I meet a Pastel man in his mid-thirties named Boshell who has twelve-year-old twins, a boy and a girl named Will and Daisy. Boshell's hair and irises still have a decent amount of pink pigment given his age, but the poor twins have no pigment at all. They are so ghostly pale that they're completely blind.

"Harlow is having twins too," Stavros tells them, and brings them over to touch my tummy.

I lift my shirt and they smile as they feel around for the babies. Daisy even leans her ear to my tummy to see if she can hear them. Due to their poor condition, they seem younger than their years.

"There's a boy and a girl inside," I say. "Just like you two."

It makes my heart sink to see the condition they're in. They're so weak and frail. *It's not fair.* We stay with them for a while, and I learn from Boshell that he and his partner Holly, like many other Pastels, were sent to Summer as a part of the peace offering. I knew of the peace offering, Alex had told me, but I wasn't sure if Jax was aware. *Now I know.*

Boshell says Holly was pregnant at the time and the two had been desperate to escape for the sake of their babies.

"Where is Holly now?" I ask.

Boshell's eyes grow sorrowful. "She died giving birth."

"Oh, I'm sorry."

"It was a long time ago," he says, "And I can't really complain. She left me with these two beautiful gifts." He takes both kids in his arms and kisses them on the top of their heads, one after the other. "They are my world."

After saying our goodbyes, we meet two female Zeeks, both in their mid-twenties. Right away I notice something's off with their colouring; they have a soft peach hue. It's unusual. And their heights and statures are more like those of Magentas than those of Pastels.

The first girl, named Destiny, is pleasant enough and says hello to me, but the other one takes one look and me and freaks out.

"Those monsters! Look what they've done to you." She leaps up from her chair and comes straight up in my face. Her eyes stare fiercely into mine. "How did you escape?"

"I…um." She's practically standing on top of me, and I can feel the heat of her breath on my face. My eyes leave hers, looking to Jax for help.

"Her story isn't the same as yours or the others, Luna," he says. "And it's a long one. I think we'd best save it for another day."

She shoots me a dark, questioning look. "You didn't choose this, did you?"

Regret stabs at me. "I made a mistake," I say.

Her eyes grow large and her nostrils flare. "GET OUT!" She whirls on Stavros, her face filled with pure rage. "GET HER OUT!"

Jax dives between us, curls his arm around my waist, and ushers me out. Luna's wild shouts arouse the attention of Boshell, and he comes rushing out to see what's happened.

Jax whisks me out of the hut entry and away from the madness.

"I'm sorry," he says once we're outside. "I had no idea Luna would react that way."

"I don't blame her," I say, and I mean it. "I knew how evil Vallons were before I met up with Alex, and I was very foolish to do what I did. I don't know what the Vallons did to Luna in Summer, but I'm sure it was terrible. I'm not upset with her for judging me."

Jax goes to say something but stops when he sees Stavros heading over. *Darn.* I want to know what he was going to say.

Stavros apologises about Luna too, and I tell him not to worry about it.

"I think we caught her off guard," he says. "Don't worry, she'll cool down after a while."

Stavros offers to show me around the village, and I accept.

Jax declines. "I'll stay and keep Acacia company."

As soon as we start walking, Rebel follows, running straight to Stavros' side with a panting smile.

"I take it she was yours?"

"Yeah, she was." He gives her a playful rough around behind the ears. "I wish I could keep her here, but it's not really an option. And anyway, I know Zannah loves having her around. How is she anyway?"

"Zannah?" I shrug, my brows crinkling. "I wouldn't know. Your sister doesn't really speak to me, but she did save my life recently, so I am grateful to her."

"Yeah, Jax mentioned that when we were out front." He lets out a dry chuckle. "I wouldn't worry about Zannah giving you the cold shoulder. She has a tendency to ward off any girls who get too close to Jax. I'm surprised she's trying her back-off tactics on you though. We've all been aware of Jax's feelings for you right from the start."

Here we go again. "You all act like the way Jax felt about me was obvious, but it's never been obvious to me."

"You mean *feels* not *felt*," he corrects, as I continue to speak.

"Only the once ever," —the night that he came in to check on me after Ogre's funeral—"did I think *maybe* he was interested in me for more than just my help. But even then, I wasn't entirely sure. He's very guarded most of the time, and not all that easy to read."

A young Yellow boy, sitting on the lap of his mother, sees us walking past and gapes at me in horror. He quickly turns his face away, burying it safely in her bosom. *Great! Now I'm scaring children.*

"You're right. Jax is guarded, but he has to be in his position." Stavros picks up a stick and throws it for Rebel to run and catch. "You'll find the more you get to know him, the more his walls will come down. He's a different Zeek entirely when he's out with Oscar, Kieran, Zannah, and me. We've all grown up together, so he's not afraid to relax and be himself around us."

"Well, unfortunately I'm not going to get the chance to know him any better," I say, feeling choked up about it. "I'll be gone in a few weeks."

"Is that what you want?" He pauses to cast me a curious glance. "Are you happy to go with the Vallon to Summer? You do know you'll be in extreme danger there, don't you?" There is a sense of strong warning in his tone.

I lower my gaze. "No, it's not what I want, but Winter isn't safe for me to live in either. I'm screwed either way."

"Are you still in love with the Vallon?"

What? I hadn't realised when he'd offered to show me around, he was really just looking for an excuse to give me the third degree.

I can feel his eyes still on me, waiting to assess my response, but I refuse to look at him. "What happened between Alex and me was a lapse in judgement."

"I'm curious then, how *do* you feel about Jax?"

Seriously? Stavros obviously isn't afraid to get deep fast. I wish I'd said no to the walk. He hasn't even shown me anything, we've only been walking and talking. "What's with all the loaded questions?"

"Interrogation has always been my speciality, it's how I got Nix's guys to talk."

Not willing to completely open up, I say, "It doesn't matter how I feel about Jax, it won't change anything, especially now. I've done too much damage. There's no going back."

"You'd be surprised at what's possible. Love is a strong emotion, it can survive a great deal of anguish, and the heart is a very forgiving muscle."

His words are powerful and tug at my insides. *Does he really believe that Jax still cares enough about me to forgive me?*

"Anyway, enough with the heavy." He heads towards one of the huts. "Follow me. I've been told there's something I really need to show you."

22

DECISIONS

-HARLOW-

The hut Stavros takes me to is a quaint library. There isn't a large selection of Zeek written books available to choose from, but I come across a few titles that look interesting. Stavros says Jax told him I loved books, and that the library would be a *must know* if I was going to be staying here. After this, he takes me to see a few of the small marketplaces, the farm, the school, the firepit gathering, and the lake. Everywhere we go, Drakes stop and stare, and I wonder if they all find me as terrifying to look at as the young boy had. I am pleasantly surprised to observe all the different coloured

Drakes mingling socially. At one point I even witness a Hazel guy and Yellow girl kiss.

The topic of Jax has been dropped, *thank goodness*, and we move on to the topic of how he and Acacia first began their relationship. He says when he first came to live here, he'd felt the chemistry between them right away, but because of their different races he'd wanted to wait a couple of months before letting his feelings be known. He said he'd arranged their first date as a surprise by setting up a romantic picnic by the lake, and he'd asked Destiny to sneakily bring Acacia over, by pretending she wanted to go for a leisurely walk with a friend.

"Acacia was impressed by my efforts," he says, and the loving smile he wears says a thousand words. "And she'd admitted right away she had feelings for me too. But she was worried about what the Drakes would think and what the repercussions would be if they found out we were entering into a mixed-race relationship in their village."

"Well, you obviously got around it," I say.

"I went and spoke to Dakari about our dilemma, and he was surprisingly relaxed about it. He said he wasn't opposed to our separate races mixing, as long as our actions didn't affect the village. He merely warned that if we, or any child conceived by our mixed-race relationship, started posing a threat to the village or any of his tribe members, he wouldn't hesitate to have us banished immediately."

"He said something along the same lines about me to Jax."

"Dakari is a good leader," Stavros says with respect. "Life here is a lot more pleasant and relaxed, and as you can probably see," he says, giving an open gesture. "Inter-colour relationships aren't an issue. Dakari has a system which works on merit, not colour status. You get what you get because you've worked hard for it and earned it—not because you're entitled to it."

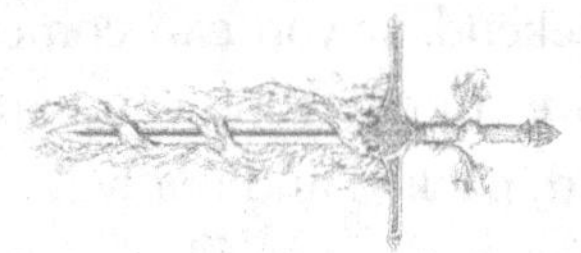

When we get back to the hut, Jax and Acacia are sitting in a couple of cane chairs on the wooden deck to the side of the hut entrance. Jax is cradling Atohi, which is a strange sight, but it's nice to get a glimpse of him with his guard down. Atohi is awake, and as I get closer, I see his eyes. They are unique—in a very cool way. Indigo eyes. I wish I had eyes that colour. *Maybe you should have fallen pregnant to a Ruke,* I joke to myself. *Or Jax, his eyes are amazing too.* I mentally slap myself. The second part of my joke is sad, wishful, and more of an agonising taunt than funny.

"What do you think?" Jax asks. "Could you handle staying here for a few weeks?"

I sit down in the empty chair beside him, while Stavros lifts Acacia up, steals her chair, and then draws her back down to sit on his lap. "I think it's great here," I say. "The library even has a few Zeek books I haven't read."

His lips quirk up into a smile which shows his dimples. "That's good, I'm glad."

It's been a long while since I've seen those beautiful dimples of his. Seeing them again almost makes me cry. "Where will I be sleeping?" I ask. "I didn't realise you were bringing me here to stay, or I would have brought my pack of clothes."

"Don't worry," Acacia says, before Jax has a chance to respond. "You can stay down our end on a mattress in Atohi's room, and I'm happy for you to borrow some of my clothes. We're a similar size."

Jax looks over at me. "I didn't tell you about the plan beforehand, because I was afraid there was a chance Dakari would say no to my offer. He's not a big fan of the Vallon race and given your circumstances…well…" His eyes begin to wander. "I wanted him to meet you in the flesh, so he could see for himself that you're not going to be a threat to his tribe or village. Now that he's met you and has accepted my offer, you have two options. You can either stay here, take Acacia up on her kind offer, and I can bring out your pack of stuff next weekend, *or* you can come back with me for the week, say your goodbyes to everyone you care about, and I'll bring you back next weekend, packed and ready."

I sit quietly for a moment, considering my options. I know the choice I should make, but it's not the choice I'd prefer. It's Zavier's birthday on Thursday, and I want to say goodbye to him—and Minty, Tatum, and Floss. "I prefer the second offer," I say honestly. "But I understand it's riskier, so if you'd prefer me to stay now, then I will. I don't want to make life difficult for you."

"I agree with Harlow," Stavros says. "She's got to be able to say goodbye to her family and friends, and what's more, it will also give Luna a week to warm up to the idea of having her around on a semi-permanent basis. Come back on Saturday though, not Sunday. The Drakes are having their festival of masks that night. It's really exciting to be a part of. It will almost be like a welcoming party."

"You should stay for it too," Acacia says to Jax, "You've never been a part of the festival of masks before."

"I can't. It's too dangerous for the huskens and me to travel back after dark."

Stavros cocks his head in a thoughtful manner. "Why don't you stay the night?"

"I don't know." Jax doesn't look like he wants to. "I doubt I'd be able to stay out here a full night. My presence would be missed during the evening. It wouldn't go unnoticed."

"I'm sure you could work something out," Stavros says, but he doesn't push the matter any further than this.

Jax notices me admiring Atohi and asks, "Do you want to hold him?"

My gaze shifts to Acacia and Stavros. "May I?"

Stavros laughs at my question, while Acacia says, "Of course you can."

Jax stands up from his chair and leans down to place Atohi in the curve of my good arm. A strange feeling settles over me as I gaze down at this small baby in front of me. I gulp. *I will have two of these soon.*

The rest of the afternoon turns out to be very enjoyable, and I feel somewhat relaxed, which is almost surreal given how treacherous these past couple of months have been for me. Acacia brings out some nibbles and drinks, and we spend most of the afternoon sitting on the deck chatting. Stavros' personality is very forward and direct, but he is also quite witty and funny. I get to hear Jax chuckle a few times, which is nice. I haven't seen much of this side of him, only small glimpses here and there. Stavros is right, Jax is different around him, his walls seem to disappear altogether.

Stavros entertains me with escapades from their past, and Jax warns if he keeps it up, he'll be forced to strangle him. I find the story about Zannah's bra being glued to the front of Oscar's warrior vest hilarious, especially now, given I know how much those two detest each other. And I also laugh out loud at the story about the boys tipping a whole bucket of stinky seafood on top of Zannah's bed while she was sleeping in it.

"That seafood stunt was all Stavros and Oscar," Jax makes sure to say—accepting no responsibility. "I know better than to get on the wrong side of Zannah."

"Man, did I cop a few hard hits for that one," Stavros laughs. "Zannah still gets bitter about it, even now. That girl's biggest problem is she can give it, but she can't take it."

"She's grown up a lot," Jax says in her defence. "She's still got a razor-sharp tongue, but she's a brilliant warrior. I don't know what I would have done without her lately."

As it gets to three P.M. Jax lets me know that we need to leave, so I help Acacia clear the table and put a few things away. I really like Acacia. She seems wholesome and kind. I'm actually delighted about staying here for a couple of weeks. I could really use a friend like Acacia in my life, even if it is only a temporary solution. Her presence alone has a serene, calming effect on me.

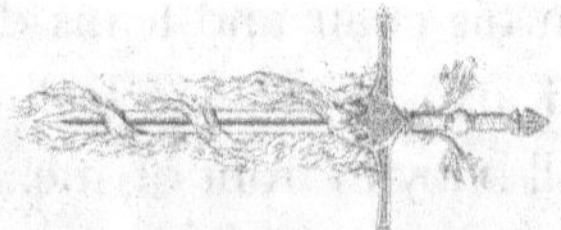

"Are you honestly okay with this arrangement?" Jax asks, as we make our way back to the sled. "I don't want you to think I'm palming you off, because I'm not. I'm trying to do what's best for you. You're not safe in the caves, and it seems awfully cruel to confine you to the restricted area of the medical chamber for the next couple of weeks. It's not much of a life."

"I know, and I think staying here is a great idea. Thank you for doing this for me. I actually had a really nice time today; it was relaxing. Stavros and Acacia are very warm and welcoming."

His lips twitch into a semi smile. "I had a nice time too. I miss having Stavros in the caves. He's always been like a brother to me. I owe him my life."

Since we're talking and already touching on the subject, I throw out a question I've been longing to know the answer to. "Is it true that I was a big part of the reason why Nix was plotting to have you killed?"

Jax tenses a little, and I'm worried he's going to close off on me again. "There were a lot of reasons why Nix wanted me killed. We fought about everything, especially when it came to the colour system."

When we get back to the sled, Jax helps me to put my jacket and bandana back on. "I can't believe you kept this," he says, tying the bandana up at the back. "And that you've been wearing it."

"Do you want it back?"

"No, of course not." He spins me around to face him, and tucks in a few red wisps from my face. "I like that you wear it."

My heart flutters at his slight show of interest, and I wish he'd say more, but he doesn't. I'd give anything to know what he thinks of me now. Despite Stavros' encouragement, I can't imagine Jax's feelings for me could be the same as they once were, not when he knows I'm pregnant to a Vallon.

What does it matter? I ask myself. *You'll be gone in a few weeks. There's no use in finding out. Let him go. He deserves better than you, anyway.*

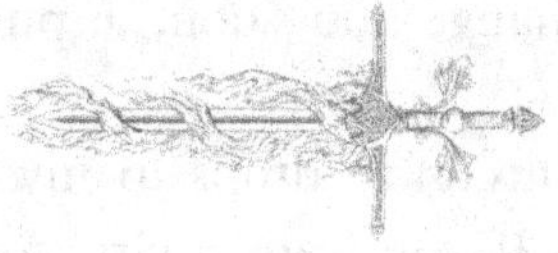

Getting me back into the caves is a far more stressful experience than getting me out. One of Jax's warriors sees me from behind and starts calling out "Zannah, Zannah"—thinking I'm her.

My pulse jackhammers, and I want to say something like, "I can't talk right now," to get him to shut up, but my voice is nothing *at all* like Zannah's.

"It's not a good time," Jax says, his tone stern. "We'll be back later."

By the time we get to the medical chamber, I'm overheated with stress; and going by the beads of sweat coating Jax's forehead, he must have been feeling the pressure too.

"I should've stayed in Spring," I say, slipping off my glasses and bandana, and throwing them on the bed. "I've made things harder for you."

"No, you shouldn't have. It was a close call, but we weren't caught. It's fine." He assesses my stressed, sweaty features with knitted brows. "Are you okay?"

"Yeah, I'm fine. It's you I'm worried about. I had a dream you were killed, and I don't want it to come true."

"That sounds more like a nightmare," he says, raising a brow. "Don't worry, I'll be careful." His eyes fix on mine, and his gaze intensifies, revealing a mixture of affection and confliction.

I know I should leave it alone, but unable to control myself, I ask, "How can you bear to look me in the face, knowing what I've done?"

"You've got a face that's hard not to look at," he says, and a smile flitters across his lips, showing off his dimples. "We all make mistakes, Harlow; I've made a few of my own lately. It's life."

"My mistake was a big one, though," I press.

"So was mine." All traces of his smile slip away, and his expression grows serious. "I should never have rushed things. It was foolish of me. By forcing change too soon, I put you in danger with Electra."

Feeling ashamed, my gaze drops to my hands. "And now I'm putting you in danger. If you were smart, you would've left me out in the forest that day."

"If I were smart things would be very different between us, and you would never have ended up in the forest."

If—But not now. Not after everything that's happened, is what I read from his comment. He might have forgiven me, but the damage is done. I've lost my chance with him.

We share an awkward goodbye, and he lets me know he'll be sending one of his warriors back to guard me during the night. It's kind of embarrassing. I bet his warriors will be counting down the days until next weekend, when I'm officially out of their hair for good.

23

MIXED EMOTIONS

-ZAVIER-

eing back at work sucks. My body might be healed, but it still hates me, and I'm afraid I'm going to feel this stiff and decrepit for the rest of my life.

Harlow said Jax was taking her somewhere this weekend, but she didn't know where. *I wonder if she's back.* I'm curious to find out where he took her.

Minty wipes the last of the scraps off the bench and tosses them into the bin. "Hey, Grandpa," she snaps. "Hurry up and sweep the floors already. Do you want to visit Harlow tonight or not?"

Minty has been tired and stressed all day, making her far more bitchy than usual. She'd never admit it, but I think she's actually worried about Harlow's wellbeing. Strangely enough, their forced living arrangement actually did their relationship some good. They seem to have bonded a bit. *Who would've thought?*

"By the way, I think your other girlfriend is coming," she says, referring to Floss. "I saw her waiting outside."

"Yeah, I know. I invited her." I pick up the broom and start sweeping. "She started her new job today, and I figured she might want to talk about it."

Minty glances over at me with curious suspicion. "You two seem to be getting a lot closer these past few days. You haven't even been bickering as much."

"It's not like that," I'm quick to say. "I know she's struggling at the moment, and I'm trying to be there for her, because I know it pleases Lexan."

"You know, if Floss wasn't Magenta, I would encourage you to go for her." I sense frustrated compassion in Minty's voice. "She's changed a lot these past few weeks, and it's obvious she genuinely likes you."

"I keep telling you, it's not like that with Floss and me," I say defensively. "And anyway, I thought you were warming to Harlow?"

"I am warming to Harlow as your friend—not as your girlfriend. It hurts me to watch you fawn over her when I know your feelings are never going to be reciprocated." She sighs. "At the risk of sounding like a broken recorded, I'm going to say this to you once more, in the hope it will sink in." Her gaze is sharp. "You need to do us all a favour and let Harlow go in the girlfriend sense. Be there for her, be her friend, help her if you must, but stop hoping for more than her friendship." She sighs. "I only say this because I care about you, my friend, and I don't want to see you heartbroken."

Even though I'm already well aware I have no chance with Harlow, hearing Minty's candid advice still stings. The problem is, I don't know what to do with my feelings, it's not like I can just click my fingers and magically switch them off.

We go back to cleaning, but a few minutes later a loud scream startles us both, and without hesitation we dash out of the kitchen to see what's happening. I automatically bring the broom with me, and Minty manages to snatch a knife from the chopping block on her way out the door.

Lucy must already be onto the situation, because I can hear her snapping and growling outside.

Another two screams ring out. The first one sounds like Floss, but the other scream sounds low and gravelly.

"You stupid mutt," the gravelly voice yells with venom, and Lucy yelps. "Get back."

I leave the front doors to discover Floss racing over towards me. "Help, it's Rae."

I'm brought to a jolting halt as she throws herself in my arms, almost knocking me backwards. There's blood on her clothes—not a lot, but enough to concern me.

Minty walks a few steps further out but doesn't continue. "She's brought the whole gang again."

Lucy continues growling and snapping, sounding even more ferocious.

"We know that you're hiding her," Rae shouts. "And it's only a matter of time before we find her. The Commander knows all about the baby now, and she wants Harlow to pay for her crimes. She might have got away with plotting my son's murder, but she won't get away with this."

"Get back," the others shout to Lucy as Rae speaks. "Get back, mutt."

Mindful we are no match for Rae's gang, the three of us stay where we are and watch as Lucy does her best to round them up. Eventually the growls and shouts fade as Rae and her gang are forced back down the passage, away from us.

"We can't go and see Harlow now," Minty says. "It's too risky."

Floss is still holding onto me tightly.

"Are you alright?" I pull back so that I can take a look at her. "Where are you hurt? Is it serious?"

"The blood isn't mine, it's Rae's. Lucy tore at her arm to get her to release me."

"I wonder what the gang did to get Lucy off Rae?" Minty paces anxiously at the entry. "I heard her yelp."

I find it strange how attached Minty has become to this husken, especially given how annoyed she was about having it around when Harlow first moved in.

"She must be okay," I assure her. "She still went at them pretty fiercely after that yelp."

"I hope you're right."

"If what Rae is saying is true, if the Commander really does know about Harlow and wants her convicted, then why send Rae to capture her? Why wouldn't she send some of the warriors?" Floss asks.

"Because Jax is the head warrior," Minty says, her tone matter-of-a-fact. "And if she believes Harlow is carrying his child, then she knows he would protect her."

"But I'm sure there's still a few of Nix's old followers she could send," Floss puts forward. "If she wanted to keep it from getting back to Jax, I'm sure she could."

The answer clicks in my head. "If she gets Rae to kill Harlow and makes it look like a revenge kill, she gets to keep Jax onside," I say. "She's trying to play her cards right to avoid retaliation from her son."

Floss mulls on what I've said for a moment, and then comes back at me with, "Well, why not just kill Jax too? Problem solved."

"He is her only living son," I point out. "If he dies, her bloodline dies."

"If Jax were to be killed, and Azazel dies, who would be in line as the next Commander?" Minty asks curiously.

"I don't know," I answer honestly. "But I'm sure one of their rich relatives would happily step up to the position."

"I wonder if they'd be any more lenient when it comes to our colour system." Floss scowls.

Lucy comes trotting back through the entryway, panting with a self-satisfied expression. Minty places the knife down on a nearby table and thoroughly checks her over from head to tail. "They must have only kicked her," she says with relief. "She's not bleeding or lame."

I sigh. "What should we do now then?"

"Let's head to your place for now," Floss suggests, taking off her blood smeared jumper. "I think we should all stay together in case Rae and her gang are still lurking around."

Minty agrees we should stick together, and after locking up, we all head back to my cavern.

"The lounge is mine," Minty grumbles, making a beeline straight for it. She flops down onto it and tosses an arm over her eyes to block the light. "My head is throbbing. Tell me you have some painkillers left."

My body is aching all over. "I have two nauclea latifolia roots left, we can have one each." I head to the bench to grab the roots. I toss one to Minty and pop the other one in my mouth.

After taking a good look around, Floss asks, "Where's Lexan?"

"I don't know, probably with your *mother*." There is a heavy accusation in my tone, yet I don't exactly know why. It's never really been an issue to me before now. I think I'm on edge.

"Hey…" Floss shoots back defensively. "She's Harlow's mother too, you know."

"Yeah, I know, I'm sorry," I say earnestly. "Minty's foul mood must be rubbing off on me."

"Whatever." Floss' expression is bitter as she makes her way into the kitchen area where I stand. She hoists herself onto the bench-top, using it as a seat. "You're just upset that we're not going to see Harlow tonight."

I *am* upset about not being able to see Harlow tonight, but it's not the only thing bothering me. Minty's words sit heavily on my chest, crushing down on my heart like an anvil. I'm well aware Harlow only sees me as a friend, she's made this very clear, time and time again. I don't know why I keep holding onto dead hope.

Floss scowls in my direction, her eyes prickled with jealousy. I wish she wouldn't do this. When she's not busy throwing tantrums or pulling faces at me—like she is right now—she actually looks very pretty, like Harlow. She keeps hitting on me lately, and I keep pushing her away, *but maybe I shouldn't. Perhaps I should give her a chance?*

I struggle with the idea. It's not so much Floss' colour that bothers me—although, if I'm being honest, it does kind of bother me a bit—it's more about the difference in the two girls' personalities. If only they weren't so different, it would make this decision far less difficult. Harlow is fun and easy to get along with, whereas Floss is the polar opposite. *But...* Floss is available and interested, whereas Harlow already has two powerful men fighting over her. A Commander's son and a Queens's son. I'm not even in their league.

Minty was right when she said Floss has improved a lot. Floss used to be a real mega-bitch when we were growing up. Some of the things she's said to both Harlow and me over the years have been that nasty and degrading, I sometimes wonder why I even bother speaking to her.

Up until the whole Ogre debacle, she was a Pastel hater, *so why such a big turnaround all of a sudden? Why pick me?* I might have stood up for her, but it didn't necessarily achieve anything. I had the sludge kicked out of me. *I'm weak.*

Floss could easily get a big bulky Magenta if she wanted to. *Although,* I suppose I shouldn't be too flattered over her interest. Anyone would be a massive upgrade when compared with Ogre. Ogre might've been strong, but he was ugly, and when it came to personality, he'd made Saul look decent—and that's saying something.

Perhaps she's following in her mother's footsteps out of interest. It's not like she hasn't made the reference to me before. I'll finally give in and fall for her, and then she'll link up with some arrogant Magenta jerk and keep me around as a side dish, like Krista does with Lexan.

My other concern is she might only be interested in me because I'm interested in her sister. She could be getting off on the challenge—it may not be personal.

"What?" Floss asks, and I realise I've been unintentionally staring. "Why are you looking at me like that?"

"I'm trying to figure you out."

"What's there to figure out?" She returns my stare with puckered brows. "You know me better than anyone else does."

If this is true, then it's very sad, because I don't really know her at all.

I want to test something, but I don't really know if I should. I'm confused and hurting, and I probably shouldn't be making any rash decisions right now. Regardless, I move towards her, mind racing and heart thumping.

"What are you doing?" she asks warily, but I don't answer.

My hand cups the back of her head, and as I pull her towards me, I detect a glint of nervous excitement in her eyes. I close mine and lean in the few extra centimetres, allowing my lips to brush softly against hers.

She doesn't respond right away, which surprises me given how excited she'd looked. I thought this is what she wanted.

She starts to respond for a second and then sharply draws back. "I genuinely like you," she admits. "So, if you're only using me to fill a void, tell me now, so I know where I stand. I don't want to read too much into this and get my hopes up if it's only a onetime thing."

Her raw openness stuns me. I hadn't realised her feelings for me were serious. Deep down, I honestly assumed I was like a game to her—a challenge she wanted to win to prove something to Harlow.

I owe her the truth. "I don't really know how I feel about you," I say. "I have mixed feelings. You haven't always been very nice to me, and even now, you're not always the easiest Zeek to get along with."

"And the real reason is you're still in love with my sister, but you've finally realised you can't have her, so you figure I'll do."

Hearing her spell it out like this makes me feel like an arsehole. "I'm sorry. I shouldn't have done that. It was selfish."

I go to step away, but she grabs hold of my shirt and pulls me back to face her. "Zavier, wait." She wraps her legs around my waist and squeezes, forcing my body to hers, and her lips press fiercely into mine, hungry with lust and wanting.

My whole body responds to her in a way I hadn't expected. I'm tingling all over. *I want this.* My lips leave hers to trail her neck, and she arches her spine and moans excitedly.

"What the Frost, you two!" Minty leaps up from the lounge. "Are you insane?"

Floss reluctantly pulls away and gives Minty a dirty look—which Minty returns with a heavy sigh.

"You know what, fine." Minty throws her hands up. "At this point I don't really care what you guys do, but can you please at least take it to the nook so that no passers-by see you? In case you've forgotten, you are not exactly from the same colour status, and we already have enough problems to deal with."

24

SECRETS REVEALED

-HARLOW-

Jax pops in early on his way to training. He converses with Kieran for a few minutes and then tells him to go home and rest up for a few hours, before coming across to see me in the hospital bed.

Compared with Oscar and Stavros, Kieran is much quieter and more reserved. We'd only spoken a little, but I could tell by his extensive vocabulary he must have a high IQ. *Like what in the world does "cantankerous" mean?* I didn't ask. I merely nodded along when he'd called Zannah cantankerous, acting as though I agreed. I can only imagine it means bitchy, angry, rude—or something to that effect.

"How did you sleep?" Jax is much warmer today. He's still got his stiff warrior stance going on, but he's not acting icy. I think our trip to the forest helped to ease a bit of the brittle tension between us.

"Any nightmares?"

"No nightmares," I assure him.

He pulls a chair up and sits close, fixing me with his glistening violet eyes. "Good, because I'm still alive. You don't need to worry about me."

"Lexan came in to see me last night," I say, trying to ignore the warm fuzzy feeling growing inside me. "And I asked him to tell Zavier to bring in my pack when he comes in next. I want to be all packed and ready to go, in case the unexpected happens and we need to leave in a hurry." I shuffle up the bed. "By the way, do you have any old leather straps lying around that you're not using?"

He raises an enquiring brow. "Probably. What for?"

"It's Zavier's birthday on Thursday, and I want to try and make him a present. He made me this bracelet with his mother's precious stones for my birthday," I say, holding out my wrist to show him, even though I know he's already seen my bracelet many times before. "And I thought, being as I might never see him again after this week, I'd like to make him a bracelet or a necklace. At least it'll give him something to remember me by." I reach into my pocket and pull out my and Zavier's magic rock. "I want to use this."

Seeming curious, Jax takes the rock from my hand. "What is this?" he asks, twirling it around in his fingers.

"I don't actually know. Zavier and I found it when we were kids. We called it our magic rock. It's something we've always passed back and forth to each other during our times of need, telling each other that it will keep us safe." I blush. "I know it sounds lame, and we don't actually believe it's magic, but I know it will really mean something to him if I make something special out of it."

A thoughtful look crosses Jax's face. "He means a lot to you, doesn't he?"

"He does," I answer. "He's my best friend, and up until recently, he was my only friend."

"Would you mind if I hold onto this for today?" he asks, referring to the rock. "I have an idea."

I feel anxious about letting him take it. It's special to me, and I don't want it getting lost, but I nod, regardless.

"I'm sorry, I really can't stay," he apologises. "I have an intense training session to run this morning. But I promise I'll pop in later this evening if I can, okay?"

I nod. "Okay."

After Jax leaves, I slide back down into a more comfortable position. His visit might have been short, but at least it was sweet. Lexan's visit last night had been disastrous. He'd seemed all out of sorts. At first, he paced up and down the side of my bed, looking as if he wanted to say something important to me, but couldn't. I'd wondered if he was gearing up to tell me he's having a secret affair with my mum. He didn't end up saying, and I didn't want to prompt him on the off chance I was wrong.

I was also aware he might be acting strangely towards me because he's upset with the position I've put everyone in. Just knowing about my secret affair with Alex could easily get them all killed by association. The Commander would say they were accessories after the fact.

He'd seemed uncomfortable looking at me too, and I'd wished I'd kept my glasses and bandana on, because I wasn't sure if it was my colouring making him feel awkward.

Towards the end of his visit, his demeanour towards me warmed again—maybe even a little too much—and things became awkward in the opposite way. He gave me an affectionate kiss on the cheek and told me he loved me very, very much, and made me promise that I will take care of myself and the babies. It wasn't meant in a creepy, pervy way, more like in a parental kind of way, but it still felt weird because he is not my parent, and although I've always admired him for what he's done for Zavier over the years, I didn't really think we were *that* close. He's only ever treated me like Zavier's friend.

It wasn't until after Lexan left, and I had time to properly rehash his visit, that I started to freak out and question things further. Lexan's old words replayed in my head. "I'm not told much. Krista tends to leave me in the dark. It's a bit of a one-sided relationship that way, always has been."

Is Lexan my father? It would explain my colouring. In the end, I'd brushed the thought aside. *If Lexan's my biological father, I'm sure I would have been told before now.*

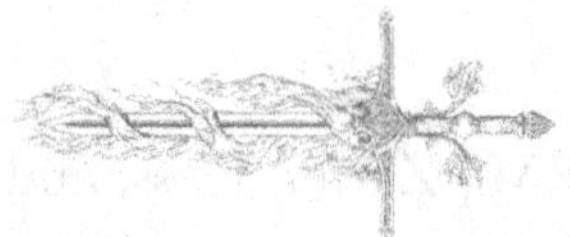

RJ comes in to see me during his lunch break. He slides his thick-rimmed glasses up the ridge of his nose, hiding his darting eyes behind the lenses. "Jax says you'll be leaving this weekend," he says robotically, but despite his hollow words, something in the way his body jitters tells me he's sad about seeing me go. "I made you something to take with you." He hands me a framed A4-sized painting of Jax with Sphinx, and I blush. "I thought you might miss Jax when you are gone," he says. "Sylvie says Jax will miss you."

"Thank you, RJ," I say, genuinely delighted. "I'm glad I got to meet you. You're a good Zeek and a great friend."

I stare at the portrait in awe. I can't believe I get to keep this. It must have taken him forever to paint. He's done such an amazing job; it's so lifelike. He's even managed to capture Jax's violet eyes, right down to the sparkle. *I love those eyes.*

"About Jax…" I say, broaching a topic that has been gnawing at me ever since our last conversation, "and Alex for that matter… Do you think they're only drawn to me because of my twin connection?"

"I don't know Alex well enough to speak for him, but I know Jax, and his feelings run deep. I'm certain the twin connection helped draw him to you initially, but there still has to be an attraction, and there are many other emotions that come into play. Many."

RJ doesn't say anymore on the subject, nor does he linger. He says goodbye and good luck and then heads back out with flushed cheeks.

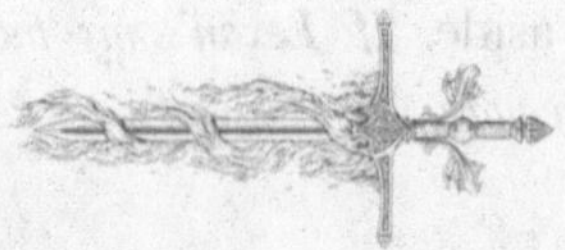

At around seven P.M., Zavier, Floss, and Minty come in to see me. They apologise about not coming the night before. Apparently, Rae had rounded up Floss and threatened her to give up my whereabouts. *That wretched woman is like a dog to a bone.*

"Don't worry, we haven't seen her or any of her gang around tonight. We made absolutely certain we weren't being followed before coming here," Minty assures me.

Zavier places my pack on one of the chairs, and I sigh a breath of relief. "Lexan told me to bring this."

Thank goodness he got it here okay. Little does he—or anyone else— know there's a jar of red vertic switz ink hidden inside the lining.

"Did Lexan say anything about the visit?" I ask curiously.

"No why? Was there something else I was supposed to bring?"

I shake my head. "No. He was acting a bit weird when he came in last night, that's all."

Zavier steps up to my bedside. "Weird, like how?"

"I'm not sure exactly. At a guess, I'd say he's probably upset that my indiscretions have put you all in extreme danger…" I pause a moment. "Which is fair. I really shouldn't have involved you all."

Floss snorts. "Like he can talk."

Zavier shoots her a look of warning, and she shrugs it off like she couldn't care less.

"Lexan's having an affair with our mum, isn't he," I say.

Zavier chokes on a response.

"I think you should tell her," Floss says, and Zavier looks as if he wants to take her outside and strangle her. "I think she has a right to know the truth before she goes."

"It's not up to me to tell her, it's up to Lexan," Zavier says through gritted teeth. "And you should learn to keep your big mouth shut."

"She's half figured it out for herself," Floss argues. "Go on and tell her the rest."

"What's going on here?" I sit up straight. "What aren't you telling me, Zavier?"

His eyes gaze into mine and he bites his lower lip with a look of angst.

"What aren't you telling me?" I urge, although I'm afraid I already know the answer.

"At this point, I suggest you tell her," Minty advises. "She's already in far more danger than the rest of us anyway, and Floss is right. She does deserve to know the truth before she goes."

Zavier reluctantly nods and then sucks in a breath. "Lexan is…" His eyes won't meet mine. "Uh…he's…"

"He's our father," Floss finishes for him. "He and our mother have been sleeping together for years."

It feels like I've been delivered a solid blow to my chest, and for a second, I forget to breathe.

"Wow, Floss, real smooth," Zavier says accusingly.

"Hey, at least I got all of my words out instead of stuttering like an idiot."

"You two stop it right now!" Minty's voice blasts. "Take a look at Harlow."

Hot tears spill down my cheeks. *Lexan is my father.*

Why was Floss told the truth, but I wasn't? How come Minty knows? I'm more hurt by their secrecy than the revelation itself. Everyone knew the truth, but nobody bothered to tell me.

I am not the one-off defective freak I'd always thought I was, I'm the product of an inter-colour affair. No wonder Floss had been so quick to warn me off Jax; she knew the truth about why we'd turned out this way, which meant she knew what the outcome of an inter-colour relationship looked like. I am the sorry outcome, and now I've gone and made the same terrible mistake—*only worse*. Chances are my children won't fit into any mould. They won't fit anywhere—except maybe the forest, and this is assuming Dakari would allow two half-Vallon babies to stay. The worst thing is, I can't even guarantee they won't pose a threat to his tribe, because I know for certain one of my children has the grave potential of being a threat. *He is a killer, my killer, who is now going to be born as my son.*

I haven't thought much about this since the day RJ served me the terrible news. I've been in denial, but now it's like everything is pushing down on top of me, threatening to suffocate me.

"Harlow." Zavier cups my good shoulder. "Harlow, I'm so sorry you had to find out like this. Are you okay?"

"How could you keep this from me?" I let out a sob. "You're supposed to be my best friend."

"We are best friends. I love you to pieces. You mean everything to me. I was only trying to protect you."

"For frost's sake," Floss curses behind him, and then storms out.

Minty gives Zavier a shove. "Zavier don't be an insensitive idiot. Go after her. I'll stay here with Harlow."

"No, stuff Floss. I'm livid with her." His forehead pinches. "She did this on purpose to cause problems between Harlow and me."

"Harlow had a right to know," Minty presses. "She really should have been told before now, and that's on Lexan. He obviously wanted to tell her last night, but he couldn't bring himself to do it. Floss is right, it's better that Harlow knows the truth before she goes."

"Whatever. If you want to play team Floss, then you go after her," Zavier says resentfully. "I came here to see Harlow. I've only got her around for a few more days."

I feel like saying, guys, I'm right here, stop speaking about me like I'm not, but I can hardly bring myself to breathe, let alone speak.

"You're such a fool," Minty says with frustration, and then turns to give my arm a light friendly squeeze. "I'm going to go and find your sister." The tone she uses with me is much lighter than the tone she just used on Zavier. It's actually far more friendly than I would have expected coming from Minty. "I'll be back soon, okay?"

Minty isn't the affectionate type, especially towards me. *She must be warming to me a little.* Trust it, I've finally managed to crack through that hard shell of hers, and now I'm leaving the caves for good.

"Harlow," Zavier's attention is back on me. "Are you okay?"

"How long have you known?"

He winces, appearing afraid to answer. "Since Lexan took me in when I was a kid. He told me the truth, trusting I would help to look out for you girls."

"Is that why you became my friend? You were simply doing it as a favour to Lexan?" I feel like I've been gutted with a blunt knife. *Ouch.* Zavier was the only Zeek kind enough to befriend me when none of the other Pastels would. I've always loved him for this, but now I feel like I've been scammed.

"No, of course not." His words come out thick and choked. "Think about what you're saying. We were inseparable long before I moved in with Lexan. I've loved being your friend. I've loved you."

"Then why didn't you tell me the truth about Lexan?"

"I was trying to protect you," he says with such pure sincerity, it's hard not to believe him. "I thought I was doing the right thing. I was trying to keep you out of danger."

"But you told Floss," I accuse.

"I didn't tell Floss. Floss figured it out. She busted them sneaking around together."

"When?"

"A few months ago, before the whole Ogre debacle."

"Nice of her to tell me," I say bitterly. "And what about Minty? How come she was told, yet I wasn't?"

"She wasn't meant to be told, and I was completely against telling her, but Lexan filled her in anyway, believing he was doing me a favour." Zavier lets out an accentuated sigh. "Minty found out Floss had been staying in my nook, and presumed we were sleeping together, so Lexan set her straight about Floss being his daughter to get Minty off my case."

"Were you sleeping together?" I ask, my curiosity now piqued. I know this part of the story isn't really any of my business, but regardless, I'd like to know the answer. It was around the time of Ogre's funeral that Floss started dropping hints about her feelings towards Zavier.

A flash of guilt crosses Zavier's face. "No." His eyes evade mine. "Not back then."

"Not then, but you are now?" I should leave it alone, but I can't. I feel jealous. Not because I want Zavier for myself in that way, but because I feel like my best friend is being stolen away by my sister. It's stupid and I know it. I should be happy for them. I want to be happy for them, but it's hard, especially now when I'm so mad at them both about other things. *They are sharing secrets I'm not a part of. I'm on the outer.*

"It only happened once." He swallows and then adds, "Last night, actually."

"And Minty obviously knows," I say. "That's why she wanted you to go after her."

"I'm sorry. I didn't want you to find out like this."

I cast him an irritated glance. "You mean you didn't want me to find out at all."

"Maybe." He gives a sheepish look. "I still don't know how I feel about Floss. It's complicated. Are you mad? You seem mad."

"I'm mad that you didn't tell me about Lexan." I pause a beat and then add, "But I'm not mad about you and Floss." I mostly mean it, or at least, *I want to mean it.* "I have to admit," I continue, "it does make me feel a little weird inside. I knew she liked you, I mentioned it to you the other day, but I wasn't sure if you felt the same way. Clearly you don't even know the answer to that question yourself."

"You are the one I've always been in love with," he says, with a small flicker of yearning in his eyes. "You're the one I wanted."

I hadn't expected him to come back at me with this. Now I feel bad. I don't know what to say in return without hurting him. I do love him—he's my best friend, and he's cute—but I think of him more like a brother than a lover.

"Don't worry," he says, clearly picking up on my anxious vibe. "I know where I stand with you, and I'd rather not make things any more complicated between us before you leave. I'd like to part on good terms." He pauses, and then adds, "On that note..." An uneasy, almost delirious laugh escapes him. "I have something else I need to tell you, something I *had* actually planned on telling you today, before I got forced into telling you everything else." He leaves my bedside to go and grab my pack. "Do you remember the time when you woke up from your coma, and you thought everyone was acting weird?"

I think back and nod. "*Yeah...*"

"It was because your dad—I mean Saul—had been attacked by a Vallon who gave him these." He opens up the pack and grabs out a rag, which he unwraps to reveal a shining red voltz.

I snatch the voltz from his hand. It feels much warmer than I'd expected. "Why was Saul given this?"

"The Vallon knew you were in a coma—clearly you must have told Alex as Ruby—and he warned Saul if he didn't use the voltz on you, he would come back and kill him. I hadn't believed Saul at the time when he'd told me, I thought he was making the whole thing up, but after hearing your story about your relationship with Alex, I've come to realise he was indeed telling the truth."

My heart leaps into my throat. "Does this mean Saul knows about Alex?"

"I don't think Saul really knew what was going on, and I don't think he wanted any part in it. He just off-loaded the voltz to me and asked that I use them on you. All Saul was worried about was protecting his own arse."

More dots connect.

"That's why he came in to see me that night, I knew it was out of character for him to visit me." I ball my blanket up in my fist, feeling angry at myself for all those years I wasted craving his acceptance, unaware he wasn't my real father. "And this also explains why he'd been so interested in you and all of your movements for the week following. I thought it was weird for him to be so interested in you all of a sudden."

A flash of Alex enters my mind, and my heart comes to a standstill. This information being brought to light changes everything. Alex helped bring me back from my coma. He'd risked himself to save the Harlow side of me before we'd ever even met here on Zadok.

That's why he hadn't come to see me until the earlier hours of the next morning. He'd told me he'd run into a few obstacles back home. I hadn't realised the obstacle had been Saul, but it makes sense now. Alex knew who Saul was when he'd told me to hide in the hunting sled. When I'd questioned him about knowing Saul, he'd said, "It's a hunter thing", which I'd found suspect, but I'd blown it off. There were more pressing issues at hand.

Guilt fills me. To think, I was *so* angry with Alex for standing me up, I'd told him off. Little did I know he'd been busy saving me. *Why didn't he say something? He should have told me.* I've spent all this time resenting him with a passion. I'd convinced myself that he never truly cared about me, that he'd used me and left me to die—and now I find out about this. *Damn it, Alex!* I feel completely guilt-ridden.

My emotions spike all over the place. Had Alex come to fetch me straight away, instead of waiting for over six weeks, I would have happily gone with him believing it was the right choice, but so much has changed these past two months, and my feelings towards Jax have grown exponentially. While human Alex is fun, cheeky and openly affectionate, the Slater side of him seems harder and scarier. Jax, on the other hand, is honourable and true. I admire him and his goals, and I share his beliefs.

Unaware of where my thoughts have taken me, Zavier takes my hand, and I can see the apology in his eyes before he says it. "I'm sorry I kept this from you until now. I don't really know why I did." His words are low pitched and filled with regret.

"Who else knows about the voltz?"

"I had to tell Minty and Floss last night, but other than them, only Saul."

"What about Jax?" I ask curiously. "He was at the medical chamber when the commotion broke out, wasn't he? I thought I heard his voice." I also remember how distracted he was when I saw him. He'd seemed on edge, all warrior, with his guard up.

"He was there, but we managed to keep the voltz hidden from him. He knew Saul and I were up to something suspicious; although he didn't know what." Zavier gives my hand a light squeeze. "You have no idea how nervous I was about using the voltz on you. I had to take a leap of faith and hope and pray I was doing the right thing."

More conflicting emotions flood through me. I might be angry at Zavier for not telling me about Lexan, but he has risked a lot for me lately. He's actually been a much better friend to me than I've been to him.

"Thank you for everything you've done for me lately," I say, and Zavier blinks in astonishment. "I know you've taken a lot of risks to help keep me safe, and I want you to know I appreciate it." I swallow hard against the lump in my throat. "I wish you'd told me about Lexan earlier. I'm still upset with you over that, but I don't want to fight, not when we have such little time left."

"What about everything else?" His hand tenses nervously.

"Everything else I can forgive you for. I've kept my fair share of secrets lately too, but for you to keep my real father a secret from me my whole life cuts deep. Especially when you were aware how much Saul's psychological and emotional abuse affected my childhood."

"I'm sorry. I thought I was protecting you. Lexan made me promise I would never tell another living soul."

"I'm mad at him too," I say accusingly. "And my mother. Floss and I should have been told a long time ago."

I'd already resented my mother before learning this, but now I almost hate her. I can't believe she let that arsehole treat us the way he did, especially when he wasn't our biological father. *I wonder if he knows the truth and if this is why he's always been so callous towards us.*

"What can I do to make things right?" Zavier asks. "I don't want us to part on bad terms. Even if you're not going to be around, you're still my best friend, and I want it to stay that way—always."

"Just give me a couple of days alone to think things through. I'm feeling pretty mixed up right now, and I don't want to say anything I might regret. It's your birthday on Thursday, tell the others to come in with you and we'll do a little medical chamber party." I force a smile. "But for now, you should really go and fix things with Floss. I don't believe she was trying to cause trouble. I think she honestly thought I should know the truth."

"You want me to leave now? Is this what you are saying?"

"Please," I say, feeling the burn of hot tears behind my eyes. "I promise things will be okay between us on Thursday, just give me some time to process everything."

He leans down and kisses my cheek. "I don't want us to lose our friendship."

"Don't worry, we won't."

As soon as he leaves, I burst into tears. It seems like all I ever do is cry lately. I need to toughen up. I never knew life could be this damn complicated—that it could hurt this much.

After half an hour of sobbing my heart out, Jax and Oscar enter, and like a child, I yank the blanket up over my head.

"What are you doing?" Jax asks, sounding amused, but as he peels the blanket back, his face registers shock. I can only imagine how awful I look. "What's wrong?" he asks.

"Don't worry about it. It's nothing, I'm fine."

He cocks his head. "I don't believe you, Harlow. Come on, talk to me."

"I might go and get a cup of bean-brew," Oscar says, clearly looking for an excuse to duck out. "Do either of you want one?"

We both answer, "No."

Once Oscar's gone, Jax's lowers the bed rail and his strong arms carefully scoop me up, placing me on the edge of the bed in a seated position. After this he drags a chair across, facing it opposite me, and sits so close his legs interlace with mine. Despite my current state of depression, warm tingles swirl through me at his touch.

Eyes now on mine, he reaches out to clasp my hand and tenderly strokes it with his thumb. "Tell me what's wrong."

"I can't," I say, and then burst into tears.

My cheeks burn with embarrassment. I don't want him to see me this way, but my emotions are too built up inside to control.

When I don't stop crying, he releases my hand and cups my chin, "Hey," he says, leaning in closer. "Harlow, please, why won't you trust me?"

The feel of his hands on me, and his warm breath on my face—as well as having his legs touching mine—is enough to send my entire body into a frenzy. I might not be sure how I feel about Alex, but I know for certain how I feel about Jax. I would give anything to be able to wrap my arms around him and pull him in for a kiss.

If only it wasn't too late.

"It's an incriminating story. If I tell you and it's discovered, it'll make you an accessory," I say, drawing back from him, before I make an impulsive decision I'll live to regret.

He lets out a light, non-humorous laugh, "All of your stories seem to be incriminating stories." He gets up, pushes the chair back and parks himself on the bed next to me. "I'm already harbouring a number of your secrets, so why not tell me the rest?"

I fidget nervously. "If I do tell you, will you promise to keep it to yourself? I don't want anyone else to find out the truth."

"Of course."

"I found out Saul's not my real father. Lexan is." Jax looks surprised but not completely shocked. "My whole existence has been a lie."

"Come here." He wraps his arms around me, making sure to be careful of my bad shoulder. "I'm sorry, Harlow."

His embrace feels warm, nice, and not at all rigid like usual. *It feels a little too nice.* My emotions spike out of control again. All of Jax's walls are down, and he's not afraid to show me he cares. I can't believe after everything I've put him through, he still cares enough to console me in this warm and affectionate way.

"Zavier filled me in on a lot of other things too," I say, wiping my wet cheeks with my sleeve. "But learning Lexan is my real father, and I've never been told, is what's hurting me the most. The worst thing is, Zavier has known about this ever since he was a young kid, yet he's kept it to himself until now. He says he didn't tell me because he was trying to protect me."

Jax's eyes grow large with sympathy. "Zavier and I might not see eye to eye, but I can tell he really cares about you, and if he says he was keeping this secret from you to protect you, then I believe he thinks he was doing the right thing, whether it is or not."

Jax holds me in his strong arms for a long moment while I struggle with my inner turmoil. It hurts being this close to him, knowing I can never be with him.

Eventually, the yearning becomes too much, and I draw my body back from his. "Can you pass me my pack please," I say, pointing to it.

His arms leave me to reach for it, and after handing it to me, I unzip the side and pull out one of the glowing rags to unravel.

"Why do you have that?" He stares questioningly at the voltz. "Did he give it to you?" I notice he doesn't refer to Alex by his name.

"Not exactly. Alex gave them to Saul when I was in the coma. He ordered Saul to use the voltz on me or he'd be back to kill him. Zavier said you knew something sketchy was going on, but you didn't know what. He said he didn't fully believe Saul's story about the Vallon either, until he found out I was pregnant to one."

Jax's relaxed body goes back to being tense and stiff, as I thought it might. "Does this mean Saul knows about you and…Alex?"

"No. Zavier says Saul didn't really know what was going on. Saul just off-loaded the voltz onto Zavier and told him to use them on me. He was probably pleased to be able to use Zavier as his fall guy in case the voltz were discovered. All Saul was worried about was saving his own hide."

Jax's face darkens, and he seems to be considering something as he stares intently at the voltz. "And Saul's never questioned you about the incident?"

"No, he's never mentioned a word about it."

"If a Vallon was showing any kind of interest in my daughter, I'd be fighting for answers."

I shrug with my good shoulder. "Chances are Saul is aware I'm not really his daughter. That's probably why his care factor towards me is zero."

"It doesn't matter if he's your real father or not. If he's chosen to stay with your mother and help raise you, then he should be there for you one hundred percent." Anger pours off Jax in waves. "You don't need to share the same blood to be a good parent, you just need to be there and have a heart."

I blink, feeling too shocked to speak. I'm not sure if his words hold double meaning, or if I'm reading more into this than I should because of my out-of-control feelings for him.

"Are the voltz of any use to you?" I ask, desperate to break the tension. "Because you can have them. Use them as you please. I don't have any use for them."

"That reminds me," he says, his attention snapping back to me. "I have something to give you." He reaches into his pocket. "I hope you don't mind, but I had an idea, and I went with it." He pulls out two leather cord necklaces, both of which share two separate halves of my and Zavier's magic rock. "I figured this way it'll keep you both safe, and it gives you something to remember each other by."

"They're like friendship necklaces," I say, thinking back to a heart-shaped friendship necklace Jade and I had shared in the human world. My half of the heart had FRI, and hers had ENDS. I accidentally lost my half, and she'd never let me forget it. I'll make sure I don't lose this one.

"Thanks, Jax, this was a great idea. I love them, and I know he will too." Acting before thinking, I lean in to give him a hug. He stiffens for a second but slowly relaxes and hugs me back with warmth.

I hear the wooden door creak as Oscar enters. "Should I come back later?" he asks.

Jax releases me from his arms, and I draw back with hot cheeks. "No, stay," Jax tells him. "I should really get going. I've still got heaps of things to do before tomorrow." His violet eyes gaze into mine with a hint of compassion. "Are you going to be okay?"

I sneakily slip him the two glowing rags with the voltz. "I'll be okay," I say, forcing a smile. "Thanks for being here for me, it means a lot."

He stealthily shoves the voltz into his pocket and stands. "I'm always around if you need me, Harlow. Remember that. All you have to do is ask."

25

GOODBYE, MY FRIENDS

-HARLOW-

I don't get any visitors over the next few days, not even Jax. Zavier had been kind enough to stuff a few new SCI-FI books in my pack as hidden extras. I'd smiled when I found them and got stuck into one right away. He knows me too well. He really is the greatest bestie ever. I don't know what I'll do without him. The resentment I'd felt towards him lifts and is replaced with gratitude. Jax was right. Zavier honestly would have thought he was doing the right thing by keeping me in the dark about Lexan. I still don't agree with his decision, but I've chosen to accept it.

The only two Zeeks I get to see are Oscar and Sylvie. Poor

Sylvie; I feel sorry for her. She's had to do a lot of extra shifts because of me. She, Tandy, and RJ are the only ones working in the medical chamber whom Jax deems trustworthy. She insists she doesn't mind doing the extra hours and assures me she's being heavily compensated for it, but I still feel awful about it all the same.

Jax must be shelling out a lot of goods for my safety lately. I'm sure I'd probably faint if knew what he'd offered Dakari in order for me to be able to stay in Spring for the fortnight. He is too kind to me. I really don't deserve it.

"Hey, Red Hot," Oscar says, wearing a cheeky grin. He steps up to my bedside. "How's the shoulder?" He and I have been chatting a lot during the evenings. I like Oscar. He's a flirt and very full of himself, but his happy-go-lucky nature often reminds me of the charming side of Alex I had fallen for. I find myself missing that side of Alex, but I've been too burnt by his other less-appealing side to still feel the same affection for him I once had. He may have saved my life, and I'm grateful, but it doesn't change the fact that he flew off in a terrifying fit of rage and left me alone and heartbroken in the middle of the danger zone. Whether he came back or not is irrelevant. What he did was selfish and careless. It was still a good fifteen minutes before Jax found me, and anything could have happened during that time. I'm just lucky it was Jax who found me first and not a predator.

"Jax said to say sorry he hasn't come in to see you the past few days, but he's copping a lot of heat at the moment and is being heavily watched."

"That's okay." I fake a carefree smile, but I'm afraid my disappointment bleeds through.

"You wouldn't want to see him at the moment anyway, trust me." Oscar gives an exaggerated wink. "In all the years I've known Jax, I've never seen him this angry—Zannah either. They are both walking around like ticking time bombs."

I try digging for a bit more information, but Oscar evades my questions, telling me he'd rather leave the details for Jax to share.

I sigh. This means I'll probably never find out.

Leaving the topic of Jax's current dilemma, Oscar fills me in on some of the controversial conversations that had taken place at Haydn and Stace's funeral the other day. He says nobody believed the cover story they concocted about the couple killing each other in a heated argument. "There was a lot of whispering and finger pointing during the service, especially from Roc, Austin, and Feeney. They were all part of Nix's gang, and they're a tight bunch."

"Well, what's going to happen?" I ask.

Oscar shrugs, a lopsided grin tugging at his mouth. "Nothing. Those Zeeks can believe whatever they want. Nobody has any proof."

He also mentions that Feeney had sworn black and blue he'd seen a couple of fish-folk swimming past the side of the boat.

I'd learnt about the fish-folk at school. Some swear they are real, while others swear they're a myth. They are the equivalent to human mermaids, only they appear far less friendly going by the creepy drawings I've seen.

"Do you believe him?" I ask.

Oscar laughs. "No, not at all. Feeney will say anything for a rise. He loves the attention."

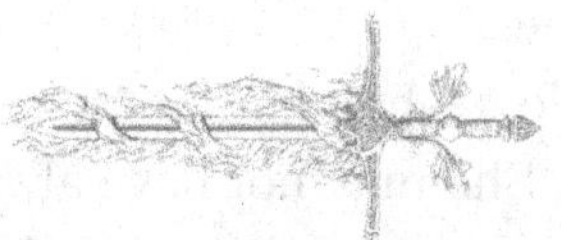

By Thursday, I'm actually looking forward to seeing Zavier again. He and Floss are the first to enter, followed by Minty, Tatum, and Lexan. I hadn't known Lexan was coming. I fidget awkwardly in his presence. I don't know how to act around him now that I know the truth. And to think, I'd wished I had a father figure like Lexan. A father who would love and support me no matter what— just as Lexan has always done for Zavier. Never in a million years would I have guessed Lexan was my actual dad. I begrudge all of those years of love and support I've missed out on. He should have told me. I feel completely ripped off.

I smile and say, "Hi," hiding my true feelings behind an indifferent expression. It's best to keep things civil. I'll be gone the day after tomorrow, and I suppose it's good of him to have made the effort to be here.

Minty and Tatum have a present for me. "This isn't how it's supposed to work," I tell them. "It's Zavier's birthday, not mine."

Tatum pulls an embarrassed, toothy expression. "Just to clarify, Minty picked the present."

I open the wrapping paper to find a book. It's called Frenemies. I laugh. "It's very fitting, thank you."

When I call Zavier over to give him his present, Floss' eyes flash with jealousy. Worst of all, I know she's going to be even more jealous when she sees what the present is, but Zavier is still my best friend, and this shouldn't have to change because the dynamics of their relationship have changed.

"I'm sorry, I didn't wrap it," I say, pulling the leather corded necklaces out of my pocket. "I figured we should both be kept safe, so I got it halved." I've totally stolen Jax's line and credit and passed it off as my own, but I know if I told Zavier who'd come up with the idea and gotten it made, he'd probably refuse to wear it out of spite. He smiles wholeheartedly and slips one over his head before sliding the other one over mine.

My eyes dart to Floss when he does this. I shouldn't really have to feel guilty, but I do. She may not have always been the best sister to me, but I don't want to see her hurt. I do love her.

"Floss, come here." I beckon her over.

She looks unenthused but strolls over, anyway.

When she gets close enough, I reach for her hand. "I know we haven't always been close," I say. "But I blame that on Saul. He pitted us against each other from a young age." The resentful part that still lurks within me hopes Lexan hears this and feels bad about it. "I do really love you, and I am going to miss you."

Floss' lower lip quivers and I can tell she is on the verge of tears. "It's hard to love you when I'm so jealous of you," she admits.

I find this perplexing. "I don't understand why you're jealous of me. I'm not someone you should be jealous of. My life is a mess."

"You have an allure about you that I don't. Even now, when you are pregnant to our enemy, you still have two Zeek guys trying to win you over." She shoots Zavier a pained, resentful look. "Nobody even likes me."

My eyes flick to Zavier's too. *Please Zavier, take the hint,* I beg inside my head. *Show her some affection. There's nothing I can say that'll make her feel better. She needs you to show her that you care.*

Responding as if he received my inner message loud and clear, Zavier wraps his hand around Floss' free one.

"It's not true," he tells her. "I like you."

Her frown turns upside down within an instant.

The evening takes a nicer, lighter turn after this. Everyone, including Minty—I blink in shock—gives Floss a hug, and tells her that they care.

Soon we all end up chatting as a group, sharing memories, gossip, and telling jokes. Lexan never mentions anything about being my father, and I'm glad. I'd rather not get into it. He acts like nothing has changed, and I follow suit.

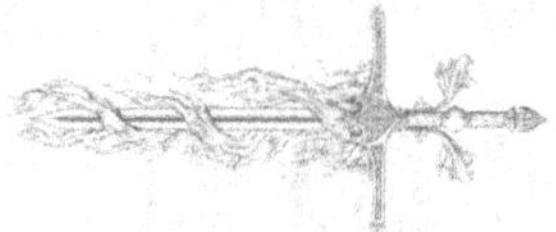

The next day rolls over and I receive another visit from Zavier who has come to give me my final goodbye. I let him know I was proud of him for showing Floss the affection she was craving last night, and he tells me they've had a heart-to-heart, and he's going to try and give her a fair shot. He says their colour difference is an issue and bothers him a little bit, but he figures if Lexan and Krista have managed to make their secret relationship work all these years, then he doesn't see why he and Floss can't make it work too.

I still haven't seen Jax since the night he caught me crying, and I can't help but feel disappointed. As wrong as it is, I'd secretly hoped I'd get to spend a little more time with him.

It's probably better this way, I tell myself. *You would have only grown more attached, which would make parting with him even harder.*

2 6

AN IDEA TO SELL

-HARLOW-

It's Zannah who wakes me up early the next morning. She reefs back my blanket while I'm still sleeping, scaring me half to death.

"You're awful!" Oscar mutters under his breath.

"It's time to get you dressed," Zannah says matter-of-factly. "Jax sent me in to help." Her eyes flick in Oscar's direction, and I detect a snarky glint behind them. "He didn't trust Oscar's hands not to slip."

Oscar scoffs in annoyance. "You're so full of it, Zannah." He stands, casts her an irritated glance, and then leaves.

My arm isn't as sore as it was, so I don't need as much help this time around, but my tummy has grown a lot in a week, which Zannah is very eager to point out as she buttons up her pants on me.

"I want all of these items sent back with Jax, got it? You're not keeping any of them."

I suppress an eye roll. "The thought never even crossed my mind," I say. "Besides, I don't think these clothes will be suitable for where I'm going. I hear it's like a furnace in Summer."

"Yeah, we'll see," she says with annoyance.

Okay... Whatever that means? I don't bother to bite this time around, I'm too tired to play her games.

As soon as I've finished getting ready, Zannah grabs my pack, and we meet Oscar out in the main medical chamber.

"Here you go, Slave-boy, you can do the honours. My job here is done." Zannah hands Oscar my pack to carry, and he slings it over his shoulder with ease.

"See you again in two-and-a-half weeks," she shouts, her back now to me as she struts off. The tone she uses makes it sound like a threat.

"Can you imagine dealing with that thing on a daily basis?" Oscar remarks, and I laugh at his use of the word "thing". I also laugh inside at the thought of her bra being glued to his warrior vest, but I keep this little piece of amusement to myself. I'm not sure which of the two would have been more upset about it, *him or her?*

Oscar spends our whole walk to the warrior cavern bitching about Zannah. He says he's had a gutful of her constant bitchy attitude and snarky remarks. He also says if she was one of the guys, he would have thumped her by now.

"She's just so full of herself," is what he boils it all down to, and again I laugh inside. It's like the pot calling the kettle black.

As we step inside the warrior cavern, I take one look at Jax, and my knees grow weak. The few days apart seemed to have made my feelings for him grow stronger, not weaker. *Damn.*

His eyes meet mine and he smiles, revealing his dimples. "Are you all set?" he asks.

"I think so." My tummy does a flip, not only because I'm talking to Jax, but because it feels weird to think this is my final moment in the caves.

Oscar tosses my pack into the back of the sled. "Be safe!" he tells Jax. "I'm going to go have a few hours rest and then I'll be alright to cover for tonight."

Jax nods. "Thanks. Add it to the list of IOUs."

"I'm starting to run out of paper," Oscar says teasingly, and then he gazes over at me. "I'll see you again at send-off."

I say bye to Oscar and then hop into the sled. Jax chucks in a few extra things, finishes hooking up the huskens, and then slides in beside me. "Hooray for the weekend," he says, and I note tension straining his voice. "I've never been so keen to leave this place."

It's still dark outside and not nearly as nice as last time. Sleet falls from the sky and there's a harsh chilly wind gusting which blows the frozen rain straight towards our faces.

"Here, take this." Jax hands me his leather shield to use as a blockade for my face.

"What about you?" I ask. "What about your face?"

"I'll be okay."

It feels like forever until we cross the Spring border. When we cross, I place Jax's shield down and sigh in relief.

"Thank God that's over," I say and Jax lets out a small chuckle.

His face is splotched red from being exposed to the harsh conditions. He still looks good, though. *More than good.* I'm certain he could fall face first in a mud puddle and still look amazing.

Our trip through the forest is void of any conversation. Jax isn't a big talker at the best of times, but I'd hoped we'd get to chat a little more given it's the last time we'll get to spend together alone. I consider striking a conversation, but he seems too preoccupied with his thoughts to speak.

After parking the sled, he automatically helps to lift me out. He also helps me slip off Zannah's jacket before leaving my side to unhook the huskens. They pant excitedly at his side as he comes back to grab the packs. He slings my pack over one shoulder and another—much heavier looking pack—over the other.

I feel useless. "Can I help at all?"

"No, it's fine. I've got it."

After trekking a whole kilometre on foot with only the sounds of birds singing and the crunching of dead leaves under our feet, I ask, "Is everything okay?"

"Yeah, why?"

I slide my hands into my pants pockets to avoid fidgeting. "I don't know, it's just… You haven't really said much."

"It's been a rough few days, and I have a tendency to keep rehashing things." He rolls his shoulders, like he's trying to ease the tension. "I'm sorry. I haven't meant to seem distant."

Rehashing what? I wish he would elaborate. I don't want to sound nosey by prying. "Do you want to talk about it?"

There's a pause. "No, not really." His hesitancy tells me his issues have something to do with me. "It's mostly politics related," he says evasively.

"And a little bit Harlow related?" I press.

"Maybe a little bit." Despite the smile he offers, I can feel tension circling within him, although I'm fairly certain it's not directed towards me personally. "You're out of the caves and safe for now, which has been my main priority."

"What about you? Are you safe? Oscar said you were copping a lot of heat."

He gives a slight tilt of the head. "For now."

I'm not reassured. "What does 'for now' mean?"

"It means I have a lot of tough decisions to make soon, but I don't really want to talk about any of those right now. I want a night off where I'm not the Chief Warrior or the Commander's son. I want to have a night where I'm just Jax." His tone is frustrated, but again it doesn't feel directed at me.

I understand there must be a tremendous amount of pressure on his shoulders lately, especially with all the drama I've caused on top of his usual duties. It makes total sense he would like a night off to...

Wait… Rewind. Does this mean he's staying the night? Something inside me tingles. I'd assumed he'd be dropping and running—that this was going to be the last I'd see of him until the big hand over.

"Okay…then," I say, suppressing a smile. "Just Jax it is."

After travelling a little further, I ask, "Have Destiny and Luna been injected with vertic switz ink? Is this why they are built like Magentas and have a peach hue?"

Going by their appearances, I'd come to the conclusion that they must have been a part of the vertic switz injection trial Alex had told me about. He'd said all of the injected Pastels had been executed. I'm guessing Luna and Destiny escaped before the slaughter.

"Yes, they said they were injected with the ink." He casts me an enquiring sidelong glance. "Why?"

"I know how Luna feels towards me, so I'll keep my distance, but do you think that Destiny would be prepared to talk to me?"

"Probably, why? Are you nervous about what'll happen to you if you go to Summer?"

"No…well…I am, but that's not what I want to talk to her about. I have an idea I would like to run by her. It's something I've been thinking a lot about since our last trip out here."

"What's the idea?" He eyes me with aroused interest. "Are you going to run it by me too?"

"Yes, of course, but only after I've spoken to Destiny first."

He seems stumped by this, but he doesn't press the matter.

When we reach the village, we are once again greeted by the two Yellows with their hounds. The atmosphere is a lot lighter and relaxed compared with last time. Everyone's tone and body language seems friendly as they converse. One of the Drakes even gives me a nod of acknowledgment.

They eventually allow us through unchaperoned, and we head straight over to the "hut of misfits" as Dakari had called it.

Stavros is all smiles as soon as we enter, and Acacia comes to greet me with a welcoming hug.

Stavros glances at the two packs on Jax's shoulders. "Two packs?" His brows rise. "Does this mean you are staying the night? Please tell me it does."

"I'm staying."

Stavros gives an excited fist pump. "Yes! This is going to be awesome. You'll see."

"Where should I put these?" Jax asks.

Stavros beckons us over to Atohi's old room. "I've moved Atohi in with us this morning, and I've set up his room for you two to sleep in tonight."

"But I only just told you that I was staying," Jax says.

"You know me, I always like to be prepared for the unexpected." Stavros' tone is playful. "That, and I was planning on twisting your arm if you'd decided otherwise."

We step into the room to find two single mattresses laying side by side on the floor. I blush at the implication.

Jax shoots Stavros an "I'm going to kill you" kind of look, and Stavros shrugs light heartedly with a grin. "Like I said, I like to be prepared."

After setting the packs down, we make our way back out into the common area, and Stavros urges Jax to come outside and have a look at the area he's fenced off for the huskens under the hut. I don't follow them. I figure it'll give Jax a chance to punch him.

Acacia hands me a cold drink, and we take a seat on a couple of the cushioned wooden chairs.

"Are Will and Daisy here?" I ask.

"No." Acacia runs her fingers through the ends of her thick black hair, untangling a set of knots. "Boshell has taken them out to the lake for a paddle."

"It must be a real challenge, given their frailty and lack of vision."

"It can be," she admits, "but Boshell never lets them out very far, and he usually takes one of us with him to have an extra set of eyes. We suggested that he take Luna today." She gives me a warm smile. "We figured it would give you a chance to settle in before seeing her. She can be quite confrontational when she wants to be."

"Don't worry," I say. "Confrontation isn't new for me. I seem to attract it." I pause a moment and then ask. "Does this mean Destiny is still here?"

She cocks her head in thought and then nods. "I'd say so. I haven't seen her leave the hut. She's probably having a lie-in."

I bite my lower lip in deliberation. "Do you think Destiny would be willing to have a quick talk with me before Luna gets back?"

Acacia appears staggered by my question. "Ah… I'm not entirely sure. But I can ask her if you'd like?"

I nod. "If you could, that would be great."

Acacia leaves her drink on the raw-timber coffee table and heads to the end section of the hut where Luna and Destiny reside. She's gone for a good five minutes before returning, and I imagine Destiny's answer had been, "No".

To my delight, Acacia gives a friendly smile and says, "Destiny said you can go in."

Acacia sits back down, while I duck to the other end to see Destiny. I enter her room to find her lying down on a mattress, propped up by colourful cushions. There's a book beside her, she's obviously been reading. *I wonder what kind of books she's into.*

"Hey," I say, feeling nervous all of a sudden. "How are you?"

She's not quite as amicable now that she's aware my current condition is due to my own free will. *I'm not a victim like her and Luna. I've chosen this.*

She gives me a look which says cut the niceties and get to the point. "What do you want?"

"You and Luna were injected with the vertic switz ink, weren't you?"

Her expression grows tight, and her one-word answer is clipped. "Yes."

"Do you feel stronger? Can you see better?"

"Yes." Her eyes narrow. "Is there a point to these questions?"

I take a step closer to the mattress. "I have an idea I want to run by you, but I was hoping I could ask you a couple more questions first, if you don't mind?"

She clasps her hands together and grits her teeth, seeming annoyed. "Go on then."

"How long ago were you and Luna injected? And have there been any negative side effects as well as the positive ones?"

She casts me a suspicious glance. "Why? Have you been injected too?"

"I have… Kind of. But that's not why I'm asking."

"Luna and I were injected around two years ago, and there haven't been any negative physical side effects as far as I'm aware." She pauses and then adds, "But the psychological scars of the torture we endured while we were captive in Summer remain."

"I'm sorry. That's terrible."

She brushes off my sympathy, and I don't blame her. She probably doesn't think it's genuine.

"Okay, now it's your turn to spill. What's your big idea?"

"I was tattooed," I say, "and so far, besides my wounded shoulder, I feel much stronger and healthier. I can see, smell, and hear better—"

"How nice for you. Now what's the idea?"

"Ever since I came here last time, I can't get the image of Will and Daisy out of my head. They are frail and blind, and I'm afraid they won't live very long lives." I can tell by the way Destiny's eyes flash heavenward, she's starting to lose patience with me, so I cut to the chase. "The point is, I have some leftover ink in my pack, and I was wondering whether it would be a good idea to speak to Boshell about using it on them. This way they can gain the benefits we've gained and live longer, fuller lives."

She jerks up, her face filled with anger. "Let me get this straight, you want to inject those poor innocent children with Vallon ink, is that what you're saying? This is your big idea?"

"I know it sounds terrible, but it makes sense, doesn't it? It would help them. It would make them stronger."

She makes a disgusted sound in her throat. "You're lucky Luna isn't here to hear this, or she'd pounce on you with the ferocity of a fuegor."

"But if—"

"No! I've heard enough. This conversation is over. I think it would be best if you leave now." She picks up her book and holds it up in front of her face, enforcing the fact this conversation is done.

Feeling disappointed, I leave. I'd expected her to be a little more receptive to my idea, but she's obviously been too scarred by what's happened to her to appreciate the benefits associated with what I'm suggesting. If there are no negative side effects from being injected with vertic switz ink, then I don't see why we shouldn't use it on the kids. I feel like it would be crazy not to use it on them. The ink could be their one chance at being able to live normal lives.

Jax and Stavros are back inside, sitting with Acacia, who is now cradling a very grizzly Atohi.

Jax gives me a questioning look as I plonk heavily on the seat next to his. Clearly, I must look as deflated as I feel. "I take it things didn't go well?"

I shake my head. "No. Destiny didn't like my idea."

We all get to chatting, and Stavros asks me how my goodbyes went.

I give a brief, "They went as well as they could go, I suppose."

He offers a knowing, sympathetic look. "It's hard, isn't it? Saying goodbye to your old life."

Once the others get back, Stavros pulls out a basket with a natural craft selection inside. "I'm creating a mask for tonight's festivities, who's in?"

"Me!" Will and Daisy yell excitedly, although their exhausted bodies don't show the same amount of enthusiasm.

Luna says "hello" to Jax as she helps to place Daisy down on one of the floor cushions, yet not surprisingly, she acts as if I'm not there. Going by the uncomfortable look on everybody's faces I think it bothers them much more than it bothers me. Being ostracized is *definitely* not a new experience for me, and at least this time I can see where the problem stems from. I've had Zeeks treat me far worse for much less.

Boshell pops Will down beside Daisy. "We'll make some masks together, and then you two will need an afternoon rest before going out tonight," he tells them.

Stavros gives them each a pre-carved mask, and Boshell and Luna help them rummage through the basket, picking out texture items that they think feel interesting. The kids excited yells must have alerted Destiny that they were home, and she comes wandering out to sit down on the floor near the action.

"I'm going to look fearsome," Will says, pulling out a few bluntly jagged pieces of bark.

Daisy appears to be more attracted to the softer items like feathers and flowers. "I'm going to look pretty."

Boshell gently brushes his hand along the side of her face. "You're already pretty."

She touches her face too and her expression dulls. "My face doesn't feel pretty. It doesn't feel like Luna's"

"What makes you say that Luna's face is prettier than yours, if you can't see it?" Boshell asks, and Destiny's gaze flicks to mine for a split second.

Could she be re-considering my suggestion? I really hope so.

Daisy shrugs. "Her nose feels bigger, and her eyelashes feel longer."

"A big nose is a bad thing. Your face is much prettier than mine, trust me," Luna insists.

Luna doesn't actually have a big nose. Her features are refined, typical of most Pastels, it's just bigger than Daisy's delicate button.

Stavros sets out some paint trays and brushes, before handing the rest of us a mask each to decorate. "Come on everyone, let's get creative."

Will and Daisy finger paint their masks, while the rest of us paint with brushes, and then Boshell and Luna help the kids glue on their selected bits and pieces.

Jax's paint job is much more impressive than I'd imagined it would be. As for mine—*well*—I think Jax's laugh says it all.

"Where's RJ when you need him?" I say sheepishly.

"Think of it this way," Jax teases, and it's good to see he's already slipped into his more casual self. "Compared with your self-portrait, I'd say it's a masterpiece."

"Okay, Funny Guy," I shoot back light-heartedly. "You wait. Once my mask is fully finished, it's going to be the standout piece of them all."

After everyone has completed their creations and set them out on display, Jax and I wander around the room to view them all. Jax and Acacia's are definitely the best *by far*. Stavros' is humorous, Destiny's is plain, the twins' are adorable, and as for mine—I clench my teeth together and cringe. It turns out blind children are able to paint better than I can.

Jax pauses in front of mine again, and I can tell he's trying to hide a smile. "Well, *technically* you weren't wrong. You did say it would be the standout piece."

Stavros takes one look and laughs out loud. "That's really something, isn't it?" He elbows Jax playfully. "Hey, at least you won't lose her in the crowd tonight."

We all chip in to pack up the mess, while Boshell takes the twins to bed for a rest, and Acacia makes lunch. Apparently Boshell, Luna, and the kids ate a big brunch at the river, and Destiny says she isn't hungry—that she'd rather get back to her book, which leaves only the four of us and Atohi eating together.

A light warm breeze ruffles through my dreadlocks as I take a seat out on one of the cane deckchairs. The air smells earthy and feels wholesome and refreshing. I could easily get used to living here for the next couple of weeks.

"You look different with red eyes and dreadlocks," Jax observes, and I can feel his gaze resting on me. "Actually, you look different all over."

"Different as in—bad?"

"No, just different."

I wish he would elaborate.

Midway through eating lunch, Destiny wanders out onto the deck and pauses directly across from where I'm sitting. Her peach eyes zoom in on mine. "Luna and I would like to have a talk with you."

"What… Now?" I say, taken unawares.

She nods, and I rise from my chair, feeling anxious yet hopeful all at once.

I'm praying for the sake of Boshell's kids Destiny has discussed the vertic switz idea with Luna and had a change of heart.

However, there's a chance she might only be bringing me in for an earbashing.

As I step away, Jax's hand grabs hold of my arm and gently tugs me back. His expression is concerned. "Are you alright with this?"

"I'm good," I say with a reassuring nod.

He accepts my answer and releases my arm.

Luna is standing, arms folded, at the entryway to their room. Her face is set hard like a glacier. "Destiny told me about your idea." Her words are like ice. "First of all, where'd you get the ink, and is it legit?"

"Alex left a small jar with me after he'd tattooed me. It's the real deal. It's the exact same ink he used on me."

"I take it Alex is your Vallon lover?" Her gaze flicks to my tummy accusingly, and I nod, not appreciating the reference.

"Is the ink you've been tattooed with red, or are you red because you are pregnant to a Red?"

"Both." I slip off my bracelet to reveal my tattoo, and the two girls flinch, appearing equally repulsed. I'm aware I'll be touching on a sore subject, but still I ask, "What colour where you both injected with? Was it amber?"

There's a frosty pause before Destiny answers. "Yes."

"And do you both feel stronger for it? Can you see better?"

"We were much stronger when we were first injected, but the initial effects seemed to fade rather quickly," Luna says, confirming what Alex had told me. "However, I must admit, we are still physically and visu-ally enhanced in comparison to what we were before we'd been inject-ed." She presses her lips together, her face pinched with discomfort. She's clearly pained about what she's planning on saying next. "Destiny and I have discussed your idea at length, and although we don't like the thought of injecting Boshell's children with Vallon ink, we do acknowledge that you have a valuable point, and it's worth talking to Boshell. In all fairness, it should be his choice to make, not ours."

"I don't think they should be injected like you two were," I say, and it earns me a dirty look from both of them. "I think they should be given a small tattoo like the one I have."

"Why?" Luna asks.

"A tattoo is permanent and has lasting effects whereas the injection effects fade over time. That's why you started off much stronger than you are now."

I give them a run-down of the different methods, parroting what Alex told me, and once I'm done, Destiny offers to get Boshell.

A few minutes later, Boshell enters. His enquiring eyes meeting mine. "Destiny says you have something you'd like to discuss with me?"

Destiny steps in behind him. "Brace yourself," she warns. "Harlow's idea is hair-raising, but we believe it's worth consideration."

Thanks, Destiny, I think sarcastically. My hands are already trembling with nerves as it is. I'm afraid Boshell will take offence to my suggestion. His children are his world. He's bound to be protective.

"Since meeting Will and Daisy and seeing how frail they are, I've been tossing about an idea which I believe will help to give them a better quality of life." I pause, my eyes flicking to Luna's momentarily for encouragement. She doesn't give it to me. "The only problem is..." My voice hitches. "The cure has to do with Vallons."

The word Vallons makes him jolt with a look of dread and doubt.

I hold out my wrist to show him my tattoo. "This is a vertic switz ink tattoo, and as you know, Destiny and Luna were injected with vertic switz ink. It gives you improved strength, sight, hearing, smell —the lot. We might still have the facial features of Pastels, but our physiques and senses are far superior. Vertic switz ink could be the key to a better life for your children. It could improve their body strength and all their senses."

I can see the dial ticking behind Boshell's eyes while he absorbs my suggestion. "This is all well and good," he says, a little more calmly than I'd expected. "But how am I supposed to get this vertic switz ink?"

"That's the thing," I say with burning cheeks. "I have some in my pack."

"You have some?" His eyes flick between the three of us, and his face fills with apprehension—like the idea *just got real*. "Does this mean you're offering us some of this special ink?"

I nod.

"At what price?"

"No price," I say, feeling slightly offended by his assumption.

"Is it safe to use?"

"I can't guarantee anything, only that we three are fine." I'm too afraid to make any promises for certain without hard evidence.

His brows dip, heavy with thought. "Do you really believe this ink will improve their strength and senses?"

Again, I nod. "I really do."

"We do too," Luna says, speaking for Destiny and herself. "We don't like the idea of using Vallon ink on the kids, but we do think it will give them a better quality of life. It all depends on whether you are comfortable with the idea or not."

Boshell wears the expression of a desperate man who's just caught a glimmer of hope. "I'd sell my soul to the enemy if it meant giving these kids a better chance at a normal life. If you all believe that the ink won't hurt them, then I'm all for it."

I give Boshell the same explanation I'd given Luna and Destiny regarding the tattoo verse the injection, and he agrees with me that the tattoo sounds like the better option for the kids.

"Would you mind if I let the others in on what's happening?" I ask. "I didn't want to discuss the matter with them until I'd spoken to you first."

"No, of course not," Boshell says, in an easy-going tone. "We're all family here."

I head back out to the deck and fill the others in on my idea and Boshell's response to it. Stavros and Acacia take the news well and seem to think I'm on to something positive, but Jax looks annoyed.

"It's certainly worth a shot," Stavros says, agreeing with me. "They are such cool kids. It would be nice to see them get a bit more quality to their lives."

"What's wrong Jax? Do you think it's a bad idea?" I ask meekly.

"No, the idea makes sense. I'm just surprised that you've waited up until now to mention you have vertic switz ink in your possession." His accusing gaze meets mine. "Where is it?"

"It's been sewn into the lining of my pack. I've kept it hidden."

"Has it been used on anyone else?" His tone holds as much accusation as his gaze. I don't understand why he is getting all worked up about this.

"No," I shake my head. "Only me."

"Relax, Jax." Stavros cups his shoulder and gives him a pointed look. "We're not in the caves anymore." He turns his attention to me, "Harlow, why don't you grab the jar of ink so we can all take a look at it."

"Okay." I nod agreeingly and head inside to Atohi's room.

I pick up my pack, break apart the stitches in the lining, retrieve the leather pouch, and take it straight to Jax.

"I'm sorry about before," Jax says, pulling out the seat next to him for me to sit, and I imagine Stavros must have had a word to him while I was gone. "You caught me off guard, that's all. I don't understand why you insist on keeping everything a secret from me. I'm always left finding things out with a bang when it comes to you. I keep asking you to have faith in me, yet you won't. Why do you refuse to trust me?"

"I do trust you."

"You sure have an odd way of showing it."

I bite my lip. "I'm sorry."

He sighs. "I think your idea about tattooing the kids has positive potential. I'm just praying it works the way you expect, otherwise there'll be a lot of disappointment, and everyone will blame you. I don't want that. I want you to enjoy your stay here. If you'd shared your idea with me, we could've put it forward together, and that way if it doesn't work, I could've helped shoulder the blame."

"I believe it will work," I assure him.

"I hope you're right." He opens the pouch and pulls out the small jar of fluorescent fluid. "So, this is it?" He stares curiously at the jar's contents. "I wonder what would happen to me if I used it?"

Speaking before thinking, I say, "You shouldn't use it. You'd lose the beautiful colour of your eyes."

Those beautiful eyes dart to mine in surprise.

My whole face turns to fire. *Oh my God, I can't believe I said that aloud.*

Thankfully, Boshell walks out to break the awkwardness. "Stavros said you've brought the ink out. Can I see it?"

Jax passes Boshell the small jar.

"Be careful with it," I warn them. "It's all I have, so if you drop it, and it smashes, it's gone."

Boshell stares at the jar inquisitively. "I find it hard to believe this strange ink could be the answer to all of my kids' problems." He gives the jar a shake. "I'd like it if we could get the kids tattoos done as soon as they wake up. I'd rather it be done now when everyone is here, and we have the extra support."

"It won't work instantly," I remind him. "It kicks in gradually."

"Does this mean, they won't be able to see anything at the festival tonight?" His face falls in disappointment.

"I highly doubt it." I smile sympathetically. "But they should be able to see the next one."

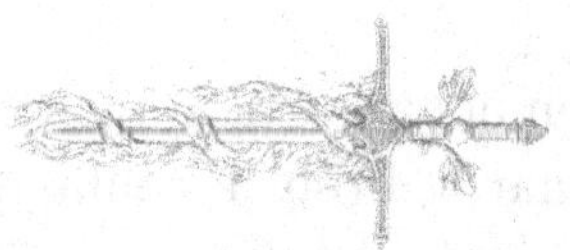

An hour later, the kids wake up, and Boshell talks to them about getting a magical tattoo that will help them feel better. Under Jax's advisement, he doesn't mention anything about improved strength, sight, hearing, and smell. Jax thought it better not to get their hopes up in case my idea doesn't turn out as expected.

Will is all for getting a tattoo, even after being told it might hurt a bit, but Daisy is scared.

"You don't have to do it." Boshell holds her in his arms, cuddling her tight. "But it should make your arms and legs work better, and ease some of the pain you feel on a daily basis."

"I will hold your hand the whole time," Luna says, taking Daisy's hand in hers.

Stavros sterilises the needle and then goes to hand it to Boshell, but Boshell shakes his head.

"I'd rather someone else do it while I cuddle them." Boshell gazes down at Luna, and I detect underlying chemistry, even though there's got to be more than a decade between them.

"Don't look at me," she says. "I might be agreeable to this idea, but I still feel extremely uncomfortable about it."

Stavros looks to me and holds out the needle.

"Uh…no. I think we've all established that my artistic skills suck."

"I'll do it." Jax walks over and takes the needle from Stavros' hand. "I just need to know what and where."

"It doesn't have to be very big," I remind them.

Jax pops two nauclea latifolia roots in Boshell's hand. "Get them to chew on these, it will dull the pain of the needle."

Boshell pops one of the roots into Daisy's mouth and hands her to Luna. "Let's do something small on their inner wrists, similar to Harlow's," he says, plopping down next to Will.

"I want a blade so I can be a warrior like Stavros," Will says eagerly.

Stavros laughs. "I'm not a warrior anymore, kid."

"What about a star?" Boshell counters, and then slips the remaining root into his son's mouth.

"Okay," he agrees unenthusiastically. "But a blade would be cooler."

Will gets his star done first, and then Daisy gets a simple crescent to represent her friend Luna. Will was extremely brave and barely made a peep during the process, whereas Daisy cried into Luna's shoulder. I could tell Jax felt awful about inflicting pain on her, but she was very well-behaved and stayed still thanks to Luna's strong and loving arms. You can tell Luna loves Boshell's kids. She treats them as though they're her own.

FESTIVAL OF MASKS

-HARLOW-

As the sun descends in the sky, Stavros drags out two wooden pull trolleys, and then he and Jax fill them with blankets, our masks, and some drinks and nibbles.

"Who wants a piggyback to the lake?" Stavros asks with enthusiasm, and both kids excitedly squeal, "me".

"I'll take Will, and you can take Daisy," Stavros says to Jax, and then his gaze shifts to Luna, who looks pretty this evening in a mint hippie-styled dress. The colour works perfectly with her peach tones.

"You and Destiny can pull the trolleys," he tells her. "They're not too heavy."

I step forward. "What should I take?"

"Nothing." Jax's voice is firm and final. "You've got a bad shoulder."

Acacia steps out into the common area wearing a yellow hippy-style dress with a feather necklace. She looks even more radiant than Luna. My cheeks flush with heat as I realise tonight's festival of masks must be a semi-dressy event among this lot. I don't own a dress, let alone anything nice. The only reason I even look half decent is because I'm wearing Zannah's warrior gear.

Noticing my deflated expression, Acacia hands Atohi to Luna and strolls over. "Come with me." She takes me by the hand and leads me into her and Stavros' room. "I have an emerald dress in here with your name on it." She steps over to her make-shift wardrobe and takes a dress off the rack. "Here it is." She holds it out to show me. "What do you think?"

I think it looks wonderful, but I feel embarrassed about having to borrow it. "Are you sure you don't mind lending it to me?"

"Of course not, don't be silly. Are you going to need my help getting it on?"

"Yes please," I say. "My shoulder is still giving me a bit of trouble."

Acacia is way gentler than Zannah when helping me to get dressed. There is a mirror in the corner of the make-shift robe, and after she finishes tying up the back, I make my way over to it. My refection is a pleasant surprise. I've never worn anything like this before—at least not as Harlow. I would almost go as far as to say I look pretty. I have curves in all the right places now—minus the swollen tummy—and I'm no longer pale and washed out. I look like a woman.

"You look beautiful," Acacia says, gazing at my reflection from behind.

"Thank you." I blush. "I'm very grateful for your kindness."

A warm chuckle escapes her. "Please… It's my pleasure."

By the time we leave the room, everyone is outside and ready to go. As I exit the hut Jax looks up and nearly drops Daisy. His double take tells me he's impressed… His full-faced grin tells me he's very impressed. Feeling his eyes on me like this makes my insides flutter.

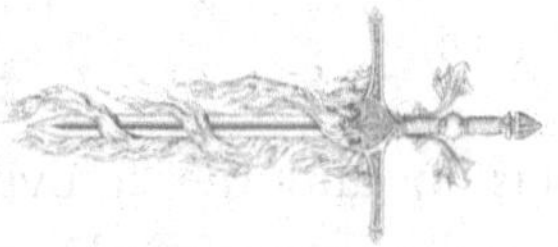

By the time we arrive, the gathering area is already jam-packed with Drakes in masks. The land on this side of the village is wide open in comparison to the rest of the forest, like a big football field lined with a dozen large firepits. Half of the pits have already been lit and are dancing with bright orange flames. It's not quite dark yet; the sun is still sitting above the horizon painting the sky a mix of pinks, yellows, and purples. It's postcard worthy.

We aren't a part of the ceremony, we're here as spectators, so we park ourselves near one of the firepits down by the far end.

Luna and Destiny shake out the blankets for us all to sit on, and Jax and Stavros place the kids down. Destiny looks nice tonight too, in a flowy black dress. Although, admittedly, she's not quite as pretty as Luna.

Boshell shares one blanket with Luna, Destiny, and the kids, while the rest of us share the other. The blankets aren't huge, which means we have to sit close, which is *very* okay with me given I've ended up next to Jax.

"You look nice in a dress," he says, his eyes glittering with reflected firelight.

"Thanks. You always look good." As soon as the words leave my mouth my cheeks fill with heat. It's another *speak before thinking moment*, and I wish I could take it back.

Jax's gaze wanders to Atohi who is happily squirming around at the bottom of the blanket, and I detect a grin.

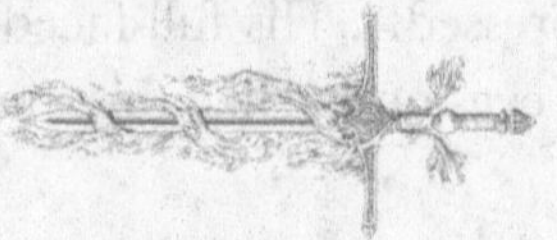

As the evening sets in and the festivities begin, excitement crackles in the air. We pull out our masks for a bit of fun, but we don't keep them on for long. It's more of a novelty. There is lots of singing, dancing, and storytelling, with forest magic thrown into the mix. The Drakes are able to make trees bend and move, flowers shoot up from the ground, rocks roll and pile on top of each other… It's spine tingling. Due to the language barrier, I don't understand anything that is being said, but their actions are powerful enough to captivate my full attention. Because Jax understands the language, he fills me in on the general gist of what's going on by giving me a brief summary after each song and story.

At one stage, Acacia leans across Jax to add, "Drakes believe in spirits, and during these festivals, they call on the spirits of their ancestors to bless their tribe and help protect them from the evil of the world."

The festival continues way into the night, and after a long while of sitting in the same position, I start to become uncomfortable. I've been using my good arm as a lever to hold myself upright, but it's struggling to continue holding my body weight. I straighten my back to take the pressure off, which catches Jax's attention.

"What's wrong?" he asks.

"I've been leaning on my good arm for too long, it's starting to cramp up."

"Here, come and lean on me." He picks me up by my waist and places me in front of him, telling me to lean my back up against his chest. When I sink back into him, he asks, "Does that feel better?"

I nod, unable to speak. The heat of his chest against my back sends warm tingles right through me. "Better" is an understatement.

He leaves one arm wrapped around me. This feels very intimate. My pulse quickens. He's holding me this way by choice.

Stavros glances across and I catch him giving Jax an "it's about time" kind of look. *Maybe Jax does still have feelings for me?*

I inhale deeply through my nostrils. Damn, he smells good; it's intoxicating. I have to fight the urge to run my hands along his legs which are straddling my thighs.

When the festivities end, my heart sinks. I don't want the night to be over, and I sure as hell don't want to leave Jax's embrace. But despite my inner protests, I force myself to do exactly that. The kids are all fast asleep and have to be gently scooped up and carried back to the hut.

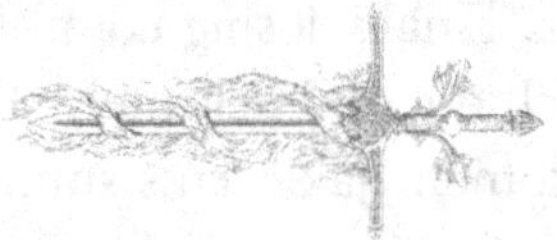

Once we're back, I say goodnight to everyone and head to Atohi's room. I don't know what to do about the mattresses. *Should I split them? Should I keep them together?* I know what I should do, but I also know what I want to do, and the problem is they aren't the same thing. In the end I decide to leave them. Jax can move them if he wants to. The choice can be his. I remain in Acacia's dress because my pyjamas are like rags. If I'm going to be lying next to Jax for the night, I want to look pretty, not poverty-stricken. I sit down on the mattress closet to the window and wait with lit-up nerves for him to come in and let me know what he wants to do. A golden glow spills in through the window from the outside fairy lights, making the room bright enough to see in. It's quite pretty actually—magical even.

When Jax eventually enters, he asks, "Are you okay with this setup, because I don't have to stay in here if you're not comfortable with it. I can sleep out in the common area."

"Don't be silly." My heart thumps. "If you're comfortable, I'm comfortable."

He smiles, strips his shirt off and then hops down on the

mattress beside me, bringing us face to face. I knew he was built, but *wow!* He looks even better shirtless than I'd imagined.

Don't look, Harlow. Turn around, face the window, and pretend he's not here… I laugh internally at my conscience. *Yeah right!*

"Did you enjoy the festival tonight?" he asks.

The sight of him, and his close proximity has me feeling warm all over. "It was great. I didn't want it to end."

"Me too. I'm not looking forward to heading back to the caves first thing tomorrow morning. I wish I could stay longer."

I wish you would put your shirt back on, I think. I can barely concentrate on what he's saying right now. It's near impossible to be *just friends* with shirtless Jax. Finally losing control and going against my better judgment, I reach out and delicately slide my fingers from his chest down to his abdomen. Jax seems stunned at first, but after a couple seconds, his tender hands find me too, and I quiver. His fingers trace my body like he's worshiping my every curve.

Desire crackles around us. This feels completely different than when I was with Alex. It's not just a heat of the moment thing, it feels deep and meaningful, like were connecting.

His face moves slowly towards mine and I can see the kindling of passion in his eyes. *Oh god, I can't believe this is really happening.* The thought of his lips on mine makes my world spin. The closer he gets, the harder my heart pounds, but just before our lips touch, he draws back and leans his forehead to mine. "I want to fight for you, tell me I should—that you want me to." His expression is pleading, almost wild.

"No." Swallowing hard, I drag my gaze away from his lips. "I can't do that. I don't want you getting killed over me. I'm not worth it."

He jerks his head back, lifting a brow. "Are you saying I wouldn't win?"

"I'm saying it's a fifty/fifty chance, and honestly, I don't want either of you getting killed over me."

His eyes survey mine, appearing conflicted. "You still have feelings for him, don't you?" When I don't answer right away, he asks, "Do you actually want to go to Summer with him?"

Great, things were finally heating up with us and now I've gone and killed the moment. *Good one, Harlow.*

"My feelings towards Alex are complicated," I answer honestly. "But he doesn't set my nerves on fire like you do. You're the one who makes my heart flutter just thinking about you." I swallow. "Ever since the day you picked me up to carry me down those stairs to the library, I've felt a spark between us, but I've forced myself to suppress my feelings for you because I know I'm not worthy of you. I will tarnish you."

"I hate it when you say stuff like that." There is a stern edge to his voice.

"It's true."

"It's not true," he argues. "And I don't want to hear it. You never give yourself enough credit."

"Or maybe you give me too much. I don't know why you're so interested in me, especially in my current state. You could do much better."

"Stop it, please." His tone grows firmer. "I'm just Jax tonight, remember? I don't want to hear this. I didn't create the colour system, and I don't agree with it. And as for your current state, it's not an issue. I'm willing to be there for you and your twins no matter what."

I blink in astonishment. My insecurities tell me that this all seems too good to be true.

I lever my head up with my elbow. "Really? Why? I just... I don't understand..."

His fingers softly trace along my side, making me tremble involuntarily. "I think you underestimate how much I care for you. I've been fighting the colour system for years, hoping to have it abolished. I figured if I could integrate the colours within our colony, just as Dakari has done here with his tribe, I could ask you out without it being a crime." He sighs. "I hadn't realised what a challenge it would be."

I can't believe the extreme lengths Jax has gone to just to ask me out. I stare in awe, taking in his ruggedly handsome features. And

his eyes, those beautiful violet eyes. I could get lost in them forever
—*only I can't.*

"I wish you'd told me how you felt earlier. It's too late now, I've
gone and ruined everything."

Jax's expression holds a glimmer of hope. "It's not too late. You
should tell Alex that you want to stay."

"I could, but where would I stay? I don't belong in your world
anymore."

"You don't belong in his either," he is quick to remind me. "You
could stay here for a little while, until I'm able to make a few
changes, and then I'll bring you back."

"I doubt things are going to change enough for us to be together,
not while your mother and Electra are running the show."

"Then I'll leave the caves and stay here with you."

Wow… Okay, that is one massive statement to make.

"No." I shake my head, rejecting the idea right away. I could
never let him do that. "The colony needs you. It will fall to ruins
without you. You're the heart of the caves."

"If this were true, I would have made more leeway by now.
Nobody wants to listen to me. I'm fighting a lost cause."

"I know you don't believe that. It's just going to take a lot more
time than you'd anticipated. These kinds of systems can take years
to breakdown. RJ told me you will succeed, but you need to do it at
a slower pace. Zeeks will learn to accept new ideas and adapt, as
long as they are implemented slowly, bit by bit."

He laces his fingers with mine. "RJ told me that *we* will succeed,
not only me."

"I can't see how I'd be of any use to you anymore; I've caused
more damage than good. You really shouldn't be interested in me,
I'm not the right Zeek for you." It kills me to say this, I want him *so*
badly, but I refuse to let him throw his life away over me. It would be
completely selfish on my part. He deserves better, even if he can't
see it himself. "I wish I were worthy of you. I really wish I were, but
I think we both know I'm not."

"Stop it!" He cups my chin. "Stop pushing me away with that
rubbish. I told you, I don't want to hear it. You only think you're

worthless because that's what you've spent your whole life being taught. I don't think you're worthless. I know you're someone special."

Hearing him say this causes my willpower to crumble. Despite knowing how wrong and selfish I'm being, I'm unable to contain my desires any longer, I dip my head and lean in for that kiss.

He lowers his forehead back to mine, stopping my lips from reaching his. The yearning in his eyes tells me he's using every bit of restraint he can muster to hold back. *I don't understand.*

"I'm not here for a one-night stand." His voice sounds breathy and strained. "It's not what I want. You mean much more to me than that." He pushes a loose dreadlock back from my face. "I'm here because I care about you. Because despite everything that's happened, I still really want to be with you."

I swallow, my cheeks flushing with heat. "I don't know how we can make this work without putting your life in danger."

His outer arm scoops me up, flips me around, and pulls me to him, settling my back into his chest. "I'm sure we could make it work if you'd let me in. And stop worrying about me, I'll be fine. It's you I'm worried about." His arm stays wrapped around me, warm and strong, and I can feel his heart pounding wildly against my back. *How can he act so calm and controlled right now, when quite clearly, he's feeling the same heat and excitement I feel? God he's good.* My respect for him grows even further. "If you still want to leave with Alex, I won't stop you. I'll be worried, but I'll let you go." His grip around me tightens contradicting his words. "I just needed you to know how I feel, before you make that decision."

I must be dreaming. I can't believe Jax has poured his heart out to me, and what's more, he's said absolutely everything I've been yearning to hear.

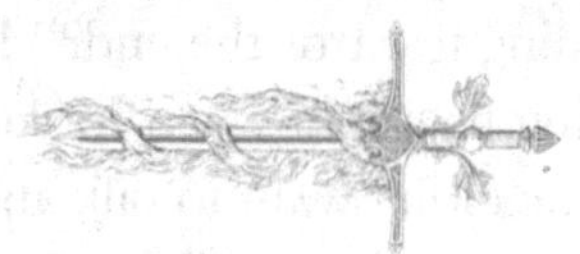

When I wake up the next morning Jax is gone, and I feel like he's taken my heart with him. I flush with lingering warmth, remembering how I'd slept snuggled in his arms all night. I find a letter on the pillow next to me.

Sorry I had to leave so early. I would've said goodbye, but I didn't want to wake you. I hope you enjoy the rest of your stay in the forest, and if you need anything, don't hesitate to ask Stavros; he's a great friend, and I know he'd be more than willing to step up and help.
Please think about what I've said.
Love, Jax.

Seeing the words *love, Jax* gives me tingles. I can't believe how open and honest he was last night.

So many Zeeks have told me that Jax has feelings for me, but until last night, he'd never fully admitted this to me himself.

I leave the room to find Stavros already awake and sitting on one of the cushioned chairs with Atohi.

"Good morning," he says, and I parrot it back. "How did you sleep?"

I take a seat next to him. "Really good. Thank you. I think it's the first time in ages that I haven't had to sleep through the constant beeps of machines."

He gives a half-hearted smile. "Jax told me you had a pretty lousy set up there, that's why he brought you here. He thought it would be nicer and safer for you. It's a good thing he got you here this weekend. It sounds like things were getting pretty savage towards the end."

"What was happening towards the end?" I ask curiously. "Oscar told me Jax was copping heat, but when I asked Jax about it, he put his guard up and said he didn't want to talk about it."

"Why does that not surprise me?" Stavros shakes his head and sighs. "Truth is, most of the colony still believes you're pregnant to him, and that he's been hiding you away to protect you."

"Well, the second part is true."

"The problem is, he was actually beginning to make some leeway with breaking down the colour system, but since the rumours started circulating, he's lost a lot of respect from fellow Purples, which means he's lost a lot of power. And to make matters worse, his mother is trying her best to force his hand into getting linked with Electra."

"Electra?" My face twists with disgust. "But she's Nix's ex."

"The Commander doesn't care about that sort of thing, all she cares about is power, and who will best fit as a fierce ruler. It's not about love."

"Do you think…" My throat constricts. "Do you think he will do it?"

"I know for certain he won't. And besides, if he links with Electra, he's a dead man. With Electra placed in such a powerful position, the Commander won't need to keep Jax around anymore. She could easily have him taken out, making Electra the heir to her title. Electra is the kind of Zeek that Azazel wants as her replacement. She's ruthless and shares her same sick beliefs."

"What do you think will happen to him if he doesn't link with her?"

"To be honest, I really don't know." His expression turns sombre. "I'm worried about him."

28

ELECTRA HAS WREAKED HAVOC

-ZANNAH-

I bounce my leg impatiently as I wait. *Where the frost is he? I thought he'd be back by now.* It's like that little girlfriend of his—or whatever she is—has him under some kind of spell. I don't understand what he sees in her. *Sure, she's pretty-ish, and he did mention something about feeling connected to her because of his father's choice to save her, but what else does she have going for her?* She's a walking menace who willingly shagged one of our enemies. Worse, she's pregnant to our enemy. Sooner or later, Jax's love for this traitor is going to get us *all* killed.

I sigh, almost growling in frustration. The nightmare we've all been through to help keep Harlow safe has been beyond ridiculous. I should've let Stace take her down without intercepting. I thought that by saving her, I was saving Jax from a path of self-destruction, but keeping her around has only put us all in more danger.

I overhead him speaking to Oscar a few days back. He said he was planning on convincing her to stay in Spring where she'll be safe. I can see why he's worried; she won't last long in Summer, but if he wants her to stay, he'd better be willing to put up a fight because that Vallon of hers seems rather attached.

I finally catch sight of the warrior sled pulling in and I dash over. "Jax!" I puff a sigh of relief. "It's about bloody time! Where the frost have you been? I've been waiting for ages."

He jerks the sled to a halt and leaps straight out. "Why? What's wrong?" His muscles coil as he snaps straight into fierce warrior mode. "What's going on?"

"Electra has wreaked havoc while you've been gone, and trust me when I say, the fact that you've been missing all night certainly hasn't gone unnoticed."

"Where are Oscar and Kieran?" he asks hurriedly. "Are they okay?"

"Yes, they're fine, but your little girlfriend's pals aren't. Your mother ordered them to be arrested. They've been taken to the cell where they are being tortured for answers."

His fists bunch at his sides. "Frost! When?"

"Last night."

"Who's in with them?"

"Electra, Roc, and Austin."

A wave of panic passes across his face. "Quick, help me unhook the huskens. I've got to get down there."

29

THIS IS TORTURE

-ZAVIER-

(twelve hours earlier)

As we finish cleaning up, an eerie feeling washes over me.

I pop the broom away and crack open the door to the dining area, giving it a scan. "Hey Minty, where's your mutt?"

She tosses her hairnet in the bin and walks over to me. "I don't know, probably waiting out the front, why?"

"Something feels off."

She pushes the door open further and scans the area as I had. "Lucy," she calls. "Lucy, where are you?"

Silence, nothing.

"Rae must be out there again." She goes back to grab some knives from the knife block. "We need weapons."

"You'd think if it was Rae, we would've heard Lucy barking and growling." I frown. "It's almost too quiet."

She hands me one of the knives. "There's only one way to find out."

We keep on high alert as we walk through the dining area to the exit.

"Lucy," Minty calls again and then whistles. "Here girl."

As we get closer to the exit, we spot Lucy lying limp on the ground. Before I can stop her, Minty screams and runs over.

"Minty, wait!" I yell lunging towards her, but it's too late, someone darts out from the shadows and grabs her from behind.

To my gaping shock, it's a warrior. Minty tries desperately to slice him with her knife but she doesn't stand a chance against his might. His big meaty hands snatch the knife from her and toss it to the ground with a clank.

"Don't worry, Sweet Cheeks." There's a sickening sleaziness to his voice. "Lucy's only napping."

My gaze snaps to Lucy after he says this. There's a dart sticking out from her side. It rises and falls as she breathes. *Good*, they've only tranquillised her. Not that I'm a fan of the mutt, but I know she's become a loyal companion to Minty, and she'd be devastated if anything happened to her.

Minty might be physically weaker than the warrior, but her spirit is strong, and she hits and kicks with fury, trying her best to break free from his grasp. Her struggles are soon met with a sickening crunch and she shrieks.

Enraged, I charge over with my knife raised and ready to plunge. I'm fully aware I don't stand a chance of overcoming the warrior, but I'm willing to die trying. "Let her go."

The warrior might not be as tall and bulky as Jax, but he's still solid, and he wears the savage face of a killer.

"Zavier, watch out!" Minty shouts, but my reactions are too slow. I've only made it halfway over to them when another warrior slams into me from behind, causing me to drop my knife. His body is hard and forceful. I feel like I've been smashed by a solid block of ice.

The warrior keeps hold once he's caught me, crushing me to him with his fierce grip. "You are under arrest. We are here to take you in for questioning, by order of the Commander."

I wonder which crime we are being questioned about? A thousand frantic thoughts race through my mind in the space of a second. *Maybe it's all of them.*

Besides a few pained whimpers from each of us, Minty and I keep our mouths shut as the warriors viciously lug us off to one of the cells. I hate being this weak, and I hate that I'm going down without a fight, but after that arsehole callously re-broke Minty's arm to subdue her, I've grudgingly accepted there's no point in continuing to fight these guys. It's obvious by Minty's lack of struggle she's thinking along the same lines. We are severely outpowered by brute strength.

There's also no use trying to verbally defend ourselves, because we are guilty as sin for a number of crimes.

Electra is waiting in front of the cell and gives Minty and me a chilling grin as the warriors carry us inside. "Good work. Now tie them up," she commands, her voice cool and cunning.

The cell is all limestone with only small holes in the passage wall to look in and out from. The Commander before Azazel used a different set of cells with bars, but they were abandoned when a captured Purple escaped. He'd frozen the metal bars with his winter magic and then smashed them to smithereens.

The warriors force us each onto a metal chair and bind our hands and legs with ropes.

I notice there's a third chair, and a few minutes later Floss is dragged in. But unlike Minty and I, she hasn't come quietly. She kicks and screams and calls out all sorts of profanities to the warriors as they drag her in. By the looks of it, they've needed to use two warriors to bring her in. It's kind of embarrassing when your new girlfriend is tougher than you.

"Zavier, Minty!" she cries when she sees us, and her expression suddenly darkens with fear. She mustn't have known we'd already been brought in.

She struggles even harder, giving the warriors all she's got. "I thought you said this had to do with Elgar's death?" she shouts in fury. "I thought you said that you had new incriminating evidence against Harlow and me. If Harlow and I are the ones you're after, then why are they here?"

Without responding to any of her questions, they slam her down onto the chair with force. She yelps but keeps kicking and thrashing, and they struggle to hold her still enough to tie the ropes. The warrior who had brought me in—Roc, I overheard him being called—jumps in to help them, and before long Floss is bound too. Her chair rocks as she continues to fight.

"Rae's wrong you know," she shouts. "We had nothing to do with Elgar's death. We are being framed!"

Electra enters and struts straight up to me, singling me out. Her gaze is sharp like shards of ice. "Where is Harlow?"

I try to keep my expression as blank as possible, and shrug. "How should I know?"

"Austin," Electra says, giving a quick tilt of the head.

Austin seizes me by the shoulder and within an instant his hand turns to ice. A sharp burning sensation rips through my whole side, and I cry out pain.

"Stop it!" Floss shouts, and a look of satisfaction crosses Electra's face. "Stop it, you scumbags. Leave him alone."

Eventually Electra holds up her hand and Austin stops. "Let me try this again." Her wicked eyes glint. "Where is Harlow?"

"I don't know." My voice comes out strangled. "We're not on speaking terms at the moment."

Again, she gives a tilt of the head, and Austin grabs my other shoulder, sending another sharp burning sensation straight though me. I grit my teeth to restrain myself from crying out this time around. I want to appear tough, but it's a struggle. A small, pained groan still escapes me, and for a moment my vision swims.

Floss continues to shout and curse at them all, but no one pays her any attention.

"We can keep this going all night," Electra says to me. "Or you can give up Harlow's location, and we can talk about swinging you a deal."

"Swing what deal? I don't even know what I've been brought in for."

"You are here because we've been led to believe that you have information on the whereabouts of a wanted felon. Now listen to me carefully because I'm not here to waste time. If you be a good little Pastel and tell me where we can find Harlow, I will let you and your other little friend there," she points to Minty, "walk."

Well even if I was considering telling her—which I most certainly wasn't—there's no way I would go through with it after that degrading comment. "I've already told you; I don't know where Harlow is."

"Okay…" A sinister grin twists her lips. "Let's try this from another angle then, shall we?" She redirects her interest to Floss. "Tell me, Pastel lover, where is your sister?"

"Go frost yourself," Floss spits, and Electra doesn't even have to signal Roc into taking action, he snaps straight into torture mode, and Floss lets out an ear-piercing scream.

Panic shoots through me, and my emotions rotate between anger, fear, and guilt.

"Hey," I shout. "If you are going to torture anyone, torture me."

The evil grin plastered on Electra's face tells me she's enjoying this. "Silly boy, don't you see? By torturing her, I am torturing you."

They try Floss a few more times, but neither of us break, so they move on to Minty. Austin, the savage beast, seems intent on using Minty's weak spot as his hit zone. He snatches up her broken arm and summons frost to ice-burn the skin around the protruding bones. I cringe as she shrieks at the top of her lungs. I can't stand to watch or listen to either of the girls being tortured. Electra is right, it really is more torturous to watch them suffer than to be tortured myself. I feel like breaking just to make their pain stop, but I know if I do, there will be repercussions for others. Plus, I also don't trust that once these Purple pricks get what they want from us, they won't just kill us anyway. While they still think we have information, we are useful to them.

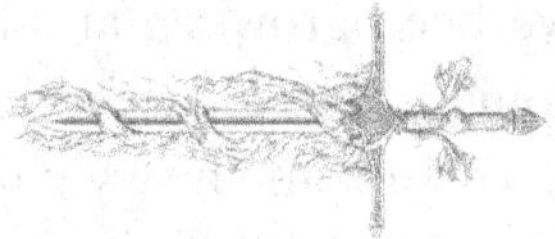

Electra hadn't been kidding when she said that they could "keep this going all night". As the hours drag on, the torture session intensifies, yet no matter how much violence they inflict upon us, none of us break. We've been ice-burnt, ice slapped, kicked, punched, strangled, and had sections of our hair near-yanked out of our heads.

The pain is intolerable; I've barely recovered from my last beating. I can hardly move. My body wasn't made for this brutality; it's not coping. I'm fairly certain even if I do survive this, I won't live to see my twenties. I'll be too broken down to support myself.

Electra calls the warriors out for a bit, probably to discuss their next plan of attack. Whatever the reason, I'm thankful for the breather. I gaze at Floss, and my heart sinks. She has two black eyes and blood dripping down from her nose and mouth. Minty's face looks good in comparison, although her broken arm hangs awkwardly, a mess of blood and bone.

Minty's face isn't as beat up because she hasn't given as much cheek to the warriors as Floss has. Minty can be tough and a total bitch when she wants to be, but she's smart enough to know when to keep her mouth shut. Floss, on the other hand, is completely erratic, and today she's chosen to come out volatile and swinging.

I'm fairly certain Floss is partially insane—in fact I could guarantee it—but I find myself admiring her courage. She's been so tough and brave throughout this whole ordeal and never once has she faltered even in the slightest.

"I love you," she says thickly. "I thought I should tell you just in case we don't make it through this."

"I love you too," I reply, and despite the horrendous situation we're in, Floss' eyes light up.

She hadn't expected me to say it back. The love I feel for her isn't the same intense love I'd felt for Harlow. But ever since I've forced myself to accept that Harlow and I are just friends, my feelings towards Floss have been growing, and after watching the way she's handled herself tonight, I feel like they've grown further.

"What I wouldn't give for some heavy painkillers right now," she says forcing a smile. The cut on her lip re-opens with the stretching of the skin, and blood dribbles down to her chin.

I sure hate seeing her like this. I wish I was strong enough to break out of these ropes and do something. If I had the chance to kill these guys for what they've done to her, I would do it without hesitation.

I turn to Minty who is sitting ultra-quietly, staring into space. "I'm sorry, it's my fault you're here."

"I don't blame you." Her words are crisp. "I knew what I was getting myself into."

The warriors return soon after this, followed by Electra, and it's back to another round of torture for us all.

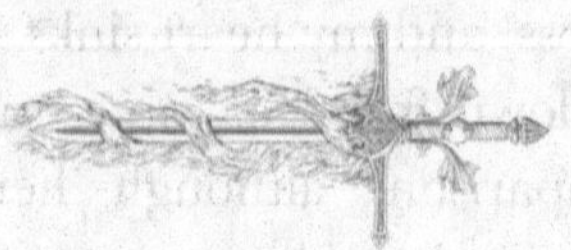

Minutes feel like hours, and my battered body is growing weaker by the second. By what feels like my hundredth round of torture, I end up slipping in and out of consciousness. At one stage I wake up disorientated, not knowing where I am, but Austin is quick to remind me.

He grabs a fist full of my hair and reefs my head backward. "Did you enjoy your little nap, Pretty Boy?" A sickening chuckle escapes him. "You're up again."

"It looks like you're struggling, Little Pastel," Electra says, and I imagine she's snarling. I don't know for sure though, because my eyes are so swollen, they're almost sealed shut. "I doubt if you'll survive much longer, so why don't you give me the information I need, and I'll get Austin to carry you straight to the medical chamber."

I can barely speak, but I manage a hoarse, "Screw you," which grants me a personal ice slap from her. *Frost, does it hurt.*

"Electra!" A booming voice shouts, and despite my earlier animosity towards Jax, I find myself exhaling with relief at the sound. "What is going on here!"

30

WHAT I WOULDN'T GIVE TO KILL THIS BITCH!

-ZANNAH-

I manage a glimpse through the small gaps in the limestone wall and wince. Jax's little girlfriend's pals look far worse than the last time I'd come down. The poor boy looks like he's merely hanging on by a thread. I have to admit, I'm both surprised and impressed that they haven't squealed. They are much tougher than I'd given them credit for.

"Electra!" Jax's whole frame radiates pure and utter rage. "What's going on here?"

Electra's head jerks up, and even through the small gaps I can still capture the sadistic grin that stretches across her face.

"The Commander's son has arrived." She leaves the cell to meet us at the entry. "How nice of you to finally join us." She pauses dramatically. "Where exactly have you been?"

Jax doesn't fold or show any signs of weakness or fear. That's what I love about him. He always manages to stay so strong and focused even under the direst of circumstances.

"Let them go!"

"I'm sorry, but I can't do that." Electra smiles smugly. "They are being detained by order of the Commander."

I clench my fists at my sides, squeezing them tight. *Geez, I'd love to whack her one—straight in the gob. Icy bitch.*

Jax straightens, making him look even taller than he naturally is. "Under what pretence?"

"New evidence has come to light regarding Elgar's death. We've been led to believe the murder was staged by Harlow and Floss. They purposely used poor Trey as their fall guy, knowing full well that you'd be able to get him off on self-defence."

Jax's jaw clicks, but he manages to keep his composure. "You're lying. You've set them up. Why?"

Blanking his questions, Electra cocks her head, and gives him an interrogating look. "Where's Harlow?"

"Gone, now let them go."

"Gone where?"

"Probably dead. She must've escaped the caves; we haven't been able to find her."

She sniggers. "Now look who's lying."

"What do you really want?" Jax cuts to the chase. "I know you. You wouldn't go to this much trouble for a murdered Magenta, especially someone as degenerate as Elgar."

"I want you to agree to your mother's request."

I scoff in disgust, and she snarls at me. It's the first reaction I've gotten from her since standing here. I have so many comments sitting on the edge of my tongue right now—and I'd absolutely love to let them rip—but I work hard to contain myself. I don't want to make things any harder for Jax. I have a habit of causing trouble when I open my mouth.

A flash of disgust crosses his stoic mask. "Not a chance."

"Well, you'd best be saying goodbye to your little pets."

He bristles. "You can't kill them."

"Watch me." A devilish gleam lights her face as she gives a distinct nod of authority to Roc and Austin. They respond to her signal without hesitation, sending cold shockwaves through two of the prisoners. Harlow's sister screams in agony while the boy passes out. I turn my face away. It's sickening to watch. I'm not afraid of bloodshed, but I don't believe in picking on the defenceless. I like a fair fight.

"Stop this!" Jax launches forward, shoving his face in front of Electra's in warning. Sphinx follows his master's lead, hunkering aggressively at his side, ready to pounce at his command.

"Link with me, and I will let them go," Electra challenges.

"That's blackmail."

"They're criminals, and quite frankly, so are you. Most of the colony believes that you should be in there with them. You are a disgrace to your title. The Commander is only letting you off lightly because you're her son."

Lightly? I can't help but scoff again. If I were Jax, I'd rather be tortured to death. Anything would be better than being forced to link with this mega beast. *How dare she say those things to him. Who does she think she is?* She has no title. She's just Azazel's pathetic minion.

Electra goes to give another signal to Roc and Austin.

"Wait!" Jax booms, thrusting a palm out. "I'll consider it."

"Not good enough," Electra hisses and continues with the signal.

This time both girls scream.

"OKAY! OKAY!" Jax's stoic mask slips. "I agree to the request."

Flabbergasted, I jerk to face him. "What? No!" I can't believe he just agreed to the request, *is he insane?* If he links with this bitch, it's game over for all of us.

Recomposing himself, he steps even closer to Electra, bringing them nose to nose. "Now let them go."

"I don't think so." Her features tighten with challenge. "You're not the one in charge here, your mother is. I'll let them go once we are linked."

"I want them released and taken to the medical chamber now, or there will be no linking." The pure ferocity spiked in Jax's deep angry voice is enough to make Electra back up a step. I don't think she was expecting this reaction from him. She thought she'd won—that she had it over him.

"I'm not completely unreasonable," she says re-finding her feet. "Let's negotiate, shall we? If you confirm to your mother that you are indeed accepting her request, there will be no more torture. I will unbind them, and they can stay in the cell moving about freely until such time as we are linked."

Jax's fierce purple eyes continue to bore into hers, never wavering. "They can't stay in there. They need medical attention."

She considers his comment. "I can't permit them to leave, but..." She leaves her words hanging in the air for a moment. "I will allow a medic inside the cell to treat them under the watchful eyes of the warriors."

"Okay," Jax nods grudgingly. "But I want my warriors in there."

"Roc and Austin are your warriors," she says, taunting him with an unnatural sickly-sweet voice.

"We all know that's not true," I pipe in, and both their gazes flash to me. "Their loyalty is to you, and we don't trust them."

"You don't trust them?" Electra raises her brows to me. "That's interesting. Tell me again, exactly how did Haydn and Stace die? I don't believe it was a lovers' quarrel turned ugly. I knew them well. They were happy." There might be a dangerous edge to Electra's tone, but this bitch doesn't scare me—I death glare her. As far as I'm concerned, she's a pathetic wannabe Commander, and I could easily take her out, just like my brother took out Nix. Azazel would have me killed for doing it, but it would be worth it. "And strangely enough," Electra continues, returning my glare, "I don't remember seeing you at their funeral. A coincidence? I think not."

"Let's compromise," Jax says, in a desperate attempt to re-steer the conversation at hand. "I'll use one of my trusted warriors, and you can use one of yours. More importantly, no one will touch the prisoners. They are only there to guard them."

Electra's penetrating gaze holds mine for a few seconds longer before snapping back to his. "Fine," she concedes. "Go and see your mother, agree to her request, and we have ourselves a deal."

"Done." Jax takes off in haste, and I follow.

I wait until we're out of earshot before opening my mouth. "What the Frost was that? What are you doing? What are you thinking? You can't link with that mega-beast." I shake my head in frustration. "I can't believe you've agreed to this."

"I'm not planning on going through with it," he assures me. "I'm just trying to save Harlow's friends and buy some time until I can figure out my next move."

"Do you want me to go back there and keep an eye on them until you return?"

"No," he says, a little too fast for my liking and I take offence. "I want you to go find Kieran and send him back.

"Why Kieran? Why not me?"

"Because…" he says, letting out an agitated breath. "I don't trust you not to say or do something that you shouldn't, especially if Electra keeps pressing about the Haydn and Stace issue."

"I kept my mouth mostly shut, didn't I?" I shoot back in annoyance.

"Zannah, please, get Kieran and then meet me at the medical chamber. If Sylvie's not on—which I'm guessing she won't be—ask one of the others to fetch her, special request of Jax."

"Fine," I grumble. "I'll meet you there."

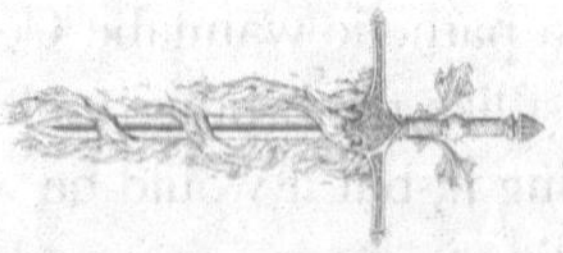

I find Kieran, give him a brief summary of what happened between Jax and Electra, and then tell him to head down to the cell until further notice. He asks a handful of questions which shows he's concerned, but much like Jax, his expression doesn't give much away.

I'm a cutthroat fighter. I'm able to take down warriors double my size in sparring matches, but hiding my emotions is something I've always struggled with as a warrior. I'm absolutely infuriated by this vile agreement taking place, and I'm certain it's written all over my face.

When I get to the medical chamber, Sylvie isn't on, so I send Tansy to get her while I man the front desk. There are two medics on, Harper and Iris. When Harper sees me, she comes scurrying over to say "hi". She's sweet enough, but a little bit too girly-girl for my liking. I can't stand the way she giggles when she speaks. I sit there and nod in annoyance while she goes on about how her friend went out on a date with Oscar last week—*gush*. If only she knew how little I give a frost.

Sylvie arrives in time to save me from ripping my hair out.

"Sylvie," I say, cutting Harper off mid-sentence. "Let's head straight over to the restricted area, shall we? Jax is on his way."

Harper flounders a moment, stunned by my abrupt break-off in conversation, but she recovers quickly and then turns her attention to Tansy, who seems far more interested in all she has to say.

As Sylvie and I make our way across, Jax enters the medical chamber and hurries over to join us. He is sweating heavily, the only visible indication of how truly stressed he is.

After closing the wooden door to the restricted area, Jax fills Sylvie in on all of the new developments and asks her if there is any chance she would be willing to help him out once again.

"I'm sorry to keep dragging you into all of my problems, but I promise you'll be heavily compensated, as always," Jax assures her.

Sylvie shifts uncomfortably. "What exactly do you want me to do?"

"I need you to go down to the cell and tend to the prisoners. Clean them up, check their wounds, and do whatever is necessary and possible within the restrictions of the cell. I would love to get in there and take a good look at the prisoners myself, but I know Electra won't let that happen."

After covering a few other concerns, Jax moves on to the topic of hardcore painkillers.

"I want you to inject them all with morphine," he says, "but there's a catch. I want to lace two of the needles with this."

He pulls a leather pouch out of his pocket, and from it, he plucks out a small jar of fluorescent red fluid.

"What's that?" I ask, leaning in closer to get a better look. "Is that? *No*, it can't be."

Sylvie isn't shocked or amazed by the jar of glowing fluid Jax is holding out to her. She merely swallows nervously.

"Why do you have vertic switz ink?" I ask, feeling put-out that this is the first time I've seen or heard about it. Jax usually keeps me in the loop. *Not this time apparently!* It seems I'm only good enough to confide in when he needs my help.

"Harlow had it. Alex gave it to her."

"You mean Slater?" I correct.

He shoots me an irritated glance. "Does it really matter either way?"

Drawing us back to the point, Sylvie asks, "Which two do you want me to use it on?" *Good question*, I was wondering the same thing.

"The two Pastels. I'm worried they won't make it, especially the boy."

"Has Harlow been injected with this ink?" I ask, suddenly curious.

"Harlow has a small tattoo on her wrist," Sylvie says when Jax fails to answer. "I saw it when I took her in for surgery."

My eyes narrow to Jax and he puts a hand up. "Not now, Zannah, please. Grill me later." He redirects his attention to Sylvie, his expression serious—verging on hopeful. "What's your verdict?" he asks. "Will you do this for me? I understand what I'm asking of you is dangerous, and I feel awful putting you in this position, but right now you're the only hope I have of keeping those Pastels alive."

No pressure, I think sarcastically.

Sylvie sucks in a shaky breath. "Yes, I'll do it, as long as you have one of your most trusted warriors in there to protect me in case something goes wrong."

"Kieran's already down there," I say, which seems to bring a goofy smile to her face. This encourages me to add, "He's single too, you know."

She blushes and turns her face away.

"Zannah." Jax gives me a "what's wrong with you?" kind of look. "Really?"

I shrug. "What? She seems interested, and he's single. I thought I'd put it out there. They seem well suited, don't you think? They're both super intellects."

Deliberately ignoring me, Jax gets back to the topic at large and asks Sylvie to get the pain meds out of the locked cupboard for him. Together they make up the syringes, two laced with ink, and pop them into Sylvie's jacket pocket.

"I'll go and sort out the rest of the supplies we'll be needing," Sylvie says.

As soon as she leaves the restricted area Jax's eyes snap to mine. "You're as bad as your brother, you know that? Neither of you know how to be subtle."

31

PLAN IN ACTION
-ZANNAH-

When we get back downstairs, Kieran is standing outside of the prison cell, while Roc and Austin are both still inside. I look around. There is absolutely no sign of Electra.

"What's going on?" Jax asks.

"Electra has gone to see the Commander," Kieran informs him. "She says she doesn't trust you."

"The feeling is mutual," Jax mutters under his breath.

As we stand around waiting in deafening silence, I notice Sylvie secretly checking out Kieran, and I forcibly have to bite off all of the comments springing to mind. It's so blatantly obvious she likes him. She should really take the leap and ask him out.

Feeling restless I step over to one of the gaps in the cell wall and take a good look at the boy. His chest is rising and falling. He's obviously still alive, but he looks close to death. I doubt even the ink will help him at this point, although I hope it does. I don't want his death weighing on Jax's conscience. I know he's already beating himself up over this.

The Pastel girl doesn't look quite as bad as the boy, but her arm closest to me is hanging at an unnatural angle. Exposed bone sticks out from her raw, bloodied, and frostbitten skin. I shudder. *That's got to hurt.*

My eyes travel to the Magenta. Her face looks the worst, it's swollen and covered in blood. *I wonder why Jax didn't want her injected with the ink too. She's Harlow's sister after all.* Then again, maybe he doesn't want them looking too much alike. I'd always assumed it was the pregnancy that'd turned Harlow red, but since finding out about the ink, I've reconsidered. If these two Pastels start turning red over the next few weeks, it's going to cause a stir with Electra. I hope Jax is prepared with a cover story.

Electra eventually returns and after examining the contents of the medical tray first, she okays Sylvie and Kieran to enter. She's brought down one of her other trusted warriors to replace Roc and Austin. It's Feeney. I roll my eyes. *Yay.*

"You may untie the two Pastels," Electra tells her warriors. "But leave the Magenta tied until the medic is out."

"That wasn't the deal," Jax argues.

"She is too wild and unpredictable. I assure you she will be released once only the two warriors inside."

Jax doesn't push the matter any further, and if I didn't know any better, I'd say it's because he actually agrees.

Sylvie works on the boy first, and Jax and I stay to watch. She manages to rouse him a little, but he can barely hold his head up, so she ties the tourniquet and holds his hand in a fist.

After Roc and Austin leave, Jax strikes up the topic of the linking ceremony to get Electra's attention. This is all part of the plan. He'd discussed it with Sylvie and me on the way down here. He'd said he would distract Electra with the topic of the linking ceremony, while Sylvie discreetly administered the meds. He didn't want Electra examining the needles contents. He was worried if Electra caught sight of the syringes before Sylvie was able to administer the meds, she would demand to check what's in them, and she'd know right away that the needles were laced.

"Tell my mother to book the ceremony for Saturday, three weeks from now."

It must kill him to say this because it kills me to hear it. And to think, there are plenty of women in this colony who would give their left arm to be Jax's nexus—*me included*—yet, Electra is only using him for his status.

Electra casts him a suspicious glance. "Why the long wait? I thought you would be desperate to get your little pets back out."

"Three weeks is hardy a long wait."

She props her hands on her hips, eyes narrowed. "I think you're stalling."

"I think you should be pleased that I'm showing enough interest to set a date."

While Jax and Electra banter back and forth, I keep my eye on Sylvie, watching with a thumping heart as she injects the meds. Her hands are shaky, but thankfully, it's only Kieran who seems to pick up on it. He is clearly curious as to what's going on, but he's smart enough not to draw any attention to her.

The injection instantly wakes the boy, and he screams and writhes like she's just set him alight. Sylvie leaps back, face anxious, and then moves to the other Pastel who reacts just as violently to the laced meds.

Electra's eyes flick in the direction of the cell, but they don't linger. She doesn't seem overly alarmed. No one enjoys being poked and prodded after being tortured half to death. She must assume their pain-filled screams are a natural response.

I glance at Feeney briefly to make sure he isn't getting suss. *Nope.* He's too busy trying to eavesdrop on the conversation going on out here to detect corruption going on under his nose. I bet he's jealous, *poor poppet*. I've seen him giving Electra the eye once or twice.

Harlow's sister refuses to sit there and cop the needle silently. After seeing how the other two had reacted to the meds, she doesn't trust what's going on. She screeches in panic and rocks violently on her chair, like she's afraid Sylvie's about to stake her with a hot poker.

"What have you given them? What's in the syringe?"

I want to tell her to sit still and shut up, but if I interfere it will only make matters worse. Her questions capture Feeney's attention, and he swings to face them. Thankfully her injection isn't laced, so the contents won't arouse his suspicion.

Sylvie brings the syringe to Floss' arm, and she starts thrusting around like a mad thing, making it difficult to administer the injection.

"It's just pain relief," Sylvie tells her for the fourth time. "Trust me. Jax has sent me here to treat you all. It will make you feel better."

During the commotion, the Pastel girl drags herself up off the floor, and she stumbles over to the wall where I stand. My jaw drops. I don't actually know that I can refer to her as a Pastel anymore. Her colouring has already transformed to a deep rosy pink and she appears sturdier. I hadn't expected the effects to be so instant, I thought it would take a couple of weeks. *We're in trouble*. This isn't going to go unnoticed.

"Can you tell Tatum to stay away from here—from me?" She might look stronger, but her voice is weak and scratchy. "Please. It's not safe for her to be seen near me."

"Hey," Feeney shouts, his voice stern, and then click, he registers the sudden change in her, and his eyes snap to mine. "What's happened to her? What have you done?" He races over. "You! Prisoner, get away from the wall."

"Please," she repeats, eyes begging, and then she stumbles away from the wall and back to her chair.

"Electra!" Feeney calls. *Big mouth*. "Electra!"

The alarm in Feeney's voice instantly grabs Electra's attention.

She breaks away from her conversation with Jax, and charges over. "What is it?" When she catches sight of the two former Pastels, she whirls on Jax. "You've tricked me," she snaps, her eyes bulging with rage. "What have you given them?"

Jax keeps his face perfectly composed. "Pain meds."

"Pain meds aren't pigment and body altering. You're lying; you've done something to them."

"The pain meds have been combined with adrenaline." He looks them over and gives a nonchalant shrug. "They must have reacted to the dual dose. It happens sometimes." Electra doesn't look as if she believes him. I'm certain she doesn't know what to think. I doubt she'd be able to guess the truth. "Don't worry Electra, I'm sure their symptoms will wear off as soon as the drugs leave their systems, although I would like them to be given the pain meds for the next few days." Electra goes to protest but Jax cuts her off. "You want them to stay alive and well, because if any of them die between now and the linking ceremony, our deal is off. I made sure to put this condition in writing when I'd agreed to my mother's request."

We stay for another half hour watching intently, and even though Electra doesn't buy Jax's cover story, she seems satisfied that whatever he'd given them wasn't a miracle cure. The Pastel prisoners are still moaning and suffering.

Sylvie eventually comes out to gives us a report while Electra carefully listens in. She says both girls should be okay, but they'll need regular dressing applied to their ice burns.

She nods her head to Minty. "Her arm won't heal perfectly straight. I've tried setting it in place the best I can, but without proper surgery and pins…" she winces. "I wasn't even able to apply a full cast because of the open wounds and ice burns."

"Don't worry, you've done well," Jax assures her.

"About Zavier," she pauses, her expression strained. "I'm not sure if he's going to pull through. He's suffering from a concussion, and along with all of his burns, bruises, and swelling, I suspect he might have a few cracked ribs and a fractured shin, but it's hard to know for certain without scans." She winces once more. "I'm hoping there's no major internal damage or bleeding. His body was already in bad shape due to what happened with Elgar, and now…" She doesn't finish.

Jax places his hand on her arm and nods in thanks. "I really appreciate your help."

"I'd like to stay for a few hours and monitor them," she says. "Will this be possible?"

Monitor them or Kieran? I think cynically, but then I decide she actually does care about the prisoners' welfare.

Jax glances at Electra, who is looking more worn down and sleep deprived by the minute. Big dark rings circle her lower eye lids. "I'll allow it." Her words are clipped. "But if any of you double cross me, things will turn ugly fast. Do I make myself clear?"

"Understood," Jax says with a nod.

They are both treading carefully. Jax is playing it cool because he wants Sylvie in there, and Electra is allowing it, because she's afraid if the boy doesn't make it, Jax will renege on their agreement.

"And what about getting some mattresses sent down for them to lie on?" Sylvie suggests. "The ground is cold, hard and unforgiving."

"Yes, that's a must," Jax agrees, not bothering to confirm the idea with Electra this time around. "We'll get three sent down from the medical chamber."

We leave soon after this, and Jax asks if I can go to the medical chamber and arrange for the mattresses to be brought to the cell, while he informs their families of their current situation.

"I'm sure they are all worried sick." His brows dip. "And I need to find Lucy. I'm hoping she wasn't hurt while trying to protect the Pastels."

"Do you know who Tatum is?" I ask.

He nods. "Yes, she's Minty's girlfriend, why?"

"The little Pastel asked me to warn Tatum to stay away from her, for her own safety."

"The little Pastel is Minty." He gives me a sharp look, acting as if I should already know this. "Although, I wouldn't really call her a little Pastel anymore." He exhales a drawn-out breath. "Thanks for letting me know. I'll make sure she receives the warning." As the passage splits and we head our different directions, Jax shouts, "I'll meet you in the warrior cavern in an hour. If you see Oscar, tell him to join us."

"Yeah, yeah," I reply unenthusiastically. Why do I always get all the crappy jobs?

3 2

ROSY PINK

-ZAVIER-

*P*ain... It's all I feel. It consumes me. I feel so broken; I almost wish Electra's guys had killed me. To say it's been a rough couple of days would be the understatement of the century. It hurts to breathe, it hurts to chew, it hurts to go to the toilet. Even lying completely still hurts. Thankfully, Floss and Minty are doing a little better than I am. They're moaning and groaning in pain too, but they're moving around more freely.

When I'd first woken up—the day after we'd all been tortured—Minty and Floss had filled me in on the agreement Jax and Electra had made. I seriously can't believe it. This whole interrogation was a

273

charade. It was never about Elgar's death and Floss' and Harlow's involvement in it; it was about blackmailing Jax so he'd agree to linking with her. We were the bait, and Jax had been foolish enough to bite. It's a completely reckless move on his part. By saving us, he's put himself and our whole colony in grave danger. Electra has the same beliefs as Nix, which means Pastels will suffer. *Although*—going by the rosy strands of hair strewn across my pillow, I'm not sure I can classify myself as a Pastel anymore. This goes for Minty too. Her hair and irises have darkened to a soft rosy colour, and her entire physique looks curvier and stronger. *I wonder what they gave us to make us change so much.* You'd almost believe that we were in the same predicament as Harlow, however, the chances of me being pregnant are ZERO—*or at least I bloody-well hope so*—otherwise I have much bigger problems at hand.

Floss comes and curls her body around mine. It hurts, and I wince, but the feeling of her warm body against mine brings me comfort. I've come to enjoy being the object of her affection. She kisses my forehead and then my cheek, momentarily drawing my mind away from the dire situation we're in. "Hey, Muscles." Her hand squeezes my bicep and I wince. "I can't believe how broad you are now, it's kind of exciting."

"Don't get too excited," I warn. "You're actually hurting me."

"Sorry." Her hand leaves my arm, and she uses her elbow to prop herself up. "Your rosy tinge has faded a little," she says quietly, while scanning my face. "So has Minty's. It's weird. I wonder what they gave you? Jax made out like you were having some sort of reaction to the meds, but I figured you were given something special on purpose. I'm certain Electra suspected it as well. Sylvie hinted as much when Minty asked her about it, she said you would never have survived the night if they hadn't given you those specific meds, and she winked."

Jax has saved me again. I sigh. *Now I'll have to be nice to the guy—if I ever make it out of this cell, that is.*

Minty comes and sits cross-legged on my other side, peering down at Floss with a chastising look. "You shouldn't be all over him like this," she warns in a hushed voice. "You aren't meant to be together. You're breaking the laws of the colour system. Roc is watching, he'll tell Electra."

Floss sniggers. "What are they going to do to me, Minty? Throw me in the cell? Torture me?"

"They will kill you," Minty says firmly. "You know as well as I do that breaking the rules of the colour system is a crime punishable by death."

"Pushing aside the fact that you and Zavier aren't 'technically' Pastels anymore—so I'm not 'technically' breaking any rules—do you seriously believe that we're getting out of here alive?" Floss' tone is snarky. "The only reason that psychopath is allowing us to be looked after and kept alive is because she still needs us as leverage. Jax has only agreed to linking with her to save us, so she needs to keep us living and breathing until the day of the ceremony. Once they're linked, we'll be worthless once more, and it'll be bye-bye to the prisoners."

"Knowing her, she'll probably have one of her warriors come and finish us off during the ceremony, while Jax is preoccupied," I spit out with a great deal of effort.

A look of despair glazes over Minty's face. "If this is true, it means I'll never see Tatum again. I'll never get to say goodbye."

I push aside the pain and move my arm so I can lace my fingers with Minty's. "I'm so sorry, Minty, I really am."

33

LIFE IN THE FOREST

-HARLOW-

The week passes by quickly with no major hiccups. Stavros, Luna, and Destiny have been out working during the weekdays, so I've spent most of my time divided between Acacia and Atohi—and Boshell and the twins. The twins are already showing signs of improvements. They've gone from near white to a soft pink and are able to see—just enough—to start doing some of their smaller daily tasks without being aided. Boshell has thanked me repeatedly to the point where it's getting embarrassing, but I must confess, it's kind of nice to be appreciated for once.

My shoulder is feeling *much* better. It's almost fully healed, which is a miracle given it was only two and a half weeks ago that I was speared with the shard. I'm guessing I've got the vertic switz ink to thank for this positive development too.

I glance up from my book as Luna sits down on the cushioned chair opposite me, cradling a warm cup of bean-brew. We haven't spoken much. I've tried to stay out of her and Destiny's way as much as possible.

Stavros and Atohi are the next two up, and I offer to take Atohi while Stavros makes them breakfast. He is halfway through making it when we hear the sound of Rebel barking, and I leap from my chair in delight. I fly out onto to the deck with Atohi on my hip, my heart pounding excitedly, but I'm brought to a sharp halt when I discover it's Zannah heading over with Rebel and Lucy. There's no Sphinx, so I'm guessing this means there's no Jax. My heart sinks in disappointment, but I'm pleased to see Lucy again.

"Lucy." I make my way down to ground level and give her a pat. I still can't believe I'd finally been given the husken I'd always wanted only to have to part with her a month and a half later.

"Hey, Zannah," I say as she gets closer, but predictably, I don't get a smile or "hey" back.

"Jax couldn't come." Her face is hard, and her tone is abrupt. "But he said to give you this." She hands me a folded piece of paper.

"Oh. Okay, thanks." Feeling uncomfortable about opening it in front of her, I slip the note into my pocket.

"Zannah!" Stavros jumps down off the desk and rushes over to hug his sister. "And here I was thinking you'd forgotten about me."

After drawing back, she nods her head to Atohi, who's become restless in my arms. "Wow, he's getting big. How old is he now, two —three months?"

"Try four months." Stavros puts his arms out to take Atohi from me. "He was only a few days old when you last saw him. That's how long it's been since you came to see us." He holds Atohi high and proud, showing him off properly to Zannah.

She tickles his toes and expresses a bit of interest, but all the while she seems distracted—distressed even. Eventually she asks, "Is there somewhere we can go to talk?"

Stavros' light expression grows more serious. "Sure."

"I can take Atohi inside," I offer.

Stavros hands him back to me. "Thanks. That would be helpful."

I'd like to ask Zannah what's wrong—it seems serious—but I know better than to press my luck with her. She obviously doesn't want me in the loop, or she'd come out and say it. Not to worry; I'll see if I can pry the information out of Stavros later.

They are gone for quite some time, and Jax's letter burns in my pocket. I'm eager to read it, but I'd prefer to do it in private in case it says something negative, and I burst into tears. A bunch of awful thoughts spring to mind. *Maybe he's changed his mind about me? Or maybe the truth has been discovered and the Commander has locked him in one of the cells? Or perhaps he's agreed to link with Electra?* I cringe at the last one.

When Acacia gets up, I pass Atohi to her and head straight to my room. I plonk on the mattress and pull the letter out, peeling it open with shaky hands.

I'm sorry I couldn't make it out with Zannah today, things are pretty tight for me at the moment. I hope you are doing well and Luna and Destiny are being nice to you. I miss seeing your face.

Love, Jax

I smile at the *miss seeing your face* part, but other than that, his letter doesn't really tell me anything. It's a short and sweet, nothing kind of letter. *At least it's sweet,* I assure myself. *Perhaps I'm overthinking things.*

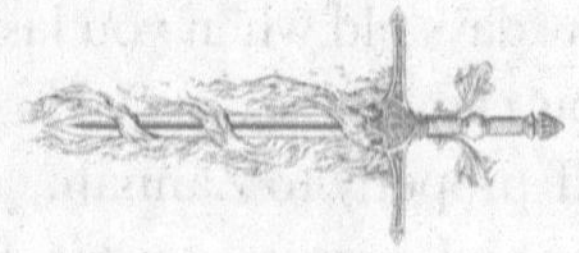

During the late hours of the morning, Destiny takes Atohi while I help Acacia make lunch. Everyone in the hut has been invited to join, and we head out to sit on the sun filtered deck. Acacia parks herself down on the end next to Stavros—who sits across from Zannah—while I head down to the opposite end and sit next to Boshell and the kids—thinking it will be the more pleasant, safer option. A dirty glare from Luna informs me I'm wrong. I squirm. *Maybe I should have sat this one out.*

Zannah and the two Peaches—as I've decided to call them— appear to get on really well. My mood deflates as I observe how casually they interact with one another, chatting and laughing. I hate that I'm so often on the outer.

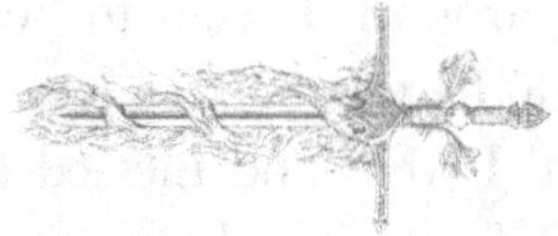

Zannah doesn't stick around for the afternoon; she heads straight back to the caves after lunch. As soon as I've helped Acacia carry in the plates and clean up the mess, I head back outside in search of Stavros. I find him under the hut, picking through a bunch of boxes which have been stored in a pile down the far end.

"I've been expecting you to come and find me," he says, without looking over his shoulder to see who it is. "I know why you're here, and I'm very sorry, but I can't tell you anything."

I come to an abrupt halt. "Why not?"

"I've been asked to keep my mouth shut. According to Zannah, I've already told you more than I should have."

"I don't understand why you can't tell me anything. Why the secrets?" Some of my earlier thoughts spring back to mind, making me feel nauseous. "Is Jax in trouble because of me?" When Stavros doesn't respond, I throw out my next question. "Has he said yes to linking with Electra?"

Stavros swings to face me. "Please don't push me for answers. For the record, I think you should be let in on what's happening, but it's not up to me. It's up to Jax. And as a part of the warrior code, I can't tell you."

"You're not technically a warrior anymore," I point out, which is cheeky, but I'm desperate for answers. "So, maybe you could hint at what's going on and I could guess the rest?"

"I might not technically be a warrior, but I'm loyal." He gives me a pointed look. "And Jax is my best friend."

My cheeks fill with heat. "Okay, fair enough. I'm sorry. It was worth a shot though, right?"

I turn to walk away, and he stops me. "Harlow. You are going to choose Jax aren't you? You're not going to leave with the Vallon?"

This issue has been haunting me all week. "My heart chooses Jax," I answer truthfully. "But I'm worried I'll do him more harm than good by sticking around. I seem to be a magnet for trouble. And you said it yourself, he was making leeway with breaking down the colour system until I went and messed everything up for him. He would be better off forgetting about me and dating a Purple. It would be almost selfish of me to stay."

"Trouble magnet or not, you have his heart and I know for sure he'll be devastated if you leave."

I know I shouldn't, but I take this opportunity to press the matter once more. "Are you suggesting *I* am responsible for the *trouble* that's going on right now?"

"No. I'm suggesting that if you love someone enough, they're worth the *trouble*."

Stavros' final words repeat over and over in my head as I wander back inside. I appreciate what he's said, but I still struggle to believe I'm worth the trouble. Jax is the Commander's son, he could have anyone. *Why choose me? A Red with baggage.*

While heading to my room, I notice Luna stand up from one of the cushioned chairs and follow me. Not what I need right now. I feel like being left alone.

As she gets closer, I whirl around to face her. "What's going on?" I ask cautiously. "Why are you following me?"

She keeps her voice level but threatening. "I want you to stay away from Boshell."

I jerk up straight. "Excuse me?"

"You heard me. I've seen you trying to use your charms on him too. Now stay away."

I'm taken aback, speechless for a few seconds. "Luna, Boshell is double my age. That's a little creepy, don't you think?"

"Says the girl carrying a set of evil Vallon twins."

Her statement stabs at me, but I speak evenly, trying not to let it show. "I understand your issue with my pregnancy, and because of this, I've been trying my best to stay out of your way as much as possible. I don't want to fight with you."

"Then stop making a pass at every man you come in contact with. Guys might like to show you attention, but it doesn't mean you have to throw yourself at them all."

Anger shoots through me, and I feel like snapping, but thankfully Acacia steps in to stop me from saying something which would only make matters worse.

"Luna, stop this at once; you're completely out of line."

Luna turns on Acacia, finger pointed. "You told me she was only staying here while she was waiting to be taken to Summer with her Vallon, and then next thing I know, she arrives back on the night of the mask festival cozying up to Jax."

"You don't know the full story," Acacia insists. "It's best if you stay out of it."

"I will happily stay out of it if she stops trying to work her magic on Boshell too. I've seen the way he's been looking at her lately."

"It's not like that," I pipe in angrily. "He is just grateful to me for helping his kids."

Luna pounces on me, eyes wild. "I'm the one who helps him with his kids." She stabs a finger at her own chest. "Me. They are my family."

"Okay, enough of this." Stavros comes charging in the front entrance, looking rather annoyed, which is rare for him. "Harlow, come with me," he beckons. "Let's go for a walk."

As I make my way to Stavros, Luna storms off to her room. I really don't know whether I should consider taking Jax up on his offer. Staying here on a more permanent basis might end up being a problem.

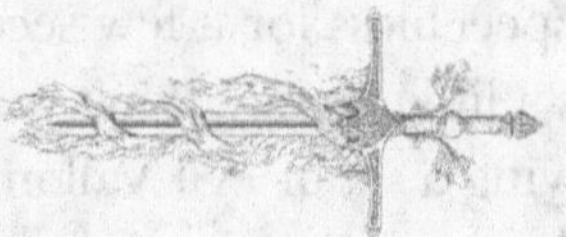

When we get outside, I apologise for the disruption, but Stavros waves it off.

"I've been expecting Luna to lash out. I'm surprised it took as long as it did for her to explode."

"I know it looks bad," I admit. "But I'm not the whore she thinks I am. I've only ever slept with Alex—that's it—and it was only the one time."

He gives me an awkward sidelong glance and chuckles. "Okay, thanks for sharing."

"I don't want you or Acacia to think I'm that kind of Zeek, because I'm really not. I made an impulsive decision in the heat of the moment. It was a mistake."

"Don't worry, we don't think anything of the sort."

There's a wooden bench facing one of the many pretty luminous gardens which are spread sporadically throughout the village. Stavros walks straight over to it and takes a seat. "Come." He pats the spot next to him. "It's easy to forget about all of your problems when there's a view like this in front of you."

He gives my belly a curious glance as I sit. "Only the once, huh?" he says with a sympathetic smile. "That's pretty unlucky."

"Tell me about it."

In a friendly, reassuring gesture, Stavros cups my good shoulder with his hand and gives it a light squeeze. "I wouldn't worry too much about what Luna says. She's been through some traumatic experiences in her life, and they've left her with trust issues. She's feeling a little insecure at the moment, that's all."

We sit silently after this, both staring at the beautiful glowing garden, lost in our own thoughts. Stavros is still acting like his light, easy-going self on the outside, but there's a haunted look in his eyes which tells me something terrible is going on back at the caves. I wish he would let me in on what Zannah told him. It's so frustrating to know something is wrong without knowing what that *something* is. Jax got upset with me for not telling him about having the vertic switz ink, yet he hardly tells me anything. He's set double standards. Trust needs to work both ways.

There is no use trying to push Stavros for answers again, he's not going to budge on his morals, so I chose this moment to touch on another question which has been nagging at me since my first visit.

"Stavros… What happened to Luna and Destiny in Summer? Do you know?"

His eyes swivel to meet mine, and he tilts his head, regarding me carefully before saying. "Destiny said she and Luna were used as slaves and beaten and abused regularly by some of the Queen's guards." He cringes, clearly picturing it. "She also said the paler of the Pastels died by the dozens during their first couple of months in Summer, because the heat was too extreme, and the workloads were too gruelling for their frail bodies to handle."

I shiver with repulsion. Alex had said as much.

"How did they escape?"

"Luna was raped by one of the Queen's guards early on," Stavros states, and a sickening feeling claws at my insides. "So, after she and Destiny had been injected with the vertic switz ink—as a part of some experiment—they noticed their strength and senses had improved significantly, and they took their revenge. Luna got Destiny to lure the guard into one of the lower chambers, pretending to be interested in a bit of hanky-panky, and then they killed him with his own blade and escaped out the window."

Disgust pours through me, making my throat close up. I have no words. No wonder Luna despises me. I'm a constant reminder of a time she'd rather forget.

"You really don't want to go there, Harlow," Stavros says, in gentle warning. "Summer is not a nice place for Zeeks. You should stay with us. Acacia loves having you around, and Luna will warm to you eventually. It's just going to take time."

"Is there really going to be enough space for me?" I ask. "I'm already taking up Atohi's room, and soon I'll have two crying babies of my own to add to the mix."

"Space is relative. If Pastels are able to survive in tight quarters and get by, I don't see why we can't all manage. And on a selfish note, it would be nice for Atohi to have little friends to grow up with. Especially friends who are going to be 'different'—" he uses his fingers to make air quotes, "like he is."

34

IT'S TIME

-ALEX AS SLATER-

My heart is pumping hard and fast. Come on, come on, come on. *Leave.* Everything is set out in place, ready to go, and I'm feeling quietly confident that I should be able to sneak Ruby in unnoticed. Now all I have to do is sneak out unnoticed. However, today of all days, Kenneth is sticking around like a bad smell.

He never lingers after we've finished unloading the carcasses; he's usually keen to leave. Especially lately, we haven't exactly been getting along. I can't stand the snitch. *I wonder if he's lingering because he suspects something is up.*

"Raven has been crying to Jacinta about you again." He crosses his arms over his chest and glances down his nose at me, doing his usual *I'm superior to you* act. "She doesn't understand why you've been giving her the cold shoulder ever since our linking ceremony. She was hoping you could remain friends."

Seriously? I can't believe we're back onto this subject again.

"Leave it alone, Kenneth."

I'm sick of Raven being pushed in my face. I'm not trying to be an arsehole, but how many times can I say, "I'm not interested", before everyone gets the point. I don't want Raven, I want Ruby. If only Ruby had been born a Vallon—not a Zeek, it would make life so much easier.

I've been dreaming about Ruby a lot lately—and our children. I've even been dreaming about her in her Zeek form. I can't wait for us to be together again. I'm looking forward to supporting her through the last part of her pregnancy. I've already missed most of it, *although* I would have only missed the first month and a half if it wasn't for Jax's warriors interfering. I grit my teeth. I feel like I've been ripped off. Ruby should already be here with me. We could be guessing genders together and selecting baby names. I hope one of them is a boy. I've always wanted to have a son and call him Axel. It has all the same letters of Alex yet it's a different name entirely. It's an anagram, and I think that's kind of cool.

A dream from last night pops into my head, and I smile. It feels weird to have so many dreams these days. They were few and far between before because I'd usually wake up on Earth. There was barely any time for me to dream, however, whenever I did dream it was always about her.

There are times where I find myself wishing I could go back to Earth. Human Ruby was bold, sexy, and exactly my type. *Hell*, I'm pretty sure she'd be most men's type. I'm still attracted to Zeek Ruby, her face is sweet and angelic, but she's less foxy and more cowardly. I understand that her Zeek life has been far more challenging than her Human life. She was born weak and vulnerable this time around, and it's killed her confidence. I'm hoping this will change once I get her here. She won't need to worry about colour status or Magentas and Purples trying to kill her; she'll be safe and cared for. I'll tell her how pretty she is and how lucky I am to have her.

"I don't know what Raven sees in you." Kenneth shakes his head. "You're a lost cause."

"I don't know what Jacinta sees in you," I retaliate. "You have a face only a mother could love."

He gets huffy, tells me to grow up, and storms off—which is exactly what I'd hoped would happen.

I wait a good five minutes after he's left, just to be sure, before taking off to the border.

I'm coming Ruby!

TOUGH CHOICES

-HARLOW-

"Harlow," Stavros' hand softly shakes me awake. "Harlow you need to hop up now, it's time to go."

My eyes don't want to open. "Okay," I say, giving my lids a firm rub. "I'll be out in a minute."

It's a struggle to get up and get dressed. I've hardly slept. My nerves are on edge. I spent the first half of the night freaking out about seeing Alex again, and then when I finally got to sleep, I found myself at Jade's place. She said she's doing much better now, and that Byron and Carrie are finally opening up to the idea of her being in contact with me.

"You'll have to try to move something in front of them," she'd said, eyes alight. "That way they'll know for sure I'm telling the truth."

I'd agreed I would try because I knew it would make her happy —but personally I'd much prefer it if she'd keep our visits to herself. I don't really feel like playing Casper the friendly ghost to satisfy everyone else's curiosity, I just want to be able to hang out with her and enjoy our time together.

Jade had soft, mellow music playing through her surround sound speakers. It was soulful, calming, and I'd tapped along trying to distract myself from my inner turmoil. Noticing my interest, Jade told me the artists name was Ben Howard.

"He's great, isn't he? His music has really helped me get through these past few months."

"If only I could take one of his CDs back with me," I'd said. *Not that we have CD players.*

Jade laughed. "CDs are a thing of the past, Rubes. What you need is Spotify, then you'll have all the music you could ever wish for at your fingertips."

She showed me her Spotify library and played a few other artists she's into. I contemplate asking her to put on my favourite Chili Peppers album, but immediately reconsider. *I died to the sound of that CD.*

At one point, I considered talking to Jade about my dilemma with Alex and Jax. I was interested in her opinion. But in the end, I decided against it. I didn't want her fretting about me. I wanted her to believe I'm safe and happy in a much better place.

A much better place… The words repeat in my head. Perhaps later today I might finally be in a much better place emotionally, but at the moment, I'm an emotional wreck.

I wish I could click my fingers and this morning would be over and done with.

I want to stay in Spring and wait for Jax. He's the one who holds my heart, and he's made it clear that he wants me to stay.

Alex had his chance with me, and he blew it. *He hurt me.*

It's going to be tough for a while, and Jax and I probably won't get to see as much of each other as we would like, but I know for certain he is worth waiting for. My only concern had been that I'm not worthy of him, and that I come with baggage, but Stavros has assured me several times now that my colour and pregnancy aren't an issue. Even last night before we all went to bed, he made sure to remind me of this, and added, "Jax has always been in love with you, and he will be absolutely devastated if you leave."

I think he's secretly afraid that when I see Alex, I'll change my mind, and break his best friend's heart.

It blows my mind to think Jax has been in love with me for years. The Commander's son, in love with a pitiful Pastel. *It's crazy.*

Stavros shared the same story Acacia had told me the first day I met her, only he'd given more details. He'd said Jax never wanted me to find out how much I truly meant to him until he'd succeeded in breaking down the colour system. He hadn't wanted to risk my integrity or my safety.

Too bad I ruined my own integrity by sleeping with a Vallon.

My mind flicks to Alex, and I wince. As much as I'm certain Jax is the one for me, I feel guilty about hurting Alex, especially after Zavier's confession about the voltz. It turns out Alex has done far more for me than I'd first realised, which means he isn't the complete and utter jerk I'd had him pinned as a few weeks ago. He actually does care about me. And he swears he did come back for me that day in the forest.

It's too late. While I was busy hating on him for leaving me to die —*or so I'd thought*—I'd fallen for Jax, and I'd fallen hard. Just the sight of Jax turns me feverish.

Jax is a little intense and hard to read at times, but I feel safe with him, and I appreciate that he puts me and my safety first.

Alex is certainly more forward, affectionate, and easy to talk to, but right from the start, I'd always felt like he was putting Lucas first, which might not have been as much of a problem if Lucas wasn't my killer. Twin brother or not, I'll never be able to understand how Alex could put my murderer first. Especially when he'd been there to witness the horrendous attack. *It makes no sense.*

The more I think about it, the more I wonder how I let myself fall for Alex in the first place. The warning signals were all there. I should never have let him in. *Alex and I were a mistake.*

Alex's cheeky smile and golden eyes flash to mind, diluting my resolve. He did go out of his way to take me to my parent's place as a nice surprise. And he'd waited at my sister's place every day after I'd woken up from the coma on Zadok, hoping, but never knowing, whether I'd even show up. He was the reason Zavier was able to bring me back from the coma. He's the reason I'm still alive.

Stop it! I warn myself. *The goods do not outweigh the bads. Think about it, because of him you are pregnant with Lucas. Your killer is growing inside you.* I'm both shocked and appalled by my own mental snap. The idea of Lucas being my son still makes me sick to my core. I grow nauseous just thinking about it. I shake my head trying to fling this thought from my mind. This is a detail I'd prefer to deny than accept. I don't want to hate my own son. I have to believe he will grow to be a different person—Zeek/Vallon—this lifetime around.

Alex once said, "He wasn't born a bad person, our parents made him this way." *Maybe if I'm a good parent, he won't turn bad?* The thought still sickens me. I reconsider. *Maybe the twins should be split up? Lyla can stay with me and the boy can go with Alex.* RJ said Lyla belongs with Jax, but he didn't mention anything about the boy.

Stavros pokes his head back in the doorway. "Harlow, what are you doing? We've got to go."

"Sorry." I pop on my friendship necklace and shove Jax's letters into my pocket. "I'm ready now."

I don't know why I insist on keeping his letters on me at all times. They've kind of become my security blankets. I figure if I can't have Jax with me at all times, I can at least have a piece of him with me.

Stavros' eyes do a quick scan of the room. "You're not packing anything?"

"No."

He smiles in relief. "Good choice."

The sun hasn't fully risen, and the tall trees of the forest block the horizon, leaving us with minimal light to see by.

"Will there still be any fuegors out?" I peer about anxiously as we leave the safety of the village fence.

Stavros chuckles. "No, they tend to keep their distance from the outskirts of the village. Don't worry, by the time we get further out, the sun will have risen, and they'll all vanish into hiding."

It's been a nice week and few days since my debacle with Luna. We've managed to keep out of each other's hair as much as possible, and to make her happy, I've kept my distance from Boshell and the twins whenever she's around. The twins have improved dramatically this week and have become very independent, Will especially. They've gone from a soft pink to a proper pink, not far-off Tatum's pigment depth, only they have more of a rosy tint. It's so exciting to see them active, exploring and trying to learn more about their new visual world.

I've actually done a bit of exploring myself this week. It's been relaxing to wander around and enjoy the village, without having to constantly look over my shoulder in fear of being attacked.

The Drakes stare and whisper when they see me pass by, but no one is trying to kill me. The stares don't particularly bother me. I'm used to dealing with unwanted attention; my whole Zeek life has been about standing out for all of the wrong reasons.

Sonja found me wandering around the food markets over the weekend and introduced me to her brother Woody. He was *extremely* tall with green fuzzy hair, grown out, unlike most Drakes. I'd looked up at him in amazement, trying to grasp what it would be like to tower above everyone, even other Drakes. It was seriously like meeting a tree. Woody's Zeek wasn't as easy to understand as Sonja's—not that she's all that easy to understand either—but I'd managed to latch on to enough words to get by.

They'd bought me lunch and spoken about how wonderful it is that Jax is taking a stance against the Zeeks' rigid colour system. They said come the day Azazel passes on, the entire Zeek colony will change for the better, and their alliance with our race will strengthen and flourish.

"Are you alright? Are you nervous?" Stavros cuts into my thoughts.

A burning sensation starts at my core and crawls up my wind-pipe, making me feel like I want to puke. "I'm absolutely terrified."

It takes us a long while to get to the dual fallen tree trunks. Stavros, who is usually quite talkative, doesn't say much at all. The closer we get, the more tense he becomes, like he is slipping back into his old warrior mode.

Alex arrives before we do. We can't see him from where we are, but we can hear him asking Jax where I am.

"She's coming," Jax says, his voice full of tension. "Just wait."

"What do you mean she's coming?" Alex's tone is far more agitated and aggressive than Jax's. "I thought you said that you were going to deliver her to me personally. I can feel she's close, but I can't see her. You're hiding her."

Stavros picks up the pace beside me. "We need to move faster."

We hurry on, zig-zagging around the trees and their protruding roots. Within a matter of minutes, Jax, Oscar, Zannah, and Alex come into view. Alex is shirtless, like the first time I met him, and his vertic switz tattoos glow brightly in the dim light of the early morn-ing. Oscar and Zannah have their blades out and ready, but Alex and Jax still have theirs sheathed. *That's a good start at least.*

Given his position, Alex sees me first. "Ruby," he calls, there's a delighted glint in his eyes. He's excited to see me, and he's not afraid to let it show.

Ouch. My heart twists. *Please don't smile at me like that.* I'm about to let him down, and I feel awful.

I head straight to Alex, fighting the urge to glance at Jax as I pass. I'm afraid if I look his way, my feelings for him will show on my face. I don't want Alex to know Jax is the reason I want to stay. I don't want them to fight.

Alex looks me up and down in his usual flirty way, and I cringe inside knowing we have an audience. I can only image how uncom-fortable this must be for Jax to witness.

"Wow, you really are Ruby Red now," he says as I get closer. He reaches over to clasp my hands, and I let him. It would be more awkward if I pulled back right away. I want to let him down gently. "You look beautiful." His face is aglow—until he detects the conflict in mine. "What's wrong?" His expression dims, and his smile dries up completely.

Oh, God, I can't do this. I really, really, don't want to hurt him. My heart is pounding so hard I'm afraid it might burst straight through my ribcage. I bite my lip, trying to think of the right words to say, but I don't know that there are any.

"Rubes," he prompts.

My lower lip quivers involuntarily. "Alex, I'm so sorry." My fingers squeeze his. "But I can't come with you."

"What do you mean?" I can hear a note of panic in his voice.

"I mean I want to stay. I don't want to leave."

He stares at me wordlessly for a moment, and then his eyes spark into a fierce, fiery blaze. "You son of a bitch!" he shouts in pure and utter rage, and he charges past me, straight to Jax. "I knew you would do this to me."

"Alex, wait!" I chase after him. "What are you doing?"

They both unsheathe their blades before coming in contact with each other, and I hear the clank as they collide with heavy force.

"Alex stop! Please!"

Oscar and Zannah descend upon Alex, one on each side, setting their blades against his neck. He doesn't seem to notice or care. He's lost in rage.

"You couldn't keep away from her, could you?" The words blast from his mouth. "That's why you wanted to keep her another four weeks. It wasn't because of her shoulder, you wanted to use that time to win her over."

Their biceps bulge and their blades shake in the air as they press firmly against one another with pressurised force.

Jax's voice is booming. "She needed the four weeks to heal."

"Take a good look at her," Alex roars. "She's mine, she's a Red, and she's pregnant… TO ME!"

"If she's *yours* and you care so deeply, then where exactly were you for the first month and a half of her pregnancy, while she was left crying into her pillow every night. Huh? Why'd you wait so long to fetch her?"

"You should never have been anywhere near her and her pillow."

I need to get between them before things get out of hand. There are blades everywhere, but I don't care.

"Harlow! No!" Stavros catches on to my intentions and races over to grab me, but he's too late. I take the risk and I jump in between the two guys, facing towards Alex.

"Alex, please don't do this," I beg "It's not Jax's fault. I want to stay. It's my decision."

"Harlow, get out of here, now," Jax says behind me. "It's too dangerous."

Alex's eyes blaze down at me, filled with anger and hurt. "Do you have any idea of the shit I've had to go through just to be here today? I've risked everything for you."

"Zannah, Oscar, put your blades down," Jax commands.

"What?" Zannah sounds outraged.

"Put them down."

Alex nods his head towards Oscar's lowering blade, eyes fixed on me. "Why don't you take it?" he says with venom. "That way you can slice it straight through my heart."

"Alex, I'm sorry. Please, let's talk."

"I don't want to talk. I want you to come with me. You are pregnant to me; you belong with me, and you know it. We have a connection that you and Jax are never going to have. We have history."

I *am* pregnant to him, and we might have history, but it's not all rainbows and sunshine. *I want to be with Jax, I'm in love with Jax.* I should be saying this out loud, not in my head, but I'm afraid Alex will kill Jax if he knows the truth.

"She'll die in Summer," Jax says, in protest. "It's not safe for her there. If you truly care about her, you'll let her stay."

Alex applies further pressure against Jax's blade. "Nobody is asking you. Stay out of it!"

"She's already told you what she wants," Jax presses on. "You should listen to her."

In a swift manoeuvre, Alex swivels around, blade and all, and I catch a flash of the sharp biting edge slicing the air towards Jax's throat.

The warriors are fast to react, raising their blades straight back to Alex's neck.

"You deceived me," Alex hisses through gritted teeth. "I should kill you."

Alex must have nicked Jax because a few droplets of blood land on my shoulder. I panic.

"Alex, please! Don't hurt him." My voice is verging on hysterical. "Please, let him go." This only angers him further and he forces forward, pressing the blade harder against Jax's skin. I grab Alex by the waist and try to force him back with all of my weight. "Please, don't hurt him. Let him go, and I'll come with you."

"Harlow don't do this," Jax warns. "It's too dangerous for you to go with him. You could be killed."

"Alex please," I continue to beg, ignoring Jax's protests. Guilt rips at my heart.

Alex's eyes lower to my face, and I can tell I'm finally starting to get through to him. His expression has gone from fierce to torn.

Despite my ultra-distressed state, my next sentence comes out controlled and steady. "Put your blade down, let Jax go, and I promise I'll come with you."

Alex considers this for a second, and then gives in, lowering his blade.

Regardless of his stand-down, Zannah and Oscar don't budge from their positions, and I don't entirely blame them. I'm not sure how badly Alex has cut Jax, and I'm too afraid to turn and look.

"Lower your blades," Jax says, his tone drenched with defeat.

I've had to reject him in order to save him. My heart bleeds. This is not how this meet-up was supposed to end.

"But he—" Zannah begins to protest, but Jax cuts her off.

"Let them go."

I long to spin around and say goodbye to Jax, but I can't bring myself to take the risk. I know if I see his face, I will fall to pieces. I won't be able to leave. *Oh, God. Why did it have to come to this?*

Not wanting to stick around, Alex grabs me by my hand and leads me away.

I can feel Jax's eyes following me, and I blink like rapid-fire trying to fight back the tears.

Goodbye, Jax. I love you.

WHAT THE FROST WAS THAT?
-ZANNAH-

I watch in disbelief as Jax allows Alex to drag Harlow off without a proper fight.

"What the frost was that, Jax?" I snap in anger. "What are you doing? Are you going to let him drag her away? You heard her, she wanted to stay, she was bullied into going with him."

Stavros looks as shocked as I am, but he's not saying anything. *Coward.*

"We could have taken him," I insist. "He was outnumbered, why'd you keep insisting we put our blades down?"

The composure Jax is trying to keep is shaky, he looks like he's on the verge of crumbling any minute. "If we took down Slater, I would have lost her anyway. She said she didn't want me to fight for her. She didn't want to see either of us getting hurt."

"How very noble of you to comply to her wishes," I bark sarcastically. "That's brilliant Jax, bravo." I fake a hand clap. "Now she's off to Summer where she'll probably be abused and killed like the rest of the Zeeks who've been abducted or sent there."

"Watch it, Zannah." Stavros casts me a look of warning. "That's enough."

Nice. He's happy to say something to me, but not to Jax.

"No, you know what Stavros, if you want to stand there saying nothing like a little bitch, that's your call, but I'm pissed. I've been laying my life on the line for that girl for months. I've even killed for that girl, because I didn't want Jax to lose her. I couldn't bear the thought of seeing him lost in despair. And now the idiot has gone and given her up without a proper fight."

"What would you have me do, Zannah?" Jax's tone is grave. "Kill him? Have you kill him? Harlow would have never forgiven me. Slater is the father of her children, and it's plain to see there's still a connection between them. I could tell just by watching." Raw emotion fractures his usually stoic expression. "She didn't even look at me once."

"And not to mention, Slater is the Queen's son," Oscar pipes in, finally finding his voice. "If we'd killed him, it would mean an out-and-out war between our races."

Jax dabs at the cut on neck with his fingers, smearing the blood. "Zannah said you told Harlow about the backlash of the pregnancy rumours, and my mother's ridiculous request for me to link with Electra." He says, eyeing Stavros accusingly. "You shouldn't have. It wasn't your place."

"Maybe I shouldn't have," Stavros admits. "But you should have. And anyway, we all know that's not why she left. She left to protect you. She didn't pack anything. All her belongings are still in the hut. You heard her. She wanted to stay."

Jax's face darkens with sorrow. He's hurting, I can see it, but it's his own fault. He's an idiot for letting her go without a fight.

Stavros tone softens. "She's in love with you; she told me. You're the one who holds her heart."

I glare in Stavros' direction. "What's the point in sharing this with him now, Stavros? It's useless information. The point is, she didn't stay. She is currently off to Summer with her super-ripped ex-lover—probably to make some more babies—while he," I say, stabbing my finger at Jax's chest with force, "is three days away from linking with a mega-beast—who is also going to want to produce a little heir to the title. And once Jax has outlived his usefulness, Electra will have him assassinated without any remorse, just like Azazel did to Arlo. Life is just wonderful, isn't it? We should be celebrating a triumph."

Jax gives me a disgusted look, while Oscar gives me a firm whack across the back of the head. "Stop being such a bitch, Zannah. We all know it's not going to come to that, we've got plans in place. Give it a rest."

I snarl, and jab Oscar with a back-elbow to his ribs. He grunts.

"Oscar's right," Stavros agrees, giving me a reprimanding look. "Try focusing that aggressive energy on Electra instead of Jax. If anyone deserves your wrath, she does." He gazes between the three of us, his expression slipping into more of a calculated one. "Are we all set for this Saturday or what?"

Oscar grins. "Let's just say it's going to be one explosive ceremony."

GOODBYE, JAX. HELLO SUMMER
-HARLOW-

My legs may be longer and stronger than they used to be, but they are still short compared to Alex's, and he is moving so quickly, I'm struggling to keep up. The terrain is shaded and uneven, and I'm nervous I'm going to twist an ankle.

"Alex, please, slow down," I say, through heavy pants. I snatch my arm back. "I'm struggling to keep up."

He comes to a halt, scoops me up into his arms, and then keeps going at a swift pace. "We can't slow down. We need to get back to Summer before they discover I'm missing." He notices tears sliding down my cheeks and gives an irritated grumble. "Why are you crying?"

Like it's not obvious. "What will happen if you're discovered missing?" I ask, ignoring his question.

"We don't want to find out, that's why we need to hurry."

Alex carries me the entire way to the Summer border, and during this time I watch as a myriad of emotions pass across his face. A couple of times he opens his mouth as if to speak, but no words leave his lips. This is restrained for Alex; I've never known him to hold back. Unlike Jax, he usually likes to air what's on his mind. I'm glad he's biting his tongue. I don't want to get into anything right now. I'm too heartbroken to speak. All I can think about is Jax and how much I must have hurt him. I should have said goodbye, but I was too scared of the backlash. *I regret it now.*

"We're on the edge of the border," Alex says, and his forehead scrunches. "This is where it starts to get tricky." He puts me down in front of a large, rolled rug and unravels it. "I need you to hide in here; don't worry it's clean. I had it newly-made especially for this purpose. I needed an inconspicuous way to sneak you in." When the rug is fully unfurled, he points to two pillows inside. "I brought one for your head, and one to protect your tummy. Hopefully it won't come to this, but if any of the guards come charging at me, I'm going to have to place the rug down to fight them off." His eyes meet mine with all seriousness. "Now, if for some reason I don't win the struggle and they drag me away, I want you to promise me you'll wait until we're fully out of sight before making a beeline to the forest." He brushes a hand over my hair. "I don't want you or the babies getting hurt or killed."

"Okay." My voice wobbles.

I'm so not ready for this. Stavros' words play over in my head, "You really don't want to go there, Harlow. Summer is not a nice place for Zeeks." I think about what happened to Luna, and I wince. Seeing how on edge Alex is about sneaking me into Summer is terrifying. I'm not welcome here, nor do I belong. I don't want to live in Summer with Alex. I want to stay in Spring where it's safe to raise my children—*our children.*

"Where are you taking me?" I ask.

"To my chamber…" He thinks this over for a second and then corrects himself. "I mean our chamber."

Our children, our chamber. The word "our" suddenly sounds like a curse.

"Does anyone else know I'm coming?"

He must sense unease circling within me, because he answers my question with a hint of compassion. "No, of course not. Crossing the border is going to be hazardous, I won't lie, but I've got a plan in place, and once I get you to our chamber, you'll be safe. No one is going to hurt you; I'll make sure of it."

I look down at the rug and swallow hard. *A least it's a nice pattern,* I think, trying to distract myself from the gravity of the situation. It's abstract, swirled with a mix of reds, oranges, and ambers. *It's very Vallon.*

"Are you ready?" he asks. "The sooner we do this, the sooner it's over."

I'm not ready, and I don't know that I'll ever be. *I don't want this.*

Without answering, I lay down flat on my back, placing my head on the pillow that Alex has carefully set out for me. He picks up the other pillow and places it over my tummy before rolling the rug back up, hiding me inside.

He lifts the rug with ease, and I feel the motion as he rests it on his shoulder. "I'm sorry if this is a bit rough," he says. "But it's the best I could come up with."

With each step he takes, I'm bounced around within the confines of the rug.

Instead of stressing about what might become of me if the guards catch Alex sneaking me across the border, I lose myself to the solitary darkness and the new carpet smell. I feel quite comfortable in this cocoon, even with the bouncing. I could easily hide in here forever and pretend that I didn't just throw away a promising future with Jax.

Alex continues to walk for what feels like an age, and my body heats up to an extremely uncomfortable temperature. *Wow, it's hot here. VERY HOT.* Droplets of sweat roll down my skin, soaking into the rug. *Okay, so maybe hiding in here forever isn't such a great idea after all. I'll die of heat exhaustion.*

Alex stops to speak with someone at one point, however due to the language barrier, I don't understand what's being said. They're both using gruff, guttural tones to converse. I'm unable work out whether they are annoyed with each other, or if this is the natural intonation Vallons use when they speak.

Despite being dreadfully overheated, I shiver. *I'll be living with Vallons now. The enemy. I can't believe I agreed to this.*

Alex says, "Guten abend," to a few more Vallons along the way. A girl's voice parrots back first, followed by a couple of guys.

Eventually I hear a clank of a heavy door closing, and I sigh with relief as the rug I'm ravelled in is placed down onto a solid surface.

Alex unrolls the rug with care and gazes down at me. "Are you alright?"

Sweat drips from his temples. He looks as overheated as I feel. My skin is slick and feels itchy from rubbing against the carpet fibres.

"I'm fine." I sit up, drawing in an anxious breath before gazing around. It turns out Alex's chamber is far less creepy than I'd imagined it would be. I had pictured a place resembling Biblical hell. I'd envisioned a red haze in the air and tall flames blasting up the walls with carvings of demonic creatures torturing screaming victims.

On the contrary, Alex's chamber reminds me of an old Gothic church from the human world. It's enormous and grand, with a high arched decorative ceiling and stone walls. There are also two large lit candle chandeliers, which have the entire chamber flickering in a soft glow of yellow.

I take in the Victorian-ish style furniture. Dare I say the button-tufted Chesterfield sofa looks inviting. It's far plusher and more luxurious than anything I've ever sat on. And wow, the matching four poster button-tufted bed... *I plan on never knowing how soft that bed is, because I won't be sleeping in it.*

I wipe a drip of sweat from my brow before it slides down into my eye.

The only thing I wasn't wrong about was the extreme temperature difference. It truly is suffocatingly hot here. The heat is even more intense than the Australian summers I faced back on Earth —*and trust me, they were HOT!* Especially in the suburb of Penrith at the base of the Blue Mountains. I remember a day it was so unbelievably hot there, sections of the tarmac had melted on the surface, making it sticky. A young teen who had been foolish enough to step on one of the melted sections—in an attempt to show off to his friends—had lost one of his thongs to the sticky black tar. Jade and I had laughed.

Alex breathes a sigh of relief, drawing me back. "That was as intense as I'd feared. I thought for sure we'd been spotted by one of the guards at one point. I was half expecting a set of fireballs to come blasting our way. I kept super low and ran as fast as I could."

"Yeah, I felt the bouncing."

He disappears for a moment and comes back with a glass of water for each of us. I take the glass from his hand and guzzle the entire contents down in one go.

I don't understand why crossing the border is such a big deal here. Zeeks cross the Spring/Winter border all the time with no issues. The only reason we don't cross into Spring during the evening is because we know we'll be eaten. Summer must have much stricter rules set in place.

"Well, this is our chamber," Alex says with an open-armed gesture. "What do you think?"

I shrug, finding it hard to fully appreciate anything given the circumstances. "It's nice."

"It's *nice*," he repeats, acid dripping from his voice. He plonks down in front of me and drags me closer to him. "You wanted to talk, so let's talk. Why are you hating on me?"

There are quite a number of reasons why I'm "hating on him".

When I don't answer right away, he says, "It's because of Jax isn't it? He's probably spent the past four weeks whispering in your ear, warning you against me, 'the big bad Vallon'."

"My resentment towards you has nothing to do with Jax," I answer defensively, although it's not entirely true. Being around Jax

—who is loyal, gallant, and dependable—has helped open my eyes to all of Alex's faults and flaws. "I'm upset with you because you left me."

He jerks back, his eyes wide with disbelief. "You told me to."

"Not the second time," I say. "The first time. You told me our relationship was finished, and then you took off and left me, alone and vulnerable in the danger zone. You left me to die."

"No, I didn't." He shakes his head. "I came back for you, I told you that." He reaches for my hand, but I pull back, unwilling to let him touch me.

"I was out there for a good fifteen minutes on my own before Jax found me. Anything could have gotten me in that time. When Jax first approached, I thought he was a predator. I honestly thought I was going to be attacked and killed."

"What are you saying? Jax is your new hero now because he swept you up and took you back to the caves?"

"What?" His juvenile reply leaves me feeling stumped. It's completely off track. "Can you push your jealousy for Jax aside for one minute and actually listen to what I am saying? I'm angry with you because you left me, and because you were always so quick to defend your brother, even though you're fully aware of all of the wicked things he's done. You told me you loved me, and you'd do anything to keep me, and then as soon as we got into an argument over your brother, you took off, leaving me crushed."

"It was stupid of me to take off, I realise that now, but you're not an innocent victim here either. You killed my brother, which consequently obliterated my human spirit. That piece of me is gone forever now because of you. Of course, I was going to be upset about it."

Again, he seems to be missing my point, and I take offence at his spiteful swipe. He knows I didn't mean to hurt him. I did what I had to do to protect my sister and nephew.

"Say what you like," I spit with resentment. "But I *was* an innocent victim when your brother killed me. You should know; you witnessed the whole thing."

"Why are you throwing this back in my face? Are you blaming me for not saving you? Because trust me, I tried."

"You know what, forget about it, Alex. You're missing the point. You obviously don't give a damn about my feelings."

"Yeah? Well, you obviously don't give a damn about me. You didn't even want to come with me. I've done so much for you, yet I mess up once and you paint me as the biggest arsehole on Zadok. If it wasn't for me, you'd be dead already. I'm the reason you're still here. If your fate had been left up to Jax you—"

"Why do you keep bringing up Jax?" I ask, cutting him off with annoyance. "Leave him out of this."

"Because I know you've been sleeping with him," Alex growls, and I flinch at his tone. "He's the whole reason you wanted to stay."

"What?" Jax is the reason I wanted to stay, but I'm not sleeping with him. I don't understand why everyone always jumps straight to this conclusion. "Jax and I have never even kissed. And even if I was sleeping with him—which I wasn't—it would be none of your damn business. *You* broke up with *me*, remember?"

"If you weren't sleeping with him, then how did he know you've been crying into your pillow every night, huh?" He lifts his chin, raising both brows in question.

"Because Zavier told him."

His eyes drill into mine. "Does this mean you were sleeping with Zavier then?"

"My goodness, Alex—*seriously?*" My patience is disintegrating by the second. He is acting ridiculously jealous and unreasonable. "Zavier is my best friend, and you're the only guy I've slept with here on Zadok, so stop with the jealousy act and take some responsibility for your actions." I face him front on, trying to keep my expression as earnest as possible. "I'm sorry I killed Lucas, and I'm sorry about severing your link to Earth. I know I really hurt you, and it eats at me, but you really hurt me too. I'm sure I won't remain upset about this forever, but at the moment I still feel raw inside, and I can't just pretend like everything is fine between us. I need time."

His whole demeanour changes, and he stares back at me, with hurt puppy dog eyes. "I'm sorry too. I didn't realise how badly I'd hurt you." His hand reaches for mine again, and this time I let him take it, even though something inside me screams, *"DON'T TOUCH ME!"*

"I was actually really excited about seeing you today." His fingers tighten around mine. "I've missed you like crazy these past couple of months, and I really want to make things work between us."

Hearing him say these words makes me wince. How can I be so annoyed with him, yet feel such sympathy towards him all at once? He'd been excited about seeing me, and then I'd rejected him, which would have stung, *but* then he wounded Jax and forced me to break Jax's heart, which in turn, has shattered mine. None of us have gotten what we wanted out of this.

"After I'd cooled down, I came back to tell you how much you meant to me," he continues, "but Jax was already there, and I was afraid if I revealed myself, we would end up getting into a fight. I held back to keep the peace."

"You didn't seem to mind picking a fight with him today," I say, my eyes flicking to the blood stains on my shoulder with accusation. My anger spikes at the memory, making my sympathy for him fade. "How badly did you cut him?"

"Not badly, only enough to get my point across." Alex's vulnerable expression vanishes, and his eyes flash green with jealousy once again. "He's lucky he's the Commander's son, or I would have killed him." His hand releases mine. "Say what you like, but I know there's chemistry between you two, and I know he would've been the one pushing for you to stay."

"It's not any of your—"

He slings a hand up, cutting me off. "Stop. I know where you're going with this, and I don't want to hear it. I need to have a wash and go to bed. It's nine P.M. here, I'm physically and emotionally drained, and there's no point in staying up if we're going to continue arguing all night." He stands and gestures to a table.

"There's plenty of food if you get hungry, and the washroom is down the end." He points. "This chamber is yours too now, so do whatever you want to do, make yourself at home, just don't open the door to anyone, or we'll have much bigger problems to deal with than Lucas and Jax."

He takes off towards the washroom with a broken expression, leaving me feeling completely torn between my anger and guilt. I don't want to hurt Alex, but I can't smile and pretend like everything is okay. Despite his apology, I still don't feel like he gets where I'm coming from. And even if we are able get past our problems, I don't feel the same way about him anymore. I still care for him, but I'm in love with Jax. *I want to be with Jax.*

After the world's quickest wash, Alex comes back to say. "By the way—the bed is yours too. I only have one, and I don't bite in my sleep, so if you get tired later on... Well..." he sighs. "It beats sleeping on the sofa."

My eyes flick between him and the bed, and I gulp.

"But like I said before," he adds, raising his hands in surrender. "Do what you want to do, I'm not about to force you to do anything."

He goes to bed, while I spend the next few hours lying on the rug pretending to myself that this is just a nightmare I will soon wake up from. Every time I picture Jax's violet eyes gazing into mine, my heart sinks deep down into the pit of my stomach. If only I could rewind time. I would go back to the night of the mask festival and hit repeat over and over again.

After a while, I force myself to get up. I need to eat something. I'm not all that hungry, but I'm sure the twins probably are, and I'm starting to feel lightheaded. There's plenty of fruit sitting in a fancy bowl in the middle of the table. I grab a deg and wander around inquisitively while eating it. The chamber really is enormous. It's bigger than the entire hut I was living in, which managed to house nine of us. It would've eventually needed to house eleven of us if I'd stayed as planned. My hand goes to my tummy, and I give it a light rub. I'm not sure what kind of life I'm going to be able to give these children in Summer. I don't want them to be prisoners in this chamber because of my terrible mistakes. I want them to be able to live semi-normal lives. They could've had semi-normal lives in Spring. They would've even had Atohi as a friend to grow up with.

I already miss my little hut family—minus Luna. Spring had really begun to feel like home.

DISAPPOINTMENT

-ALEX AS SLATER-

I wake up the next morning, hoping to find Ruby in bed next to me, but my heart sinks as I roll over to find an empty space. Feeling anxious, I hop up, still dazed and take a look around. We didn't leave things in a very good place last night, and I'm afraid she might have tried to slip out of the chamber while I was sleeping.

I breathe a sigh of relief when I spot her. She's sprawled out on the rug on the floor. She couldn't possibly be comfortable, so I scoop her up and carry her to the bed. She's certainly not a small, scrawny Pastel anymore. She's a Red, and a damn fine one at that. I love her deep red hair and fuller figure. She looks lush and womanly, more like Human Ruby, although we'll have to do something about her tattered, threadbare clothing. After placing her down, I kiss her forehead, wishing I could kiss her lips. I'm so disappointed with how everything has turned out. I thought she'd be keen to make things work between us, but instead she's holding onto resentment. I understand why she's upset with me, but I don't understand why she's *so* upset with me. If I'm willing to overlook what she did to me and my brother, then I can't see why she can't forgive me for leaving her alone in the forest for fifteen minutes. *Honestly,* I feel like if anyone should still be upset, it should be me. I'm the one who lost a brother and the other half of my life that day, and I'm the one who's been making the most effort. I've risked my life multiple times to save hers and I've shared my vertic switz ink. *What has she done for me besides cause problems?*

Regardless, I'm still hoping we can sort things out. I'm not ready to give up on us just yet. I still really love her, and I want to be there for her and our twins. I'd like to be the dad I never had. My first one was an abusive junkie and my second was all tough love until the day he died.

As I leave for work, I notice a small piece of folded paper on the rug where Ruby had been lying. Curious, I lean down to pick it up. On closer inspection I discover there's a second piece of paper folded inside the first.

I unfold the outer piece expecting it to be a drawing or something innocent—*how wrong I am.* The handwritten words bounce right off the page, hitting me in the face.

Sorry I had to leave so early. I would have said goodbye, but I didn't want to wake you. I hope you enjoy the rest of your stay in the forest and if you need anything, don't hesitate to ask Stavros; he's a great friend and I know he'd be more than willing to step up and help.

Please think about what I've said.

Love, Jax.

. . .

As my eyes continue to flash between, *I didn't want to wake you* and *Love, Jax,* I feel all of the blood drain from my face. *They were sleeping together. Ruby lied to me.*

With trembling hands, I open the next letter and read it too.

I'm sorry I couldn't make it out with Zannah today, things are pretty tight for me at the moment. I hope you are doing well and Luna and Destiny are being nice to you. I miss seeing your face.

Love, Jax

Filled with rage, my hand clenches around both letters, scrunching them into the curve of my palm.

That sly son of a bitch! I should have killed him.

Unable to contain myself, I charge back over to the bed. "You lied to me," I growl, scaring Ruby awake. "You made out like I was being paranoid and jealous over nothing, but it wasn't nothing. You've probably been lying to me all along."

"What?" She jerks up dazed and confused.

I peg the scrunched letters straight at her head. "I found your little love letters. Why don't you tell me again that you've never slept with Jax, *huh?*"

Ruby picks up the scrunched letters, her face registering alarm. "Did you go through my pockets?"

"No, I didn't go through your pockets," I spray with irritation. "I found them on the rug. And don't you dare try to turn this one around on me. You're the one in the wrong here. You're the liar."

"I wasn't lying when I said you are the only one I've been with," she says, and I don't believe her. "Nothing has actually happened between Jax and me, but you were right when you said there's chemistry between us."

Jealous rage burns inside me. I feel like picking her up and throwing her across the room. *Of course, I'd never physically hurt her,* so I reach for the next best thing. I grab the ornament on the bedside next to her, and send it flying across the room with a crash. When I'm done with it, I grab the candleholder and send it flying too.

Ruby pulls her legs to her chest and cowers.

Her frightened reaction bothers me. *Okay, I shouldn't be throwing things in a tantrum—but it's still me, she knows it's me. I'm not my brother.* "What are you doing?"

"You're scaring me."

Hearing her say this stings. As livid as I am, I don't want to scare her. I need to leave now before I do or say something I'll regret.

I storm out and slam the door behind me, making sure to safely lock it before I leave. I don't want anything happening to her while I'm at work. I still really love her, *even if she is a lying bitch!*

She should have told me the truth from the start. I wouldn't have liked it, but I'd prefer her to be honest with me. I don't like being made a fool of.

I shouldn't have insisted she come with me. I should have left her where she was, like she wanted, but I wasn't ready to lose her, or our children. For the past month she and our children to be are all I've dreamt about. We were a family. We'd seemed so happy. I thought if I got her here, and I was able to show her just how much she meant to me; we could make it work. She honestly means everything to me.

When I get out to the stables, Kenneth is already there. I hate working with him, but I have no choice; only royals are supposed to hunt.

While Kenneth is busy hooking the horsens up to the cart, I fetch the weapons, ropes, and sacks. Still lost in rage, I toss everything into the cart with such a loud crash, it spooks the horsens. The horsen closest to Kenneth bucks instinctively almost giving him a hoof to the face. It's a damn shame it missed, actually. Seeing Kenneth taken down by a horsen might have cheered me up a bit.

"Hey!" He turns on me with flared nostrils. "Watch it! What exactly are you trying to pull?"

"Calm down, Mama's Boy," I say. "You're alright."

He storms over to me, eyes blazing, and I can tell he wants to hit me. I find myself praying he will so I can hit him back. I'm itching to punch something, and if it's not Jax's face, Kenneth's would certainly be the next best thing. "You can finish hooking the horses up," he orders through gritted teeth. "I'll pack the cart."

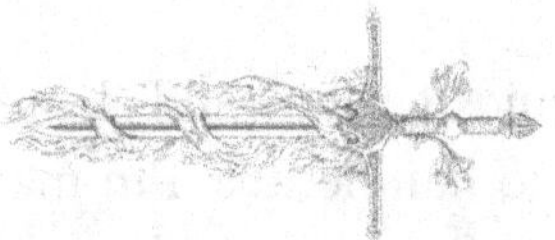

Kenneth and I manage to get through the rest of the Summer day/Spring evening without saying another word to each other. Our only form of communication is through the hand gestures we use when hunting.

Kenneth can tell I'm in mega foul mood, yet amazingly, he doesn't press me on the matter, even though I sense he's curious.

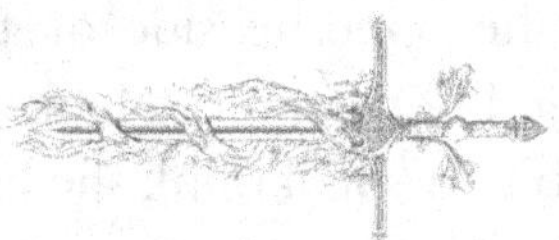

When I get back to my chamber, I pause at the door, taking a few deep, calming breaths before unlocking it. I'm still angry with Ruby, but I don't want to blow up again. I can't afford to cause any more damage to our already fragile relationship. I need to stay in control and talk this out civilly.

My eyes do a sweep of the chamber as I open the door, only to find Ruby still curled up on the bed where I'd left her. I hope she's at least gotten up to eat something. The twins don't need to suffer just because we're fighting.

As I click the door shut again and re-lock it behind me, her head lifts. "Alex?" she says, in almost a whisper.

"Yes, it's just me," I reply, slipping off my blade sash and dumping it at the doorway. "You can go back to sleep."

She sits up and looks over at me. "I wasn't actually asleep. I haven't been able to get back to sleep. I've been too worried about you. I didn't know if you'd…" she cuts her sentence short and winces. "I think we should talk."

We should talk, but I feel sticky and sweaty, and I have blood on my arms from carrying the carcasses. "I need to have a wash first," I say. "I'll be back."

I was hoping the quick wash would clear my head. No such luck. I still don't know how to handle this. I'm mad, *really mad,* but I don't want to push her away. I want her to give me a chance.

Ruby is still on the bed, and for some reason she has her knees pulled tight to her chest again.

"I'm not going to hurt you," I say, feeling insulted. I shouldn't have to spell it out for her. She should know me better than this.

"You're pretty scary when you're angry, especially as a Vallon." She bites her lip and waits a beat before adding. "But I understand I'm responsible for your outburst this morning. I should have been honest with you."

I step around to the opposite side of the bed and sit down, keeping my back to her. I don't want to look at her, because I'll cave. She needs to grovel a bit, or she'll think she has it over me. "Yes, you should have," I agree.

The sad reality is, *she does have it over me.*

"I didn't want to lie to you." Her words come out choked. "But I was afraid if I told you the truth about how I really felt, you would kill Jax."

I pump my fist against my leg in agitation. *Stay in control,* I chant in my head. "Are you in love with him?" It hurts to ask, but I need to know where I stand.

She swallows hard. "I have strong feelings for him, but I wasn't lying to you when I said nothing has happened between us. We slept in the same room together once, and he held me while I slept, but that's it. Other than the one occasion, it's only been words passed between us."

I feel like she's driven a knife into my chest and twisted it. "I don't believe you."

"Believe what you want but it's true. Not that it should matter because we weren't together. You broke up with me, *remember?*"

I feel like arguing the point, but she's right. In my fit of rage, I had broken up with her. I'd even been foolish enough to entertain a reconciliation with Raven as a way of getting over her. It was stupid, selfish, and a waste of time. Ruby is all that I want; she's all I've ever wanted.

"I don't know what to do," I say, surprised by my own honestly. "I know I should probably take you back to the forest, but I don't want to lose you. And I don't want to lose the chance to be a father to my children."

"What are we going to do when the twins come?" she asks, and her tone sounds sincere, not mocking. "Are you going to deliver them? And what about when they cry? Will their high-pitched sounds echo off these stone walls, alerting other Vallons of their existence?"

I hadn't really thought about any of this. I know I should have, but I've too been busy worrying about other things—like how I was planning on sneaking her into Summer undetected.

"Who would have delivered them if you stayed? *Jax?*" Saying his name prickles my tongue.

"I doubt it. Jax wasn't staying with me in Spring, but there were plenty of others who would've been more than willing to help me."

"Where were you staying?" I ask curiously. "I gather from Jax's letters it was somewhere in the forest, but where in the forest? Were you camping out at the Drake village?"

I feel her wiggling uncomfortably on the bed. "I don't know if I can trust you with the truth."

Shocked, I spin around to face her. "What's that supposed to mean?"

"When you get mad, you go off, and I'm afraid you'll lose control and say or do something that will jeopardise the Drakes."

"I'm not Lucas," I say with a harsh edge.

"No, you're not, and I'm not comparing you to him, but you do really go off when you're upset."

Her low opinion of me has me feeling majorly offended, and I want to argue her point, but I'm determined to stay in control. I close my eyes and let out a long, pained breath.

Noticing my wounded expression, she softens, "Alex, I'm sorry. I didn't…"

"I don't want things to be like this between us," I say, and I mean it. I'm willing to overlook what's happened with her and Jax if it means getting back on her good side. I crawl across to where she sits and place my hands on her knees, which are still risen to her chest, protecting her swollen belly. "I'd like to wipe the slate clean and start again. You're here now, and it took a lot of effort for me to get you here, so do you think you could at least give me a chance?" I gaze into her red irises, searching for any remnants of her feelings towards me. "There's only a month and a half of your pregnancy left, so why don't you give me that time, and if you're still not happy with me by the end of it, I'll take you back to the forest."

She takes a long moment to think it through, and I hold my breath, afraid she's about to turn me down. "I suppose what you're asking is fair. But I want to work on our friendship first. I'd hate to rush into something and make promises, only to end up in another fight."

I'm afraid this is her way of telling me that she no longer has those kinds of feelings for me. But if she's willing to stay, there's always a chance I'll be able to win her over again. I'll do whatever it takes.

"Okay, sure," I nod. "Friendship first."

POWERFUL PURPLES
COMING SOON...

October 15th 2021

Born in Queensland, Australia, 1984, Nikki Minty rose into this world with a wild imagination. As a young girl, she would lay in bed with her family of a night, co-telling stories about the big bad wolf and his turbulent adventures.